THE GREAT AW

1825–1826

FURY

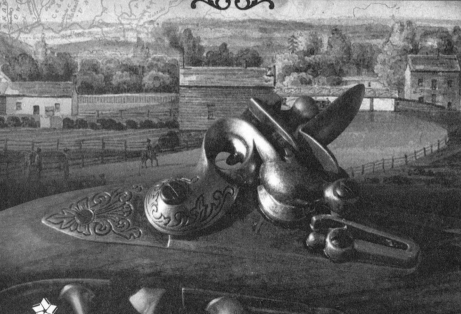

HOWARD
Fiction

BILL BRIGHT &
JACK CAVANAUGH

Award-Winning Authors of *Proof, Fire,* and *Storm*

Our purpose at Howard Books is to:
*Increase faith in the hearts of growing Christians
*Inspire holiness in the lives of believers
*Instill hope in the hearts of struggling people everywhere
Because He's coming again!

Published by Howard Books, a division of Simon & Schuster
1230 Avenue of the Americas, New York, NY 10020

Fury © 2006 by Bright Media Foundation and Jack Cavanaugh

www.howardpublishing.com
www.thegreatawakenings.org

ISBN 13: 978-1-58229-573-2
ISBN 10:   1-58229-573-5

10 9 8 7 6 5 4 3 2 1

HOWARD is a registered trademark of Simon & Schuster, Inc.

Manufactured in the United States of America

For information regarding special discounts for bulk purchases, please contact Simon & Schuster Special Sales at 1-800-456-6798 or business@simonandschuster.com.

Edited by Ramona Cramer Tucker
Interior design by Tennille Paden
Cover design by Kirk DouPonce, www.DogEaredDesign.com

Scripture quotations are taken from the *Holy Bible*, Authorized King James Version.

DEDICATION

To Reverend Charles Finney and all preachers of revival,
past and present. May God bless your efforts as you work
tirelessly to bring revival to this troubled world.

FOREWORD

Wide awake at 5:00 a.m., I finally finished devouring the manuscript for this novel. I did it without even the faintest aroma of coffee. In everyday life, the only thing more potent than a pot of coffee is a captivating story like *Fury*.

My dad wrote more than a hundred books and booklets during the course of his lifetime. He always told stories to illustrate his points, but in 2001, at the age of eighty, he published his first novel.

At the age of eighty-one he slipped the bonds of this earthly life, but during his final stretch on this planet, he coauthored seven novels. For the final four he teamed up with Jack Cavanaugh to create the Great Awakenings Series. This is the last of that series—and the last novel that will ever bear my dad's name.

He came to understand that a great storyteller is the most powerful person in any culture. Stories change the way we think. Stories inform who we are. Jesus knew this 2000 years ago. Hollywood knows this today.

During the final three years of his life, we spoke often of the need for Christians to once again discover who God really is. For years I repeatedly heard him say, "The most important thing we can teach another believer is who God is." At one point he even said, "We can trace all of our human problems to our view of God." He understood that it is all about God—which brings us to the need for revival.

My dad yearned for revival. Up until the day he passed on he ardently believed God would send revival. In fact, he believed God had told him He would send it.

This novel, along with it's three predecessors, was part of my dad's encouragement to those of us who remain behind to continue to ask God to send another revival to this land we call America. It's happened before. It can happen again.

On behalf of my dad and Jack Cavanaugh, I invite you to pull up a comfy chair and turn back the hands of time almost two hundred years as they transport you into the world of a young man named Daniel Cooper.

By the way, coffee is optional.

Brad Bright
National Director
DISCOVER GOD

ACKNOWLEDGMENTS

Jack's heartfelt thanks go to—

David and Ginger Darval, who on December 5, 1975, presented him with a multivolume set of books featured great preachers in history and their sermons. For thirty-one years it has been a source of personal inspiration, an instruction guide for sermon preparation, and now research for this novel. David—who knew that when our kindergarten teacher introduced us on the playground, fifty years later you would still be a constant friend? May God bless you and your family.

Freelance editor Ramona Cramer Tucker, cheerleader and editor; managing editor Philis Boultinghouse, and the staff of Howard Books, the Best Christian Place to Work in America for the fourth consecutive year. I'm glad someone else has recognized what authors have known for a long time.

And Steve Laube, agent and confidant.

CHAPTER 1

Once again his best friend had betrayed him.

Sixteen-year-old Daniel Cooper sat sulking, hunched against the winter night, atop a wooden barrel behind Gregg's casket shop. A shaft of moonlight sliced the blind alley into two halves. Daniel sat in the dark half, in a dark mood.

He wanted only two things in life: to play his music, and to be left alone. Was that asking too much? Yet every time he played, someone showed up, drawn to the music like flies to honey.

"Why can't they just leave me alone?"

He stared at Judas, his black recorder. He used to call the woodwind Faithful Friend because it understood him. It never judged. And it always reflected his mood. Lately, however, he'd renamed it Judas for obvious reasons.

Even so, it was a sweet betrayal. If a soul could sing, Daniel's soul would be mistaken for a recorder—a lone, haunting voice that did not belong to this world. Most people he knew preferred a lively fiddle or a foot-stomping banjo. Not Daniel. When he played the recorder, his very being vibrated with matching pitch.

Clutched in his hand, the instrument was silent now. So was the street, which wasn't surprising at this late hour.

"Dare we try again, old friend?"

He lifted the mouthpiece to his lips.

Closed his eyes.

And played.

The alley came alive with music. A mournful tune that wafted from wall to wall to wall, surrounding him, penetrating him. Daniel's soul sighed with pleasure.

He'd played less than a minute when a discordant animal noise slashed the melody. Frowning, Daniel lowered the recorder and listened.

The night lay under silent stars.

Daniel was certain he'd heard something. Possibly a complaining cat. He cocked an ear in the direction of the street. Whatever it was, it was gone.

Once again the recorder touched his lower lip, but before it uttered a note, the noise repeated itself.

A painful moan. A wounded cry.

There was a scuffle on the cobblestones, then another moan.

Daniel's heart seized. This time it didn't sound like an animal.

Just then a man stumbled into the mouth of the alley and collapsed. He whimpered. Tried to get up. Collapsed again.

Startled, Daniel's first impulse was to flee. But brick walls on three sides blocked his escape.

The man in the alley lay facedown, his breathing ragged and labored. He obviously needed help, though Daniel was at a loss as to what to do.

Setting the recorder aside, he slid off the barrel.

Two cautious steps and he pulled back, stopped short by an unseen, high-pitched voice. Like a child playing a game. Only it wasn't a child. And if this was a game, Daniel didn't want to play.

"Come out, come out! Where are you?"

The man on the ground heard the voice. It stirred him to life. Whimpering, the man's hands clutched at the icy cobblestones. He dragged himself deeper into the alley.

"Come out, come out!" sang the voice.

Daniel reversed his direction and dove behind a stack of barrels. Then, scrambling to the balls of his feet, he crouched, ready to explode out of the alley like a ball shot from a cannon.

It was at that moment that Daniel realized he'd left his recorder sitting in plain sight atop the barrel. He rose up to reach it, then stopped.

At the mouth of the alley, the voice had taken shape. A silhouette stood against the streaking moonlight.

Broad-rimmed hat.

Shoulder-length hair.

Knee-length travel coat.

And in the man's right hand—a knife large enough to gut a bear.

"Asa, he's gone."

Camilla Rush stood, one hand worrying the other, in the doorway of the study.

"Did you look in the—"

"I think I scared him off." Her voice quivered as she spoke. Her eyes, normally a portrait of compassion, revealed a tender soul that was as attractive to Asa Rush now as it had been two decades ago, when he first fell in love with her.

"When I went to slop the hogs," she continued, "I thought I heard somebody behind the barn. I stopped and listened. Then I heard music. Oh Asa, he has such talent."

Asa slammed shut his book. Chair legs scraped against the floor. He reached for his coat and hat and cane. "A man can't support a family playing a pipe. Where did you see him last?"

"Running into the forest. When he finished his song, I clapped. Then, when I went to tell him how beautiful it was, all I saw was his back disappearing into the woods." She stepped aside.

Asa's cane struck the floor with force as he strode past her. "Don't wait up."

"Go easy on him, Asa. It's been hard on him."

"It's been almost a year. Long enough for him to know we have rules in this house. Long enough to know I expect him to obey them."

"There you are!"

The silhouette at the mouth of the alley held his arms wide. The voice was playful, but the blade in his hand deadly serious.

From his hiding place in the back of the alley, Daniel could hear the hunted man but not see him.

"No . . . no . . . please, no," the man pleaded. "I haven't told anyone, I swear."

The hunter threw the man's words back at him in a singsong voice. "I won't tell . . . I won't tell . . . Please don't hurt me!" Then the hunter's tone changed. Hard. Menacing. "You know, I believe you. Honestly, I do. But do you know why? I'll tell you. I believe you because it's hard for a man to tell anyone anything when he has no tongue. Harder still when he has no heartbeat."

The hunted man's whimpers turned to grunts. From the scratching and the way the barrels shook, Daniel feared the man was trying to claw his way up them. The stack shuddered and threatened to topple. Daniel braced them from his side.

There was a scuffle. Then a scream bounced off the same walls that, moments earlier, had provided sweet acoustics for his recorder.

The stack of barrels gave an earthquake rattle. Daniel looked up just as one of the barrels tipped over the edge toward him. He ducked. It hit him on the back with force, flattening him. He winced and bit back a yelp of pain as his head slammed against the cobblestones, the side of his face resting in a slushy patch of melting snow.

When he opened his eyes, to his horror, his head stuck out from behind the last barrel. He could see the length of the alley . . . and be seen . . . if he didn't scoot back.

At that instant, a mirror image of his fall occurred on the other side of the barrel. The hunted man's head hit the ground, his face toward Daniel. He was dirty, bloodied, eyes scrunched in pain. Then he opened them.

Both men's faces lit with recognition.

"Braxton!" Daniel mouthed.

He knew it was a mistake the moment he formed the name, because his bloodied mirror image began to say his name in reply. "Da—"

Braxton never got a chance to finish. A hand grabbed him by the hair and lifted his head. A flash of silver crossed his neck.

Braxton's head hit the ground a second time. This time, however, nothing reflected in his eyes. The light in them had gone out.

Daniel began to shiver with fear. He bit back a whimper. If the killer heard him . . . or if Daniel moved, so would the barrel on top of him. And, for all he knew, he could set off an avalanche of barrels.

All he could do was lie still.

Not breathe.

And stare into the lifeless eyes of Emil Braxton.

Daniel's heart jumped at the sound of whistling. But whistling was good, wasn't it? If the killer had spotted him, he wouldn't be whistling, would he? He'd be killing. Whistling was good.

Then it stopped.

Braxton's head moved away from Daniel. Was dragged away.

The back of the killer came into view. He pulled Braxton by one arm, then dropped it. Braxton's lifeless arm hit the ground with a fleshy *thud*.

The killer straddled the body. He searched Braxton's pockets. Then, when he grabbed Braxton's shirt to roll him over, the killer's head crossed into the moonlight. His hair fell to one side, revealing a tattoo of a coiled snake on the back of his neck.

From the street came the clatter of an approaching carriage. The killer crouched. His knife, looking eager for more blood, poised for action.

The carriage stopped at the end of the alley.

"There you are," said a voice that was familiar to Daniel.

The killer relaxed.

A portly man in a carriage climbed down and entered the alley on foot. "Did you find—" A cry of revulsion cut short his sentence. "Why didn't you warn me? You know I can't stand the sight of—"

Retching echoed in the alley.

Daniel watched as the man slipped on an icy patch, catching himself on the side of his carriage. Steadying himself with a hand on the wheel, he took several minutes to recover.

Meanwhile, the killer finished his business with Braxton. Heaving the dead man onto his shoulder, he strolled toward the carriage as casually as a sailor carrying a bag aboard ship.

"The deed is done, payment is due," said the killer.

Averting his eyes and steadying himself all the way around the carriage, the man climbed into the seat. "Just get rid of that thing. Come to the store tomorrow. I'll have your money."

With his free hand, the killer touched his hat to signal farewell.

The man in the carriage took several deep breaths.

Then Cyrus Gregg—Daniel's employer and his uncle Asa's best friend—grabbed the reins and drove away in the carriage.

CHAPTER 2

Daniel Cooper had no memory of how he made it home. He balanced on shaky legs on a frozen tree limb outside his bedroom. His hands shivered, but only partially from the cold.

Something rustled nearby. Daniel's head snapped in that direction. He expected to see a dark figure emerge from the night with a broad-rimmed hat that concealed murderous eyes, hear the *swish* of a long coat, and feel the cold steel of a blood-stained blade against his neck.

To his relief he saw nothing but shadows and heard nothing except night sounds and the pounding of his heart in his ears. His throat had constricted needlessly. This time. But that didn't mean there wouldn't be a next time.

After watching the killer haul Braxton's dead body out of the alley, Daniel managed to crawl from beneath the barrel that had pinned him to the ground. He exited the alley but not before retrieving his recorder.

Had the killer seen it? Daniel had left it in plain sight atop a barrel. He'd found it lying on the ground. If the killer had seen it, would he know it belonged to Daniel? Cyrus Gregg, the man in the buggy, would recognize it as Daniel's. Almost daily Gregg's voice cut through recorder music to call Daniel back to work. All the killer had to do was mention to Gregg he'd seen a recorder in the alley.

They would come for him. They had no choice but to come for him. He could lie and tell them he'd left the recorder in the alley. That he went back for it later and saw nothing out of the ordinary.

Tightening his grip on the tree limb, Daniel closed his eyes and took a deep breath to steady his nerves. The breath came in irregular stutters.

Feeling no calmer for the effort, he opened his eyes and fixed them on the immediate problem. His bedroom window was closed. He remembered leaving it open. At least he thought he remembered leaving it open. At the moment he couldn't be certain of anything. Watching someone you know get murdered has a way of shaking up a man's memory.

It was the suddenness of death that unsettled Daniel the most. It just seemed wrong that a human life could be extinguished as quickly as one would snuff out a candle.

Daniel forced his mind back to the window. With his recorder tucked in his waistband, he straddled the three-foot span between the tree and the second-story window sill. Now came the tricky part. He let go of the steadying branch and stretched past his right foot, attempting to worm his fingers beneath the sash.

The window held fast. It was locked. Daniel grimaced. Not so much from the effort, but because a locked window meant his Uncle Asa knew he had sneaked out of the house and was probably sitting in the front room lying in wait for him.

With a groan, Daniel pushed off from the window sill and shinnied down the tree. He brushed off his clothes and stared at the front-room window, lit by a cozy, warm orange glow but camouflaging the white-hot fury that awaited him on the other side. The last time his uncle caught him sneaking out of the house, Daniel had to listen to an hourlong lecture on how youthful disrespect for authority will lead to the downfall of civilization. He dreaded the lecture's sequel.

For ten minutes Daniel paced outside, delaying the inevitable. Uncle Asa's wrath was only part of the problem. There was the matter of the murder. He had to tell someone, and his uncle was the logical choice. The appearance of Cyrus Gregg in the alley complicated things. Not only was Gregg his uncle's best friend, he was one of the most respected men in town. Even now Daniel had a hard time believing Gregg had anything to do with it. But he had seen Gregg there!

Daniel needed time to think. Maybe he could tell his aunt first, get her reaction, which would certainly be less volatile than his uncle's. That's what Daniel liked most about her. She listened to him and didn't judge him. Unlike Uncle Asa, who was always too busy yelling to listen.

He couldn't put it off forever.

Daniel took a step toward the front door. He stopped, turned away, and paced another five minutes despite the fact that the killer might be looking for him . . . even now hiding in the shadows watching him.

Finally—and not because he concluded his uncle was the lesser of two evils—Daniel braced himself for the onslaught and went inside.

"Daniel? Is that you? Oh, Daniel!"

Laying aside her Bible, his aunt Camilla catapulted from her chair and rushed toward him, her arms outstretched. "Thank God, you're all right. I've been praying for you!"

Daniel allowed himself to be wrapped in her embrace. The top of her head came to just below his chin. Her warmth and the smell of her hair comforted him on a deeper level than he thought possible.

"You're shivering!" she cried, holding him tighter.

A glance around the room revealed they were alone. The ogre must be upstairs in his den. Daniel allowed himself a moment to relax.

All too soon his aunt stepped back. Holding on to his arms, she looked up at him, her eyes brimming with concern.

Camilla Rush was a kindly woman with a round face framed by black hair pulled back and pinned up. If you asked her, she would say she was plump. Daniel thought of her as soft. If you asked, she would also point to the lines around her eyes as cruel indicators of advancing years, nearly four decades now. But Daniel loved the way her skin framed her eyes, the perfect setting for two azure pools.

She brushed dirt from the side of his face. Daniel winced.

"You're hurt!" His aunt took a closer look.

Daniel touched his temple. It stung. Until now he wasn't aware he'd been injured. It had probably happened when the barrel fell on him.

"It's nothing," he said, turning away from her.

"It's *not* nothing," she insisted. "Come over here by the fire. Let me look at it."

The scrape itself didn't concern him, except for the fact that it was evidence something had happened. Something that begged an explanation.

His aunt's eyes narrowed. She sensed he was hiding something. "Daniel, have you been fighting?"

"No ma'am."

She looked him in the eyes and believed him. *She believed him!* Was it any wonder he was fond of her? Uncle Asa would never believe him.

"We should put some ointment on those abrasions," she said. "You wait here. I'll get a damp cloth."

She wasn't gone long. Just long enough for Daniel to realize that now would be a good time to tell her what happened. He could gauge her reaction. Of course, she'd insist on telling Uncle Asa. Tonight.

No that was too soon. Daniel needed time to think.

He moved closer to the fire where his aunt had been sitting when he came in. Her Bible lay open on the Pembroke table. It was her practice to pray with an open Bible. She'd read a verse or two, then pray, read another verse, and pray, letting the text guide her. He bent over the book, curious as to the subject of her prayers tonight.

"Luke, chapter fifteen," he muttered.

Anger sliced into his gut like a knife. He was familiar with the text. A lost sheep. A lost coin. A lost son.

He straightened up, furious. Is that how she thought of him? A prodigal? A wastrel? An ungrateful son who squanders his inheritance?

"Here we are," his aunt said, carrying a small basin, a towel, and a bottle of ointment.

She set the basin on the table next to the Bible, dipped an edge of the towel in the water and reached toward him. "Now . . . are you going to tell me what happened?"

Daniel stood stiff and silent as she dabbed his temple.

"Your uncle and I were worried sick," she said. "He went looking for you."

Daniel grabbed his aunt's wrist. "He went looking for me? How long ago?"

Before she could answer, the front door slammed open. The ogre himself stormed into the room in a rage, his head down, his cane leading the way. Bent over and grumbling, he looked like an angry bridge troll.

"I searched everywhere," he groused, "and found no sign of—"

When he looked up and saw Daniel, his eyes narrowed to murderous slits, and his jaw did that clenching thing that made him look like a bulldog with its teeth sunk into someone's leg.

"There you are!" he bellowed. "Where have you been? I've turned Cumberland inside out looking for you!"

For a man with a serious limp, he could move quickly if sufficiently motivated or angered.

"Asa, calm yourself," Aunt Camilla said. "He's home safe. That's what's important."

Asa looked at his wife, the towel, the basin, and the scratches on Daniel's face. "You've been fighting!"

"I haven't been fighting," Daniel replied.

"Then how do you explain those?" His cane jabbed the air in the direction of Daniel's face.

"I haven't been fighting," Daniel insisted.

"I've seen enough fights in my day to recognize the aftermath of a common brawl when I see it. Tell the truth for once in your life. Who have you been fighting?"

Daniel's chest swelled with so much anger, he thought it would explode. His teeth clenched, he sidestepped his aunt and made his way toward the stairs.

His uncle's words hit him in the back. "We're not finished. Come back here!"

Daniel paused on the first step. Without turning around, he said, "Yes, we are."

He waited for the response he knew would come.

"If you have something to say to me, turn around and face me like a man."

Daniel allowed himself a wry smile. There was nothing his uncle hated more than for someone to turn his back on him. With that small victory, Daniel bounded up the stairs two at a time.

"Go ahead, run away. That's what you're good at, isn't it?" his uncle shouted.

CHAPTER 3

Sitting on the edge of his bed, Asa Rush let his shoe drop to the floor. He resisted throwing it down. He wanted to throw it. Needed to throw it. Needed to throw something.

"You should talk to him," Camilla said as she brushed her hair in front of the vanity mirror. "If you don't, you'll never get any sleep."

"Talk?" Asa scoffed. "There's no talking to that one. All he does is sit and stare into the distance. I've had better conversations with cows."

Camilla laughed. Her hair, when let down, fell to her hips. "You're exaggerating."

"I am not! The boy's a stone statue."

He wrestled with the buckle on his remaining shoe. The leather tongue was worn, creased nearly to the point of breaking. If he tugged too hard . . .

The tongue ripped from the shoe. For a second he stared at it dumbly between his thumb and forefinger.

It was all the excuse his dormant rage needed. With a cry of frustration, he threw the leather tongue across the room, followed by the shoe.

His outburst and the sound of the shoe hitting the wall gave Camilla a fright. A hand flew to her chest. "Asa!"

"We needed those shoes to last the winter!" Asa shouted, defending himself.

"That's no reason to throw them across the room!"

"It's the only reason I had."

He sat slumped over with one sock on and one sock off, his chest rising and falling as though he'd just carried a heavy load up the stairs.

Asa Rush had always thought of himself as physically average and mentally unremarkable. He'd never been the best-looking man in a room, but neither had he been the worst. He'd never been the smartest man, but neither was he the dullest. At age forty-two, he continued his average ways. Like most men his age, his hair was showing streaks of gray, he needed glasses to read, and his muscles and bones were beginning to ache in places they'd never ached before.

Camilla crossed the room and sat next to him. She placed a hand on his hand. "I've never seen you like this," she said softly.

"The boy does manage to bring out the worst in me, doesn't he?"

"You've worked with troubled boys before," Camilla said. "Is it so different that Daniel is your nephew?"

Asa stood. He couldn't sit still. He had to pace. Camilla folded her hands in her lap and watched him—one sock on, one sock off—limping back and forth, occasionally steadying himself with a hand to the edge of the bed. It took him a few moments to find the words.

"I don't know why, but for some reason, my inability to reach Daniel strikes at the heart of my entire professional life. For years now I've felt like a failure. For some reason Daniel exacerbates that failure a hundredfold."

"Asa Rush! Don't say such things! I won't have it! You're not a failure. Everyone looks up to you. They wouldn't entrust the education of their children to you if they didn't have the utmost confidence in you."

"That's not enough," Asa said. "That's not why I became an educator. I wanted to do more than teach mathematics and science and philosophy. I wanted to mold them, to influence them."

"As Dr. Dwight influenced you at Yale."

"Yes," he said.

"Surely, in all these years you've . . . what about—"

Asa cut her off. "No. I've had some good students . . . some competent students . . . but none who are any better off than they could have been in any other classroom."

He knew Camilla was trying to help, but she didn't know the depth of his sense of failure. Any listing of students' names would only make things worse.

Staring at the hairbrush in her hand, Camilla asked, "Why have you never told me you felt this way before?"

Asa smiled wryly. "A man doesn't easily admit his failures, not even to himself."

His confession did, however, lessen his rage. Now his injured foot began to ache. He lowered himself once again onto the edge of the bed.

"I still think you should talk to Daniel," Camilla murmured. "Something happened out there tonight."

"The fight."

"He was shivering when he came home, and I think it was more than the cold. He was scared."

Asa hunched, as though settling in. Camilla was right, of course, but he didn't want to do this tonight. He was cold and tired, and because of Daniel he'd have to get up early in the morning to finish grading the papers that would have been done if he hadn't gone on a wild goose chase all over town.

"Every year he becomes more and more like his father, wouldn't you agree?" Camilla asked.

Changing the subject was her subtle way of gloating. She knew he would go. That she'd won the argument. Now she would attempt to make his defeat more palatable with small talk.

"He may look like his father, but he has his mother's stubborn streak," Asa said.

He snatched the spare sock from the floor and put it on. Pushing off the bed, he went to get his shoe.

"What are you doing?" Camilla asked.

"Putting my shoes on."

"You're only going down the hallway."

Retrieving his shoe, Asa headed back to the bed. "A man in bare feet is a man with no authority. That's why the president of the United States always wears shoes."

Camilla laughed. Making her laugh was Asa's way of giving in to her.

"Was it this difficult for you when Dr. Dwight asked you to try to win over Eli?"

"That was different. I knew I was reaching Eli. Daniel's nothing like his father that way."

"How did you know you were reaching Eli?"

"Every chance he got, he pounded me into the dust."

Camilla laughed again.

"But with Daniel—" Asa shook his head. "It's as though he doesn't hear me."

"You never gave up on Eli."

"I wanted to."

"But you never did."

"No."

Camilla linked her arm in his. "Then don't give up on his son."

Sitting Indian-style on his bed, Daniel listened to the voices coming from the other room. Though he couldn't make out the words, he knew they were talking about him. Whenever their voices got loud, they were talking about him. A sudden thud made him jump. The voices got louder still.

Daniel grinned. The thought of his reserved, ordained uncle throwing things struck him as humorous.

He pulled the recorder from his waistband, the instrument that had set the evening's events in motion. Earlier, seated just as he was now, Daniel had begun playing it. His uncle yelled down the hallway, telling him to stop, saying it was too late to be playing a musical instrument.

Daniel shouted that he'd go outside to play. The answer came back instantly. No, it was too late to go outside.

That was his uncle in a nutshell. The man who quoted rules, making them up on the spot—Daniel was certain—to get his way.

Well, Daniel was tired of it. Rules were for little kids. He was sixteen. Old enough to take care of himself. He didn't need someone's rules to tell him when to go to bed, when to get up, and when he could play his recorder.

That was when Daniel had gone out the window. It wasn't the first time, and it probably wouldn't be the last.

Daniel examined the recorder to see if it had suffered any damage in the scuffle. Holding it to the light of the lamp beside his bed, he thought he saw a scratch. He tilted it to get a better look while running a finger the length of the flaw. He picked at it with a fingernail. Bits of it came off. Holding his finger closer to the light, he examined the jagged black flecks. They felt sticky. They . . .

He dropped the recorder and recoiled as though it had bit him. Pushing himself away from it, he furiously wiped his finger on the bedspread.

The black flecks were blood.

Braxton's blood.

Curled up and pressed against the headboard, Daniel stared at the black recorder in horror. He shuddered. The shudder turned into a shiver that took on a life of its own. He wrapped himself up in his own arms. When that didn't stop the shivers, he pulled the bedspread over him.

The recorder rolled off the edge of the bed and clattered against the wooden floor. He made no effort to retrieve it.

The bedspread captured his body heat, and after a time the shivering stopped. With the warmth came drowsiness. Daniel's eyelids grew heavy. He fought to keep them open, afraid of what he'd see if he closed them.

He knew it was a losing battle, but he fought it anyway. Eventually, time and fatigue, as they always did, proved themselves stronger than his will, and Daniel dozed off . . .

His dream had no sound.

Braxton's head fell in slow motion, hitting the shiny, wet cobblestones, bouncing, knocking drops of sweat and spittle and blood in the air like some kind of grotesque ballet of liquids. Braxton's eyes were fixed with fright, as if his last conscious thought was the realization he was dying. They stared directly at Daniel—only inches from his face. And because this was a dream, Daniel was helpless to look away or to close his eyes.

He tried to scream and found he had no voice. He tried to run even though he knew he was pinned to the ground.

The next thing Daniel knew, he was underwater. There was barely enough light to see. Broken pieces of wood floated all around him. Among the debris were two figures. A man and a woman, from their dress. Lifeless, they floated toward him. Like Braxton, their eyes were open but unseeing.

Daniel knew who they were before he could make out their facial features. As with Braxton in the alley, despite every effort, Daniel couldn't turn, couldn't swim away. Some unseen force forced him to look at them, to look into the eyes of his dead parents.

All of a sudden, he couldn't breathe. There was no air underwater. And he knew what it must have been like for his parents when they drowned. Still conscious. Lungs bursting. Inhaling liquid. Saltwater filling their lungs. The drowsiness of death blanketing them, but not before they had time to know they were sinking to the bottom of the sea and that they were dying.

With a violent gasp, Daniel threw back the bedspread and sat up with a jolt. He greedily inhaled one gulp of air after another.

It took him a moment to realize he was in his bedroom. Voices came from the other room, the same conversation he'd heard earlier. He had fallen asleep for a matter of minutes.

His heart was pounding wildly.

CHAPTER 4

Standing with his hand on their bedroom doorknob, Asa had both shoes on, but the one missing its tongue was loose and sloppy. He gave it a chagrined look. It would have to do.

"When you go in there, listen to him," Camilla said.

"This is going to be the quietest conversation in the history of mankind," Asa replied.

Camilla wasn't listening. She was too busy telling him what to do. "Be patient with him. I don't think he's gotten over his parents' deaths yet."

"Of course he hasn't. Neither have I."

His admission took the wind out of Camilla's sails. They hadn't spoken of Eli and Maggy's deaths in months. And though she knew Asa's pain over the loss of his sister and best friend had to be enormous, never once had he admitted such to her.

Camilla went to him.

"Sometimes I look at the boy and think that somehow Eli's been raised from the dead." Asa blinked back tears. His voice broke. "I miss him horribly, Camilla."

"As do I," Camilla whispered.

Asa braced himself. "But grief does not exempt the boy from living by our rules. I would be doing him no favors if I let him believe he was exempt simply because life is sometimes cruel."

"Of course not, dear. You need to be firm. Firm, but patient. Go in there and listen to him."

Her sweet stubbornness brought a smile to Asa's face. He caressed her cheek with his hand. "Yes, dear."

His one shoe flapping, his cane clicking on the hard wood like a talon, Asa sounded like some kind of wounded bird flopping down the hallway.

Stopping outside Daniel's door, Asa took a deep breath to calm himself. He took a second for good measure.

"Daniel?" he called gently. His ear close to the door, he listened and heard no response.

"Daniel?" he said a little louder, this time adding a triple rap with his knuckle.

Still no response.

The boy could be asleep.

Asa opened the door quietly. "Daniel?"

He poked his head in. "Daniel?"

The bed was rumpled but empty. The room chilled. Asa pushed the door open and stepped in. The lamp beside the bed lit the room with a cozy light.

The reason for both the lack of response and the chill became clear in an instant. The window was open. The wind rustled the curtains.

Asa knew instant rage. He could feel it fill his head and color his face. His chest heaving, he charged toward the window and looked out.

Everything was dark and still.

Not a sign of his nephew.

"Daniel Cooper!" he bellowed, frightening some birds pecking the frozen ground.

"Daniel!"

The night was still.

Slapping the sill with the flat of his hand, Asa pulled his head back inside. He slammed the window shut, locked it, extinguished the lamp beside the bed, and closed the door on the dark room.

Camilla was waiting for him when he returned to the bedroom. "What happened? I heard shouting."

Asa kicked off his shoes and began readying himself for bed. "The boy didn't want to talk."

Outside his bedroom window, high in the tree, Daniel heard his uncle rap on the bedroom door and call his name. He heard his uncle's cane strike the floor as he crossed the room and from on high saw his uncle stick his head out the window and bellow his name.

Daniel started to call down to him but thought better of it. The man was obviously in one of his moods.

The window slammed shut. Daniel heard it lock and saw the light in the room go out. The only way he could get back into the house now would be to break the window or go to the front of the house, knock on the door, and hope his uncle would give Aunt Camilla permission to let him in.

It looked like he was stuck outside for the night.

Just as well.

Afraid to close his eyes, he'd come outside to stay awake and think. Bracing himself in the crook of a tree limb, he scraped the last of Braxton's blood from his recorder and fought the urge to gag. With a shiver of revulsion, he wiped the last of the blood from his fingernail.

The scene in the alley kept replaying in his head. He couldn't help but think that had he acted differently, Braxton might still be alive.

Yet, like a coward, he'd hid. If he'd gone to Braxton the instant he'd seen him in the mouth of the alley, everything might have played out differently. He might have been able to help Braxton escape. If not that, at least the killer would have seen there were two of them. That alone might have frightened him away.

But Daniel would never know, would he? Because he had acted cowardly, Braxton was dead. And now Daniel was hiding out in a tree in the middle of winter.

Disgusted with himself, Daniel slipped the recorder under his coat, folded his arms against the cold, and settled himself for a long winter's night.

CHAPTER 5

Sometime during the night Daniel dreamed he was an icicle. When he stirred, he found the shoulder of his coat frozen to the tree branch. Climbing out of the tree, he moved to the barn and buried himself in a pile of hay, where he slept until morning . . .

The cows woke him. His joints aching and stiff, he did his morning chores before going inside, for no other reason than to give his uncle one less thing to yell about. There would be enough yelling when Daniel told him he wasn't going to work today.

How could he? For all he knew, Cyrus Gregg and the killer were waiting there for him. Maybe that was Gregg's plan all along. Why chase after him if he was dumb enough to come to work the next day?

Of course, Uncle Asa would demand a reason. Daniel thought up a lie. He would say that after spending all night outside, he was ill. Once Aunt Camilla learned that he hadn't run off after all, but had been in the tree outside his room when Uncle Asa locked him out, she would feel sorry for him and take his side. With every angle covered, he went inside.

His plan self-destructed almost immediately. As expected, the instant he mentioned not going to work, Uncle Asa flew into a rage. He launched into his, "If a man doesn't work, he doesn't eat," speech.

Daniel's undoing proved to be his own anger. The stiff-fingered lecture proved too much for him, and Daniel grew so angry he stormed out of the house without breakfast.

He went straight to work, hoping that Cyrus Gregg and the killer were indeed waiting for him and that they'd put him out of his misery. At least when the truth came out, Daniel would be vindicated, and Aunt Camilla would never forgive Uncle Asa for treating him so unjustly.

Then, as he fumed, a thought occurred to him. It would be just his luck that Cyrus Gregg and the killer weren't lying in wait for him. After all, Daniel's fears were based on a supposition. Maybe neither man saw the recorder in the alley. It was dark. The recorder is black. And if they hadn't seen it, not showing up for work today would raise unwanted questions that, if answered, would place him in the alley. And even if they had seen the recorder in the alley, it didn't prove Daniel had been there during the murder. He could have misplaced the instrument. Left it there by accident earlier in the day.

In fact, if they asked him, that's what he could tell them. That he'd lost the recorder and came to work early this morning in hopes of finding it.

Suddenly Daniel's dilemma didn't seem so hopeless. But that didn't mean he was safe, not by any means. He was still working for a killer.

Arming himself with the alert spirit of a pioneer entering unfriendly territory, Daniel made his way to work, determined to keep an escape route always in sight.

Gregg's Caskets of Cumberland, the largest producer of caskets in the west, consisted of an office and a showroom. The caskets were made in a cavernous workshop behind the showroom. Daniel entered the workshop by way of an employees' entrance on the side. Shop workers were rarely allowed in the showroom, the exception being when they were carrying display caskets in or out.

The workshop was deserted when he arrived. The large saws were silent. Hundreds of unfinished planks lined the far wall, filling the space with scents of poplar, mahogany, walnut, and cherry. Caskets in various stages of completion awaited the skilled workers to assemble them and line them with muslin. The more expensive caskets were stained and varnished and fitted with handles.

Cyrus Gregg employed about a dozen skilled woodworkers and three shop boys. The shop boys did whatever they were told to do, from lending an extra hand, to running errands, to being the subjects of all manner of crude jokes and pranks, to sweeping out the shop at night.

As Daniel walked onto the floor that he and Braxton had swept the night before, his footsteps echoed among the ceiling rafters. He moved cautiously, leaving the door open behind him. While it wasn't common for him to be the first person to arrive, it wasn't unusual. Not enough to make a person jumpy or suspicious. That is, unless he'd seen his boss murder one of the employees the night before.

With each step further into the shop, Daniel grew more anxious. Maybe it would be better to wait outside.

"Daniel! There you are!" Cyrus Gregg's voice boomed through the shop.

Daniel nearly jumped out of his skin.

Gregg entered the shop through the showroom door. He headed straight toward Daniel with purposeful strides. "Come here. I want a word with you before the others arrive."

Daniel's heart raced, as though knowing it had only a limited number of beats left and it wanted to get as many of them in as possible.

Suddenly, behind Daniel, a larger black figure filled the side doorway, blocking his escape.

As Gregg closed in, Daniel's feet began to fidget as though they didn't understand the delay in receiving orders to get him out of there. Given Cyrus Gregg's healthy waistline, Daniel's chances of getting past him and through the showroom to the street were not the best.

The figure in the side doorway spoke. "What are you so nervous about, boy? Have ghosty dreams last night, did you?"

To Daniel's relief, he recognized the voice. Jake, the head sawyer, was arriving for work. He strode into the shop with the easy strides of a man in charge. Close on Jake's heels were two more sawyers in conversation. They walked past Daniel as though he weren't there.

By now Gregg had reached Daniel. Taking Daniel by the arm, he pulled him aside. The man's expression was serious. His voice confidential. "Emil Braxton won't be in today. It'll just be you and Icky. I'm making you the head boy for today. Don't let me down. And tell Icky when he comes in."

He squeezed Daniel's arm for emphasis, then turned his attention to the sawyers, wanting an explanation as to why they hadn't shipped the Burlingham order yet.

Daniel's knees were liquid. It was all he could do to keep them from buckling. He had thought for sure Gregg and the killer would be measuring him for one of the shop's caskets.

Icky Kitterbell arrived soon afterward and was not at all happy to learn that Daniel had been appointed head shop boy. While he was a year younger than Daniel, he'd worked in the shop eight months longer and felt he deserved to be head shop boy in Braxton's absence. Daniel told him to take it up with Gregg, which he did, only to return a short time later, looking as though he was about to cry. Icky spent most of the morning pouting and telling anyone who would listen that he should be head boy, not Daniel.

Daniel ignored Icky and his mood. His mind was on the fact that Gregg had said Braxton wouldn't be in today. That was odd, considering Daniel had it on pretty good authority that Braxton wouldn't be showing up for work any time in the foreseeable future.

The morning passed with an eerie familiarity, as though nothing had happened the night before. As though Braxton were attending to some personal business and would be back, his usual foulmouthed self, in the shop tomorrow. But then nobody had reason to believe otherwise. Daniel was the only person in the shop who knew Braxton was dead.

On his lunch break, Daniel ventured to the alley behind the shop where he normally ate his lunch and played his recorder, though he doubted he could ever do either there again. He went to see if he could find evidence of Braxton's murder.

With no idea where the murderer took Braxton's body, Daniel's story would be reduced to his word against Cyrus Gregg's and some shadowy figure Daniel had never seen before. Daniel knew who everyone would believe.

Cyrus Gregg's family had been established community leaders in Cumberland for decades. Gregg himself was a business leader in the town. His connections with several members of the United States House of Representatives were a topic of civic pride.

Daniel was a troubled orphan who had lived in Cumberland a little less than a year and had been dismissed from school for disruptive behavior.

Evidence. If anybody was going to believe Daniel's story, he needed evidence.

It had snowed the night before, so Daniel wasn't surprised to see the alley looking whitewashed and fresh. What surprised him was the fresh pile of manure on the exact spot where Braxton had fallen. Where his life's blood had been spilled onto the cobblestones.

Why would someone dump manure there? And why today? In all the time Daniel had been working for Gregg, no one had dumped manure in this alley. And why here, in the back, against a row of barrels? It was difficult to believe that it was coincidence that the pile would have been dumped in that very spot. Unless the purpose was to hide and possibly soak up bloodstains.

Daniel looked around for something he could use to move the pile. There were shovels in the workshop, but he didn't want to risk being seen walking out with one when he had no good explanation for needing one just now.

There was nothing in the alley he could use as a shovel.

Standing over the pile, Daniel grimaced as the thought occurred to him to shove the manure aside using his foot. The pile was high enough that it would stain his pants halfway up to his knee. But what other choice did he have?

Just as he was placing his foot beside the pile and grousing to himself that he was going to smell like manure for the rest of the day, his eyes fell on the barrels.

Blood splatters.

His recorder had been splattered, so it stood to reason that some of the barrels would show blood splatters.

Stepping to one side, bracing himself with a hand on top of a barrel, he bent down over the pile of manure to get a closer look at the barrels most likely to be splattered with Braxton's blood.

"What are you doing there?"

It wasn't the voice that startled him, but whose voice it was. With hands on hips, Cyrus Gregg stood at the mouth of the alley, awaiting an answer.

Flustered, Daniel's hand slipped as he tried to right himself, and he nearly fell headlong into the pile of manure. Somehow he managed to prevent the dive.

"I asked you a question," Gregg demanded.

"Um . . . lunch," Daniel said.

That sounded odd even to him—especially when he was standing next to a pile of manure.

Reaching into his coat, he pulled out his recorder. "I always come here to eat lunch and play my music."

It was a plausible explanation. On more than one occasion Gregg had sent Braxton or come himself to get Daniel from the alley, accusing him of taking more than the allotted time for his break. Gregg was constantly accusing all his workers of robbing him of work time.

"Aya . . . well," Gregg said, "your time's up."

"It is not!" Daniel cried. "I've only had ten minutes."

"Head shop boys don't always get lunch," Gregg countered. "Hitch up a team. We have a delivery to make."

The next thing Daniel knew, Gregg was gone.

And Daniel was left standing next to a pile of manure with his heart weary from all the heavy pounding it had done this morning.

CHAPTER 6

Deliveries prompted mixed emotions among the shop boys. On the one hand, it was a chance to get out of the shop and escape the seemingly endless bark of demands. There was a certain freedom riding in a wagon to and from the delivery, even though Daniel always had to put up with Braxton's insufferable boasting the entire journey.

The unpleasant part about deliveries was that they usually involved handling dead bodies. Someone had to lift the body and place it in the casket. And someone usually meant Cyrus Gregg's shop boys. Gregg made a big fuss of offering their help to the family as a service that he included in the price of the casket.

Since Braxton was the head shop boy, he always got to carry the feet. Carrying the other end was not only heavier, it entailed lifting the shoulders while cradling the head to keep it from falling backward. This meant placing your face uncomfortably close to the deceased person's. Braxton insisted that one time he had grabbed the shoulders of a dead widow and forgot to support her head. It had snapped back so hard, it fell off and rolled around the floor.

Daniel didn't believe Braxton's tall tale for a minute, though he was familiar with the gasps of family members whenever a deceased loved one's head or arms lolled about unexpectedly.

Once, when lifting a revered minister, the man's arm had fallen to one side, slapping the head of his little granddaughter, who had been told repeatedly to stand back. The little girl was startled, but not hurt. Not until her mother and aunt flew into hysterics did she join them. For a month afterward Daniel was restricted from making deliveries.

Now, as he and Icky loaded the casket into the back of the wagon, Daniel took delight in the fact that he was head shop boy, which meant he got to carry the feet and Icky would have to worry about the head.

The deceased was no one of importance. Daniel knew that because they'd loaded a bottom-of-the-line casket, little more than a box.

After pulling on coat and gloves, Daniel climbed into the driver's seat of the wagon. The sky was clear, the air crisp.

Icky had run into the office to get directions. He seemed to take forever. And just as Daniel was about to climb down to see what was taking so long, Cyrus Gregg strutted out the side door carrying a sheaf of papers, his breath creating clouds in the cold air. He climbed into the wagon seat beside Daniel.

Using the papers as a pointer, Gregg ordered, "Head west along the Wills Creek road. We're going just beyond Braddock Run."

"Sir? Should I wait for Icky?"

"It's just you and me this trip. Let's go."

"Yes, sir." Daniel flicked the reigns, setting the wagon in motion. "Braddock Run. That's a pretty good distance."

Gregg wasn't listening. He'd turned his attention to his papers, occasionally looking up to exchange greetings with someone passing by.

Daniel couldn't help but be unnerved sitting this close to his employer. Especially when less than twenty-four hours ago, he'd witnessed the man approving of and financing a murder.

What unsettled Daniel even more—besides the fact that they were headed out of town with an empty casket in the back of the wagon—was that he'd never known Cyrus Gregg to deliver a casket personally. It was widely known that the owner of the casket company couldn't stomach death. Besides, the man was dressed in blue silk breeches and coat and wearing a dress hat.

And while Daniel was ready to concede that there were exceptions to every rule, it would stand to reason that an unprecedented personal delivery would be to someone wealthy or influential, or possibly family. But if that were the case, wouldn't the casket in the back of the wagon be the top of the line and not a mere wooden box?

The further they traveled into the hills, the colder it got and the scarcer the road traffic. Distances between houses became greater and greater. And every time the wealthy man fidgeted in his seat, Daniel expected to turn to see a gun pointed at him, with a wickedly grinning Cyrus Gregg informing him this would be a one-way trip.

Daniel scanned the road ahead for a good place to jump and run.

Cyrus Gregg cleared his throat.

Daniel gave a start.

"Relax, boy. I'm not going to bite your head off."

Daniel grinned defensively. He didn't relax.

"On our way back . . . ," Gregg began.

Back? Any mention of a return trip was good news.

". . . we'll take a small detour to pick up a machine and deliver it to my house."

"Yes, sir," Daniel said.

Papers shuffled. "Have you ever seen one of these?" Gregg asked, holding a piece of paper in front of Daniel.

It was a drawing of what looked like a wooden barrel on its side sitting in some sort of trough with legs. A hatch opened in the middle of the barrel, and there was a crank on one end.

"No, sir," Daniel said.

Gregg sported a schoolboy grin. "It's the patent drawing for a revolving washing machine. I'm an investor in the company that is producing them. My partners have shipped one to me."

Daniel stared at the picture, intrigued.

"You put the clothes in here." Gregg pointed to the hatch. "You add soap, latch the door down, and turn this handle at the end. The trough is filled with water." He sat back. "This machine can do the work of two scrub women with half the effort."

Daniel had to admit the idea was ingenious.

This pleased Gregg. He shuffled the papers and produced two more drawings. "These are our competitors. This first one forces the clothes through two sets of rollers on a vibrating frame, while this second one agitates the clothes, pounding them with four hammers which are attached to a crankshaft." Gregg spoke with animation.

Daniel was taken aback. Did Gregg want his opinion? Or was he just wanting Daniel to agree with him that his model was obviously the best machine of the three?

To give Daniel a good look at the drawings, Gregg was leaning against him. Daniel had never before been this close to his employer. His sideburns looked like sparsely bunched little white corkscrews growing on a field of splotchy pink skin.

Daniel glanced up the empty road, then focused on the two drawings. "The one on the right, the one with the hammers . . . the idea is to simulate a washerwoman's arms—the scrubbing motion—right?"

"That's right."

"Well, it's just that, from the drawing . . . it doesn't seem that it has enough leverage to be effective. I mean, I remember my mother washing clothes. She used to bear down so hard that her tongue stuck out the side of her mouth."

"An interesting observation. Go on."

"That's it. All I'm saying is that when she taught me how to scrub something clean, she told me to use plenty of elbow grease—meaning to bear down, to really give it a good scrubbing. From the configuration of the drawing, those thin wooden rods . . . well, they wouldn't generate very much elbow grease. I mean, if a woman had arms that thin, you wouldn't mistake her for a washerwoman."

Gregg laughed. "And this one?"

After another glance at the road, Daniel studied the second drawing.

"This one looks like it has better leverage, just the way it's built. And the rollers are a good idea, squeezing the clothes through them like that." A thought made him sit up.

"Yes?" Gregg said.

"I wonder what happens when buttons go through there. Big buttons. That would really foul things up, wouldn't it?"

It was Gregg's turn to sit back. He took a long look at Daniel, one that made Daniel feel good. There was approval and respect in Gregg's eyes, something Daniel had never seen in his uncle's.

"I just paid a couple of investment firms a substantial sum of money to come to the same conclusion you arrived at in just a few minutes," Gregg said.

Cyrus Gregg's words worked like a tonic, warming Daniel all over inside.

"All right," Gregg said, shuffling the cylinder washing machine drawing to the top of the stack. "What about this one? Be honest, now."

Feeling flush with success, Daniel examined the drawing. "I like the trough. It obviously holds more water than the other models, which means it probably rinses the clothes better."

"Very good! And . . . ?"

"And . . ."

Daniel stared at the drawing. Nothing came to him. He looked harder. He wanted to say something insightful, something that would impress Cyrus Gregg.

"Well, it has legs, so that it stands up higher than the others. That has to be easier on the back, I suppose."

"Yes," Gregg said but not with the enthusiasm of before.

"And . . ." Daniel stared at the drawing of the hatch. It was raised. The opening was shaded black. "What's inside?"

"You tell me," Gregg said.

"I was just thinking . . ."

An idea came to him. It took him a few minutes to work it through.

Gregg gave him time. Unlike Uncle Asa, he didn't expect an answer immediately to every question.

"It just seems to me," Daniel explained, "that if the walls of the cylinder are smooth inside, with the soap and water, it's going to get slippery, don't you think? And the clothes will just slip around and not really . . ."

The word he wanted wasn't coming.

"Agitate?" Gregg suggested.

That wasn't exactly what he was thinking, but the more Daniel thought about it, the more he liked the word. "Yeah, I guess that explains it about as well as anything else. Agitate."

"What would you recommend?" Gregg asked.

Daniel wished his uncle were here, listening to this conversation. Asa Rush held Cyrus Gregg in high esteem. And here Daniel and Cyrus Gregg were, having an intelligent discussion, and Cyrus Gregg was not only *listening* to him but *seeking* his advice.

"Rails," Daniel said. "I was thinking there should be wooden rails nailed to the inside walls, something to catch the clothes and turn them over, but not enough for them to get caught up in."

Gregg was staring at the drawing like he'd never seen it before. "A series of wooden rails evenly spaced inside to increase the agitation." With his index finger, he drew an imaginary horizontal line the length of the cylinder.

"Actually," Daniel said, "I was thinking they should be angled slightly." He reached over and showed Gregg what he meant with his own imaginary line. "That way, the agitation has a spiraling effect."

Cyrus Gregg nodded. He smiled. "Brilliant."

Daniel wasn't certain if he'd heard correctly. Did Cyrus Gregg just call his idea brilliant? Never had that word even been remotely associated with Daniel Cooper. That single word uncapped a wellspring of good feeling inside Daniel. It bubbled forth with such emotion that he had to fight back tears.

"Rome; Oneida Lake; Lock 23 is just east of Oneida Lake; Baldwinsville; Seneca Falls; Clyde; Lyons; Newark; Palmyra; Macedon . . ."

Cyrus Gregg looked on with an amused grin as Daniel named the locks of the Erie Canal from east to west. Their discussion had turned to canals when Gregg told Daniel that he was part owner of the Patowmack Canal that ran from Georgetown to Cumberland.

"Have you ever seen the Erie Canal?" Gregg asked when Daniel finished his list.

"No, but I know everything about it."

"Everything?" Gregg said, lifting an eyebrow.

"Aya," Daniel replied. "I think so."

"Then you wouldn't mind a little test. Just to amuse us along the way."

Daniel had become so caught up in their conversation, first inventions and now canals, that he'd lost track of time. Normally he would have hated the thought of a test. He'd had his fill of them at school. But then school never asked questions about things that interested him, like music and canals. Daniel saw no useful purpose for knowing what dead Romans and Greeks said or thought thousands of years ago. But facts about mankind's most recent engineering marvel? Daniel couldn't understand why everyone wasn't interested in things like that.

"What is the total length of the canal?" Gregg asked.

Daniel rolled his eyes. "Ask me something hard."

Gregg looked disappointed. "Stumped so easily?"

With a flat tone, Daniel said, "The Erie Canal is three hundred and sixty-three miles long."

Gregg nodded that was correct. Before he could ask another question, Daniel added, "It has eighteen aqueducts and eighty-three locks with a rise of five hundred and sixty-eight feet from the Hudson River to Lake Erie. The Niagara escarpment presented the greatest engineering problem with its sixty-foot rise. Nathan S. Roberts solved the problem with a double set of five combined locks—one set for ascending traffic, the other for descending traffic."

Gregg listened as though he'd just heard a mesmerizing symphony and didn't want to speak too quickly for fear of breaking the mood. "All right," he finally said. "What size are the locks?"

"Ninety feet by fifteen feet. They're designed to accommodate boats up to sixty-one feet long and seven feet wide with a three-and-a-half-foot draft. Do you want me to tell you how they function? About how the sluices, or ground paddles, operate?"

"Tell me the purpose of the lock gates meeting a chevron," Gregg said.

Daniel smiled. Gregg thought he had him on this one. "The two halves of the lock gate meet at a point, which points against the flow of the water. This keeps the locks from succumbing to the pressure of the water between an empty lock and the full force of the canal above it."

"Impressive," Gregg said. "Where did you learn all this?"

"My father collected articles. I used to sneak into his study when he was gone and read them."

"I thought your father was a minister."

"He was. But he was a lot like his hero, Thomas Jefferson. He felt an educated man should be knowledgeable in a wide variety of subjects."

"And your uncle?"

Daniel frowned. "Uncle Asa doesn't care what you have to say unless you're a Greek or Roman orator who has been dead for a thousand years."

This made Gregg laugh.

"Are you familiar at all with the Patowmack Canal? I know it doesn't begin to compare with the Erie . . . still, thousands of boats have locked through the Great Falls carrying flour, whiskey, tobacco, and iron downstream, and cloth, firearms, hardware, and manufactured products upstream."

"When my uncle brought me out here, we were going to stop awhile at Matildaville, and he was going to let me watch the lock in operation.

But then he got a headache on the journey and just wanted to get home, so we didn't stop."

Gregg pulled a pipe from his pocket and began stuffing tobacco into the bowl. "I understand your uncle no longer travels well." He lit the pipe and huffed and puffed until the tobacco caught on. "What would you say if I told you I was partner in an effort to extend the Patowmack Canal from Cumberland to the Ohio River?"

The idea was so fantastic, it stunned Daniel. "Is that possible? The engineering problems—"

"Would make the Erie Canal look like child's play in comparison," Gregg said with a tone more humble than boastful.

Daniel thought a minute. "It can be done."

Gregg laughed. "You're certain of that, are you?"

"I think man can pretty much do whatever he sets his mind to do."

"I wish my financial backers were as optimistic as you."

"It's a matter of vision," Daniel said. "And what's to stop you at the Ohio?"

"Explain."

"The Northwest Passage. You know—the one all the explorers were searching for . . ."

"Go on."

"We know now that nature didn't create such a passageway, but what's to keep man from doing what nature didn't do? After all, nature didn't connect Albany and Buffalo with a waterway."

Gregg looked at him with wonder, the type of gaze that encouraged Daniel to continue, so he did.

"Think of it. What's to keep us from creating our own Northwest Passage? Creating a waterway, a canal, that links the Atlantic and Pacific Oceans?"

"A transcontinental canal. A water passageway capable of shipping food and goods across the nation," Gregg said, catching the vision. "The fabled Northwest Passage."

"Why not? It's technologically feasible."

"Indeed. Why not?"

CHAPTER 7

So caught up was Daniel in his discussion with Cyrus Gregg about machines and canals that he forgot to be afraid of the man with whom he was riding and about where they were going. Clearly, this was not the man Daniel had thought him to be. This was not the man in the alley who had consented to Braxton's murder. Did Cyrus Gregg have a brother? Possibly a twin?

At the moment, it seemed more likely to Daniel that his Uncle Asa would be involved in a killing than the man riding in the wagon next to him.

"Take this road here." Gregg pointed to his left.

The wagon tipped back and forth as the wheels intersected frozen ruts in the main road. Barely wide enough for wagon passage, they followed a descending path, crossing over Mills Creek on a wooden bridge that complained under the weight of the wagon.

Daniel felt foolish that at the outset he'd considered jumping from the wagon to escape Cyrus Gregg. He looked forward to the return ride with great anticipation. First, to see the working model of Mr. Gregg's revolving clothes-washing machine, but also because Daniel wanted to ask Mr. Gregg his thoughts on steam.

Daniel had read predictions somewhere that engines powered by steam would someday replace the horse, just as steamboats were challenging the sail. Daniel had never seen a steam engine except in pictures, nor had he ever met someone who'd seen a steam engine. Had Mr. Gregg? Daniel was anxious to ask him. Also, to tell him of an idea he had.

If steam engines would indeed someday replace horses, wouldn't it make sense to lay tracks for these locomotive engines, as they were called, parallel to canals and pull barges with them?

Already, Daniel could hear Cyrus Gregg's voice in his head, saying, "Brilliant!"

A cabin came into view.

"That's it." Gregg sat forward in his seat and yelled in its direction. "Epps! Epps!"

Daniel pulled the wagon to a stop in front of the cabin. He jumped out and circled to the back to unload the casket while Gregg climbed out and went to the cabin door, which was standing open.

"Epps!" he shouted inside.

Daniel hopped into the back of the wagon and waited. It would take two men to unload the casket.

"Epps!"

Getting no answer from inside, Gregg walked around back, calling as he went. Daniel placed his hands in his pockets and searched the immediate vicinity for a man named Epps. He saw nothing but forest.

The shuffle of boots on wooden floorboards and a movement in the doorway drew Daniel's attention back to the cabin.

The next thing he knew, he was staring into the face of Braxton's killer.

The hat and coat were gone, but it was him. Daniel was sure of it. His imposing stature. The way he stood, feet apart, was identical to that of the man who had stood at the mouth of the alley while a whimpering Braxton clawed at the cobblestones, attempting to escape.

Piercing, gray, wolflike eyes fixed on Daniel, as though from a black den—only in this case the shadows were black facial hair. A thick, full beard covered everything on the man's face except sharp cheekbones and those threatening eyes. Attached to the man's belt was a large hunting knife, the size of the one that had slit Braxton's throat.

Daniel stood frozen by the killer's stare.

He recognizes me, Daniel thought. *He knows I was there.*

"Epps! There you are!" Gregg said, coming around from the back of the cabin. "Why didn't you answer?"

Even now, the killer didn't answer him. Not until he was done staring at Daniel, which seemed an eternity.

"You woke me," Epps said in a deep, groggy voice. He stretched like a bear emerging from hibernation.

"At this time of day?" Gregg said.

Epps turned and walked back inside.

"Where are you going?" Gregg demanded.

From inside the house Epps said something Daniel couldn't make out. With the hunter's gaze no longer immobilizing him, Daniel's thoughts turned to flight.

"Daniel, come down here," Gregg said, walking toward the wagon.

Daniel glanced around him. Now was his chance. If he was going to run, he'd have to do it now.

"Hurry, boy," Gregg said in a low voice. "There's something I need to tell you."

Had Daniel not connected with Cyrus Gregg during the ride to the cabin, he probably would have run. But the connection was strong, and it held. Against his instincts, Daniel jumped over the side of the wagon, landing in front of Cyrus Gregg. But he kept his eyes on the door of the cabin, just in case.

Gregg put a hand on Daniel's shoulder. "Listen to me, son," he said in a fatherly tone. "I meant to tell you this on the ride out here, but our conversation took such a pleasant turn, I let the time slip away. I wanted to warn you—"

Epps emerged from the cabin. Daniel took a sharp intake of breath. He couldn't help himself. Epps appeared wearing the hat and long coat that he had worn the night before in the alley. He looked exactly as he did before he killed Braxton.

"Let's get to it," he said, pulling on a pair of gloves.

Gregg tightened his grip on Daniel's shoulder. "The deceased—"

"He's back here," Epps said, walking to the rear of the cabin.

"We'll be right there!" Gregg shouted at him impatiently. Turning back to Daniel, he said, "You know the deceased. It's Emil Braxton. I'm sorry you have to hear about it this way. It was a very unfortunate accident." He released Daniel. "Go help Epps load him up. I'll explain it all to you later."

Daniel didn't move.

"Go on," Gregg urged him.

Daniel's body didn't seem to be working.

"I'm sorry to spring it on you so suddenly," Gregg said. "But you weren't close, were you? You've known him only a couple of months."

"No," Daniel managed to say. "We weren't close."

An impatient Epps bellowed from behind the cabin.

Daniel managed to take a couple of small steps. He took them alone. "You're not coming?" he asked Gregg.

"I-I'll wait for you here."

Daniel nodded. He took a few more steps.

"Take the wagon," Gregg said.

Daniel's mind was so stiff from fright, he didn't comprehend.

"The wagon," Gregg said. "Unless you want to carry the body all the way out here."

"Oh yeah . . . good idea."

Daniel managed to climb into the wagon on weak knees. The horse responded too eagerly to his command and pulled the wagon too quickly toward the back of the cabin, toward Daniel's uncertain fate.

He found Epps waiting for him.

The killer stood in front of a small storage shed. The moment he saw Daniel coming, he stepped inside.

Daniel reined the horse to a stop and climbed down. As he did, his recorder—tucked in his waistband like it always was—poked him in the side, as if in warning.

He walked to within a few feet of the storage shed but didn't go in. "Um, Mr. Epps? Mr. Epps?"

The killer appeared. "What kind of coffin business do you people run?" Epps exclaimed in disbelief. "Is everybody there skittish about death?"

"It's just that . . . we should get the casket out of the wagon first. Otherwise, we have to set the . . . um, your loved one . . . down and pick him up again, or try to lift him up, while—" Daniel made lifting motions with his hands at the same time simulating stepping up. "While . . . um, climbing into the wagon."

"I see your point," Epps said.

With his greatcoat flapping like a cape, Epps jumped into the back of the wagon with ease. Daniel climbed in at the end, and they unloaded the casket and removed the lid.

Moving with no wasted motions, Epps again disappeared into the shed. Daniel took a deep breath to steady himself and followed him.

When his eyes adjusted to the decreased light, Daniel saw Epps already holding the very dead Emil Braxton by the shoulders. The dead man's blue-and-gray-colored head lolled forward, making it look like he had fallen asleep in a chair.

Daniel stooped down and grabbed the dead man's ankles. He couldn't help but muse that this was Braxton's end of choice when moving dead people. Daniel wondered if Braxton—wherever he was right now—was aware that it was Daniel who had him by the ankles.

The dead man's shoes and pants were cold and soaking wet. In fact, the entire body was drenched.

"River accident," Epps said. "Drowned. A real shame."

Without thinking, Daniel looked at the dead man's throat. The instant he did, he regretted it. The throat was wrapped with a scarf.

Realizing what he was doing, Daniel looked up. Epps was staring at him suspiciously.

"Yeah. A real shame," Daniel said, looking aside and hefting the legs.

Daniel did his best to act as though this was just one of any number of dead bodies he had placed in a casket. He backed out of the storage shed and led Epps to the casket, where they lowered the body.

Without looking at Epps—he was afraid to—Daniel grabbed a hammer and nails from the back of the wagon and approached the casket.

"Any keepsakes?" he asked, his eyes averted.

"Any what?"

"Keepsakes. People sometimes put personal items into the casket with their loved one. Rings. Lockets. A poem or booklet. For men, sometimes their favorite weapon."

He winced the moment he said it. Having recited this little speech dozens of times, it just spilled out of his mouth without thought. But the last thing he wanted this man Epps to think about was weapons, especially the knife attached to his belt.

"No," Epps said. "Just close it."

Eager to get this over with, Daniel knelt and positioned the first nail. As he bent over, his recorder jammed into his side. It always did when he nailed caskets closed. Normally he took it out and set the recorder aside.

That didn't seem to be a wise thing to do today.

Reaching under his coat, he repositioned it and tried again. But the instant he bent forward, the recorder moved and poked him again, this time even harder.

"What do you got under there?" Epps asked.

Daniel grinned. "Nothing. I can finish closing the casket by myself, if you want to join Mr. Gregg. Possibly conclude your business with him . . ."

"I suppose you're gonna lift that casket into the wagon all by yourself?"

"We're putting it back in the wagon?"

This was not the usual procedure. Usually the casket was carried into the house for the wake. But then it didn't seem likely Cyrus Gregg and his killer would be holding a wake for their murder victim, did it?

"We're burying your loved one today?" Daniel asked.

"That's the plan."

Epps stood over him with folded arms.

Daniel readied another nail. He bent forward. This time the recorder poked him so hard, he winced.

"Let's have it," Epps insisted. "You're hiding something under your coat. Give it to me so we can get on with it."

"Thanks," Daniel said, not looking up, "but that won't be necessary."

Epps stepped closer until he was hovering directly over Daniel. He held out his hand. "I ain't got all day. Let's have it."

Daniel was curious as to what pressing business a killer might have on an ordinary day, but he dismissed the idea of asking as an unhealthy one. Instead he said, "Really, it's no—"

"Give it to me!" Epps shouted.

Seeing no other recourse, Daniel reached beneath his coat and pulled out the recorder. In an instant he saw himself using it as a club to knock Epps down and giving him time to run. But the instrument in his hand was too light for such fantasies. So he handed it to the killer.

Epps gripped it like it was a hatchet handle. "What is it?" he asked, turning it this way and that, running a finger along its wavy shape, stopping only long enough to examine the holes.

With his heart in his throat, Daniel gripped the hammer tightly. It was more of a weapon than the recorder, no match for an enormous hunting knife, but it would make a pretty good dent in whatever it hit.

"It's a recorder," Daniel said of the instrument, all the while watching for the slightest flicker of recognition.

Epps shook his head. "A recorder?"

"A musical instrument. Like a flute or a pipe."

The killer was losing interest. "Never seen one before."

At that moment Daniel couldn't have heard any words sweeter than those.

"Why're you hidin' it?" Epps asked. "Gregg not want you to have it?"

Daniel was breathing again. "Sometimes I play it when I'm supposed to be working."

"Whaddya know . . . I thought you was hiding a bottle in your drawers,"

Epps said. "Taking an occasional nip of whiskey or rum on the job. Was gonna have myself a little nip. The price of keeping silent."

"Sorry."

Daniel set to work and nailed the casket shut in quick order. When that was finished, Epps handed Daniel the recorder with a sad shake of his head, as though he couldn't understand why a young man would hide a musical instrument in his pants.

After tossing the hammer into the back of the wagon, Daniel and Epps loaded the casket. Then Daniel drove the wagon around to the front of the house, where Cyrus Gregg was waiting for them.

The sight of the casket didn't seem to bother Gregg as he climbed into the seat next to Daniel. Apparently Gregg didn't have a problem with boxed-up corpses.

Epps hopped into the back of the wagon, and Daniel was directed to a road that ascended steeply to the top of a small hill. Cresting the ridge, he saw five grave markers already in place. Emil Braxton would be number six.

The hole had already been dug. From the looks of it, it had been dug days ago and had been waiting since then for its anticipated resident to die.

Emil Braxton's casket was hefted into the ground, and Epps tossed a shovel at Daniel. Grabbing a second shovel, the two of them filled the grave.

Daniel was not accustomed to graveyard work, but it wasn't the neighborhood residents that disturbed him as he worked. It was Epps—or, more accurately, the tattoo on the back of Epps's neck. With each shovel of dirt he tossed into the grave, his hair would swing wildly to one side, giving Daniel a clear view of the coiled snake on the back of the killer's neck.

With each peek, the snake eyed him, as though it recognized him from the alley the night before.

CHAPTER 8

Daniel sat on his bed and watched the snow fall. He had an unobstructed view. The tree that had once served as his ladder to the second story was gone. Only a stump was left. And it didn't take a genius to figure out who had it removed or why.

He stood and walked to the window. It had been a long time since he'd seen it this dark outside. It was late afternoon, and he'd just arrived at home when the snow began falling. At the rate it was falling, everyone would be digging out come morning.

On the return trip from burying Braxton, Daniel had one of the most entertaining conversations he'd had in ages. For a time he again forgot that Cyrus Gregg was his employer *and* a ruthless murderer. There was no age difference. There was no social difference. They were just two kindred souls who shared a passion for machines and visions of the future.

They reached the docks on the Potomac River just as the dark clouds were rolling in. Temperatures plunged. But Gregg couldn't wait to show Daniel his revolving washing machine. He had it unpacked right there and danced to keep warm as Daniel inspected it. A giddy Gregg asked him to draw up his idea for placing ribs on the inside of the cylinder. He said he would hire a woodcarver to craft and install them.

It was quitting time when they reached the shop. Business called

Gregg into the office as Daniel unhitched the wagon.

Icky was in a foul mood. Being the only boy in the shop that day, he'd been run ragged with everyone ordering him around. He was the only one still in the shop when Daniel walked in. He was sitting on the floor with the broom next to him and the shop less than half swept.

The instant he saw Daniel, Icky was on his feet and heading out the door. He informed Daniel that he didn't care if Daniel *was* head boy. Daniel could finish sweeping the shop by himself. He was going home.

As it turned out, Icky's timing was bad. He made his proclamation just as Cyrus Gregg came into the shop. The owner jumped all over Icky for his insubordination, ordered him to finish sweeping the shop by himself, and told Daniel he was free to go home.

"Oh, and Daniel," Gregg added, "you made a long trip today thoroughly enjoyable. Get me that drawing. I want to talk more with you. You are far too talented a young man to be spending your time sweeping out the shop."

Daniel wished he had a sketch of Icky's face at that moment. It would be priceless.

Even now, standing in his bedroom, Daniel grinned at the remembrance. It was one of several sweet moments he'd experienced that day. And that fact alone made his dilemma that much more perplexing.

His life made no sense.

Did it make sense that he had just spent a thoroughly enjoyable day with a murderer? But he had, hadn't he? When was the last time he'd felt so alive?

He flopped back onto his bed and picked up a piece of paper upon which he'd drawn the cross-section interior of a cylinder, showing the placement of curved ribs evenly spaced. The drawing had come easily for him. He couldn't wait to give it to Cyrus Gregg. Couldn't wait to see his idea take shape. Couldn't wait to test the first load of laundry.

Just the thought of it awoke the little boy in him, the one that jumped up and down with excitement and without shame. For the first time in his life he caught a glimpse of his future, and he liked what he saw.

But one mention of what he saw last night in the alley, and his future would die a stillborn's death.

Daniel fell back on the bed and stared at the ceiling. *Think!* he told himself. *Think!*

Did he really have to tell his uncle about Braxton's murder? Just for the sake of argument, what would happen if he didn't? Cyrus Gregg and Epps would have committed a murder and gotten away with it. A terrible thing, certainly. But why did their wrongdoing have to ruin his life?

What if—again, just for the sake of argument—what if he, Daniel, hadn't been in the alley last night? What if he'd stayed in his room as he'd been told?

Answer: none of this would be bothering him now. He still would have had the conversation with Cyrus Gregg on the road during which they would have discovered their common passion for machines. Gregg still would have asked him for a drawing. Daniel still would have made the drawing, and he would, with unfettered conscience, take that draw-ing to Gregg in the morning and see where things went from there.

In his mind's eye Daniel was back in the wagon traveling the Mills Creek road, talking to Cyrus Gregg. He clearly remembered Gregg say-ing that if his plans continued as he hoped they would, he wanted Daniel to work with him on the canal project, the one that would connect Cumberland with the Ohio River.

It was too fantastic even to imagine. Yet it was possible, wasn't it? After all, this wasn't some fantastical schoolboy daydreaming on a lazy summer afternoon. This was community leader Cyrus Gregg who had actual plans drawn up. Plans that even now his friends in Washington were poring over. Friends with money who could turn the dream into reality, just as had been done with the Erie Canal.

And one word from Daniel would ruin it. Ruin Cyrus Gregg's dream. Ruin Daniel's future.

Now that Daniel knew the location of Braxton's body, it would be easy for authorities to verify his story. All they had to do was dig up the fresh grave and remove the scarf from around Braxton's neck. They would find that the man who was reported to have drowned had in reality suffered a fate of a more violent nature.

Daniel squeezed his eyes shut. All this mental wrestling was giving him a headache.

One memory from the night before played repeatedly against the dark curtain of his mind. The moment Braxton's head had hit the cobblestones inches from his own, the dead man's lifeless eyes had fixed on his.

Grabbing his pillow, Daniel screamed into it.

He didn't even like Braxton.

Downstairs the front door opened and closed.

Once inside the door, Asa Rush set his cane in the corner, removed his hat and scarf, brushed the snow from his shoulders, pulled off his gloves, removed his coat, stomped his feet, and made his way to the fireplace in hopes of thawing out his fingers. He whistled as he held his hands to flame.

Camilla emerged from the kitchen with a stirring spoon in her hand. She wore her baking apron, a sign that Christmas was just a few days away.

No one baked for Christmas like Camilla. Let the wealthy have their big parties and the Germans decorate their evergreen trees. Asa would willingly trade both for a slice of her apple-cinnamon bread.

"You sound happy," she said, smiling.

Asa sniffed the air. "What is that heavenly smell? Raisin cookies?"

Camilla offered him a kiss, and he gave her his cheek. Her lips were warm and moist against his cold skin.

"Heavens! You're nearly frozen!" she cried.

"Can't remember the last time the temperature dropped this quickly," he replied. "Plum pudding?"

With a playful sparkle in her eyes, she shook the wooden spoon at him. "It's a surprise. Wash up for supper. It's almost ready."

Rubbing his hands, Asa asked, "Is the boy in his room?"

"He came home early about an hour ago and went straight upstairs. He seemed happy. Is it too much for me to hope that both of you will bring a good mood to dinner?"

Asa took his wife's face in his hands and kissed her on the forehead.

"Asa! Your fingers are icicles!"

"I guarantee you a strife-free supper, m'lady."

Her innocent eyes dared to hope.

"I can make such a bold promise," Asa said, returning to the fire, "in the belief that Daniel's good mood and mine flow from a common spring."

"Something good happened today, didn't it? Tell me!"

Asa leaned close to his wife, putting his lips next to her ear, and whispered, "I'll tell you the good news if you tell me what that wonderful aroma is coming from the kitchen."

Camilla pulled away. She smiled sweetly. "So that's how it is . . ."

"That's the going rate for good news today."

Lowering her head, she gazed at him flirtatiously. He loved it when she played coy. As he had done to her, she leaned close, her lips to his ear, and whispered, "Then I'll just ask Daniel when he comes down." Pulling away quickly, she rapped him on the chest with the wooden spoon and said sharply, "Now wash up for supper."

"Daniel, tell us about your day," Uncle Asa said.

His uncle stood at the head of the table slicing a freshly baked loaf of wheat bread, passing a slice to Camilla, who passed it to Daniel.

Daniel reached for the jam. Aunt Camilla was looking at him expectantly, as though she knew something he didn't.

"It was all right, I guess," he said.

After handing his wife a slice of bread, Uncle Asa carved a slice for himself, sat, dipped it in his stew, and ate. They chewed in silence for a minute.

"Anything *unusual* happen today?" Uncle Asa persisted.

Daniel looked up at him suspiciously. Everything about today was unusual. His uncle was hinting at something. What did he know? To whom had he been talking?

Uncle Asa couldn't know too much. His tone was casual, and he asked the question with his head lowered, as though he was talking to one of the carrots in his bowl.

"We made a delivery today," Daniel said cautiously, to his stew, mimicking his uncle. "Took most of the day. Out Mills Creek road. Just past Braddock Run."

"All the way out there?" Aunt Camilla said.

From the lack of expression on Uncle Asa's face, he already knew about the delivery. So why was he asking questions? What was he leading up to?

"Anybody go with you?" Uncle Asa asked.

Irritated that his uncle was asking questions for which he already knew the answers, Daniel dropped his spoon and glared at him. But all he saw was the top of his uncle's head as he fed himself.

Daniel looked to his Aunt Camilla, who pleaded patience with her eyes. *For my sake . . . please.*

"No, I didn't go out there alone," Daniel said, for his aunt's sake. "Mr. Gregg went with me. But you already know that, don't you?"

"Cyrus Gregg?" his aunt said, surprised. "You spent the entire day with Cyrus? That's unusual, isn't it? I wouldn't think a man of his importance would make deliveries."

"It's *highly* unusual," Uncle Asa said. "However, as it turns out, it was providential for Daniel."

"Oh? Something happened?" Aunt Camilla asked, eager to hear the news.

His uncle was acting like it was his story to tell. So Daniel let him tell it.

"Seems the head boy at Cyrus's shop met with an unfortunate accident, and since he had no family, other than a distant cousin from Matildaville who happened to be visiting him, Cyrus Gregg took it upon himself to give the boy a proper burial."

Aunt Camilla's brow furrowed. She'd been expecting good news.

Uncle Asa looked straight at Daniel. "That's the kind of man Cyrus Gregg is."

"How is this poor boy's misfortune providential for Daniel?" Aunt Camilla asked.

Uncle Asa pointed at Daniel with his spoon. "You're looking at the new head boy at Cyrus Gregg's shop."

Aunt Camilla clasped her hands. "That's wonderful news, Daniel! Only . . . did you know the other boy well? Was he a friend?"

"I barely knew him, and it was only for the day—the head-boy position," Daniel muttered.

"Not by the way Cyrus Gregg was going on about you it isn't," Uncle Asa said.

"Cyrus talked to you about Daniel?"

"We had a nice long conversation about him," Uncle Asa said. To Daniel, "You made quite an impression on your boss. I don't think I've ever seen Cyrus Gregg that enthused before."

Daniel smiled inwardly. Lest his uncle see how pleased the comment made him, he lowered his head, took a bite of stew, and chewed nonchalantly.

"Seems our boy here . . . ," Uncle Asa said to his wife.

I'm not your boy.

" . . . is drawing up plans to improve one of Cyrus Gregg's inventions. A revolving washing machine."

"Really, Daniel?" Aunt Camilla asked.

Without looking up, Daniel said, "It's nothing. Just some ribs inside the washing cylinder that will increase the agitation."

"Sounds complicated to me," Aunt Camilla said.

"Cyrus was telling me he sees unlimited potential in Daniel," Uncle Asa continued. "Seems he wants to take Daniel out of the shop and give him greater responsibilities on larger projects."

"Oh, Daniel, I'm so happy for you!" Aunt Camilla clapped her hands. "You must be thrilled!"

Daniel allowed himself a smile. For her.

"There's more," Uncle Asa said.

"More?" Aunt Camilla cried.

Daniel looked up. What more?

"Cyrus Gregg has extended an invitation to us to join him at his house on Christmas Eve."

"Asa! I don't have anything to wear!"

His uncle's beaming smile and his aunt's exuberant cry led Daniel to think there was more to this invitation than just cookies and punch. "What's the big deal?" he asked.

Uncle Asa interlaced his hands, forming a canopy over his stew. He leaned forward on his elbows and explained. "Cyrus Gregg's Christmas parties are the social event of the year in Cumberland. Invitations are coveted and normally reserved for community leaders, senators, and representatives. The powerful, the moneyed, the upper crust. Men's fortunes have been known to change simply by receiving an invitation."

"I don't understand," Daniel said. "I thought you were his friend. He's never invited you before now?"

"A man like Cyrus Gregg operates on various levels. Yes, I'm his friend and neighbor. But I'm an educator. The people invited to Cyrus Gregg's Christmas party have little use for educators."

"Now, Asa," Aunt Camilla said, "don't belittle your contribution to society."

"So why did he invite you this year?"

Uncle Asa's eyes narrowed defensively. "He invited the *three* of us. If you want my opinion, he wants you there. Camilla and I are window dressing."

That's what Daniel had surmised. He just wanted to hear his uncle say it.

Men's fortunes have been known to change simply by receiving an invitation.

Daniel grinned. He couldn't seem to stop grinning even after taking a bite of stew. He exchanged glances with Aunt Camilla, who was grinning too. She was happy for him.

To Uncle Asa's credit, he let Daniel have his moment. But only a moment.

"I hope you realize what this means," Uncle Asa said seriously. "Not just the Christmas Eve social, but your relationship to Cyrus Gregg."

It was almost humorous. All Daniel had thought about since last night was him and Cyrus Gregg.

"I think I do."

"You *think* you do? You'd better do more than just think, young man."

His uncle had switched to his lecturing tone. Daniel hated it when his uncle turned the dinner table into a classroom and he was the only student.

Daniel felt his ire rising. "I know better what I'm getting into than you do!"

The instant he said it, he wished he hadn't. Not only did it provoke his uncle, which he'd intended. It opened the door to a discussion, which he didn't intend.

"Oh, you do, do you?" his uncle thundered. "I've known Cyrus Gregg for eleven years. You spend one afternoon with him and you've sized him up, have you?"

"Asa . . . Daniel . . . ," Aunt Camilla warned.

But the line had been drawn, and his uncle had crossed it. Daniel wasn't going to back down this time.

"You'd be surprised how much you don't know about your good friend, Cyrus Gregg," he said.

"Of all the insolence!" His uncle threw his napkin on the table. "You sweep the man's floors and take an afternoon ride with him, and all of a sudden you're an expert on all things Cyrus Gregg?"

"Not an expert, but I know enough to know I'd be crazy to be associated with him!"

The statement shocked Daniel as much as it did his uncle. Apparently, deep inside, he knew he could never work with Gregg. Even though he hadn't yet admitted it to himself. Even though a part of him still warmed at the remembrance of their discussion in the wagon.

Uncle Asa was out of his seat so quickly, he startled his wife.

"Asa, for goodness' sake! Sit down!"

"I'll not have a fine man such as Cyrus Greg dishonored at my table!"

Daniel fought the urge to get to his feet and take his uncle on, head to head. For once he could put his uncle in his place and prove that he didn't know what he was talking about.

Instead Daniel broke eye contact with his uncle and lowered his gaze. "I don't mean to speak ill of Mr. Gregg. I like him. I like him a lot."

"And well you should!" His uncle came at Daniel around the table, leaning on it in absence of a cane. "What is it with you? Every time folks try to help you, you turn against them. You treat them as though they're the enemy!"

"Asa . . . please," Aunt Camilla begged.

With his uncle hovering over him, Daniel felt trapped. Belittled. Suffocated. He didn't like the feeling. He pushed back his chair and stood. At full height, now he was looking down at his uncle.

His aunt reached across the table and tugged at his shirt sleeve to hold him back. "Daniel . . ."

Uncle Asa's face was red and glistening. His eyes were charged with anger. But there was pain too. Behind the angry sparks there was pain.

Every time folks try to help you, you turn against them. You treat them as though they're the enemy.

Was this argument still about Cyrus Gregg, or was Uncle Asa talking about himself and Aunt Camilla now?

Daniel's presence in the house had been hard on all of them. Some of it was Daniel's fault. But some of it was his uncle's fault too. And that was something his uncle would never admit.

"All I'm saying is that I know some things about Cyrus Gregg," Daniel said. "I can't work with him. After Christmas I'll start looking for another job."

"No. Not good enough!" his uncle replied.

"Daniel, dear, what is it about Cyrus that bothers you? Maybe if you talk to him . . ."

Daniel shook his head. "Talking will do no good. Now, if you'll excuse me . . ."

He turned to leave.

His uncle caught him by the arm.

Daniel tugged to get free. His uncle's grip held.

His uncle's eyes locked on to his. "First, you decide you don't want to attend school. You promise to find a job. Now, for no good reason, you want to quit that job, just when one of the most influential men in Cumberland takes an interest in you. All you want to do is play that blasted pipe day and night. Well, that's not good enough!"

"It's not a pipe! It's a bass recorder!"

"I don't care!" his uncle roared.

Aunt Camilla whimpered as though she'd never seen her husband this angry before.

Daniel and his uncle glared at each other for what seemed an eternity.

When his uncle spoke, he did so with great restraint. "You have a job. Tomorrow you will go to work. Christmas Eve, you will attend Cyrus Gregg's party with your aunt and me. You will work through your personal differences with Cyrus Gregg because that's what men do. They don't run away every time something happens that doesn't suit them. Do I make myself clear?"

"Cyrus Gregg is a murderer."

His uncle's grip on Daniel's arm failed.

Aunt Camilla gasped.

They stared at him dumbly. But Daniel didn't regret saying it.

"I saw it. Last night in the alley behind the shop. Emil Braxton, the head boy? His death wasn't an accident. He didn't drown. His throat was slit."

Aunt Camilla cried out.

"Now I know you're lying," his uncle said. "Cyrus Gregg is incapable of—"

"I know. He can't stand the sight of blood, or death. So he hired a killer, the man he says is Braxton's cousin. I'm telling you, I saw it. The murder. And Mr. Gregg arranging to pay the killer when it was done."

His uncle was shaking his head. "I can't believe that the man I've known all these years . . ."

"It explains why he rode out to Braddock Creek, doesn't it? To make sure the body was disposed of."

"You saw the body?" his uncle asked him.

"I helped the killer lift it into the casket."

Aunt Camilla's eyes were wide with horror. She held her hand over her mouth to stifle the sounds coming from it.

"And you saw that he wasn't drowned. That there was a cut across his throat sufficient to kill him?"

"His clothes were wet. And the killer had wrapped some kind of scarf around his throat to hide the wound."

"I see," said his uncle.

Daniel did, too. His uncle didn't believe him.

"But the boy was killed in the alley last night, and you're certain you saw Cyrus Gregg there, in the alley?"

"When Braxton's throat was cut, he fell inches from me," Daniel said, hating that he was pleading.

"You witnessed the whole thing, and the killer just let you walk out of the alley?"

"I was hiding."

"So he didn't see you?"

"No . . ." A residue of doubt kept him from saying it emphatically.

"And Cyrus Gregg. Did he see you?"

"No, I don't think so."

"Daniel," his aunt said, her voice muffled, "I've known Cyrus Gregg all my life. He is not the sort of man who would—"

Uncle Asa cut her off with an uplifted hand. "The wound," he said to Daniel. "From here to here?" His uncle made a slashing motion from ear to ear.

"Yes."

"A deep wound?"

"Deep enough to kill him."

"Such a wound would leave a lot of blood."

Daniel saw where he was going. "Someone dumped a pile of manure on the spot early this morning. I don't think it was by accident."

"Grab your coat," his uncle said.

"Asa? What are you doing?"

"Go on." His uncle motioned Daniel upstairs. "Get your coat. I want to see this untimely placed manure pile."

Daniel excused himself to his aunt and made his way up the stairs. He felt badly about ruining Aunt Camilla's dinner, but it wasn't his fault. Behind him he could hear his uncle attempting to apologize.

Aunt Camilla wasn't making it easy for him.

Good.

CHAPTER 9

Camilla was in bed when Asa returned. He eased the door closed, and the latch clicked softly. Waiting for his eyes to adjust, he moved cautiously across the room.

"I'm not asleep," Camilla said.

A rustle of bedclothes and the lamp beside the bed sprang to life.

"I was trying not to disturb you," Asa said.

"I've been waiting for you. How did . . . oh, Asa!" She wrinkled her nose. "Heavens, Asa! That smell!"

"Sorry." He looked at his feet. "I left my boots outside on the porch step. I thought that would be enough."

Camilla covered her nose and mouth with the blanket.

Asa stripped off his pants, socks, and shirt, wadded them into a ball, hobbled across the room, tossed them into the hallway, and closed the door. "Better?"

"It's hard to tell." She didn't lower the blankets.

Asa slipped on his nightshirt and crawled into bed. "Sorry," he said again. "After you've been around it awhile, it loses its pungency."

"Somehow I'm finding that hard to believe." Camilla lowered the blanket, took a sniff, and evidently decided it was safe to breathe again. "How did it go?"

"Daniel's in his room sulking. I managed to talk him into returning to work in the morning."

Asa pulled the covers to his chin and made nesting moves to get warm.

"In the alley . . . did you find . . . ?" Camilla asked.

"A pile of manure? Aya, we did."

Camilla shoved him playfully. It was the very response he was after.

"You know, I would be perfectly within my wifely rights if I insisted you sleep in the barn tonight."

"I don't know what we saw," Asa said, in answer to her question. "There were stains. They could have been blood, I suppose. But even if it was . . . is it human blood? All manner of things have been spilled in that alley over the years."

"So you're saying you don't believe Daniel's story?"

This was the question he knew Camilla most wanted answered. Knowing she would ask it didn't make it any easier to answer.

Before Asa and Camilla had met, she had been feverishly courted by Cyrus Gregg. From the way she smiled at him, she still held a special place in her heart for him. The one time Asa had asked her directly why she didn't marry Cyrus Gregg, she had smiled, kissed him on the cheek, and said, "I was waiting for you to come along."

It was clear Cyrus Gregg still had feelings for Camilla. On more than one occasion Asa had caught the man gazing longingly at her when he thought no one was looking. And it was Cyrus who was most directly responsible for luring Asa away from Yale. Sometimes he wondered if Cyrus Gregg did it just to get Camilla back in Cumberland.

"How can I believe Daniel's story?" Asa replied. "You know Cyrus Gregg better than I do. All I know is that if the boy had stayed in his room like he was supposed to last night, I wouldn't smell like manure and we wouldn't be having this discussion."

The room fell silent.

Then, in a small voice, Camilla said, "So you don't think Cyrus had anything to do with that boy's death?"

He knew she needed to hear him say it.

"No, I don't think Cyrus Gregg murdered that boy."

"Why would Daniel say he did?"

Asa rolled over into his sleeping position. "I have my theories, but this is not the time to test them. We've done all we can tonight." He closed his eyes.

The bed creaked, and he heard Camilla blow the lamp out.

"I'll ride by the shop and talk to Cyrus after school tomorrow," Asa said to the dark. "With a few more facts, maybe we can solve this mystery."

They fell silent. Sleep did not come readily. Camilla tossed and turned for over an hour. Asa couldn't seem to turn his mind off. There had to be a reason Daniel was lying about Cyrus Gregg being in that alley. Had the boy made up the entire story by turning his friend's accidental death into a murder? For what purpose? For some reason, the boy seemed determined to sabotage his own life.

Asa was determined not to let him.

The thought of Eli and Maggy looking down at him from heaven strengthened his resolve.

Daniel sat on his bed, his legs pulled against his chest. Prostrate before him was his black recorder. Daniel's eyes were fixed on the instrument, but his mind had wandered back to the alley, where the murder played out for the hundredth time.

His uncle didn't believe him.

While his uncle had shoveled tirelessly in search of bloodstains, Daniel didn't think that he shoveled with an open mind. The man's thoroughness was not from zeal to prove Daniel right, but to eliminate any possible reason to believe him. Which he had seemed to accomplish tonight.

Undaunted by their lack of convincing proof, Daniel knew what he witnessed in that alley.

The wind rattled his window.

Daniel glanced over at the featureless black pane of glass. It looked so foreboding. There had always been a moving portrait of branches there, painted by interior light. Tonight they were gone, cut down on his uncle's orders as punishment for Daniel's transgression. All that was left was a featureless black canvas.

The lamp flame danced beside him as though to cheer him up. He would keep the lamp lit all night. As he had done last night.

Hugging the recorder to his bosom, Daniel repositioned himself on his side, his knees drawn up.

His uncle had browbeat him into agreeing to return to work tomorrow. At first Daniel had resisted. Then, the more he thought about it, it made sense for him to go to work. If he didn't show up, Cyrus Gregg would want to know why. By showing up for work, no questions would be asked.

The way Daniel figured it, he was safe as long as Cyrus Gregg didn't know he was in the alley the night Braxton was murdered.

What's he *doing here?*

Familiar voices snatched Daniel's attention away from his pile of wood shavings. More specifically, his uncle's voice. The man had a staccato laugh that sounded like a woodpecker doing serious damage to a tree. It echoed through the shop.

Daniel glanced around, worried that someone had heard it. Icky was outside, so it was just him. Everyone else had gone home for the day.

His uncle and Cyrus Gregg emerged from the office. Talking. Laughing.

All of a sudden Daniel found it hard to swallow.

What was his uncle doing here?

It could be nothing. But a twisting pain in Daniel's gut seemed to think this visit was trouble.

Daniel tried to convince his gut otherwise.

He could be here to thank Cyrus Gregg for the invitation to the Christmas party.

His gut was unconvinced.

He could be here to gather ammunition for a later attempt to change my mind about working for Cyrus Gregg.

Daniel's gut dared to hope.

His uncle motioned for him to join them.

Daniel's grip tightened on his broom.

He closed his eyes and wished he could be someplace—anyplace—else. He took a deep breath. But even before he opened his eyes, he knew his wish had not been granted. He smelled wood shavings.

"Daniel!" his uncle called, motioning to him with increased urgency.

Daniel set his broom aside. As he approached them, he tried to read their faces.

His uncle wore the same expression he always wore—that of a stern headmaster. Cyrus Gregg underwent a transformation as Daniel drew near, as though he was afraid to face Daniel.

The Cyrus Gregg that stood before him was unlike the Gregg Daniel had seen before. He appeared smaller. Vulnerable. He stared at his own feet. The change was unnerving.

Either Daniel had slowed, or he wasn't moving fast enough. His uncle came to him, taking him by the shoulder. It was a harness of flesh by which his uncle steered his boys at school, often against their will.

"I was just telling Mr. Gregg about our little excursion last night," his uncle said.

A panic bomb exploded inside Daniel. He stopped dead in his tracks. His gaze jumped to Cyrus Gregg, not knowing what to expect.

Gregg kept his head down and didn't look at Daniel.

"You told him about last night?" Daniel mumbled.

"And the night before," his uncle said. "What you told me you saw."

Daniel must have backed away, because his uncle's grip on his shoulder tightened. "You . . . you . . . told him?"

"Matters such as this are best handled directly and forthrightly," his uncle said.

"E-e-mil Braxton was . . . *murdered?*" Cyrus Gregg's voice trembled. His eyes were red and wide with disbelief. He didn't look up.

"I saw it happen," Daniel said.

"Please believe me. I-I . . . didn't know," Cyrus Gregg said.

Daniel stared in disbelief.

"And . . . and . . . you say it was his cousin who killed him? The man we helped bury Emil yesterday?"

"Yes," Daniel said.

"He told me Emil had drowned," Cyrus Gregg insisted. "That he'd slipped on a rock, fell into the stream, and drowned. I didn't question him. I had no reason to believe he would lie to me."

"Of course you didn't," Uncle Asa said.

Encouraged by the affirmation, Cyrus Gregg turned to Uncle Asa. "Emil's cousin—maybe deep down I knew. I've never liked men like him. A man without roots. A frontiersman. You know the kind . . . stays one step ahead of civilization. Has no use for God's laws."

"In your profession, you have to work with all kinds of men, Cyrus. That's what has made you a good businessman. Let me ask you something. Is the boy's cousin still at the cabin?"

"I don't know," Cyrus said. "He was very secretive about his personal affairs."

Daniel was finding it difficult to digest Cyrus Gregg's testimony. "But I saw—"

"Me in the alley?" Cyrus Gregg lifted his gaze pleadingly to heaven, then to Daniel. Tears filled his eyes. "As I told your uncle, the night before last—is that correct?"

Uncle Asa nodded.

"That night I did not venture out of the house. I can't explain what you saw, only that it wasn't me. It wasn't me."

In his mind Daniel clung desperately to what he knew to be true. He was certain it was Cyrus Gregg in the alley that night. Certain. Certain. Almost certain.

"How difficult these last two days must have been for you," Cyrus Gregg said to him. "First, seeing what you saw. And then, all day yesterday, riding next to me, believing you were sitting next to a man who had a hand in murdering your friend." Tears fell to his cheeks.

Uncle Asa rubbed his friend's back reassuringly.

Images from the night of the murder flashed into Daniel's mind.

The alley, cut in half by moonlight. Moans interrupting his music. Braxton appearing, stumbling, clawing at the cobblestones.

The killer. Standing at the mouth of the alley. Featureless. The light behind him. The knife. The taunting voice.

Braxton's eyes. Fearful.

The flash of a blade.

Braxton's eyes. Lifeless.

The arrival of a carriage.

Cyrus Gregg?

Daniel strained his memory, searching for some detail that would conclusively condemn or exonerate Cyrus Gregg. But the harder he tried, the murkier the memory became.

"I wish there was something I could do to convince you that the man you saw that night wasn't me," Cyrus Gregg said. "Failing that, I understand your reluctance to continue working for me."

None of this was making any sense.

"I will give you a letter of recommendation with which to secure a new position. I only regret we will not be working together." Cyrus Gregg chanced a smile. "Yesterday, talking with you about inventions and the future . . . well, it was as though I'd discovered a long-lost son."

Daniel felt as though it was he who should feel guilty.

"Show him your drawing," Uncle Asa said.

Daniel shook his head. "No, it's—"

"Drawing?" Cyrus Gregg asked.

"For that machine of yours that washes clothes," Uncle Asa said.

Cyrus Gregg turned to Daniel. "You designed the agitation ribs for the cylinder?"

Daniel shrugged, admitting that he had.

"May I see it?"

Fishing the sketch out of his back pocket, Daniel handed it to Gregg, who glanced excitedly at Asa as he unfolded it.

Cyrus Gregg began nodding immediately as he studied the drawing. "Yes . . . yes . . ."

Daniel couldn't help himself. He smiled when he saw the effect the drawing had on Cyrus Gregg.

"May I show this to a woodcarver?" Cyrus Gregg asked. "Of course, I'll pay you for your design."

"Would it help if Daniel went with you when you spoke to the wood-carver?" Uncle Asa offered.

"I wouldn't want to force Daniel," Cyrus Gregg said.

"I think it would be good for both of you," said the man who never hesitated to force Daniel to do things. "What do you say, Daniel?"

Daniel fidgeted. He didn't want to go. But more than that, he didn't want to tell his uncle he didn't want to go. "I guess I could go with you."

"Are you certain, son?" Cyrus Gregg asked. "I would very much like a chance to redeem myself in your eyes."

Uncle Asa glared at Daniel. "Cyrus, I apologize for my nephew's insolence."

"Think nothing of it, Asa," Cyrus Gregg replied. "Given the circumstances, it's understandable."

"That's very kind of you, Cyrus, but there's no excuse for Daniel's rude behavior."

"Daniel," Cyrus Gregg said, "would it be convenient for you to accompany me tonight? You could finish sweeping, and I'll take you home afterward."

"Splendid idea!" Uncle Asa cried. "Have dinner with us, Cyrus. Camilla would be so pleased to see you."

"Any other time and it would be my pleasure," Cyrus Gregg replied. "However, with the Christmas party tomorrow evening, there are a multitude of details demanding my attention. Please offer my regrets to your lovely wife."

"Of course," Uncle Asa said. "It was thoughtless of me to ask. We're very much looking forward to tomorrow night, aren't we, Daniel?"

"Yes sir," Daniel muttered obediently, though he hadn't agreed yet to go. "I'll just finish sweeping." He motioned to his broom.

Since there were no objections, he walked away. His uncle and boss carried the conversation into the office. The door closed.

Icky blustered into the shop, stomping off snow and cold. He'd been outside unloading wood. "That all the sweeping you got done?" he wailed. "You've just been leaning on that broom the whole time, haven't you? Waiting for me to come back and do all the work. Well, I'm not going to do it. And if you run to Mr. Gregg, I'll tell him to his face that you—"

"Shut up, Icky."

"Shut up? Shut up? You can't tell me to—"

"Shut up and go home."

Icky stared at him suspiciously. "Oh no you don't! Mr. Gregg's coming through here, isn't he? And you know it. You want him to see only you sweeping. He'll say, 'Where's Icky?' and you'll say—"

"Go home, Icky!"

Icky looked at him, looked at the office door, then back at him.

"Go!"

Icky wasn't entirely convinced it was safe, but it was clear he wanted to leave.

Seconds later Daniel was alone. To the rhythmic *whoosh, whoosh, whoosh* of the broom, he tried to make sense of Cyrus Gregg.

Could it be he was wrong about Gregg being in the alley? Could it have been another man who looked like Gregg?

The man in the alley got sick when he saw Braxton's body. But Cyrus

Gregg wasn't the only man to be sickened by blood . . . only the most joked about.

Had he mistaken the man in the alley for Cyrus Gregg simply because it was something Cyrus Gregg would do?

Daniel's head was swimming. He worked faster, hoping the exertion would clear his mind.

The night of the murder seemed so distant. At the time, the only thing he knew of Cyrus Gregg was the no-nonsense way he ran the shop.

And look how quickly Uncle Asa and Aunt Camilla rose to his defense. They'd known him for years.

One other thing. Daniel had to admit that the man he rode with yesterday—the man who at times acted as giddy as a boy, the man who could see the future of transportation—was not the man he thought he was.

Despite what he had seen in the alley, Daniel found it increasingly difficult to believe that Cyrus Gregg was capable of murder.

CHAPTER 10

The ride out to the woodcarver was a repeat of yesterday, only colder. Daniel drove the wagon while Cyrus Gregg talked about how he was going to test the washing machine's cleaning abilities before installing the agitation ribs and again after installation. Having listened to Icky whine incessantly all day, intelligent conversation was a balm to Daniel's ears.

Every now and then, Cyrus Gregg would look over at Daniel and fall silent, and Daniel would feel guilty. Then Gregg would start talking again. Before long the man was once again at a full gallop, and Daniel would find himself smiling.

He was reluctant to admit it, but maybe his Uncle Asa was right—

Right about accompanying Cyrus Gregg to see the woodcarver.

Right about Cyrus Gregg.

Right about the opportunity to work with Cyrus Gregg.

It wasn't easy for Daniel to admit that his uncle was right. Perhaps his pride had kept him from seeing the truth about Cyrus Gregg.

No longer.

Daniel smiled to himself. Beside him, Cyrus Gregg rattled on about applying for a patent for the agitator wings, which he was now calling them, unaware that Daniel had just made a momentous decision.

"Mr. Gregg, about what happened earlier—"

"Down this road, Daniel." Cyrus Gregg pointed to a narrow road guarded by twin elm trees.

From the accumulation of snow, the road had not been recently traveled. Daniel had passed it on a number of occasions but had never gone down it.

Passing between the trees, Daniel tried again. "Mr. Gregg, about our previous conversation—"

"No need to apologize, Daniel. You saw what you saw."

"Yes. About that—"

A hail from a man emerging from a heavy patch of woods cut him off. Cyrus Gregg returned the hail. Daniel pulled back on the reins.

"No, keep going," Cyrus Gregg instructed. "He'll meet us at the workshop."

A modest house appeared just ahead. Cyrus Gregg directed Daniel toward the back where there were two additional structures—one no more than a shed.

Cyrus Gregg jumped out of the wagon while it was still moving and hurried into the larger building, throwing open the door as though he owned it. Daniel secured the horse and followed him.

The familiar scent of cut wood greeted him. The interior was similar to the shop he worked in, with some of the same equipment and a few other pieces Daniel didn't recognize.

From the looks of it, the floor hadn't been swept in over a week. Stacks of lumber were covered with dust and wood chips. Two caskets were propped upright against a wall. The top of one lay on a workbench with a partially completed design carved into it.

While Cyrus Gregg warmed himself at the fire, Daniel took a closer look at the coffin's craftsmanship. It was incredibly detailed. A rose-and-leaf pattern.

"Excellent work, wouldn't you agree?" Cyrus Gregg said, turning his backside to the fire. "Noland does special jobs for me. He's the most skilled woodcarver this side of Philadelphia."

Daniel traced a wood-carved rose with a light finger. "It seems a waste to use such talent to fashion a few agitators."

"Lesson number one: never waste your time with mediocre or questionable talent. Always employ the best available talent and reward them well for their work."

Daniel looked up. It was almost as though Cyrus Gregg had read his mind earlier. As though he knew Daniel had had a change of heart.

Cyrus Gregg dispelled that assumption. "I'm sorry," he said, his face downcast. "For a moment, I forgot myself. You must understand. I'd gotten my hopes up and—"

"Mr. Gregg, about that . . ."

The door banged open.

A tall, dark figure filled the door frame.

Daniel gasped. He took a step back.

For an instant, the figure in the door looked like the killer. Only for an instant, but that's all it took for Daniel's heart to seize.

Instead of a knife, the man in the door wielded an ax. He pointed it at Daniel. "Watch out behind—"

Daniel bumped into one of the upright caskets. It slid against the wall. He turned to catch it but couldn't.

It landed with a crash and a cloud of dust.

"What are you doing in my shop?" the man bellowed. Then, to Cyrus Gregg, "What's this boy doing in my shop?"

Without waiting for an explanation, the man tossed his ax aside and examined the fallen casket. He began to lift it.

"Let me help you," Daniel offered.

"Stand aside!" the man shouted.

Daniel moved out of his way.

Close to him now, Daniel could see that the man looked nothing like the killer. His forehead was huge and his nose bulbous. His face was clean-shaven. His size made him appear better suited to being a logger than the woodcarver who fashioned such delicate designs.

With titan hands the man gripped the sides of the casket and lifted it back in place.

Now that everything was in order, Daniel dared to take a breath.

Cyrus Gregg got right down to business. He approached the man and handed him Daniel's drawing. "This is what I want you to make for me."

Without an introduction, until now Daniel wasn't certain this man was Noland, the woodcarver. The man removed any shred of doubt by the way his expert eyes studied the sketch.

"Who drew this?" Noland asked.

A head motion from Cyrus Gregg indicated Daniel.

"You drew this?"

"Yes, sir."

"Who gave you the idea?"

"No one! It's my idea, my drawing."

Noland looked skeptical.

"I was with him when he came up with the idea," Cyrus Gregg said. "Can you make them?"

"Of course I can make them," Noland scoffed. "When do you want them?"

"A week."

"Impossible. It'll take a week to soak the wood."

"Soak the wood?" Daniel asked.

Cyrus Gregg's eyes lit up. "It's a fascinating process. By soaking the wood in vats, he . . . may I?" he asked, pointing to the back door.

Noland's attention was still on the drawing. He looked up and shrugged with indifference.

Cyrus Gregg took the shrug as assent. He led Daniel to the back door.

"Prepare yourself," Cyrus Gregg said. "You're about to see wood twisted into shapes you never thought possible."

He opened the door. A blast of wind staggered them. Lowering his head, Cyrus Gregg met force with force. "He soaks the wood in this shed," he shouted over the gale.

The distance between the building and the shed was no more than ten feet. Snow had accumulated between the buildings. Gregg negotiated it with high steps. Daniel followed.

Just before the shop door closed, from inside Noland hollered, "Gregg! How much are you going to pay me for these things?"

Cyrus Gregg looked back. Low enough so that Noland couldn't hear him, he said to Daniel, "He always asks for twice the amount a project is worth, and he has a reputation for bullying his customers into paying what he asks. Not me. But it doesn't stop him from trying. You go ahead. I'll join you in a few minutes."

The door to the workshop closed, and Daniel was alone. He reached for the latch on the shed door. It was stuck. Frozen. He rattled it and tried again. Reluctantly, the latch clicked. Daniel eased the door closed, keeping it slightly ajar.

Crossing the threshold into the shed was like stepping into a muggy summer night. Four open furnaces with throbbing orange coals warmed the interior. Parallel workbenches supported two rows of vats of various size. The air was heavy and smelled of trees after a hard rain.

Of course, Daniel said to himself, sticking a finger in one of the vats. *He has to keep them from freezing.*

Behind him, the door slammed shut. Daniel's head snapped around. The wind wailed. Ever since the alley he'd been jumpy.

He poked a piece of wood in one of the vats. It disappeared and then resurfaced, belly up, like a dead fish.

As Daniel's eyes grew accustomed to the dim light, he began to notice all manner of twisted shapes protruding from the rafters above and beneath the benches. It looked as though he'd wandered into a forest thick with corkscrew tree limbs and twisted roots protruding from the ground. With a little imagination he could see them reaching for him, trying to grab him.

Having walked to the far end of the shed, he turned and made his way back between the benches, careful lest one of Noland's discards snag his pants leg.

He'd expected Cyrus Gregg would have rejoined him by now. He considered going back to the shop but decided to wait. Cyrus Gregg had been anxious to show him the shed, and he didn't want to deprive him of the pleasure.

Squatting, Daniel took a good look under one of the benches. In a box of discards, he found a flat piece of wood about the size of an agitator blade, and twisted almost exactly in the shape he'd depicted on his drawing. In his mind, he could see it being attached to the inside of a cylinder.

He held on to it, eager to show Cyrus Gregg.

Several more minutes passed and no one came.

Daniel made a move toward the door, then stopped. If he went back into the shop, he could very well be barging into the middle of negotiations. He doubted either man would take kindly to that.

Several more minutes passed.

Daniel spent the time imagining the conversation at the dinner table tonight, the reaction of his aunt and uncle when he told them he'd had a change of heart and would work with Cyrus Gregg after all. Both would be pleased. Then his uncle would spoil it with a lecture about hard work and responsibility and warnings not to mess up such a fine opportunity.

Daniel found himself smiling, wondering if with his new position Cyrus Gregg would pay him enough money to allow him to move out of his uncle's house. The more he thought about it, the larger his smile became.

The smile faded when he realized he was still alone in the shed. Now he began to wonder if he'd heard correctly. Cyrus Gregg did say he'd join Daniel in the shed, didn't he? It would be embarrassing if the two men were waiting for him in the workshop. Wondering what had happened to him . . .

In his mind he could hear Noland quipping, "We thought you'd fallen into one of the vats, and we were going to have to fish you out."

He'd waited long enough. He decided to go back into the workshop.

Gripping the latch, Daniel leaned into the door, expecting resistance from the wind. He bounced off. The door didn't give an inch.

As before, he rattled the latch and tried again.

No good.

He rattled harder.

The door didn't budge.

First, you knock over his project. Then you get stuck in his shed. Not very impressive, Daniel.

Working the latch again, Daniel put his shoulder into the door with force, enough to cause the entire shed to shudder. Strips of unnaturally shaped wood fell out of the rafters, one plopping into a vat with a splash.

The door held.

Thoughts of the shed collapsing or of ripping the door off its hinges stopped Daniel from any further attempts.

Daniel looked at the door helplessly. He knew what he had to do, but he didn't want to do it. He knew what it would sound like—a little boy who locked himself in a shed and got scared. But what other choice did he have?

"Mr. Noland?" he shouted. "Mr. Gregg? Hello? The door's stuck and I can't get out!"

He listened for a response and heard only the wind.

"Mr. Noland! Mr. Gregg!"

He tried the latch one more time until his fingers hurt. He stepped back. Looked at the door. And decided all he could do now was wait. Cyrus Gregg knew where he was. Eventually he and Noland would come looking for him. They'd find the latch frozen. It would be embarrassing, but they'd understand there was nothing he could do.

He only hoped that the outside of the latch was just as frozen as the inside. The last thing he needed was for a grinning Noland to work the latch with ease.

Folding his arms, Daniel settled against a workbench and waited.

Finally the door latch rattled.

"Daniel? Daniel, are you in there?"

Daniel grinned at Cyrus Gregg's voice.

"The latch. It's stuck," Daniel called. "I couldn't get out!"

"Stand back!" Noland shouted through the door. "Don't do anything. We'll get you out."

Daniel took a step back, not knowing what to expect, but having visions of the big man knocking the door down.

At first there was nothing. Then a *click* as someone worked on the latch. Odd. It almost sounded like it was being unlocked.

The door swung open.

A man stood in the doorway. Dark. Rimmed hat. Long overcoat. Long hair. With a knife big enough to kill a bear. Or Emil Braxton.

"Well well well," Epps taunted. "What do we have here? Looks to me like we've cornered ourselves an alley rat."

CHAPTER 11

Towering behind the knife-wielding Epps stood Noland. Behind him, peeking around both men, was Cyrus Gregg with a half-smile.

Did Cyrus Gregg find the expression on Daniel's face comical? Or was Gregg simply pleased with himself by the way he'd lured Daniel into the trap?

"Let's not make this messy, alley boy," Epps said, stepping into the shed.

"No," Daniel replied, "let's—" Grabbing a vat, he threw it at the advancing killer.

Epps fended it off with a forearm but got drenched with oily water. Wood chips stuck to his beard and coat. He growled in anger.

Daniel was running out of room. Retreating a few more steps, he seized another vat and threw it. Then another—only that one proved to be too heavy and he managed only to tip it over, sending a wave of water over the killer's shoes.

Noland had entered the shed behind Epps. The narrow space between the benches worked to Daniel's advantage. Only one of them could get his hands on Daniel at a time. Still, it was two against one, with both of them larger than he.

Three against one if you count the hunting knife, Daniel thought, his eyes fixed on the threatening blade.

Daniel grabbed at anything. He found wood strips hanging from the rafters. Frantically he pulled, searching for something with which he could defend himself. Those that were too short or thin or blunt, he chucked at the advancing killer, who ducked and weaved. One stick found its mark, hitting Epps just below the eye, drawing blood. It didn't stop him. It didn't even slow him.

Just then Daniel's fingers wrapped themselves around a substantial piece of wood. He pulled it down. It was corkscrew-shaped, with a point at the end. Short, but the most promising weapon so far. He leveled it at Epps like a sword.

It worked. Epps stopped. He sized up Daniel's weapon . . . and burst out laughing.

Behind him, Noland peered over his shoulder, saw Daniel's corkscrew sword, and laughed too.

"Gregg! You gotta see this!" Noland bellowed over his shoulder.

Noland and Epps leaned to one side as Cyrus Gregg stepped into the shed so he could share the laugh.

Daniel saw his chance. He lunged at Epps with his corkscrew sword.

Deftly Epps sidestepped him, letting Daniel's momentum carry him within reach. With a step as smooth as a dancing partner, Epps slipped behind Daniel, his left hand cupping Daniel's chin, pulling back, while his right hand pressed the deadly edge of his knife against Daniel's throat.

"No!" Noland and Cyrus Gregg both protested at the same time.

"Not in my shed!"

"Not here! In the woods!"

Daniel felt a trickle of blood drip down his neck as the pressure of the blade eased.

"It would make too much of a mess," a shaky Cyrus Gregg reminded Epps.

Of course, it was an excuse. Cyrus Gregg didn't care about making a mess in Noland's shed. It was just that the sight of Daniel's blood would make him sick.

Any relief Daniel felt for the reprieve was cut short by the pain of Epps grabbing a fistful of his hair and yanking his head back. The knife remained level across his throat.

"Walk," Epps said, giving him a shove.

One by one they exited the shed. Cyrus Gregg first, followed by Noland, followed by Daniel and Epps walking in step. To keep Daniel from getting any ideas as they crossed the threshold, Epps gave his hair an extra yank.

They passed through the shop without conversation. As they exited the other side, Cyrus Gregg issued final instructions. "A shallow grave. The animals will see to it that his body is unidentifiable."

How many times had Daniel heard Cyrus Gregg give orders to workers in the shop using that same businesslike tone?

"And a good distance away," Noland added. "I don't want his blood attracting vermin near the house."

"I'm touched by all this sentiment, gentlemen," Daniel managed. "You can save yourselves all this trouble by letting me go."

The quip earned him another yank on his hair.

"How about if I just kill him here and drag his body into the woods?" Epps said.

Cyrus Gregg turned white. "The woods-the woods-the woods—," he stammered.

"*Deep* into the woods," Noland added.

"Then you're coming along," Epps told Noland. "You know these woods."

"Noland is coming with me," Cyrus Gregg insisted. "We have unfinished business."

Daniel couldn't believe what he was hearing. It seemed Cyrus Gregg's late-afternoon agenda had consisted of two items of equal importance: kill Daniel, and order washing-machine agitators.

"No," Epps said. "Too risky. I don't take risks."

"He's nothing but a boy!" Noland sneered.

Epps shook his head. "I don't take risks."

It was a standoff. Daniel liked standoffs. Anything that prolonged his life was fine by him.

"Fine. Wait here." Noland disappeared into the workshop and returned a minute later, carrying a casket over his head like a canoe, the same one Daniel had knocked over earlier. "He's already damaged this one. He might as well use it."

"No casket," Cyrus Gregg said. "I want a shallow . . ."

"It's not for burying," Noland said. "It's for carting." He lowered the casket onto a flatbed handcart. "We put the boy in here. You cart him into the woods. Kill him. Bring the empty casket back."

Daniel heard Epps grunt his approval.

With no objection from Cyrus Gregg, Epps shoved Daniel in the direction of the casket.

Daniel dug his heels into the ground, but they slipped in the snow and ice. He jerked to free himself. Epps shoved a knee into his back while pulling on Daniel's hair, keeping him off balance while at the same time pushing him forward.

The casket loomed larger and larger. While he'd never given it a thought before today, Daniel realized that no man should be forced to walk toward his own casket.

There was no request for him to climb in. Epps and Noland lifted him with ease and lowered him into the box. How many times had Daniel lifted a body into a casket? The difference being, of course, that the people Daniel put in caskets were no longer breathing.

With a fist in his chest, Epps held him down while Noland went back into the shop to get the lid.

Cyrus Gregg peered into the casket.

Was it curiosity? Did he wonder if a live person in a coffin looked different than a corpse?

"It hurts me to have to do this, Daniel," he said. "I hope you believe me. I really like you."

"I hope you forgive me if I don't get sentimental," Daniel replied.

His smart remark earned him additional pressure on his chest so he couldn't talk.

When Noland came into view carrying the lid, Daniel knew if he let them put the lid on the casket, he would be letting them slam the door on his life. He'd seen how quick Epps was with a knife. Braxton never had a chance. Neither would he.

Epps leaned hard on Daniel's chest. So hard he couldn't breathe. Daniel gauged Noland's approach. Epps had to let up before the lid could be put in place. The instant he did, Daniel would make his move. Shove Epps back. Kick the lid. Jump over the side.

Noland held the lid in place.

The pressure against Daniel's chest eased.

Then a fist came from nowhere, smashing into Daniel's face, knocking him senseless.

The lid came down.

Everything went dark.

Daniel blinked back the pain. He had to be conscious, didn't he? You didn't feel pain when you were knocked out. And Daniel felt plenty of pain.

Gradually the edges around the lid let in a thread of light. Daniel's ears rang as nails were pounded, securing the lid in place, extinguishing even the thread of light. All was dark once again.

He kicked at the lid. It held. He started to shout, then stopped. What good would it do? What could he say or promise that would convince them to let him out?

The pounding stopped.

Daniel couldn't see, but he could hear.

"Follow the stream road until you get to a clearing," Noland said. "Just past the clearing there is an outcropping of rocks. That's as good a place as any."

The casket jostled. It started to move.

Voices grew distant. Faint.

"Now when you hit me," Cyrus Gregg was saying, "don't hit me too hard."

"It has to be convincing," Noland said.

"Convincing, yes. But it doesn't have to be hard."

CHAPTER 12

The rhythmic trudging of his executioner's steps and the *crunch* of cart wheels marked the final minutes of Daniel's life, unless he could devise a way to escape the blade that had cut Braxton's throat.

Confined in the casket, he'd tried kicking and hitting the lid and had begun to make progress when the cart stopped and Epps yelled at him and pounded the lid back down.

Now, shivering in the dark, the rocking of the cart was a lullaby of death.

The rocking of the cart.

An idea came to him. It probably wouldn't work, but desperate men about to die don't have the luxury of being choosy.

For the next several moments, he lay as still as possible, doing his best to shrug off rising panic, no small task while reclined in one's own casket. He concentrated on the movement of the cart, tried to get a feel for it, hoping to be able to anticipate its movement.

At first he discerned no pattern of occurrence, no back and forth rocking like a ship on the ocean. After a time, however, he did notice a relationship in the size of what he thought of as the ebb and flow of the cart's motion. The higher a wheel raised, the harder it came down, and the greater the rocking motion when it did. Maybe, just maybe . . . shifting cargo in a ship's hold came to mind. More than one ship had capsized because of shifting cargo. If he could push the casket off the cart, capsize it, possibly break it open . . . Admittedly it wasn't much, but what other choice did he have?

Like a blind hunter waiting for a rabbit to jump out of a bush, Daniel waited for one side of the cart to rise. When it did, he anticipated its peak and threw himself against the opposite side of the casket the moment it came down.

His timing was off. His shoulder came up too high, hitting the lid, absorbing a good part of the effort. The casket didn't move.

Learning from his first attempt, he tried again, this time keeping his shoulder down, sliding like a pendulum. He hit the side with greater force. He tried again. On the fourth attempt, he felt the casket slide. Probably not even an inch, but it slid!

He sensed he was running out of time. What had Noland told Epps? Follow the stream road to the clearing. Clearings were flat. Flat was deadly. Daniel needed ruts and rocks. Big ruts. Big rocks.

The casket shuddered. The cart stopped abruptly

The calm Daniel had managed to scrounge up now fled.

He waited.

Epps cursed.

The cart rocked, not side to side, but back and forth. It rose, teetered, fell, and once again began moving.

The movement did Daniel no good. This was forward movement, not side to side. But at least they hadn't reached the outcrop of rocks Noland spoke of, which meant Daniel still had time. But how much?

The cart moved evenly. Had they reached the clearing? If so, Daniel was as good as dead.

When this went on for a while, he turned his thoughts to what he would do when Epps started prying the lid off the coffin. Images of shoving open the lid, knocking Epps off balance came to mind. But with them came the memory of a fist to the face. Epps would be expecting some kind of desperation move.

The cart began picking up speed.

A jolt surprised him. A big one. And he'd missed it.

He waited. Another jolt. This time he was ready. He threw himself against the side. Another jolt. He threw himself again. And again.

The casket slid. It tilted.

Epps cried out.

The casket dropped. Hit the ground hard on its side, knocking the wind from Daniel's lungs.

He'd hoped the casket would break open like an egg. It didn't. It rolled.

And Daniel rolled with it.

Epps was shouting now.

The rolling increased. Inside, Daniel was tumbling, tumbling, tumbling like a pile of clothes inside Cyrus Gregg's washing machine. The casket held together, a tribute to the workers with whom Daniel worked. He wished they hadn't done such a good job.

Over and over, he went, getting sick, wanting it to end. But it didn't. It picked up speed. He tumbled faster.

Then . . . nothing.

All was silent, except for the air whistling through the cracks.

Daniel found himself floating, falling, in a wooden cage without windows, doing a slow tumble.

Then, just as he realized that the longer he fell, the smaller his chances of survival, it came to an end.

Suddenly.

Painfully.

Asa gripped a note in one hand and the reins to his coach in the other as it barreled down Centre Street toward Gregg's casket shop. The sun was going down. On a gray, overcast day like today, he couldn't see it, but it was time, and the low clouds were getting darker.

The dark day matched Asa's mood.

Just as he was settling down in front of the fire to read the newspaper, a boy showed up at the house with a hastily written note from Cyrus Gregg.

> *Asa,*
> *I must speak with you. Utmost urgency. Concerns Daniel.*
> *Cyrus Gregg*

Asa's anger propelled him, despite a throbbing ache in his bad leg. On cold days and wet days, the leg refused to be ignored. Right now, it burned like fire. Asa clenched his teeth and did his best to ignore it. He had other things on his mind.

What has that boy done now?

When he'd left Cyrus Gregg's office, everything was fine. He'd managed to negotiate what he thought was a working relationship between Daniel and his boss, despite Daniel's unfounded allegations.

Cyrus Gregg had impressed him. Not many men accused of plotting murder would be so gracious to their accuser. Asa wondered if Gregg would have acted the same had he not been friends with him and Camilla.

"Yes, yes, I think he would," Asa said under his breath. "That's the kind of man he is."

Daniel, on the other hand . . . Asa was ready to wring his neck. The boy had thoughtlessly cast aside one opportunity after another. Asa was tired of it. He had run out of patience.

Trickling water roused Daniel. With a moan, he lifted his head. It felt wet. And his entire left side too. One by one his senses began returning and making reports. The reports were not good.

His insides were scrambled. His head felt like it had exploded. He was wet and shivering.

He hurt everywhere. But pain meant he was alive!

He tried to sit up. His hand splashed in water, and he hit his head on something.

The top of the casket.

Wait.

No, the bottom of the casket.

Daniel took stock of his situation. The casket had landed upside down. It had split open, and the stream was running through it.

He shoved the shell off of him and kicked away a portion of the lid. He managed to sit up. He found himself sitting in a pool in the middle of a shallow stream. The water was freezing. His fall had broken through the ice.

Struggling to his feet, his teeth chattering, he looked up from where he had plunged. Coming down, he remembered it being higher than it was. The cart on the road was unmanned.

A movement upstream caught his eye. *Epps.* He'd found a trail from the road to the stream and was coming down it.

Epps stopped and caught Daniel's eye. He shook his head and smiled slyly.

Daniel got the message. He may have thought he'd escaped, but he hadn't.

With Epps upstream, Daniel turned downstream. He splashed his way out of the water to the slippery, muddy side, looking for some way back up to the road.

He glanced over his shoulder just in time to see Epps slip. His feet flew from under him, and he landed hard on his tailbone and slipped the rest of the way down the slope. He grabbed at branches and dug his heels into the mud in an attempt to slow himself down.

But his momentum was too great. One foot found a rock. Instead of slowing him down, it flipped him over onto his belly. Like a coin deposited into a tray, the slippery path deposited Epps into the river.

He slid across the ice and slammed headfirst into some rocks. He lay motionless.

Daniel couldn't believe his good fortune. He turned to run before Epps had a chance to get up.

But something stopped him. As badly as he wanted to put distance between him and Braxton's killer, something deep inside kept him from running away.

He stared at the man lying on the frozen stream.

Epps had yet to move a muscle.

Daniel took a step toward him.

Now another voice inside Daniel spoke up. *What if Epps is only acting hurt to draw you in?*

What a fool he'd be to walk into the arms of a killer when he had a chance to escape. And he had every right to run, didn't he? The man had tried to kill him!

Daniel took a tentative step toward the fallen man. Then another. And another.

Epps moaned.

Daniel stopped.

Slowly the killer lifted his head. His head hanging, he took inventory, just as Daniel had, and managed to get up on all fours.

He saw Daniel. Reached for him. He tried to get to his feet but couldn't seem to maintain his balance. Sliding back down with his back against a rock, he stared at Daniel with glazed eyes. Blood streamed down the side of his face.

"Just give me a minute," Epps said. "No need to make this hard on both of us. You know you have no place to run."

Complete sentences. That's all Daniel needed to hear. If the man could speak in complete sentences, he couldn't be that hurt.

Daniel turned and sloshed his way downstream as fast as his legs and the terrain allowed. With every step it felt as though someone were hitting him in the head with a hammer.

The door to Cyrus Gregg's office was ajar. Asa stepped inside. The front room was dark and unoccupied.

"Cyrus?"

"Asa? Thank God, you've come. I'm back here."

The front room had two desks with chairs on one side for salesmen and on the other side for customers. On top of the desks were catalogs of caskets and palls and related funereal items. On the far side of the room was another door, lit by an unseen flickering light.

Passing through it, Asa found a disheveled Cyrus Gregg slumped in his office chair, pressing a towel to the back of his head. His hair was mussed, and his face flushed.

"What happened to you?" Asa hurried toward his friend. Asa had never seen Cyrus with a single hair out of place.

"Daniel," Cyrus said.

"Daniel?"

Cyrus Gregg blinked, finding it difficult to focus. He nodded. Tears filled his eyes.

"Daniel did this to you?"

As angry as he was with Daniel, Asa had a hard time believing that the boy would assault anyone.

"I suppose I'm to blame," Cyrus Gregg said.

Asa bent over to get a better look at the back of his friend's head. Cyrus lifted the towel for him to see. A bump the size of a large walnut had formed at the base of his skull. The towel was red with blood.

"He followed me in here as we were preparing to leave for our meeting with the woodcarver. In retrospect, I should have asked him to wait for me at the wagon." Cyrus Gregg replaced the towel and winced. "I needed to get some cash to pay the woodcarver." He motioned to an empty cash box on top of his desk.

Asa put two and two together. "Daniel hit you over the head and stole your money?"

"I'd been meaning to deposit the money in the bank," Cyrus Gregg said. "I know better than to let it accumulate to that amount."

"How much was in there?"

Cyrus Gregg looked him in the eyes. "Over five hundred dollars."

"Five hundred dollars!" Asa exclaimed.

"I know, I know. That's why I say it's my fault. What young man, seeing that kind of money, wouldn't be tempted? It was just too much for Daniel."

Asa rubbed the back of his neck. If Daniel had done this, it was a side of the boy he'd never seen before. "What could he possibly be thinking? Did he really think he could get away with it?"

"I don't think he meant to leave behind any witnesses," Cyrus said.

The comment stunned Asa. "Do you really believe Daniel meant to kill you?"

"I don't know." Cyrus shook his head sadly. "Is it more likely to think he knew exactly how to hit a man over the head without the possibility of killing him?"

Asa didn't know what to think. "We need to have someone tend to that. Let me help you up."

Cyrus stopped him. "I should probably send for a physician."

"My coach is outside. Let me take you home. It's not far. Camilla can tend to you while I go for the doctor."

Cyrus's eyes quickened. "Now that you put it that way, I can't think of any better balm than the ministrations of your lovely wife."

Leaning heavily on his cane, Asa assisted Cyrus to his feet and ushered him to the carriage. A minute later, with the winter wind assaulting his face, Asa transported Cyrus Gregg to his house.

And all the while he wondered what sort of bedevilment could have possibly come over Daniel to get him to commit such a terrible act.

CHAPTER 13

Daniel shivered uncontrollably as he burst through the front door of the house. He went straight to the fire in the front room. He couldn't soak the warmth from the flames fast enough.

"Asa? Is that you?"

Aunt Camilla appeared, removing her apron. Her face lit with shock when she saw Daniel. "Good heavens! What happened to you?"

Daniel's jaw was clenched so tight from the cold he couldn't answer her. He let his shivering speak for him.

His aunt came halfway toward him, then turned and went back, disappearing down the hallway. Daniel heard cabinet doors opening and closing.

She reappeared with an armload of blankets. Tossing two of them onto the sofa, she unfolded a third and wrapped him up in it. She repeated the process with the second blanket. The third she spread as a seat cover on the sofa.

"Here . . . sit down." She guided him to the sofa.

Daniel basked in her mothering. It was as comforting as the fire.

"I'll get you some hot tea."

Exhausted, Daniel sank back in the sofa. It felt good to rest, but the warmth felt better. He stood and moved closer to the flames, then had an idea. Getting behind the sofa, he pushed it closer to the fire.

That's where his aunt found him when she returned. If she objected to his rearranging her furniture, she didn't voice it.

Setting the teacup down on her Pembroke table, she moved it within Daniel's reach next to the sofa and perched on the edge next to him.

Daniel drank some tea. The warmth traveled down the back of his throat all the way to his stomach. It was a heavenly sensation.

His aunt looked at him anxiously. He could tell she was trying to be patient.

"Did you have some kind of accident?" she asked.

Daniel tested his jaw. The tea seemed to have lubricated it enough that it was working again. "Is-is Uncle Asa home?"

"No." She looked at a clock on the mantel. Her eyes widened, as if fearing the worst. "Oh Lord! Was he with you when—"

Daniel shook his head. "Cyrus Gregg—"

"Cyrus Gregg was with you?" She put a hand on his arm. "Is he all right?"

She cared for him! Daniel could see it in her eyes. How could she? How could she not know what kind of man he was?

She might just as well have slapped him.

Daniel steeled himself with another sip of tea. "You want to know what happened? I'll tell you. Your Cyrus Gregg just tried to kill me."

"No!"

She pulled back from him. Stared at him, as though he was the monster, not Cyrus Gregg.

Daniel expected as much. It would be a waste of words to try to convince her. And if she didn't believe him, what chance did he have with Uncle Asa?

All of a sudden, Daniel felt uncomfortable even sitting next to her on the sofa. He stepped closer to the fire and stood, his back to her.

"Daniel, surely there's some sort of—"

He whirled around. "Explanation? Some sort of misunderstanding? Possibly I misunderstood Mr. Gregg's intentions when he lured me into a shed and locked the door. Or maybe I misread him when he sicked his two hired hands on me and had me nailed into a casket and carted into the woods to have my throat slit! You're right—maybe I have misjudged the man. Maybe that's just Cyrus Gregg's way of saying he really likes me."

She stared at him in horror.

A carriage passed by the window.

Daniel ran to the window and pulled back the curtains.

His uncle and Cyrus Gregg rode cozily together like twin oysters in a black shell.

The sight of them together threw Daniel into a turmoil of indecision. His instincts told him to run. He'd listened to them, done it their way, and it had nearly got him killed. He had no friends here.

Daniel pulled the blankets off his shoulder and threw them onto the sofa next to his aunt.

"Daniel?"

He didn't answer her. He didn't have time to. A single thought possessed him. He had to get out of the house.

No more talking.

No more listening to reason.

There was only one person he could trust. Only one person who could save him, and that was himself.

His foot was on the first step of the stairs when a plan began to take shape in his mind. By the second step the plan had clarified enough for him to reverse his course.

His aunt was looking out the window now. "Good. It's your uncle and Cyrus Gregg. We can all sit down and clear this up."

Daniel wasn't listening to her. He grabbed the two blankets from off the sofa and vaulted up the stairs, taking them two steps at a time.

Halfway down the hallway he stopped long enough to open a cabinet and grab a handful of candles and a tinderbox.

In his room he tossed the candles and tinderbox and blankets onto the bed. Dropping to his knees, he retrieved a haversack from beneath the bed. Next he grabbed handfuls of clothes and began stuffing them into the haversack.

He could hear the front door open.

"Camilla," Uncle Asa called. "Cyrus needs medical attention. He's been hurt."

"Hello, Camilla," Cyrus said weakly.

"Oh dear!" Aunt Camilla cried. "Let me see that!"

Daniel threw the candles, tinderbox, and a small utility knife from the bedside stand into the haversack. He tried to stuff the blankets in, but after the first one fit only halfway, he pulled it out and tied the haversack closed.

Downstairs the voices had turned to mumbles until—

"Daniel's here?!" Uncle Asa bellowed.

"Upstairs," Aunt Camilla said. "He's had some kind of—"

"You-you saw him?" Cyrus Gregg asked.

Daniel rummaged under his bed, feeling with his hand until he found a length of rope.

"Yes, I'm here, you deceitful, lying murderer," Daniel said more to himself than anyone else. "And how I'd love to see the expression on your face right now, but I think I've just run out of time."

Uncle Asa's cane sounded on the stairway with surprising speed.

"I've said it before," Daniel murmured to himself, "it amazes me how fast you can move when you're motivated, Uncle. Why is it that I'm always the one doing the motivating?"

He slung the haversack over his shoulder, grabbed the blankets and the rope and double-checked that his recorder was in his waistband. The last check was second nature to him now. It was there. His trustworthy friend. Through it all, it was still with him.

The steps on the stairs were louder now. And it was more than just Uncle Asa.

Daniel ran to the window and opened it. A blast of cold air greeted him.

The tree that had been his stairway of escape was gone, courtesy of Uncle Asa. Daniel couldn't help but wonder if his uncle had foreseen this day. Until today he would have dismissed with a laugh the idea that his uncle could be involved with anything connected with murder. But then, until recently, he would have done the same with Cyrus Gregg.

Daniel tossed the haversack, blankets, and rope out the window. He threw one leg, then the other, over the sill and ducked to clear his head.

He could hear his uncle charging down the hallway. Daniel looked back just as he appeared in the bedroom doorway. Their eyes locked.

"Daniel Cooper! Don't you dare!"

Daniel dared. He pushed off and felt a rush of air, followed by a bone-jarring landing. He rolled, ending up on his back, looking up at the window.

His uncle's head appeared. "Daniel Cooper, get back up here! You have a lot of explaining to do!"

Daniel got to his feet and gathered his things.

"Do you hear me?"

Throwing the haversack over his shoulder, Daniel backed away from the house.

In the window frame, next to his uncle, a tight-lipped Cyrus Gregg appeared. His eyes flashed with anger.

Daniel didn't care. He didn't care about anything anymore.

Not Cyrus Gregg.

Not Uncle Asa.

Not Aunt Camilla.

Tucking the blankets under his arm, he turned his back on all of them and ran.

CHAPTER 14

Darkness covered the earth by the time Asa Rush returned home, un-hitched and fed his horse, and hobbled toward the house. With nightfall, the wind had turned nasty, finding all sorts of slippery ways to get past his defenses and chill him.

His bad leg ached worse than it had in recent memory, giving him a headache so severe he could barely see straight. He leaned more heavily than usual on his cane as he hobbled up the front porch stairs.

He saw Camilla in the window, watching his progress. As soon as he reached the door, she opened it for him. She was nursing him even before he crossed the threshold.

"Let me help you with your coat," she said, kicking the door shut in the arctic wind's face.

She removed his coat and hat, then his muffler and gloves and cane. She became his cane, assisting him to the sofa that was already situated in front of a roaring fire.

Asa welcomed the blaze as he would an old friend. His leg got him as far as the sofa and no farther. He collapsed onto the seat.

"I have coffee on the stove," Camilla said.

She bolted for the kitchen, as though Asa's life depended upon a quick infusion of coffee.

"Who moved the sofa?" Asa called after her.

She didn't reply. Maybe she hadn't heard him.

Asa let his head fall back. He closed his eyes and tried not to think. It hurt to think. That's all he'd done since entrusting Cyrus Gregg to the care of his housekeeper. Asa had spent every moment since then trying to make sense of his nephew's irrational behavior.

According to Camilla, Daniel had come home "cold, wet, and frightened" —her words.

Asa had asked her if he'd said anything about what had happened, if he'd said anything about money. At the mention of money, Camilla's brow furrowed. It deepened when Asa told her that Daniel was responsible for the bump on the back of Cyrus's head.

Camilla always refused to hear anything bad about someone and in typical fashion had refused to believe that Daniel was capable of attacking someone, least of all Cyrus Gregg. And when Asa questioned her further, she insisted Daniel had arrived home shortly before he and Cyrus had arrived and that upon seeing them, became frightened and ran upstairs.

But she hadn't told them everything. Asa knew his wife well enough to know when she was holding something back. She would tell him the rest when they were alone.

Somehow Cyrus had seemed to sense it, too, for he had made Asa promise that he would relay everything to him at the earliest opportunity.

"Here you are," Camilla said, setting his coffee on the Pembroke table, which was also out of place.

The rearrangement of both sofa and table suggested that Daniel had been there longer than just a few minutes.

"I don't care what Cyrus says," Camilla began, "I refuse to believe Daniel stole from him."

Asa reached for his cup and sipped his coffee. It was hot and heavenly. "The lump on the back of Cyrus's head argues otherwise."

"I've been thinking about that." Camilla sat on the edge of the sofa, her hands in her lap, her knees turned toward him. "Can Cyrus really know who hit him? The blow came from behind, didn't it? And people are often confused after receiving a blow to the head."

"All I can tell you is that Cyrus is certain it was Daniel."

Camilla appeared thoughtful.

"Tell me everything Daniel said to you," Asa said. "Tell me what you didn't tell me when Cyrus was here."

His wife didn't appear surprised that he knew. Even so, for some reason, she stared at her hands, as if finding what she had to say difficult. "He says Cyrus tried to kill him."

"WHAT?" Asa spilled coffee on himself.

Camilla rushed to get a towel and dabbed his chest with it.

While she was still dabbing, he cried, "Of all the lamebrained accusations! What possible reason would Cyrus Gregg have for wanting Daniel dead?"

"You're forgetting what Daniel saw the other night in the alley."

Asa waved that off. "That was all taken care of this afternoon. I went to the shop and told Cyrus what Daniel thought he saw. As you might expect, he was shocked and hurt. Turns out Cyrus was nowhere near the alley that night. We called Daniel over and settled everything. When I left them, they had plans to ride together to see a woodcarver about that washing-machine drawing Daniel made. At that point, everything was settled. And I have to say, considering the circumstances, Cyrus was every bit a gentleman about the whole misunderstanding. Any lesser man would have released Daniel on the spot."

"Gone isn't good enough! I want him dead!" Cyrus Gregg seethed.

Hat in hand, Epps stood wet, cold, and humiliated on Gregg's front porch. The warmth from inside the house poured out the doorway, tantalizing him.

"The boy has family here. He'll write. Or come back. That's unacceptable to me. I want him dead."

"I could kill the family," Epps said.

The offer prompted Gregg to hesitate . . . to entertain the idea. "No," he said finally. "I don't want you to touch her. Do you understand?"

Epps nodded. He understood completely. He understood that Gregg had just revealed feelings for the woman. It was a piece of information he might find useful later.

"But if I know Asa—and I do—he'll go after the boy. Who knows what might happen on the road? He could have an accident. A fatal accident. He could possibly become a victim of highway robbers."

Epps nodded. His fee had just doubled. "Tell me what I need to know about the boy and the old man."

The coffee and the fire had done their jobs. Asa felt warm and comfortable. For the first time all day the pain in his leg was bearable. Another ten minutes and he wouldn't even notice it.

"What's for dinner?" he asked.

Her mind elsewhere, it took Camilla a moment to hear what he'd said. "What? Dinner . . . yes, it's in the oven. Ready shortly. While you were gone, I packed your bag and put some food in a basket."

"My bag?"

"I assume you'll want to start out as soon as we've had dinner."

"Start out . . . ?"

"To find Daniel, of course."

Asa sunk deeper into the sofa. "You assume incorrectly."

"Surely you're going after him!"

"Surely not."

"Asa! You can't sit there while Daniel is missing!"

"He's not missing. He's run off. There's a difference."

"Not to me, there isn't! Daniel is out there in this dreadful weather."

"That's his choice."

Camilla was fuming. "So you're going to sit there in front of the fire and do nothing?"

"No, I'm going to have dinner."

"Then you're going to have to get it yourself!"

Camilla stormed up the stairs. Seconds later the bedroom door slammed.

Asa sipped the last of his coffee and set the cup on the table beside him. He folded his hands and soaked up the warmth from the fire.

A night out in the cold will do him good, he thought.

The aroma of baked biscuits from the kitchen made his stomach growl.

Daniel's stomach complained. He'd had nothing to eat since his lunch break at work.

Night's cloak covered him. Dark and cold.

He'd rolled up one blanket and tied it to his haversack. The other blanket he'd draped over his head and neck. He didn't care that he looked like a biblical shepherd. At least it kept his ears warm. Besides, no one was around to see him. Traffic on the road was sparse at best. Just to be safe, though, whenever he saw someone coming, he left the road and walked down by the river.

The inky Potomac meandered quietly in the night, his compass to the East coast. When he had first started out, he considered going west through the mountain gap. For some reason, he had turned eastward, not certain why.

Was his old home calling to him? Possibly. But what was there for him? Not his parents. And most of his friends had moved on to schools or jobs. Besides, New Haven was the first place his uncle would look for him. The man still had contacts there, and it would be hard for Daniel to live there undetected. So why east?

The sea? Were his parents calling to him from their watery graves? Some would think the thought morbid. Daniel didn't think so.

He didn't know why he chose east. He didn't know where he was going. All he knew was that he had to get away. From Cyrus Gregg.

From his uncle.

Daniel couldn't get the image of the two of them together out of his mind—standing united against him in the shop. Two peas in a pod in his uncle's carriage. It just didn't make sense that his uncle could be so close to Cyrus Gregg and not know what kind of man he was. His uncle wasn't blind. He was a smart man. He had to know.

A blast of wind knocked Daniel sideways a step. He lowered his head and redoubled his effort.

He decided it no longer mattered how much his uncle knew or didn't know. That was in the past. Behind him. His future lay before him.

A thick layer of clouds obscured the moon and stars. At times it was so dark, Daniel had to feel his way from tree to tree along the river's edge.

He began looking for a place to bed down.

After an hour or so—it was hard to tell the time in the dark—he spied an outcropping of rock that formed a shallow grotto. The opening faced south, protecting him from road and wind.

Daniel searched for and found a tree limb with which to explore the shelter. Unable to see all the way to the back, he didn't want to climb in and find it occupied.

When nothing growled or jumped out at him, he removed the blanket from his head and spread it out on the ground with shivering hands. He didn't risk a fire or even a candle—not this close to the main road.

With his haversack for a pillow, he untied the other blanket and pulled it over him and closed his eyes, hoping that sleep would come quickly.

But sleep did not come. His eyes snapped open at every sound. His heart raced. His stomach growled.

It was going to be a long, cold night.

Sweat rolled down Robely Epps's cheeks. His fury propelled and warmed him. Even if Cyrus Gregg wasn't paying him, he'd hunt down the boy and kill him.

After that humiliating rebuke on Cyrus Gregg's porch, Epps broke into a dry-goods store and equipped himself for the hunt. Not only would he catch and kill the boy, he would tie the boy's scalp to his belt to remind himself not to let other people tell him how to do his job. Had he slit the boy's throat in the shed like he wanted to, none of this would be happening.

Now, his feet sloshing in the road ruts, Epps focused on the hunt. He had tracked and killed both animals and humans. Two skills had served him well. Observation and anticipation. Learn their patterns and anticipate their moves.

With animals, patterns were largely the same for each breed. One buck acted like every other buck. With humans, each person was different. That's what made it exciting. There was no finer feeling than to know what a man would do even before he did. To anticipate his moves so precisely and to position yourself so that he came to you.

It made for a sweet kill.

Epps lived for such moments.

From what he'd learned from Gregg, he knew the boy would head east. He also knew the boy was ill-equipped for the journey, probably cold, and tired from anxiety. The boy wouldn't travel far tonight. He would find a place to sleep and hope to start fresh in the morning.

That would give Epps the time he needed to catch up to his prey. By midmorning tomorrow, the boy would be dead.

CHAPTER 15

Camilla still wasn't speaking to Asa as he packed the last of his things in the carriage. He turned and looked at the house, lit by the rosy early morning light. He debated whether or not to go in and say good-bye.

She wasn't asleep. They'd been married long enough for Asa to know when his wife was asleep and when she was giving him the silent treatment.

Tossing his cane into the carriage, Asa climbed in after it. Lord willing, he'd make it up to her tonight by taking her to Cyrus Gregg's Christmas Eve party.

Taking the reins in hand, he glanced one last time at the house, hoping to see his wife standing in one of the windows. But the house stood motionless and silent.

With a snap of the reins, Asa set the carriage into motion. He groused to himself that he was getting too old to be doing this sort of thing. He only hoped that he'd be able to find Daniel quickly and bring him and the money back by tonight. And he hoped that Cyrus Gregg had enough Christmas goodwill in him to forgive the boy one more time.

A *click* woke him. Daniel stirred, half-asleep, half-awake. He tried to lift his head. It felt like a bag of sand.

There it was again. A definite *click*.

He opened his eyes, then blinked several times to bring the world into focus.

Something sharp hit him in the forehead. Crying out from the pain, he raised an arm in defense.

Cheers came from the river.

Sitting up, he saw a barge floating downriver with two boys about his age laughing. Daniel felt his forehead. His fingers explored a small crater. There was no blood.

Another *click* sounded on the rock above him. Something fell to the ground. Daniel picked it up. It was a small piece of metal, flat and about the size of a coin. He found another similar piece, and another.

Something stung his leg.

"Ow!" he cried.

Again, cheers erupted from the barge.

The boys were making sport by pelting him with the metal.

He saw them wind up and throw again. The pieces of metal dipped and curved as they sailed toward him. One sailed wide left. The other curved right at him. Daniel ducked behind his blanket and heard a thump as the metal hit.

Using the blanket as a shield, Daniel scrambled to his feet and shouted at his attackers to leave him alone. His protests had no effect. If anything, it only encouraged them.

Daniel positioned himself behind a tree and listened to their complaints that he wasn't playing fair until the barge finally moved out of range.

He rubbed the dent in his forehead, gathered up his blankets, and prepared to set out.

The sky was clear. The air was brisk. Daniel took that as a good sign. Despite the rude wake-up call, it was going to be a good day, the first day of his new life.

Robely Epps surveyed the town as it yawned and stirred to life. From his elevated vantage point, he could see into the heart of Cumberland in one direction, and in another direction, the thinning eastern edge of town. His position also afforded him an excellent view of the main artery that paralleled the Potomac.

He shared his position with a huge bell, having forced his way into an empty church and climbed the circular steps that formed the backbone of a steeple. To keep up his strength for the anticipated chase, he chewed on a strip of dried meat.

Epps felt no anxiety over his decision to take up position here. His instincts told him the boy would not travel past the outlying section of the town on his first night. And so, like a hunter waiting for a rabbit to poke a twitching nose out of its hole, he waited for the boy to venture onto the road in search of food.

He didn't have to wait long. He spotted the boy scrambling up an embankment onto the road, having spent the night somewhere down by the river.

Epps didn't allow himself a smile. The boy owed him a life, and he would not feel satisfied until he'd collected the debt.

Chewing the last of the dried meat, he unsheathed his knife and checked the sharpness of the blade just as the first rays of the sun shot over the eastern horizon and hit the steeple.

His breathing labored from the climb up the embankment, Daniel stood with hands on his hips to catch his breath and settle an argument between his stomach and his mind.

His stomach urged him to go left, back into town where he was certain to find something to eat. His mind argued that the first order of business was to put distance between him and the town. Any delay meant risk.

His stomach punctuated its point with a growl.

Daniel took a step toward town.

His mind countered with an image of Cyrus Gregg, the businessman. The man knew everyone in town. Everyone knew him. Plus, there was the added risk of running into someone who knew his uncle.

The argument was over. His mind won. Going back into town was like crossing behind enemy lines with little to gain for it. Better to press forward. He consoled his stomach with the vague memory of a tavern a few miles down the road.

For now he had the road to himself. Hitching up his haversack, Daniel set his back to the town and began walking.

Every once in a while, he shot a glance over his shoulder. Somehow it seemed like he was being followed. Was it just nerves? Or was someone behind him?

He turned around. The road was clear.

Whatever it was, it set his senses on alert. He quickened his step. He'd be foolish to let his guard down. His uncle could very well be patrolling the streets looking for him. Not that his uncle would do so out of his own concern, but because Aunt Camilla would insist.

Daniel moved closer to the river side of the road, ready to leave the road at the first sign of trouble.

Epps thought the boy was going to make it easy for him. Walk right into his arms.

Having abandoned his sentry post in the steeple, he peered around the corner of a printer's shop and watched the boy take a step toward him. Then something must have changed the boy's mind, for he reversed his path and headed away from town.

With the patience of an experienced hunter, Epps let him go. This wasn't the time or place to make the kill.

He watched as the boy rounded a bend in the road. Then, leaving his hiding place, Epps followed him.

CHAPTER 16

From a discreet distance Robely Epps watched the boy walk into the tavern. He waited several minutes, allowing the boy to get settled inside. Then, when Epps thought it was safe, he passed in front of the tavern and traveled a distance down the road in search of a suitable hiding place. One that was concealed from the direction the boy would be traveling, yet close to the road so he could be on top of the boy before he had time to react.

A large boulder suited his plan. It was close to the road, but hidden among a cluster of trees. Epps took up a position from where he could see the front door of the tavern.

He didn't relax. His eyes were sharp and alert. His muscles twitched like those of a cat crouched and ready to pounce on a bird. He watched the door and waited . . .

Daniel opened the door of the tavern and walked into the sunlight, his stomach satisfied. It amazed him how much better the world looked after a hot bowl of oatmeal and a cup of coffee.

Above him in the trees birds chirped and chased one another from branch to branch. The morning air still had a chill in it, but the sun was warm. For a December day, it couldn't be any better for traveling.

He stretched leisurely. Up the road, coming toward him, was a heavy wagon. The first travelers he'd seen on the road today. A woman rode in the seat. A man walked the horse. From what Daniel could make out at this distance, they appeared to be farmers.

He set off toward them, his head down, the brim of his hat blocking the bright winter sun. He didn't get far before he heard voices. He glanced up.

The wagon had stopped in the middle of the road. The farmer stood off to one side. He looked like he was arguing with a huge boulder. At first Daniel couldn't make out what the man was saying. He began to get agitated and started shouting at the boulder, something about common decency.

The farmer was big and beefy, his hair gray and pulled straight back. His movements bordered on lumbering, but he looked strong. His hands were huge.

Daniel slowed, not wanting to interrupt a man who was talking to a rock. In fact, he wanted to keep as much distance from the man as possible. He altered his course to pass by on the far side of the wagon.

As he got closer, Daniel could hear the farmer asking the rock for directions. Then, just as he reached the wagon, he saw another figure in the shadows. He only caught a glimpse of it, but that was all he needed.

And that was all the man behind the boulder needed.

It was Epps—the killer!

Charging from behind the rock, Epps shoved the farmer aside to get to Daniel.

Startled, the farmer's wife screamed.

Daniel jumped behind the wagon, putting it between him and Epps. Clutching opposite sides, they locked gazes. A wooden bed and some old farm tools were the only things separating Daniel from the man he knew was determined to see him dead.

Just then the farmer approached.

Epps drew his knife.

The farmer pulled back and threw up his hands to signal compliance.

"Everyone! Stay right where you are!" Epps shouted.

The farmer's wife turned in her seat, her eyes fixed on the huge metal blade.

"We don't want no trouble!" the farmer said.

"This man's a murderer!" Daniel shouted. "He's trying to kill me! You've got to help me!"

"He's lying!" Epps growled. "The boy stole money from his employer, and he's trying to skip town. Help me catch him, and there's a reward in it for you."

Daniel didn't like the way the farmer's eyes lit up at the promise of money. "I didn't steal any money!" he insisted.

He would have pressed his case, but Epps began moving to his left. Daniel countered, moving toward the back of wagon and the open road. Then Epps changed direction, forcing Daniel back to the middle of the wagon.

His eyes darting this way and that, looking for something—anything—that could get him out of this alive, Daniel spied a pitchfork in the bed of the wagon. Epps, following Daniel's gaze, must have seen it too. He brandished his knife, almost daring Daniel to reach for the pitchfork. He would do so at the risk of losing a few fingers.

"I'm no threat to you or Mr. Gregg," Daniel insisted. "I'm leaving town. Just let me go."

"It's too late for that, boy," Epps said.

They glared at each other, waiting for the other to make a move.

To the farmer, Epps said, "I'm going to move toward the back of the wagon. When the boy comes around to your side, grab him. Got that?"

The farmer nodded that he understood.

Epps began working his way toward the back of the wagon.

Daniel countered, moving toward the front, keeping one eye on the farmer. As he got close to the farmer's wife, she eyed him warily and scooted to the far side of the bench.

The farmer reached into the back of the wagon and grabbed the pitchfork. Epps nodded his approval.

As Epps rounded the back of the wagon, Daniel had the horse by the reins. Could he swing a leg up on the horse and make a run for it? he wondered.

The horse might have read his mind, because it shook its head, and it was right. It was a plow horse, not a thoroughbred, and the wagon was heavy.

But if not that, what? Daniel was running out of options.

On one side, Epps was coming toward him.

On the other stood a farmer with a pitchfork ready to puncture him.

Daniel glanced behind him to the tavern. Could he make it? Could he outrun Epps? What then? Tavern keepers were notorious for doing almost anything for money. What was to keep the tavern keeper from handing him over to Epps?

Time was running out. Epps was getting closer.

Daniel had to make a choice. It was either him or the farmer. Not much of a choice, really. Daniel had seen Epps at work. His only chance lay with the slower farmer, if he could just manage to get past him.

Daniel committed himself to the farmer's side.

Gripping the pitchfork like he was some kind of sentry, the farmer looked him in the eye. "Run for it, boy," he said.

At first, Daniel didn't understand. Was the farmer challenging him, or letting him go?

"Run!" the farmer said again. This time, he stepped to one side.

Daniel looked him in the eye and saw no threat. He ran.

The farmer let him pass.

Epps cursed.

With his haversack slapping him in the back, Daniel put every ounce of energy he had into his legs.

He looked over his shoulder, expecting to see Epps in close pursuit. What he saw made him slow, then stop altogether.

In anger, Epps had turned on the farmer.

The farmer, however, moved faster than Daniel had thought possible.

He put himself between his wife and Epps, with the pitchfork leveled at Epps's chest. The length of the pitchfork handle gave him an advantage.

Epps looked at the pitchfork, at Daniel, back at the pitchfork, and must have decided the farmer was no longer worth the trouble.

Backing away slowly, he cursed the farmer again, sheathed his knife, and turned back toward Daniel. But he had only taken two steps when he flopped flat on his face!

Just as he'd started to run, the farmer had swiped the back of his heel with the pitchfork, knocking one foot into the other and sending Epps sprawling.

Now the farmer stood over him with the pitchfork pressed against his back, telling him to stay down.

"A man doesn't settle a score with a knife that size," the farmer said. He eyed Daniel. "Better skedaddle while the goin's good, boy. I'll hold him here long enough for you to get a head start."

"Thank you, sir!" Daniel shouted. "Thank you!"

He took the farmer's advice and ran.

Asa sat glumly, holding the reins of his carriage. After inquiring after Daniel at several places in town and coming up empty, he arrived at the grudging conclusion that the boy had left Cumberland. Adrian Marcus, about the only boy he'd been close to in school, hadn't seen him in weeks. Nor was he at Finney's Livery, which had a large loft that was popular with boys who for one reason or another couldn't go home at night.

Now Asa had to decide whether to waste any more time searching around town. If Daniel had left town, he'd have a good head start by now.

Asa straightened up, encouraged by an idea. Jake's Tavern. If the boy had left town, chances were good he'd stopped at the tavern on his way out. It was the last place to get food and drink for thirty miles. If someone at the tavern had seen him, at least he'd know which direction the boy was headed. And if they hadn't seen him, Asa could double back and search the town again.

With a sigh that signaled he'd come to a decision, Asa flicked the reins while trying to corral his annoyance. Before Daniel had come to live with them, his life had been orderly and predictable, the life of an academic. While some people would have found that life boring, Asa took comfort in it. He'd had his share of drama and excitement when he was younger. Now give him a good book, a cup of tea, a warm fire, and Camilla sitting next to him on the sofa and he was content.

The sight of a wagon coming toward him broke his reverie. A large man led the horse, walking beside it. A woman sat in the wagon. Asa could ask them if they'd seen a young man fitting Daniel's description.

But before he reached them, they turned down Centre Street and headed into the middle of town. Asa considered following them, then decided against it. He'd get what he needed at Jake's Tavern.

CHAPTER 17

Relentless. The man was relentless.

Daniel peered over his shoulder. Epps was still there. Still gaining. Twice, Daniel thought he'd lost him. Twice, he'd appeared again.

Daniel didn't know how much longer he could keep going. His chest felt like he'd swallowed a torch. His legs were wobbly. No longer could he run in a straight line. He lurched side to side.

Epps was close enough that Daniel could hear his labored breathing.

Another glance over his shoulder revealed that his pursuer continued to close the distance between them. Murder lit Epps's eyes. He reached for his blade and closed for the kill.

A couple of hundred yards back Daniel had abandoned the road after it turned inland, away from the river. He had hoped that, by doing so, he could lose Epps in the trees, but the woods had thinned to brush for as far as Daniel could see. There was no place to hide.

He stumbled up a rise and came upon a sudden three-foot drop. Mistiming his jump, his legs gave out under him and he tumbled in the dust.

His face in the dirt, a part of him gave up, surrendering to death. But he refused to listen to it.

Struggling to his feet, he looked frantically behind him. Epps was cut off from view. Not by a dirt mound as he expected, but by a three-foot black hole.

Daniel scrambled toward it and peered inside.

A cave!

The entrance had a steep but manageable grade. He snatched a pebble and tossed it inside, listening as it bounced from side to side and kept going into what seemed to be a bottomless shaft. He never heard the pebble hit bottom.

His choices were two. Risk falling to his death, or stay above ground and get his throat slit. Removing his haversack, he tossed it into the cave, then climbed in after it, feet first.

The grade proved steeper than it looked. He began to slip, then slip faster. He grabbed at roots, only to have them snap off in his hands. Sharp rock edges cut his fingers. He slid past his haversack, snagged on a root, lunged for it, and got it. It broke free from his weight, and he continued sliding, dragging the haversack with him, the dark swallowing him up.

Then, just like that, he came to an abrupt halt. His toes hit a ledge and held. But only his toes. The ledge stuck out only a couple of inches, and it had a downward slope.

Hugging the rock slide, his heart hammering against it, he lay as still as possible, assessing his situation. He was safe for the moment. He had a toehold, but just barely, and he was afraid to reposition them for fear they would slip. A glance down revealed nothing but black.

Then, everything got even blacker as Epps eclipsed the light coming through the cave entrance. "You down there, boy?"

Epps moved to one side to let in more light. What he saw must have prompted the wicked grin.

"Well, there you are! Found yourself a hidin' hole, did you? Won't do you no good. Here, let me give you a hand."

Scooting on his belly into the hole, he reached down to Daniel, who made no attempt to grab it.

"Take it! Don't make me climb down there! I'll pull you up by the hair."

To Daniel's right, the cave opened up, revealing an antechamber with a landing. Beyond that was a fissure in the cave wall. All Daniel had to do to reach it was jump sideways about four feet over a bottomless abyss from a slippery foothold.

"Take my hand!" Epps shouted angrily.

When Daniel didn't take his hand, Epps crawled closer, his hand feeling for Daniel like some kind of insect antenna.

His efforts started a small rock slide. Daniel ducked as pebbles hit him on the head and shoulders, then continued past him into the void.

Epps paused to laugh. His laughter echoed down the cave. "Sounds like that dark space below you stretches to forever, boy. Maybe I won't have to drag you outta here after all. Maybe all I have to do to send you to your eternal destiny is give you a little nudge."

Epps inched his way down farther. His fingers brushed the top of Daniel's head, trying to tangle themselves in his hair. Daniel ducked to avoid them. His left foot slipped, then held. Rocks echoed down the chasm.

Epps gave out a grunt as he reached for Daniel. His fingers wiggled in Daniel's face.

Daniel arched his back to avoid them. If he was going to make a leap, he was going to have to do it now.

Across the chasm, the ledge appeared to be an impossible distance away.

Epps slipped a little closer toward him. He was now in range to knock Daniel from the ledge. The killer's hand shot toward him.

Daniel crouched and sprang from the ledge.

He heard himself scream as he hung suspended between life and death, as though his grave had opened up to receive him, and there was nothing he could do to stop himself from falling through the portal into the next world. He wondered if his parents would be waiting for him on the other side.

He hit the ledge hard. Pain shot up his legs, then to his shoulder and the side of his head; it was the earth's way of telling him she wasn't going to let him go yet.

"That was stupid. Really stupid," Epps shouted at him.

Daniel was glad Epps thought so, because anything he considered a good idea usually had something to do with Daniel's death.

Clutching his haversack, Daniel lay on his side, stunned by the pain and realization that he'd just leaped over a bottomless pit. Then, to his amazement, Epps began worming his way out of the hole and, after a brief struggle, disappeared.

Daniel closed his eyes with relief.

His relief was short-lived. The sound of loose gravel sent a shiver through him. He opened his eyes to see a pair of legs kicking their way into the cave. Epps was sliding down the cave entrance, just as he had, his feet searching for and finding the ledge.

Ignoring the pain, Daniel stumbled toward the fissure in the stone wall. The opening was jagged, as though God had torn the rock in two.

It was a tight fit, too tight for both him and the haversack at the same time. Behind him, Epps was leaping across the chasm. He, too, landed with a cry of pain.

With unforgiving rock jabbing him in the back, scraping his nose, and forcing his feet sideways, Daniel worked his way deeper and deeper into the fissure. With arms stretched out like he was flying, he pulled his haversack after him as he went.

He could hear Epps on the landing groaning, getting to his feet, and lumbering to the fissure. As he had at the cave entrance, his hand stretched into the fissure after Daniel. His fingers snagged Daniel's haversack.

Daniel tugged to free it. Epps tugged back, scraping Daniel's knuckles against the rock. Wedged into a crack in the earth, Daniel held on, his fingers cramping. He stepped sideways a half-step and pulled, then got pulled back. Another half-step. He managed to keep this one. Then another. Then the haversack broke free. But its freedom came with a price, the sudden release causing more scraping contact between flesh and rock.

He worked his way through the fissure, toward the dark opening, navigating each step with duck and weave twists, until finally he was on the other side where he found level ground. Pulling his haversack through the crevice, he looked to see if Epps was following him.

On the far side of the fissure, Epps approached the jagged opening several times, contorting his body this way and that, trying to find the right combination that would allow him passage. But, like a key that didn't match the lock, no matter what he tried, he couldn't get in.

Standing on the dark side, Daniel allowed himself a sigh. Then, lest he celebrate too quickly, he dropped to his knees and rummaged in his haversack until he found his tinderbox. He lit a candle.

As far as the light of the small flame could stretch, Daniel saw nothing but flat ground and a cavernous ceiling. Turning around he examined the rock with the fissure. It completely sealed off one side of the cave from the other. Turning back again, Daniel ventured several more steps into the cavern and saw nothing to suggest there was another opening.

Satisfied for the moment, he found a rock to sit on and another rock upon which to place the candle. Epps's curses and threats slipped easily through the fissure, but they were the only things belonging to Epps that found their way through it.

Daniel decided to counter discord with harmony. He pulled out his recorder and began to play. The acoustics of the cave were magnificent. It sounded to Daniel as though he were playing in a cathedral.

It had been too long since he'd played. Actually, it was only a couple of nights ago, but so much had happened since then, it seemed like years, not days. The last time he played was in the alley. The night of the murder.

Daniel forced himself not to think about that night, choosing instead to concentrate on his music and the achingly beautiful voice of his wooden friend.

CHAPTER 18

The boy's long gone, Asa Rush concluded.

His backside was sore, his stomach empty, his patience worn. He was grouchy and frustrated. The man tending Jake's Tavern—Paulie? or was it Polly, like the bird?—had remembered seeing a boy that fit Daniel's description. He said the boy ate breakfast and left. Hadn't offered his name, and Paulie hadn't asked.

But now, after hours of nothing but dirt road, a biting wind, an empty sky, and the back end of his horse for company, Asa had had enough.

Years ago, when he'd chased Daniel's father all the way to Kentucky, at least he'd known where Eli Cooper was going. Asa could let him slip out of sight and not worry. This was different. Asa could only guess where Daniel was going. And he had no way of knowing whether he was getting closer to the boy or farther away.

Asa pulled back on the reins, and his horse came to a ready halt, agreeing with him that they'd come too far. It was time to turn around.

Asa cast one last look up the road. Nothing but skittering leaves for as far as he could see. The wind whistled. Asa recognized the tune.

His brow furrowed. *Tune?*

He listened harder. He was certain he heard a faint melody—one that wasn't of nature.

He coaxed his horse into a slow walk and cocked an ear, hoping to pick up the direction of the sound. But even when it grew louder, pinning down its location proved troublesome.

Stopping the carriage, Asa grabbed his cane and climbed out. He walked in circles in the road, listening, his senses alert like those of a dog sniffing the air. He left the road, took a few steps, and stopped. Then walked again until he came upon a hole in the ground, large enough for a grown man to squeeze through.

His joints complaining, Asa lowered himself to his knees and leaned into the hole. It was a cave entrance. The familiar recorder music told him Daniel was inside.

"Daniel?"

His voice traveled into the dark regions, then came back to him. The music continued to play.

"Daniel!" he shouted.

He listened for a pause in the music, some indicator that the boy heard him. The music played on.

Another shout, this one loud enough to grate his throat, yielded a similar result.

Asa crawled a little ways into the cave, scraping his palm and propelling pebbles down the slope into the abyss.

Either Daniel still hadn't heard him, or—and Asa couldn't stop himself from thinking this was the more likely scenario—the boy *had* heard him and was ignoring him. There was no letup in the music.

Asa had never liked the recorder and liked it even less whenever Daniel used it to drown him out. More than once the boy had claimed he hadn't heard Asa calling him from the bottom of the stairs.

By now Asa's eyes had adjusted to the diminished light in the mouth of the cave. He could see past the rock slope to a place where no amount of eye adjustment could make seeing possible.

He set his cane aside and crawled a little farther down the slope to make one last effort to get Daniel to hear him, bracing himself as he crawled. Then his hand slipped again.

This time his chest and chin hit rock, forcing the breath from his lungs. His elbow hit his cane, knocking it free and sending it slithering like a stiff snake toward the abyss. Lunging at it, he caught it just before it went over the edge. But in doing so, he accelerated his headlong slide toward the deepest black he'd ever seen!

Nothing he tried could stop the slide. His boots could find no anchor.

"Dear God, help me!"

Daniel lowered his recorder, certain he'd heard his name. Did Epps believe he could talk Daniel into crawling out of the cave to his death?

Still, the taunting made him uneasy. Epps could be toying with him. Diverting his attention. Had he found another way into the cavern?

Daniel eyed the fissure with suspicion. It was clear all the way to the other side. His eyes darted in all directions for as far as the candle light shined, and he saw nothing to indicate Epps had found a way in. Satisfied he was safe, he lifted his recorder and began playing again.

In the distance, beyond the music, beyond the cavern walls, he heard his name again.

"That does it."

Picking up the tinderbox and candle, Daniel worked his way deeper into the cavern where he could play his recorder without Epps interrupting him.

Camilla gave a start.

"Asa . . . ?"

The house felt empty with him away. Traveling away felt different from everyday-at-school away. All morning she'd kept herself busy, trying not to think about it.

She'd finished her morning chores, baked some Christmas cookies, warmed a bowl of soup for lunch, looked out the window for the hundredth time, and figured the time might be best spent by reading her Bible and praying.

Sitting on the front-room sofa beside the fire, she continued her Bible study in Genesis where she'd left off—the story of Joseph. She was at the verses where his brothers saw him coming from afar and called him a dreamer.

One of them said, "Come now therefore, and let us slay him, and cast him into some pit, and we will say, Some evil beast hath devoured him: and we shall see what will become of his dreams."

For some reason, when Camilla read that passage, Asa came to mind and her heart gave a start.

Why would she think of Asa then? Was God speaking to her? Trying to tell her something? Had some evil come upon Asa?

A knock on the door startled her even more.

A frightened whimper escaped from her throat.

With her hand pressed to her chest—her heart was racing, oblivious to any attempt to calm it—she opened the front door.

"Camilla, my dear! Did I startle you?"

A concerned Cyrus Gregg stood in her doorway.

"No . . . well, yes, a little. It's just that, with Asa gone . . . I was being silly, that's all."

But she didn't feel foolish. The fright she'd experienced reading about Joseph's brothers and the pit lingered.

"So Asa went after the boy?" Cyrus asked. "I figured he would."

"Yes." Camilla took a deep breath to steady herself. "He rode out this morning."

Cyrus lowered his gaze. "I hope you don't mind my stopping by like this. I was hoping Daniel had come to his senses and thought it would be easier for us to work everything out if I took the initiative. Despite what he's done, I can't help but like the boy."

"How thoughtful of you! You're so kind . . ."

Cyrus touched the back of his head and winced.

"Your bump!" Camilla stepped toward him, trying to see it. "Have you seen a doctor? Let me take a look."

"It's not serious. Nothing to concern a doctor about. Not on the day before Christmas."

"Let me determine that for myself," Camilla insisted. "Come inside. Over here. Sit on the sofa and let me look at it."

She tugged at his arm and led him inside. He sat on the sofa. Making her way to the back side of the sofa, she bent closer to get a better view of the lump on the back of his head. She lifted his hair, then probed it with her finger.

"Ow!" Cyrus pulled away. "Do all women have to do that? Show a woman a wound, and the first thing she wants to do is touch it."

While his cry of pain was real, his tone was friendly, almost playful.

"Men are such babies when it comes to pain," Camilla replied. "It's discolored, but it looks better than it did yesterday. Did you have a difficult time sleeping?"

"You have no idea," Cyrus said.

It felt good to be talking to him. Camilla was glad he'd stopped by. Hearing another voice made the house feel less empty.

Cyrus stood and faced her, the sofa between them. "How long did Asa say he would be gone?"

"He didn't." Camilla chose not to tell Cyrus he hadn't said anything because they'd been fighting.

"Do you know if he planned to return in time to be at the Christmas Eve party tonight?"

"Your party! Oh, Cyrus! In all the commotion, I'd forgotten all about it! You must think me horrible!"

"I would never think that of you, Camilla. You know that."

"You're being kind. Truthfully, I don't know of Asa's plans for tonight. I know he was excited about going before all this happened with Daniel. I suppose it depends on whether or not he finds Daniel, and if there is enough time to dress."

"I understand," Cyrus said. "It's my own fault, I suppose. I should have invited you and Asa to my party years ago."

"Asa was thrilled to be invited this year. Please believe me. He'd do anything to be there. And who knows? He and Daniel still might show up in time to get ready for your party."

"I hope so." Cyrus walked toward the front door.

Camilla followed him.

"Tell you what I'll do." Cyrus swung back around. "I'll send a carriage for you tonight."

"No, you're being too kind."

"I'm certain Asa will be tired after driving his carriage all day, and maybe this will convince him to come. Please, I insist."

"You've always been a good friend. But I can't promise—"

"Of course you can't. Still, I'll send the carriage." Cyrus smiled and gave a little bow. Before entering his carriage, he added, "And if Asa and Daniel aren't home when it arrives, well, there's nothing stopping you from climbing into it and coming to the party yourself."

"I understand the sentiment behind the offer, and I appreciate it. But I couldn't."

"My invitation stands. I don't like thinking of you sitting alone in an empty house on Christmas Eve when a short distance away I have a houseful of friends who would be delighted to spend the evening with you. And I'm certain Asa would agree with me."

With a tip of his hat, Cyrus climbed into his carriage and rode away. Camilla stood on the front porch and watched him leave.

She couldn't attend the party without Asa, she knew that. But Cyrus's offer was kind, and his visit timely. The fright she'd felt earlier was gone. In fact, now it did seem silly.

As she walked inside the house, she found herself smiling . . . wondering what it would be like at Cyrus's party tonight.

Asa was sliding down death's gullet, and there was nothing he could do to stop it.

Thoughts flashed as though they knew the cessation of his earthly thoughts and cares was but a breath away.

Camilla. He hated that they'd parted in anger. He hated that his death would cause her grief. How he wished he could have one last moment with her.

Daniel. Regret came to mind. He wished he'd treated the boy better. It was just that he loved Daniel's parents—his sister, Maggy, and Eli—so much.

Oh, Eli, when I see you next, what will I say? I've let you down, old friend. You entrusted your son to me, and I—

He'd reached the edge.

The sliding stopped. Abruptly.

Something had him by the ankle.

"Hold on there, friend!" The strong male voice came from behind.

Asa peered into the blackness. He was afraid that, if he moved to look over his shoulder, he might wrench the man's handhold free. That would be ironic, wouldn't it? So instead Asa called, "Um . . . thanks! Don't let go."

The comment sounded inane, but never having dangled over death before, Asa couldn't think of anything to say that didn't involve his predicament.

Then the grip on him slipped, and he began sliding again. The grip tightened, and he stopped.

"Whoa!" Asa shouted. "What's happening up there?"

"Sorry about that," said the voice. "I had to reposition myself . . . to get a better grip to pull you out."

"I . . . understand. You gave me a scare, that's all."

That was an understatement. Asa's swollen heart was in his throat, choking him. Hanging upside down, he found it hard to swallow, hard to breathe.

He didn't want to say anything, but his rescuer seemed to be taking his time.

"Are you still there?" Asa called.

Another inane comment considering someone had him by the ankle, but he had to ask.

"Almost got it," came back the answer.

Asa slid. A good slide this time, the right direction, one that put distance between him and death. Just a couple of inches, but it was up and that was good.

He felt a hand grab his other ankle—his bad leg—and yank hard. Pain shot up to his hip. Asa clenched his teeth and bit back a cry. But the sliding backward continued, and that's all that mattered. He was being pulled out.

Emerging into the light and out of the hole, Asa felt reborn. He rolled over onto his back, letting the pain ease, letting his head clear. After several deep breaths, breathing came easier. He inhaled the crisp afternoon air and blinked back the bright day.

"You all right, friend?"

Asa looked up into the face of a younger man with a strong nose and winning smile. He had a frontier appearance about him. His clothes were leather and heavy and worn. He wore a knee-length overcoat. He had a thick black beard.

"Thank you hardly seems enough," Asa said.

The man grinned, showing a lot of teeth. "In a way, it was almost comical, the way I found you. I happened by and saw a pair of feet sliding down a hole in the ground."

"The other end of that picture was not as comical, I assure you."

"Anything broken? Can you stand?" the man asked.

"Let's give it a try."

The man moved to his side, hooked an arm under Asa's arm, and helped him get up. Asa tested his bad leg with a little weight. It hurt, but held.

"This yours?"

Still supporting Asa, the man bent down to retrieve Asa's cane. As he did, Asa noticed a tattoo on the back of the man's neck. It depicted a coiled snake.

CHAPTER 19

"Lucky for you I came along," Asa's rescuer said.

"Thank God you came along."

"You think *God* had something to do with it?"

Asa took a hard look at the young man. "I believe God has a hand in everything. And I know for certain if you had not fished me out of that hole when you did, I'd be standing in His presence right now."

They found themselves sitting in a clearing a short distance from the cave entrance, out in the open. It appeared to have once been a camp with large rocks arranged in a circle around a blackened patch of dirt.

The sky was clear. The sun had already started along its descending arc.

After rescuing Asa, the young man helped him sit down. Then he retrieved Asa's horse and carriage from the road while Asa caught his breath and steadied his nerves. Asa learned that the young man's name was Robely Epps. He took an instant liking to him.

"Who's in there?" Epps motioned to the cave.

"My nephew."

"Does he go in there often?"

Asa hesitated. He didn't like airing his family business like so much laundry, but the chances of meeting up with Mr. Robely Epps again were remote, and the man *had* saved his life. He figured that was worth answers to a few questions.

"We're from Cumberland, up the road a piece. He's a runaway. I came looking for him."

Epps nodded, looking off into the distance as though remembering something. "Sixteen years old?"

Asa smiled. "How did you know?"

Epps grinned. "Tough age. I ran away when I was sixteen. Best thing I ever did. Made a man of me."

"And your parents? What did they do when you ran away?"

"Father. Ma was dead by then." He shrugged. "Don't know what he did. Haven't talked to him since. He probably bought himself another bottle, beat my brothers, and drank himself to sleep. That's what he did every day. Doubt he'd change his ways because he had one less boy to beat."

Asa stared at the ground as he listened. He'd heard similar stories. Over the years he'd lost a number of students to abusive fathers who pulled them out of school for one reason or another. A real shame. Some of them—like the man sitting across from him now—could have made something of themselves with an education. Asa recognized intelligence behind Epps's eyes.

"Does the boy know you're looking for him?" Epps asked.

"I think he heard me calling to him, all right," Asa replied. "We can hear his music well enough."

"So he doesn't want to be found. Why waste your time?"

Asa looked down. He'd already said more than he was comfortable saying.

But Epps didn't seem to need it spelled out for him. He stood and stretched his legs. "Do you know these caves? Any other way in or out?"

"Until today, I wasn't aware the cave existed."

The pain in Asa's leg eased to a dull ache. As Asa positioned his cane to get up, Epps took a step forward to help but backed off when Asa signaled he could do it himself.

Epps turned away, as if providing Asa the dignity of not watching him struggle to get up. Epps addressed his comment to the surrounding brush and rock. "Seems to me—and mind you, I don't mean to be telling you your business—as long as you can hear that thing the boy is playing, you know where he is."

"True enough," Asa said, wincing as he stretched his stiff leg.

"In the meantime, a search of the surrounding area would be in order. If there is no other way in or out . . ." He turned to Asa. "What's the boy's name again?"

"Daniel."

"Then Daniel will have to come out of this hole sooner or later. In that case, it just becomes a matter of time."

Asa nodded approvingly. The educator in him liked the way Robely Epps reasoned his way through the situation.

"Does the boy have a supply of food?" Epps asked.

"He left the house in a hurry. Took what he could grab in a hurry. Though he did stop at a tavern this morning."

"Which means he could stay down there through the night, or longer."

Asa reached for his pocket watch and frowned. With the short winter days, even if he were to head back now, it would be dark before he reached home. And the last thing he wanted to do tonight was guard a hole in the earth when he could be attending Cyrus Gregg's Christmas party.

"Time constraints?" Epps asked.

"No." Asa put his watch back in its pocket.

"Tell you what . . . how about if we go to the hole? You shout into it a couple of times—I'll hold your legs to keep you from falling in—and see if we can coax him out. If that doesn't work, we can search the area before it gets dark."

Asa was shaking his head halfway through the offer. "Very kind of you, but I can't impose on you any more than I already have. You've done enough. I'm sure you have somewhere to be tonight, it being Christmas Eve."

"Is it?" Epps said. "Makes no difference to me. Just another night as far as I'm concerned."

Asa couldn't help wondering what would bring an intelligent man to have so little regard for Christmas.

"Besides, if there's one thing the frontier has taught me," Epps continued, "it's that men have to look out for each other if they're going to survive. And if that weren't a good enough reason, I like the fact that you came after the boy. It's more than my father did for me."

Asa didn't argue with him. He was glad to have the company. And maybe Daniel would listen to a younger man. He could learn a thing or two from Robely Epps.

"I'm in your debt," Asa said.

"There it is, then."

Robely Epps followed Asa to the cave entrance. But before Asa had time to yell into the cave, the music stopped.

Daniel lowered the recorder. The chill in the cave had succeeded in penetrating both clothing and flesh. He got up, stomped his feet to get his circulation going, and looked around, feeling small in the immensity of it all. He'd descended farther into the cave than he'd thought. Tucking the recorder into his waistband, he turned his attention to finding a way out.

The logical way out was the way he came in. After all, he had heard Epps jump back across the chasm and scramble out, proving it could be done. But it was a safe assumption that the killer was guarding the hole, waiting for Daniel to poke his head out, and then . . .

Daniel didn't want to think about what would happen then.

How long would Epps wait before giving up?

One day?

Two?

Daniel had to find another way out.

He held the candle high, throwing the light as far distant as possible, and proceeded deeper into the cave. His footsteps echoed as he trespassed through the rock cathedral.

The walls were wet and shiny and slick, the candle lighting but a few feet at a time. He continued descending, sometimes on natural rock steps, sometimes down a slope where he tested every step.

A jagged line came into the field of light, separating rock from black nothingness. He inched toward it. As he did, a chasm yawned in front of him.

Staying well back from the edge, Daniel paralleled the chasm, looking for a way across. It stretched from one side of the cavern to the other, from sheer wall to sheer wall. There was no passageway across it.

Jumping was out of the question. At its narrowest, the chasm was easily twenty feet wide and twelve to fifteen feet deep. His candle reflected off a liquid bottom, a shallow stream. There was no way down.

Retracing his steps along the edge, Daniel inspected it again, thinking perhaps he'd missed something. He hadn't. His hope of finding an alternative way out was growing dim. Still, he wasn't ready to give up.

Daniel held the candle close to the wall, examining its surface with his palm. About a foot above his head, he discovered a thin ledge, four, maybe five inches deep. It extended across the chasm, but did it reach the other side? His candle light didn't stretch far enough for him to see.

He tested the ledge with his fingers. The rock was solid, not flaky. Tracing it away from the chasm, he found an abutment of boulders that served as steps.

Adjusting his haversack and his grip on the candle, Daniel climbed up to the ledge and scooted out onto it, his feet spread wide, his chest and cheek hugging the wet rock wall. With the candle in his lead hand, he inched his way to the edge of the chasm.

This is crazy, he thought. Even if he made it to the other side, would that be a way out of the cave?

But the known way out was more frightening than the unknown. So, taking a deep breath, Daniel continued inching his way forward.

The cavern floor fell away. Far below him, the stream was a wide black ribbon.

Daniel told himself not to look down. To concentrate on each step.

Halfway across the chasm, the ledge began to narrow. Less than four inches. Now three inches. And narrowing.

He stopped. It was still too far to jump.

Should he go back?

The image of Epps sharpening his knife came to mind.

Daniel clung to the side of the cliff. He pressed so hard against it, he could feel his heart bouncing off rock. He closed his eyes and pressed his forehead against the cold stone, attempting to calm himself.

A deep breath. Then another. And another.

Below him, the stream gurgled over loose rocks.

Opening his eyes, he caught sight of the ledge, his goal. Could he work himself along the ledge far enough to jump?

He had to try. He took a step . . . and his foot gave way.

Fear struck like lightning.

The fingers of his left hand clutched a projection. But, in doing so, he lost the candle. It tumbled downward and, after the smallest of splashes, went out.

The cavern was plunged into total darkness.

Camilla couldn't believe she was standing in the home of the wealthy Cyrus Gregg, where everything was light and bright and gay.

Earlier she'd told herself she wouldn't come without Asa.

Then she told herself she'd put on her dress and fix her hair in case Asa showed up at the last minute, because, as everyone knows, it always takes men less time to get ready than it does women.

A short while later she had found herself sitting in the front room, all dressed up.

When Cyrus Gregg's carriage had come for her, she decided to go, even though Asa wasn't there. She thanked the driver as he treated her like a lady and assisted her into the coach.

Now that Camilla was at Cyrus's home, she was glad she'd come. While she'd known Cyrus most of her life, she'd never known him to be so gallant and entertaining, the ultimate host.

She met senators and congressmen, and all of Cumberland's well-to-do. She danced with a French diplomat, sang Christmas songs, laughed, and smiled until her face hurt.

Camilla couldn't remember when she'd had such a delightful time.

CHAPTER 20

Once the sun went down, the temperature plummeted. Asa leaned close to the fire as Epps piled more wood onto it, sending embers spiraling skyward.

Asa followed the twirling path of the red sparks, watching them mingle with the stars, the same stars the shepherds of Bethlehem camped under so long ago when the sky exploded with angel song. Unlike that ancient night, it was silent. No music had come from the cave for hours.

"Warm enough?" Epps asked.

"Those last few branches helped," Asa replied.

While Asa started the fire with surrounding brush, Epps had taken the horse and carriage to get some more substantial fuel from a wooded area he said he'd passed earlier that day.

It was the end of a frustrating day. They'd spent the last of the afternoon first shouting into the cave without results, then scouting the surrounding area for another entrance to the cave. That, too, proved to be unsuccessful.

Epps stoked the fire, goading the embers to release their heat. Asa's thoughts turned to Camilla. He hated the fact that she was spending Christmas Eve alone. He could see her bundled up, buried beneath a comforter in the front room with a cup of tea and her Bible next to her on the stand. Every Christmas Eve of their marriage, they'd read the account of the nativity from the apostle Luke's gospel. Tonight Camilla would read it alone. The thought angered him.

"If we left now, you could be home before midnight," Epps said.

Mired in his thoughts, Asa looked at Epps blankly. "Huh? Oh . . . that obvious, is it?"

"I'd be willing to travel with you—you know, two men together . . . less of a target for brigands. Or, if you prefer, you could go home and I'll wait here for the boy to surface. I could escort him home. Sort of a Christmas gift."

It was an enticing offer.

Asa smiled. The more time he spent with Robely Epps, the more he liked the man. "I hope Daniel gets to meet you. He could learn a lot from you."

Epps shrugged. "Don't know about that, but after what we've been through, I'm kind of anxious to meet the boy myself. And I'm serious about my offer."

"Much appreciated," Asa said, pulling his coat tighter around him. "But I think I'll stay the night and see what the morning brings."

Daniel couldn't see a thing. He could hear his breathing—almost as fast as a dog's pant—bouncing off the face of the cliff in front of him. He could feel the cold stone penetrating his coat and pants. He could feel the rock cutting into his fingertips, and the thin ledge upon which he stood through his shoes. But he couldn't see. The instant the candle had hit the stream below, everything had gone black.

His choices were two: go forward, go back. Forward was the shortest route, but the ledge upon which he was standing diminished to the point of disappearing that way. How much farther could he go without slipping off? The way back was the safer route. It was farther, but the ledge remained wide and secure the entire distance.

A thought came to him. He could go back, light a new candle, and try again.

No. He dismissed that idea. Once he stepped off this ledge, he knew he would never step onto it again. Not in this lifetime. If he were going to cross, he'd have to do it now.

His fingers cramped. He needed to make a decision.

Forward. It had to be forward.

All right, forward. Now, can I do it? Can I do it blind?

Staring ahead into the darkness did him no good, so he closed his eyes. It was just as black, but it felt more natural. Eyes open and seeing nothing added to his anxiety.

He tried to remember every detail of his position before he dropped the candle. The distance to the other side. How far the ledge went before it got too thin to stand on. He imagined himself making his way to where the ledge gave way, getting a good toehold, then jumping the rest of the way.

That was the plan.

A blind leap into the dark.

With nothing else to do but do it, Daniel eased his way forward, feeling the ledge with his toe. He tested it first, then transferred his weight while clutching the cliff with his fingers. He took another step. On the third step, his foot gave way. There wasn't enough ledge left to hold his weight. He'd gone as far as he could go. The only thing left to do now was jump.

He opened his eyes, hoping to glimpse something that would tell him how far he had to jump. He saw nothing. Not a line. Not a shadow. Not a shape. He would have to guess.

Overshooting the mark meant he would land farther away from the edge. The danger was falling short. So the plan was simple. Jump as far as possible.

He rose up on the balls of his feet, getting the best foothold he could manage. Crouching to spring proved to be a problem when he was pressed this flat against the cave wall. His knees knocked against solid rock. Doubt niggled, telling him he wouldn't make it. It was too far. Perhaps if the ledge extended a foot or two farther, he could make it.

Daniel squinted in an attempt to silence his thoughts. They sounded too much like his uncle's.

He told himself he'd jump at the count of three.

One. He double-checked his foothold.

Two. His knees bent, hitting rock.

Three.

Daniel flung himself into the black void, stretching his arms forward, as though by doing so he could will himself to the other side. But the instant he released from the cave wall, he could feel his momentum failing. He began to fall.

In all his life he'd experienced no more helpless feeling than this. He had no control. Flailing arms did nothing. Kicking legs had no effect. He was falling, and there was nothing he could do to stop.

He prepared his feet for landing, though he could see no land. Jumping out of the tree or the bedroom window was different. Then he could see the ground rushing up. He could anticipate the landing. But now his feet stretched and found nothing.

At that instant, his chest slammed into the edge of the chasm, knocking the breath from his body. He hadn't jumped far enough!

His hands and arms slapped the cave floor. His chin hit rock. He began sliding backward into the chasm.

His fingers clawed at rock and found no hold. His feet plowed into the side of the chasm and dug for a foothold that wasn't there.

And then there was nothing to cling to.

Daniel slipped over the edge and tumbled into the void like his candle. And, like his candle, he hit the water with a splash and the light of his conscious mind went out.

"I had a lovely time tonight, Cyrus!" Camilla cooed.

Still glowing from the evening, she stood with her back against the front door of her house. Behind her all the rooms were dark—evidence that Asa wasn't home yet.

"You were a delight. Everyone loved you," Cyrus said.

Camilla lowered her gaze. Her face felt warm. It had been years since she had blushed at a man's compliment. She'd forgotten how good it felt.

"Everything was bright and festive," she said. "And you were the perfect host."

Cyrus started to object.

She stopped him with an upraised hand. "Don't. You were masterful," she insisted. "It's obvious you thrive on these events. I've never had the privilege of seeing you in this role."

"A grievous error on my part, madam. One that I'm glad has been corrected tonight."

"It was a memorable night. The food. The conversation. Everything. I wish Asa were here to enjoy it too. He was looking forward to it so much."

Cyrus took a small step back. "Should we be concerned that he isn't home?" he asked in a more somber, businesslike tone.

Camilla looked over her shoulder at the dark house. "I'm not concerned for Asa's safety, if that's what you're asking. He's no stranger to travel. As for Daniel, Asa will do whatever is necessary to find him and bring him back. Did you know that he once tracked Daniel's father all the way from New Haven to Kentucky?"

Cyrus half grinned. "I didn't know that. Like father, like son?"

"Daniel's father is Reverend Eli Cooper."

"The great revival preacher?"

Camilla nodded.

"I'm impressed. I had no idea. All I knew was that his father and mother went down in the Atlantic. So that was Eli Cooper . . . and, of course, his mother was Asa's sister."

"Maggy," Camilla said. "Asa and Eli were rivals in college. Hearing about some of their antics, it's a wonder they didn't kill each other. Then they became best friends."

"From rivals to best friends to in-laws. Sounds like quite a story."

"You'll have to ask Asa to tell it to you sometime."

"Well . . ." Cyrus shuffled his feet on the porch. "Are you sure you'll be all right here by yourself? I could send Martha—you met her, didn't you? My house servant?—to stay with you until Asa returns. Or . . . you could use my guesthouse."

"That's very sweet of you, Cyrus, but I'll be fine. This isn't the first time I've spent a night alone in the house."

Cyrus did another little shuffle with his feet. "If you change your mind . . ."

The shuffle brought him closer to Camilla. He leaned toward her and, in a half-whisper, said, "I know you won't believe me when I tell you this, but you were the most beautiful woman at the party tonight."

For the second time Camilla felt her color rise. Then, to her dismay, Cyrus continued leaning toward her. His eyes closed. His lips pursed.

She backed away, the closed door blocking her retreat. His face was inches from hers now, his lips seeking a target. An involuntary moan escaped her lips as she fumbled for the door latch.

Should she stop his face with her hand? Turn her head so he hit only cheek? Slap him? Scream? Faint? Duck and let him kiss the door?

At the last second she found the latch, pushed the door open, and stumbled inside.

"There!" she said airily. "Our front door latch always sticks in the cold weather."

She turned to him as though she hadn't noticed he'd tried to kiss her.

For a moment Cyrus appeared startled, but he recovered. "Will you come to the house for dinner tomorrow after the Christmas service? I'd love to have you as my guest . . . and Asa and Daniel, if they should come home."

"Would it be rude of me to request that I give you my answer tomorrow at church?" Camilla asked.

"My dear lady, rudeness is not part of your nature. Of course you may. I'll prepare for your company, hoping for the best." He stepped into the doorway.

"Thank you. You've always been a dear friend. And thank you again for tonight. It was a memorable party. Good night."

Camilla began to close the door with a polite but firm touch, forcing Cyrus to step back. He bid her a final good night as she latched the door.

She listened for the clatter of his carriage leaving before crossing the room in the dark and lighting a lamp. Up until the last few moments it had been a fairytale evening. She removed her dress gloves, and as she did, her gaze fell upon her Bible.

It lay open to Luke chapter 2, the nativity account. She'd found the passage in anticipation of Asa coming home.

Her comment to Cyrus had been true. This wasn't the first time she'd spent the night alone.

"But it's the first Christmas Eve I've spent alone," she said to the empty house.

CHAPTER 21

After unhitching the carriage and getting his horse settled for the night, Asa returned to the fire, his fingers frozen. The crackle and odor of roasting rabbit greeted him.

Robely Epps said he'd gotten lucky earlier when he went to scrounge up some food. But Asa didn't believe him. The man was being modest. Epps moved comfortably in this outdoor world. Asa didn't think there was anything the man couldn't do out here.

"I can add some of my wife's biscuits to the dinner," Asa said. "Fresh baked yesterday. And some cookies."

Epps grinned the widest grin Asa had seen yet. "I'll pass on the biscuits, but I'd slit your throat for one of them cookies. I've got me a whale of a sweet tooth."

Epps's response was crude, but Asa liked the man's enthusiasm. He returned the grin as he warmed his hands over the fire.

When his back hurt from standing up, Asa shoved a rock closer to the fire and sat down.

"That's got to be the gentlest horse I've ever seen," Epps said. "Had him long?"

"A couple of years." Asa rubbed his aching leg.

"I would have guessed longer. He responds to you so well."

"Picked him up from a friend who trained him well." Asa stretched his leg out and continued rubbing it.

Epps studied him for a time, then leaned forward and turned the rabbit. He poked the meat with his finger to see if it was done. "Riding accident?" he asked.

Asa stopped rubbing his leg.

"A guess," Epps said. "When I asked you about your horse, you started rubbing your leg."

Asa nodded. Once again, he was impressed. He'd spent his life evaluating the intelligence of boys and girls. From the moment he'd met Robely Epps, the man had continued to demonstrate remarkable intellectual ability and insight for a frontier man. Asa was dying to ask him about his schooling.

"Carriage accident," Asa said.

Epps didn't appear surprised. Nor did he seem all that eager to hear the details of the incident. But for some reason, Asa wanted to tell him.

"I bought a purebred," he explained. "Finest horse I'd seen since leaving New Haven. Two things about the transaction gave me pause. First, the price. It was twice as much as I'd planned to spend on a horse. But then, it was the kind of horse I'd always dreamed of owning."

"And the second thing?"

"He was high-spirited. I wasn't sure if Camilla would be able to handle him." He sighed, reliving his indecision. "She didn't like the horse. Said his eyes looked like he was possessed by a demon. Of course I scoffed at her fear and told her it was the sign of a quick mind and good breeding."

"So you told the seller of your wife's reluctance, and he lowered the price," Epps said.

"Have you heard this story before?" Asa laughed. "That's what happened. I was like a giddy boy in love. I had the horse of my dreams." He stared into the fire. "My dream turned into a nightmare."

Epps leaned forward and turned the rabbit again. Asa waited until he sat back down before continuing the story.

"We'd just celebrated our first year of marriage. And we were expecting our first child. It was a Sunday. Bright. Sunny. One of those carefree days when nothing ever goes wrong."

The fire popped and spit embers into the sky.

"We were on our way to church. The horse had been acting skittish all morning. I had a devil of a time harnessing him." Asa rubbed his leg. "We hadn't gotten far when something set him off. To this day, I don't know what did it. Maybe the horse *was* possessed by demons . . . You can figure out the rest. The carriage overturned. And when the dust settled, my leg was broken in several places."

Epps listened in silence, his head bowed.

"That wasn't the worst of it. Camilla lost the baby—and the ability ever to have children." He rubbed his leg. "This pain is a daily reminder of my foolishness. All because I wanted a purebred."

"You love your wife," Epps said.

"Yes. Very much."

"I wasn't asking. I was observing. You love your wife. The way you talk about her. It's obvious you love her."

Epps checked the rabbit again and declared it done.

As they ate, Asa couldn't take his mind off Camilla spending the entire evening alone in a dark house.

Christmas morning dawned clear and crisp. A shaft of sun woke Asa, who had curled up on the seat of his carriage halfway through the night. Every joint in his body complained as he unfolded his arms and legs and walked around. He stretched.

Epps stood a short distance away, eyeing the cave entrance. When he saw Asa, he said, "Was hoping we'd have some music this morning."

"Have you heard anything?"

"Quiet as a tomb."

Asa limped over to the hole. "If you can find some water, I might be able to come up with a pan and some coffee from the back of the carriage."

"I could use something hot."

While Asa rummaged in the carriage for the bag of coffee he was certain he'd packed, Epps went in search of water.

Shivering was the first thing Daniel became aware of. That, and the fact that his jaw ached from clenching his teeth.

He stirred. Moaned. And stirred again. Raising a hand to his head, he swished water and splashed himself in the face. He sputtered and lifted his head. It felt like it would fall off his shoulders, and if it did, he would make no effort to put it back on.

He managed to sit up. How, he didn't know. Nor did he remember sitting up. He just noticed that he had.

He thought he'd gone blind, then remembered the falling candle followed by the falling Daniel. The stream in which he sat was a couple of inches deep. He reached around to his haversack, felt around for another candle, and managed to light it.

Rock cliffs rose to impressive heights all around him. He recognized where he was and where he'd been. From down here the chasm looked a lot deeper than it had from on top.

The candle shook in his hand. He was chilled to the bone. He had to get dry and warm—something he wasn't going to do in this subterranean ditch.

Splashing to his feet, Daniel looked around. The walls were too high and slick to climb. Upstream, the water seemed to emerge from the base of a cliff. Downstream was his one viable choice.

With no idea if it was day or night, or how long he'd been unconscious, Daniel resumed his earlier quest of finding a way out of the cave.

But now he tended to think of it as a quest to get warm.

Camilla awoke to an empty bed. She reached over to Asa's side and caressed his pillow. It was cold.

"Merry Christmas, darling. Wherever you are."

There was something about it being Christmas that made the house feel emptier.

She fixed herself a biscuit and jam for breakfast and a cup of hot tea. Then she dressed for church.

Selecting her best dress, she told herself she was wearing it because it was Christmas. But while she was pulling it over her head, she was envisioning what it would look like at Cyrus Gregg's Christmas dinner table.

She told herself she still hadn't decided to accept his offer, considering his behavior last night.

But as she walked out the door, Bible in hand, the thought of coming back home after church and spending the day alone seemed unbearable.

By noon of Christmas Day, Asa knew he had a decision to make. They had heard no music coming from the cave for almost twenty-four hours.

"The boy never goes this long at home without playing that thing," Asa said.

"He could have wandered so far into the cave we can't hear him," Epps suggested.

"Or found another way out."

"Which would mean he's putting distance between us and him while we stand here."

Hands on hips, Asa surveyed the road. His heart argued for home and Camilla. But how could he return to her empty-handed?

"If the boy managed to find another way out, where would he go?" Epps asked.

"New Haven, most likely. That's where he was raised. He has friends there."

Epps's eyebrows raised, as though the idea surprised him.

"Think I'll hitch up the horse and head on down the road a piece. See if I can find anyone who has seen him." Turning his back on the cave entrance, Asa headed toward his carriage.

"Is the boy partial to the sea?" Epps asked.

"Not that I'm aware of."

"He could get a job on the docks."

"No, he did that for a while. I've never heard him say a good word about the experience."

"So you think he's going east because of his friends?"

Asa stopped and thought. "He hasn't stayed in touch with any of them."

"If I was a young boy running away," Epps said, "I'd go west. More opportunities. More excitement."

Asa shook his head. "Daniel is not the frontier type." He started out again for the carriage.

"What kinds of things is he interested in?" Epps asked, following. "Other than his music."

"Nothing. All he does is play that ridiculous recorder and work as a shop boy for a casket company." He stopped. "Until recently, that is . . . within the last couple of days, he's been interested in inventions."

"Inventions?"

"He designed finlike things for the inside of a clothes-washing machine. Impressed a local businessman and a friend of mine."

"There are machines that wash clothes?"

Asa laughed. "It was opening some exciting doors for him, too, which makes his actions all the more—"

A thought struck Asa. "Wait a minute! Canals! For a time, it looked like he would get a chance to work on a canal. He got excited about it!"

"Canals? Like the Patowmack? Or the Erie?"

"Epps, you're astounding! Never have I met a man so astute!"

"What did I say?"

Asa smiled. "I know where Daniel's heading. Not east, but north. He's going to the Erie Canal."

"You think so?"

"I know it as sure as I'm standing here." Asa grabbed Epps by the shoulders. "Thank you! You may not believe this, but God led you here to help me save my nephew."

"I find that hard to believe. You don't even know me."

"I know you well enough, friend."

"So then, you're heading north?"

"A day's journey at least," Asa said. "If I don't catch up with Daniel by then, or come across someone who's seen him, I may rethink it. But I have a good feeling about this."

"Then we'll be traveling the same direction."

"I thought you were going to Cumberland."

"No, I'm heading to Syracuse."

Asa smiled. "Well, do you think you can put up with an old man for the next day or two?"

Robely Epps returned the smile. "I would welcome the company. And with any luck, I'll get to meet your nephew."

CHAPTER 22

A giant, gnarled tree that had stood for centuries marked the division in the roads heading east and north. It had taken Asa and Epps about thirty minutes to pack up and reach this fork in the road.

"Are you sure about this?" Epps asked.

"Confident," Asa replied.

"What if the boy's heading east?"

Asa turned to him. "Do you think he is?"

"No."

"That's what makes me confident the north road is the right road."

"Because of what I said?"

"Yes, because of what you said. You have the most remarkable insight when it comes to people, do you know that?"

Epps nodded, which surprised Asa a little. He'd expected modesty. "I've been told I have a gift."

"So what are you doing out here by yourself, if I may be so bold? With your ability, you could be a captain of industry."

Epps scoffed at that. "Nobody does business with a man who has one year of learning. As soon as moneyed people learn I don't have an education, they hand me a broom. About all I could be captain of is the dust bin. I want more than that."

Asa saw the truth in what he said. "So what do you do, Mr. Epps?"

"I want to be wealthy," Epps said. It was obvious by the way he said it that he'd thought about it. "I don't want to scrape for a living all my life. And the way I see it, there are two ways to wealth: either become 'a captain of industry,' to use your words, which is not possible with my education, or become indispensable to those who are captains of industry, to men who have money. I'm not talking about working for them, mind you, but becoming indispensable. Providing them a service they desperately want, can't do for themselves, for which they are willing to pay handsomely. I find out what that is, and do it for them. Simple as that."

Asa nodded in admiration. "Simple as that," he repeated. "Find a need and fill it. You are a most remarkable man, Robely Epps. I wish Daniel had half of your drive and determination. So, tell me, what kinds of jobs have you—"

"Don't you think we'd better get going? The day's awastin', and who knows how much of a jump your boy has on us."

"You're right."

Asa snapped the reins and steered the horse onto the north road. With all his heart he hoped Daniel would have a chance to meet Epps. If Asa had the money, he'd hire Epps himself. But being a poor educator and no captain of industry, he doubted he could come up with the kind of money Epps was accustomed to making.

Camilla sat with her hands folded in her lap at Cyrus Gregg's Christmas table. It was beyond impressive. Roast goose. Roast turkey. Smoked ham. Cranberries. Yams. Breads and jellies of every description and flavor. Apple pie. Pumpkin pie. Berry pie. Puddings. Candies. All of it colorful and served on the finest silver and china she had ever seen.

As for the conversation, it was as sparkling as the candelabras—with the mayor of Cumberland and his wife, who seemed much too young for him and who was more overwhelmed than Camilla by the dinner and surroundings and guests, the pastor and his wife, the district superintendent for the Patowmack Canal and his fiancée, and the widow Worthington, Cumberland's wealthiest citizen.

Normally, Camilla would have felt out of place among such elite company, but Cyrus—bless his heart—had treated her like the guest of honor from the moment she stepped in the door. All the other guests had followed his lead so that by the time the main course was served, Camilla herself believed she belonged here with them.

During a lapse of conversation, she wondered how Asa and Daniel were doing in the wilderness. But the thought vanished almost as soon as it appeared. It took a concerted effort on her part to keep up with the conversation and festivities at Cyrus Gregg's Christmas dinner table.

Logic told Daniel the stream would lead him to the river. He was beginning to wonder if the river was in China.

He was sore from the fall. Exhausted from shivering. His feet were wet and numb. Daniel tried to warm himself with images of sitting beside a fire. Here, inside the cavern, he could not sit and rest. The floor was frigid water. In one place the ceiling had dropped to two feet and Daniel had to get on his belly and crawl. He was beginning to think he'd never see the sun again.

He shuffled through the water, stepping on stones that had been polished smooth over hundreds of years. His head was down. His eyelids drooped. The water sparkled from candlelight.

Or was it candlelight?

There were two hues of sparkle. Yellow and white. The white sparkles extended upstream, beyond the reach of candlelight, all the way to—

The opening was small, but fresh air gushed with the promise of sky and sun. Daniel dropped his candle and ran to it.

He had to get down on his hands and knees to see out. And there it was. The Potomac River, lolling in the winter sun! All of a sudden a ferocious feeling built within Daniel, the kind a convict might have looking through prison bars at freedom. It was as though his life depended upon his getting out through that opening. That if he didn't get out now, he'd be trapped in this cave forever.

The opening was small. Too small to climb through. Daniel clawed at the edges and the stream bottom, pulling away loose rock. The opening grew a bit wider, but was still not big enough.

"This is not my grave! This is not my grave!"

He looked around for a large rock, something he could use as a hammer. But all the rocks in the stream were smaller than his fist.

Then he had an idea. Scooting back some, he sat in the icy stream and leaned back, supporting himself with his hands and arms. With dripping feet, he kicked at the edges of the opening.

The kick jarred his teeth, doing more damage to him than to the cave opening. He kicked again. And again. His kicks took on a rhythm. Then the rhythm took on a fury that bordered on obsession, fueled by anger.

"This . . . is . . . not . . . my . . . grave!" he screamed with each kick.

The side of the opening crumbled, giving way. Not all the way. But it gave, and that fed Daniel's fury until, finally, a huge section of rock broke loose. Daniel kicked it down a slope and into the river.

He had never seen a more satisfying splash.

Pulling his haversack off his back, he tossed it through the hole and climbed out after it. Lifting a hand to shield his eyes, he squinted against the hazy sky.

He stood on the gentle slope beside the river, unable to see over the rise. A wind flew over it and embraced him with icy arms.

His thoughts turned to getting warm, but first he had to check something. Staying low, he made his way to the top of the rise and peered over it. He took his time about it. He hadn't come all this way to get killed out of carelessness.

The vista was flat. Daniel saw no sign of Epps. He had no idea in which direction to look. Having become so disoriented in the cave, he had to guess as to where the entrance was located.

He scanned the surrounding terrain a second time. Then a third. A feeling of comfort came over him as he concluded that Epps had given up and moved on.

The relief he felt was twofold. One, he felt safe. Two, now he could get warm.

Scrambling around the slope, Daniel piled up twigs and branches and anything that looked like it would burn. Before long, he had himself a good-size fire next to the river.

He stripped off his wet clothes and pulled on drier—not dry, since the falling and crawling in the stream had seen to that—clothes. It seemed to take forever to get warm, but at last the circulation returned to his hands and feet and face and he stopped shivering. He couldn't imagine ever wanting to leave this fire.

Laying down beside it, his eyes grew heavy. Before long, he was asleep.

CHAPTER 23

Rested and dry and warm, Daniel stood at a crossroads in front of a gnarled tree. It was one of those trees that looked like it had been around forever.

How many people had passed by this very tree in its lifetime? Settlers coming west for the first time. Soldiers in the war with the French and Indians. Soldiers in the War for Independence. It would be a safe bet that George Washington himself rode past this tree, the way everybody in Cumberland talked about him. And before him, Indians.

And now Daniel. Not anyone of any importance. One of hundreds of forgettable people who came to this crossroads and made decisions that altered their destinies.

East?

Or north?

Daniel's future hung in the balance.

East was the logical choice. The safe choice. He knew East. New Haven. He'd worked at the docks before and could do so again. He could track down some old friends.

On the other hand, New Haven wasn't all security and good times. It had its ghosts too.

North was a trek into the unknown. That was part of its allure. A fresh start. And it also had a grand canal. But what would he do there?

Who would hire him? He knew how to play the recorder and sweep floors. How many jobs were there for recorder-playing shop boys?

In the East he could go back to where he'd worked before. It was hard work, but it paid better than sweeping.

East was the smart choice. Daniel turned eastward . . . but he saw nothing but ghosts in that choice.

Turning north, he started walking at a brisk pace.

All day during the climb out of the river valley Epps had sidestepped Asa's inquiries about the specifics of his employment. He was quite chatty, though, when it came to his upbringing in Matildaville.

With the road to themselves, it being Christmas afternoon, Asa listened as Robely Epps described a small town with two main streets—Canal Street and Washington Street—with a market, a foundry, a gristmill, an inn, a sawmill, an ice house, the canal company superintendent's house, and workers' barracks. Epps, his father, and seven brothers lived on the edge of town in a house that was little more than a shack.

Matildaville, named after the wife of its founder, Revolutionary War hero Light Horse Harry Lee, served as the headquarters of the Patowmack Canal Company. Life revolved around the waterway as boats locked through the Great Falls, hauling manufactured products and firearms upstream to Cumberland, and iron, whiskey, flour, and tobacco downstream to Washington, D.C., Boaters frequented the town while waiting their turn to go through the locks or to enjoy an evening before continuing their journey.

"My father worked in the ironworks foundry," Epps said. "He measured a man by the strength of his arms. Every night when he came home, he made it a point to prove his superiority. With games of strength, if he was in a good mood. By beating us if he was drunk."

"Among your brothers, you were . . ."

"The strongest."

"I was thinking more in terms of age."

"Age didn't matter. Pa had to whip the strongest to prove he was top dog. But I was second oldest."

"So you always got the worst of it."

"Aya." Epps pointed. "How about over there? That looks level." He pointed to a small clearing off the road.

"And none too soon," Asa replied. "My back is killing me."

The sun had disappeared behind the mountain, and the air had turned cold. Asa was ready for a fire.

Having done this before, the two men worked with a minimum of words to set up camp. As he had the night before, Epps provided the meat for the meal. This time it was squirrel.

While Asa was grateful for the hot food, the manner in which Epps provided it was weird to the point of eerie. Asa would look up and notice the man was gone. It was never for long, and Asa would never hear a shot, or a rustle of leaves or branches. The next thing he knew, Epps was walking into camp with the kill.

"Good meal," Asa said later, wiping the grease from his fingertips. "Always amazes me how much of an appetite I work up when all I've done is ride in a carriage all day."

Epps tossed a bone picked clean into the fire. "Always had a taste for the little critters."

Asa stood and stretched. He walked back and forth, trying to limber up his leg.

Epps stretched out too, but without getting up. "I suppose you'll be heading back, come morning," he said, reclining against a log.

Asa stared past the trees into the black night. "If only I had some indication that I was heading in the right direction . . . I was hoping to come across someone who had seen him on the road. But this being Christmas . . ."

"He may not be traveling by road."

"The thought had crossed my mind. I don't know . . . Do I give it another day, or am I wasting my time?"

"You already know what I think."

"Aya. And I'm sure you'll be proved right. But I have a wife to think about. She's been sitting alone in a house for two days worrying about me. If I decide to stay away any longer, I need to get word to her."

Epps picked up a small knife and began cleaning his fingernails while Asa paced.

"I've got to go back," Asa said. "I feel like I'm chasing the wind out here."

Having made the decision, he sat down.

Epps said nothing.

"Aya. Come morning, I'll start back," Asa said more to himself than to Epps. "Maybe when the boy settles down, he'll have the decency to write to us and tell us where he is."

Epps made no reply. He'd taken to flipping the knife at a piece of firewood. It would stick, he'd retrieve it, and throw it again.

The sound of someone approaching brought them both to their feet. At the sight of both of them, the rider stopped, keeping his distance. He eyed them with suspicion.

"Greetings!" Asa called out.

"Good evening," said the man with a cautious tone.

Even wearing a greatcoat, it was evident the man was portly. His sideburns were red and his face pink, which was the only flesh showing. Two unblinking eyes, set close together and cowering in the shadow of his hat brim, glared at them.

"I'm Asa Rush, from Cumberland. This is Robely Epps. Care to join us? We can offer you a hot cup of coffee."

"Thank you, no," the man said. "I must be on my way."

"It's late. Not safe to travel, if you ask me," Epps said.

The man looked Epps up and down and did not hide his distaste. "All I ask of you is that you keep your opinion to yourself."

Asa allowed himself a satisfied grin as he noted Epps's lack of response to the rude remark. Epps didn't appear to take offense, nor did he back down. He looked at the traveler with a steady gaze, as though no exchange had taken place between them at all.

"We won't detain you," Asa said, "other than to ask you a question."

The man on the horse moved a hand ever so slowly to his side. Closer, Asa assumed, to a weapon.

Epps toyed with the knife.

Asa moved between the two men, his hands up. "I'm an educator. From Cumberland, as I already mentioned. We're chasing a runaway. All I want to know is if you've seen him. He's sixteen years old. Average size and weight, with brown—"

"Haven't seen him." The quick answer wasn't reassuring.

Asa tried again. "Are you sure? You see, we've been traveling for—"

"Haven't seen anyone on the road except the two of you. It's Christmas, you know. Now, if you'll let me pass . . ."

Asa recognized a stone wall when he saw one. He took a step back from the road.

Just then a low, haunting melody wafted through the treetops, trilled, and rose in pitch.

Asa recognized the instrument. "Daniel!"

His eyes darted here and there but couldn't seem to pinpoint its direction. The music surrounded them.

"What is this? What's going on?" The man on the horse pulled a pistol from his coat. His fear made the horse skittish. It pawed the road.

"Easy . . . easy! It's my nephew!" Asa cried. "This is the first we've heard of him all day!"

The man on the horse was spooked. His eyes darted this way and that.

"It's the musical instrument he plays," Asa explained. "A recorder."

"I know what a recorder sounds like," the man snapped.

"Then you know it's not a weapon," Epps said. "Put that gun away."

The pistol remained at the ready in the man's hand.

"Are you going anywhere near Cumberland?" Asa asked the man on the horse.

"I don't see how that's any of your business," came the answer.

"If you could deliver a message to my wife," Asa said, digging into his pockets for a piece of paper he'd put there for this purpose, should it arise. "Or if that's too much trouble, if you could see that it got to a Mr. Cyrus Gregg at Gregg's Caskets of Cumberland, I would—"

"Cyrus Gregg? You know Mr. Gregg?" The man's whole demeanor changed.

"Yes," Asa said, amused at the turnabout. "I know Cyrus."

The use of Cyrus Gregg's first name impressed the man even more. He fumbled with his pistol, unable to put it back in his coat fast enough. Once it was away, the hand shot forward.

"Timothy Watkins, at your service, sir."

Asa shook the offered hand. "Pleased to meet you, Mr. Watkins."

"It would be an honor to deliver your message to Mr. Gregg," Watkins said with toadylike enthusiasm. "And if I may assist you gentlemen with any other business, it would be my pleasure."

Epps scoffed with disdain.

Asa turned aside to gather his thoughts. He struggled to find the right words to say to Camilla. As he wrote, the music filled the forest while Watkins babbled from atop his horse, speaking to no one in particular, because Epps had stopped listening to him.

"I had the privilege of assisting Mr. Gregg some months back in a highly personal matter," Watkins said with pride. "You see, I'm an accountant at the Bank of Green Ridge, and Mr. Harrison—the owner of the bank—entrusts all of his personal accounts to me. So, as you might expect, when Mr. Gregg frequented our establishment in need of an accountant for a local matter, Mr. Harrison pulled me aside confidentially . . ."

Asa finished writing. Folding the paper into an envelope, he addressed it to Camilla. He handed it to Watkins, who oozed with respectability as he received it.

"I assure you, sir, this message is as good as delivered," he said. "You will not regret entrusting Timothy Watkins with your missive."

Epps rolled his eyes.

"Thank you for doing this, Mr. Watkins," Asa said. "May I pay you for your services?"

"Yes!" Watkins' eyes lit up. "But not with currency, sir. I will consider myself reimbursed if, the next time you see Mr. Gregg, you will speak favorably of me. Remind him that I was the accountant at the Green Ridge bank who assisted him. I'm sure he'll remember me, but it doesn't hurt to remind a man of his stature, does it? Mr. Gregg must meet so many people. But, if I may boast, he said my work for him was exemplary. That's the very word he used—*exemplary!*"

"Are you sure you won't join us for a cup of coffee?" Asa asked.

Epps cringed at the offer. Asa pretended not to notice.

"Thank you, no," Watkins said. "I must be about my business." He placed Asa's message in an inner pocket and patted it to indicate it was secure there.

"Thank you for your assistance, Mr. Watkins," Asa said.

Epps had turned his back and was sitting at the fire.

"Don't forget," Watkins added as he rode off. "Timothy Watkins from the Bank of Green Ridge."

"I'll remember," Asa called after him.

"I can't forget fast enough," Epps muttered.

As Timothy Watkins, accountant, disappeared into the dark, Asa relaxed by the fire.

"Change of plans," Epps said.

"Daniel's nearby." Asa flicked a finger at the unseen sound of a recorder. "Can you tell how much of a lead he has on us?"

Epps looked up to the treetops. "Hard to say . . . with the mountain . . . the trees . . . the clear night. Sound's a funny thing. I once heard a bear roaring and thought it was coming from a cluster of rocks in front of me. Turned around and found myself staring the critter in the snout."

"What did you do?"

Epps shrugged as though the answer was obvious. "Killed myself a bear."

High in a tree, Daniel sat wedged among the branches, enjoying the voice of his recorder as it sang to him. Contented, he played with his eyes closed.

He felt comfortable there, having spent hours in the tree outside his bedroom window. The one his uncle had chopped down to spite him. Sitting here tonight, it was as if the tree had been resurrected.

He also felt safer up high than he did on the ground. Any number of predators could pounce on him as he slept. Up high, bundled up like a cocoon, he'd sleep better.

Earlier, beside the river, after drying off and restoring circulation to his hands and feet, which had been frozen in the cave, Daniel had felt human again. The absence of any sign of the killer Epps all afternoon cheered him even more.

He'd done it. He'd escaped. Come morning, with the rising of the sun, a new chapter would start in the life of . . .

"Daniel! Daniel Cooper!"

The recorder fell from Daniel's lips and the music died.

He refused to believe what he'd heard.

"Daniel Cooper!"

His name echoed among the trees.

Daniel wanted to blame the recorder for giving him away, but he knew it wasn't the instrument's fault. He should have waited. A day. Two days. When he was certain Epps was nowhere near.

With a grunt, Daniel shoved the recorder inside his coat. Epps had killed his good mood.

Glum, Daniel folded his arms and listened with disgust as his name bounced among the trees. In some ways, it sounded like his uncle's voice at home when he stood at the foot of the stairs and yelled up at him.

CHAPTER 24

Daniel, secure in his tree nest, wasn't aware he'd dozed until he awoke with a start. Human coughing roused him.

About fifty feet from the base of the tree, Daniel saw a man hunched over a pile of kindling. Hands struck sparks. A horse stood nearby, tied to a bush.

Another cough interrupted the fire-starting, then a sniff and the appearance of a white handkerchief waved like a flag under the man's nose. He exhibited all the signs of needing a fire.

But why did he have to choose this spot?

The man gave no indication he knew anyone was watching him. Men often do things when they're alone they don't do when they're not alone, and Daniel watched as the man did three of those things in the course of lighting his fire. The man thought he was alone.

He was the nervous sort, bumbling about, unaccustomed to the outdoors. He jumped at every sound and spent much of his time peering into the dark with a hand in his right pocket, which Daniel imagined held some sort of weapon. But after a time he settled down and situated himself with his face to the road and his back to a tree. Snoring soon followed.

Feeling no need to relocate—the man was no threat—Daniel nestled in for the night. But he kept his senses on alert in case.

161

Cuddled against the collar of his coat, Daniel felt his eyes growing heavy. They'd gone down for the third time when he saw it.

A shadow moving among shadows. And this one was the worst kind of shadow. The kind with two legs.

Now Daniel couldn't be more awake. The shadow skulked from tree to tree. It was coming straight toward him.

He tensed.

Did it know he was in the tree? Was it coming for him? If it wasn't, and he moved, he would alert the shadow to his presence.

Frozen by indecision, Daniel tracked the shadow as it glided toward him. Then it was gone.

Daniel sat forward, straining to see where it went. It appeared to have melted into a tree.

For several breathless seconds, he searched for it and found nothing, as though the shadow was some apparition that had completed its wicked business and vanished.

But then the shadow took shape. It stepped from the tree and into the moonlight.

Daniel's heart sank. The shadow's evil business was not finished.

"Epps!" he mouthed.

There was no mistaking the broad-rimmed hat or the way his flowing coat rustled as he moved. Daniel would have preferred an apparition.

Epps's course was dictated by the uneven terrain, but it was clear he was headed in Daniel's direction.

Daniel took stock of his situation. Unless he could sprout wings, he had no options. He'd waited too late. Epps had him treed.

But did Epps know it?

Hope sparked in Daniel.

It was the rim of Epps's hat that tipped him off. Not once had the killer looked up. Maybe he didn't know Daniel was there!

Daniel held his breath again as Epps made his way to the base of his tree and rested his hand on the trunk.

From his vantage point, Daniel stared down at the top of the killer's hat. Was Epps thinking about his next move? His hand was steady.

Then Epps began making his way toward the sleeping man.

Daniel wanted to shout. To wake the man. To warn him. But something stopped him.

Self-preservation? Yes, but not only that. There was something about the way Epps approached the campsite, as though he was taking a stroll in the park.

While the sleeping man snored, Epps walked to the fire, warmed his hands, poked the fire with a stick, then tossed the smoldering stick into the man's lap.

"Wha—!" The man bumbled himself awake, shoving the burning stick off his lap, and in doing so, knocked his hat off. He eyed Epps with alarm, groping for the pistol that had been resting on his chest.

That the gun didn't go off in all the fumbling was amazing. Even from a distance Daniel could see the barrel of the gun shaking.

"Put that away, Watkins," Epps ordered.

"You! What are you—? How dare—"

"Aya, it's good to see you again too."

It was clear Watkins was flustered. Holding the gun with one shaky hand, he felt for his hat with the other shaky hand and, with difficulty, placed it on his head.

"I couldn't say anything back there at camp," Epps explained, "so I waited until my partner was asleep before coming to find you."

"Say anything? Find me? Why would you want to find me?"

"I work for Cyrus Gregg," Epps said.

Watkins sneered down his nose at the long-haired intruder. "I don't believe you."

"Doesn't make it any less true."

The gun stayed up. "What is it you want of me?" Watkins asked. "Do you want me to deliver a message for you?"

"No, I want you to give me something. I want the letter you placed in your pocket."

The man's free hand went to his pocket, almost as though he thought the letter would jump out and fly to Epps on its own.

"The letter was entrusted to me," Watkins said.

"Cyrus Gregg will be angry if you deliver it to him."

"That is none of my affair. I gave my sacred pledge that I would deliver this letter, and deliver it I shall."

Epps held out his hand. "Just give me the letter."

"Never, sir! I will guard it with my life!"

Watching in the tree, Daniel groaned. "Wrong answer," he muttered.

Epps scratched his beard. "Last chance, Watkins. I'm telling you, it's in your best interest to give me that letter."

"Is it now?" Watkins sat up straighter, bolder. The gun no longer shook. "Do you know what would happen to me if word got back to Green Ridge that I had forsaken my pledge to—?"

Epps kicked the burning fire on the man, who raised his arms to protect himself from the flaming sticks and embers. Quick as a panther, Epps was on top of him, knife drawn.

In two seconds it was over.

The dead man's head lay to one side. His throat was cut. Like Braxton's.

"And what's going to happen when word gets back to Green Ridge that you're dead?" Epps said to the corpse.

His hand slipped into the man's coat and came out with a piece of paper that Epps unfolded and read. Bending over what was left of the fire, he touched the paper to the flame. It flared, blackened, and was gone.

Epps showed no other interest in the man other than to say to him, "By the way . . . Merry Christmas."

Robely Epps paused at the edge of camp. Everything was as he'd left it, including Asa Rush curled up, sleeping, in his carriage.

Moving to his spot beside the fire, which was little more than dying embers, Epps pulled the blanket up around his neck.

"Anything wrong?" Asa's head rose up inside the carriage.

"Squirrel didn't agree with me."

"Doing better now?"

"I'll be fine by morning. Thanks."

The carriage jostled. The head went down.

Epps got himself cozy under his blanket.

For a while tonight he had thought he was going to have to kill Asa. Then the boy had made his presence known.

Epps was glad. He didn't want to have to kill the old man any sooner than he had to. He liked him.

CHAPTER 25

Unable to sleep in a tree near a fresh corpse, Daniel ventured deeper into the forest. He stumbled through the woods, across the frozen ground and over patches of snow, anxious to put as much distance between him and Epps as possible.

He found another tree suitable for nesting, but sleep eluded him.

When morning came, his eyes were bleary, his nerves jumpy, and his legs distilled to jelly with fear.

It didn't help that he hadn't had a meal since yesterday. His stomach was a hollow pit. But he was more afraid than hungry, so he kept going, casting frequent glances over his shoulder.

By midmorning, exhaustion overtook him. He searched for and found a large evergreen tree. While other trees made better beds, daylight forced him to find something lush in which he could hide.

Shinnying up the tree, surrounded by the scent of pine needles, his hands sticky with sap, Daniel found a limb suitable for his purposes. He lay prone on his stomach, his cheek against the branch, his arms and legs draped over the sides.

Within minutes sleep caught up with him.

"See something?" Asa asked, packing the last of their things in the carriage.

Epps stared into the woods. "Not sure. Something caught my eye. It's not there now."

Asa gazed into the woods and saw nothing. "Sleep well?"

"Never better."

Asa grinned. "The sign of a clear conscience."

He finished packing with a sense of urgency. God willing, they'd catch up with Daniel this morning. And if Daniel didn't give him any trouble, they could almost beat the letter to Camilla back to Cumberland.

"The squirrel must have settled down," Asa said.

Epps appeared puzzled.

"Last night. Your stomach."

"Oh, that!" Epps pounded his stomach with his fists. "Not a chirp out of the little fellow this morning, may he rest in peace."

"Good! Let's get going. If I remember correctly, there's a little town not too far up the road. A couple of miles, maybe. I'm hoping Daniel will stop there to get something to eat."

The two men climbed into the carriage.

"What are you grinning about?" Asa asked.

Epps's grin widened. "Am I? Guess I'm just grateful you're still around. For a while there, I thought I'd be heading out alone this morning."

"The feeling is mutual, my friend. To me, you're a godsend."

Refreshed from his nap, which left him with sap on his cheek, Daniel had just begun to climb out of the tree when he heard someone approaching.

He froze.

Epps! The man had to be part bloodhound.

But it wasn't Epps.

Ten feet below, a boy sauntered through the woods. *Beefy* was the word that came to mind when Daniel peered down at him. A huge body, but with a boy's face. His jeans and coat were threadbare. His boots scuffed. His brown hair mussed. He carried a switch in his hand with which he whacked everything within reach as he walked along.

The boy stopped and glanced over his shoulder. Daniel checked that same direction, but a branch blocked his view.

The boy swatted a tree limb and continued on his way. He came to a giant oak tree, stepped behind the tree, and disappeared.

Daniel waited. He thought it best to stay where he was until the boy finished whatever it was he was doing behind the tree. But several minutes passed, and the boy didn't reappear. Nor did he make any sound.

Intrigued, Daniel decided to outwait him.

"I'm not fibbin'. Honest!"

"You are too, Red. And I'm tellin' Pa."

"I'm shootin' straight with ya, Hughie. Trees got feelin's—just like people."

"Yeah? Then how come they don't laugh when you tickle 'em?"

Two boys walked below Daniel. Brothers from the looks of them. The older boy had red hair and freckles. The younger boy—six or seven years old—had sandy-colored hair and a rounder head.

"I'll prove it to you," Red said. "Crawl under here with me."

Daniel's breath caught in his throat as Red urged his younger brother to follow him under the evergreen. If either of them glanced up, they'd see him.

Red wiggled in the pine needles on his belly to the trunk of the tree. Hughie followed his example.

"See there on the trunk?" Red pointed. "Those are tree tears. This tree's been cryin'."

"Has not! I'm not stupid, ya know."

"Go on, touch it. Just because they're different from human tears don't mean they're not real tears. Go on!"

When Hughie refused to touch the sap, his brother tried to make him. When the younger boy resisted, they wrestled around, and Daniel thought for sure they'd seen him. But once Red succeeded in sticking his little brother's finger in the sap, he let go and the wrestling stopped.

Hughie made disgusting noises and tried to wipe the sap off on his trousers. Daniel touched the sap on his cheek and wondered how he was going to get it off.

The boys crawled out from under the evergreen.

"I learned all about trees havin' feelin's in school," Red insisted. "You'll read about it too. When you get as old as me."

Hughie was still wiping his finger on his trousers.

"Back in the olden days, everyone knew trees had feelin's. Even little fellas, like you," Red said.

"I ain't little. I'm big for my age."

"Over the centuries, men have forgotten most of what they knew in ancient times."

"Yeah? Well, how come you know about it, then?"

"I read about it, Chucklehead. I just told ya."

Hughie was still trying to get the sap off his finger. "Well, Pa's read more books than you. How come he doesn't know about it?"

"When you get old like him, you get civilized, and civilization blinds you. You and me? We ain't civilized yet, so we can understand. I'm talkin' about lost knowledge, Hughie. Lost and mysterious. You see, Hughie, a long, long time ago, there lived these three sisters. And they had a brother. But their brother died, and his body was buried beside this river called Poo."

"Poo?" Hughie laughed. "You're makin' that up."

"Will you shut up and listen? It's a river in India, an old and ancient country. The three sisters? They were real sad their brother died."

"I wouldn't be sad if my brother died." Hughie's comment earned him a punch in the arm.

"Do you want to hear this or not, Thickwit?"

Hughie rubbed his finger again on his pants.

"Anyway," Red continued, "these three sisters kept comin' back to the river where their brother died."

"Poo." Hughie laughed.

"And the three sisters were cryin' and wailin' and carryin' on somethin' awful."

With a singsong tone, Hughie said, "And their cryin' made the trees so sad, the trees started to cry. Ow!"

Red punched him in the arm again. "Shut up and listen."

"I'm gonna tell Pa you're hittin' me again!"

Red's voice took on a ghostly tone. "One day, when the three sisters were lyin' beside the river, weepin' and wailin', one of the sisters—her name was Phaethusa—"

"What a stupid name," Hughie said.

Red ignored him. "Phaethusa was cryin' real hard, and all of a sudden, the wind begins to moan in the top of the trees. She gets this real shocked look and starts complainin' that her feet are feelin' real stiff. She looks down, and . . . roots are growin' out of her toes! They're tryin' to wriggle and worm their way into the ground!"

The older boy toed the dirt with his foot as though it was trying to root. "Then her sister, Lampetia, sees what's happenin'. She gets this real terrified look and jumps up. But it's too late. Her feet are growin' roots too! Now both girls are screamin' somethin' awful."

Hughie's eyes were as big as saucers.

"But there was nothin' they could do about it. And it didn't stop there. Before they knew it, their arms start turnin' into tree limbs, and tree bark starts to wrap itself around and around their legs and their bellies!"

Red twisted and contorted his torso for effect.

"The third sister, seein' what's happenin', tries to rescue the other two. She reaches for one sister and thinks she's grabbin' her by the hair, but when she pulls her hand back, she's got a handful of leaves. And then the third sister's arms and legs start growin' into tree limbs too!"

By this time Hughie had caught enough of the story to become agitated. His feet began to dance in place.

Red grinned and continued with the story. "Then their mother hears their screams and comes runnin'. She gets real scared, because when she gets there, her three daughters are half-girls and half-trees, but what can she do? She can't stop it. So she runs from girl to girl, cryin' and kissin' them while there's still time, because now the girls' faces are turnin' into tree bark.

"The mother grabs one of the tree limbs and pulls real hard, hopin' to pull her daughter out of the tree. But the limb breaks off and the girl inside the tree cries, 'Stop, Mother! Stop! You're tearin' off my arm! Please, stop!'"

Hughie was caught up in the story. His mouth dropped open.

"And to this day," Red continued, "sometimes a girl will walk into the forest and never come out because, like the three sisters, she's been turned into a tree. And if you listen late at night, you can hear them moanin' and tree limbs crackin' as the girls try to break free, but they can't. They're trapped inside the tree forever."

With that last bit, it was evident Red had gone too far.

"Naaaaahhhhh. You made that up," Hughie said. "You're just tryin' to scare me."

"Did not. I read it in school, just like I said. A fella named Ovid wrote it a long, long time ago. And if you don't believe me, ask Mr. Tibbetts. Besides, they couldn't teach it in school if it wasn't true."

"I know why you brought me out here. You brought me out here to scare me," Hughie said with a quiver in his voice. "I'm tellin' Pa."

"Hughie, I'm tryin' to do you a favor. I don't want you to get scared when you hear girls cryin' in the woods when no girls are around."

"I'm tellin' Pa." Hughie turned to leave.

Red caught him by the arm. "OK, I'll prove it to you." His voice sounded reluctant, as though he didn't want to do it, but Hughie was forcing him. "But you have to promise you won't tell anybody about it. Do you promise?"

Hughie nodded. "I promise."

Red shook his head. "I don't know. You're awfully young."

"I promise, Red. I won't tell no one."

"OK, but just because you're my brother." He leaned close to Hughie.

From his vantage point in the tree, Daniel strained to hear what Red was saying.

"You know how sometimes people write in their schoolbooks?" Red whispered.

"Jonathan got six lashes on the back of his hands for writin' in his 'rithmatic book," Hughie said.

"Aya. Well, still people do it. In the back of my Ovid book there was this old writing. It was shaky, like some old person wrote it."

"Old people don't go to school."

"Shut up and listen. Maybe somebody's grandfather wrote it. It was some kind of magic spell."

"A magic spell?" A horrible thought formed on Hughie's face, and he began backing away from his brother. "You're not goin' to turn me into a tree, are you? I'll tell Pa!"

"Get back here. I'm not gonna turn you into a tree, Chucklehead. Will you just listen to me?" Red rolled his eyes. "It's a spell that wakes up the girl inside a tree."

Hughie's brow furrowed. He appeared skeptical but interested.

Red stepped closer to the massive oak. "For example, if you pull a leaf or a branch off a tree, all you hear is a crack. Right?"

He snapped off a twig.

Hughie did the same.

"But," Red continued, "if you wake the girl inside the tree with this spell . . . well then, when you break off a branch, you can hear her cry out in pain."

Hughie cocked his head. "You gonna do it, Red? You gonna cast the spell?"

"Do you want me to?"

A few seconds pause, then Hughie nodded.

Again Red showed reluctance before saying, "You have to tap the tree twelve times."

Hughie began poking the trunk. "One . . . two . . . three . . ."

"Not like that! You can't just tap it anywhere. Like this." Red stepped up to the tree. He loosened his shoulders and rubbed his index finger. "Three taps, four times. That's what the spell said." He bent low.

"Three to her toes." He tapped the roots three times.

"Three to her knees." He tapped a fourth of the way up the trunk.

"Three to her chest." He tapped halfway up the trunk.

"And three to her head. It said, 'On the laurel of acorns.'" Stretching, he tapped the trunk as high as he could reach, then stepped back, hands raised in expectation. "There. She's awake."

Hughie looked from the tree to his brother. "Are you sure? How do you know?"

"One way to find out," Red replied. "Break off a branch."

"Me? I'm not gonna do it! You do it!"

Red shrugged. He reached for a branch and snapped off a twig. "Ow!" he cried, using a high voice out of the side of his mouth.

Hughie's finger pointed. "You did that."

"Did not. That was the girl."

"It was you. I saw your lips move."

"Then you try it." Red stepped back from the tree.

With an eye on his brother, Hughie snapped off a twig.

"Ow!" Red cried, the same as before.

"I saw you do it that time," Hughie insisted.

"All right," Red said. "I'll stand over here, so you can see me. And I'll put both of my hands over my mouth, like this, OK?" He placed both hands over his mouth to demonstrate. "But you have to pull a really big branch off this time, so I can hear it too. Agree?"

Wise to him, Hughie eyed his brother as Red moved into position. The older boy covered his mouth.

"Press hard," Hughie said. "You have to press hard on your mouth."

Red yelled against his hands to demonstrate that he was pressing hard.

Hughie stepped up to the tree. Keeping his brother in sight, he selected a good-size branch. He grabbed hold with both hands. He checked his brother.

Behind his hands Red made muffled shouts, urging Hughie to do it. Hughie pulled.

The branch bent but didn't break.

Red rolled his eyes.

Planting a foot against a root for leverage, Hughie positioned himself to pull again. This time he gave it everything he had. The branch gave way with a loud *snap*.

"Aaahhh!" A banshee scream erupted from the tree. *"Aaahhh!"*

Terror-stricken, the limb in his hands, Hughie stepped back, tripped over a root, and fell backward. His legs were running even as he hit the ground. Staring at the limb in his hands as though it was a bloody arm, he tossed it aside. His arms became legs, pawing, pushing at the ground, scrambling to get him away from the tree.

Bawling and blinded with tears, Hughie flipped over onto all fours—arms and legs still churning—and crawled as fast as he could until his feet caught hold and he was upright, running and screaming and wailing.

He passed beneath Daniel on a dead run.

Next to the tree, Red had dropped to his knees, laughing so hard he couldn't stand. The laughter became a duet as a second voice joined his.

The beefy boy with the switch in his hand stepped from behind the tree. The two boys relived the look on Hughie's face several times, pulling branches from the tree and howling, and laughing so hard they cried.

Falling all over themselves, they disappeared into the woods, heading the opposite way from Hughie.

Daniel climbed out of the evergreen. His intended journey would take him in the same direction as Red and his friend. But Daniel went the opposite way, following the path of the terrified boy.

CHAPTER 26

"I saw what they did to you," Daniel said when he came upon Hughie, sitting at the base of some rocks, his arms wrapped around his legs.

The boy was shaking and crying. He jumped up and started to run away when he saw Daniel.

"Hughie!" Daniel said. "It was mean, what they did to you."

At the sound of his name, the boy turned around but continued backing away.

Daniel spoke with a soothing tone. "I saw it all. The sap on your finger. Your brother. The tree. And I saw the large boy hiding behind the tree."

"Dumps?" Hughie asked.

"Big fella. Brown hair. Likes to hit things with a stick."

"Aya, that's Dumps."

"He and your brother teamed up against you. Two against one. Wasn't fair."

"And they're both older than me too!"

"Want to get even with them?"

Hughie's eyes lit up, then became wary again. Skeptical. "I don't know you, mister."

"Well, my name's Daniel. And I'm just like you."

"Like me?"

"Aya. I have big people picking on me. That's why I'm out here in the woods. One of them has a thick, black beard and a big knife. If you see him, run away."

"He's here in the woods?"

"I saw him last night. He didn't see me. He wants to hurt me."

"What did you do to him?" Hughie asked.

"Nothing. I saw him do something bad. Real bad. And now he wants to make sure I don't tell anyone. So when I saw two big boys picking on a little boy, I wanted to do something to get back at them. Make things even. What do you say?"

"Are we gonna hurt 'em?"

The way Hughie asked, Daniel got the impression the boy wouldn't have objected to hurting them a little.

"No, just scare them. Like they scared you. What do you say?"

Hughie's grin was answer enough.

"Hey, Red! Red! Wait for me!"

Daniel followed at a distance as Hughie caught up with his brother and the boy called Dumps.

Red whirled on his brother. "Go ahead and tell Pa. But if you do, I'll tell everybody in school that you're a frightened little crybaby."

"I'm not gonna tell Pa. Promise," Hughie said. "I came to warn you."

Daniel urged him on. *Good boy, Hughie!*

"Warn us? Warn us about what?" Red asked.

Hughie looked from Dumps to Red. "Does he know?" he asked his brother.

"Know what?"

"About the trees and the . . ." Hughie whispered the next three words. ". . . the girls inside."

Dumps and Red exchanged grins.

"Yeah, he knows," Red said.

"Then he'd better listen, too, so he doesn't get hurt."

"What are you babblin' about?"

"You were right, Red. About the girls, I mean. He got real angry that you woke one of his girls up."

"He? Who got angry?" Red asked.

"Their father."

"Whose father?"

"The girls in the trees. Their father," Hughie said.

The older boys laughed.

Dumps scoffed. "What a dunce."

Red shoved Hughie. "You're makin' that up. And it's stupid."

"I'm not makin' it up, Horsebreath!" Hughie's expression was earnest. "He told me hisself, Red. He said if any of us woke up his girls ever again, he was gonna turn *us* into trees!"

The older boys laughed harder.

"Told you hisself, did he?" Dumps mocked.

Hughie was persistent. "I'm not lyin'. If you wake up one of his girls again, he's gonna turn you into a tree! Why don't you believe me?"

"Because you're a seven-year-old chucklehead, that's why," Dumps replied.

"Yeah. A little, half-brained thickwit," Red added.

"Oh yeah? Then, why don't you come hear him for yourselves?"

Dumps and Red stopped laughing.

"What the matter?" Hughie pressed. "Scared?"

Behind the distant tree, Daniel grinned. *Atta boy, Hughie. You got 'em now.*

Dumps shoved Hughie hard, almost knocking the boy down. "I ain't scared of nuthin', you little maggot."

"Then come see for yourself, you big oaf!" Hughie was already out of reach, but he stepped back anyway.

"You take us there," Dumps said. "But I don't hear no voice, so help me, I'm gonna skin your skinny little carcass to the bone."

Red shot a warning glance that only a brother would understand. *What are you doin'? You've gone and made him mad!*

Hughie shrugged it off. "It's this way. And you're gonna be apologizin' all over yourselves when you hear the voice."

Daniel smiled. *Good boy, Hughie!* He ran on ahead to get ready.

Several minutes later, the three boys caught up with him. Hughie led the two older boys to the rocks where Daniel had found him. Daniel was waiting for them, concealed, so he could observe their reaction. As they approached, he was stuffing a tree limb up his pants leg.

"I was sittin' right here." Hughie showed them the place.

"Yeah? Well where is he?" Dumps spread his hands, waiting for an answer.

"I didn't say I *saw* him. I said I *heard* him."

Dumps scanned the trees. "Hey! Old-man tree! Talk to me!"

Red thought Dumps was funny. Grinning, he joined in. "Hulloooooooo, Father of the tree girls! Come out, come out, wherever you are!"

They listened.

The forest was silent.

Dumps turned to Hughie with a raised fist. "I'm gonna flatten you."

Hughie hid behind his brother. "I'm tellin' ya, Red. He spoke to me. Honest!"

But his brother sided with Dumps. He grabbed Hughie by the arm and pulled him around so he was between the two bigger boys. They started shoving him back and forth between them.

"He'd have to be a pretty stupid voice to talk to you," Dumps said, pushing Hughie so hard he would have fallen down, had his brother not caught him.

"Don't say that," Hughie complained. "He'll hear you."

Dumps stuck out his chest and called to the tops of the trees. "I don't care if he hears me. I'm not afraid of no stupid voice. You hear that?"

A long, low musical note floated through the trees and surrounded them.

Now all three boys were gazing up into the treetops, their mouths open.

"Uh-oh!" Hughie said.

"What, uh-oh?" Red cried.

"He's angry. You shouldn't have done that, Dumps. You made him angry!"

The note rose in pitch and began to flutter.

"I ain't scared of no whistle," Dumps said, his jaw slack.

Hughie tried to break Red's grip on him. But the grip tightened, holding him in place.

"Where do you think you're goin'?" Red asked.

Hughie gaped at his brother with fear in his eyes. "Let me go, Red! The girl's pa said if I ever heard pipe music in the trees to run and not look back, 'cause if I did, I might get turned into a tree!"

The music jumped in pitch again. Strident. Angry.

Dumps grabbed Hughie from Red. "I'll hold him. You circle around these rocks. Whoever's doin' this is behind these rocks."

"Me? I'll hold Hughie. *You* circle behind the rocks."

"Do you want me to put my boot on your backside?" Dumps bawled. "Go!"

"They didn't mean it," Hughie called up to the trees. "Please, don't hurt us. Please!"

The sound stopped.

Dumps glared at Red, who had stopped when the music stopped. "Go. Hurry! Before he gets away!"

"Wh-what if I find someone?" Red asked.

"Then yell. I'll circle around the other way and come up behind him."

With the forest silent again, Red was getting back his nerve. He nodded and circled around behind the rocks.

The road sign had announced the town as Dry Run a ways back. Asa had yet to see the town itself when Epps grabbed his arm.

"Listen."

Asa heard it. "Daniel!"

He pulled back on the reins. The carriage halted. Epps jumped out, his ear to the wind. Asa grabbed his cane, climbed out, and joined him.

"It's coming from behind us," Epps said.

"I do believe you're right."

With a single mind, the two men returned to the carriage. Asa turned it around.

"He just started," Epps said.

"The boy can play for hours."

They rode a distance, then stopped. Epps climbed out. Listened. "Keep going," he said, jumping back in.

They did this two more times before they began searching for a suitable access road.

"There!" Epps gestured.

Asa had already seen it.

The carriage tilted side to side as it straddled a ridge, then started down an embankment.

The music was louder now. Then it stopped.

Epps cursed. "Keep going." He leaned forward, his eyes intent. "Keep going. He's close."

"Why did it stop?" Dumps asked.

"How should I know?" Hughie struggled against the grip the larger boy had on him.

Earlier he hadn't been able to break the hold his brother had on him, so what chance did Hughie have against Dumps? But that didn't stop him from trying.

"Let . . . me . . . go!" He twisted to break free.

"Shut up!" Dumps shouted. "Listen for your brother."

Just then Red appeared.

"See anything?" Dumps asked him.

Breathing hard, Red shook his head. "Nothin'."

"Maybe we scared it away."

"Maybe it went away because I apologized to it," Hughie countered.

"Not likely, Chucklehead," his brother spat.

"Shut up, Horsebreath!" Hughie spat back.

"Let's find out." Dumps peered up at the trees again.

"What?" Red cried.

"Let's find out if it stopped because Thickwit here apologized."

"And what if it starts up again?"

Dumps shrugged. "We'll just have the little maggot apologize again."

"Don't do it," Hughie warned. "I'm tellin' ya, Red. Don't do it."

Dumps and Red exchanged glances. That sealed it. "We're doin' it!" the older boys said together.

Dumps called, "Hey! Tree-god! We're gonna go knockin' on as many trees as we can, just to see how many girls we can wake up!"

"Then we're gonna pull off some arms and limbs," Red added. "Start a collection. Maybe build us a bonfire!"

A single note floated through the trees, just like before.

The two older boys exchanged grins.

It rose in pitch faster than before.

The boys' grins faded.

The pitch continued to climb.

Red punched Hughie's arm. "Tell it you're sorry."

"I'm not sorry. I didn't do anything."

Dumps got a worried look. "Yeah, tell it you're sorry, you little maggot."

Hughie glared at him. "Tell it yourself!"

Dumps bent inches from Hughie's face. "Tell it!"

"There it is again. Over there." Epps pointed to his left.

Bushes and a stream blocked their way. Epps took the horse by the reins. He led it downstream a couple of hundred yards and found a place to cross, all the while tracking the sound.

"Make it stop!" Red shouted.

"I can't! I can't make it stop!" Hughie shouted back.

The whistle was high-pitched now and trilling feverishly. The boys had turned their backs to each other to keep anything from sneaking up behind them.

Hughie grew frantic. "Someone's gonna die! Someone's gonna die!"

"I don't want to be turned into a tree," Red whimpered.

Holding Hughie in front of him, Dumps exclaimed, "If I'm gonna be turned into a tree, I'm makin' sure this one gets it first. It's all his fault!"

Dumps' voice was shaky. Red had tears in his eyes.

The music grew louder. More shrill. More frantic.

"It's comin' for us!" Hughie screamed. "I warned you. It's comin' for us!"

Hughie went berserk, screaming and wrestling to break free, but Dumps had a death grip on him.

The two older boys danced in fear, their heads whipping this way and that, expecting something to swoop down on them.

Hughie kept yelling, "It's comin'! It's comin'!"

When Dumps turned his head, Hughie stomped on his foot as hard as he could.

Dumps howled in pain. His grip on Hughie released. The instant it did, the boy was gone, running back in the direction from which they came.

"Get back here, you little—" Dumps grabbed for him, but got only air.

Red took off running after his little brother.

Dumps was hot on Red's heels.

From behind the rocks, Daniel watched Hughie run past him. That was his cue.

He set the recorder down, adjusted the tree limbs he'd stuffed down his shirt, up his sleeves, in his waistband, and up his pants legs until his appearance was that of half-man, half-tree. Branches hid his face and scraped the ground when he walked.

Moving stiff-legged, his arms extended at his sides, he rounded the rocks just in time to run into Red and Dumps.

The instant the two boys saw him, they stopped dead in their tracks. Dumps plowed into Red. They both turned as white as ghosts.

"Ahhhhhh!!" Daniel moaned. "Help me! Help me! My legs! My arms! Stiff . . . so stiff!"

He hobbled toward them. "Help me! *Ahhhhhh!* I don't know what's happening! Please, help me!"

Pushing each other out of the way, Dumps and Red screamed and stumbled and scrambled as fast as they could to get away from him.

"Come back! Help me! Help me, please! Help me!" Daniel called until he could no longer see them.

Then he stood in the road, grinning from ear to ear. He hadn't felt this good in years. He began pulling branches out of his clothes.

When Hughie showed up, the boy was smiling.

"Did they see you circle back?" Daniel asked.

Hughie collapsed to the ground. "That was sooo great! I was laughin' so hard it hurt!"

"You were masterful, Hughie. Played your part perfectly."

"That sound. You told me you'd make a sound that whistled in the trees. How did you do that?"

Daniel walked over to where he'd dropped the instrument. He handed it to Hughie, who examined it and placed his fingers over the holes.

"It's called a recorder," Daniel said.

"It scared me!"

"Even though I told you I was making the sound?"

Hughie nodded, handing it back to him.

"It's a wonderful instrument." Daniel positioned his fingers on the holes. "It can reflect any mood the musician feels. Happy, sad . . ."

"Scary," Hughie added.

Slipping the recorder into his waistband, Daniel tugged the last of the twigs out of his clothes.

"This was the best day ever, Daniel!"

"It was fun, wasn't it? Do you think they'll give you a hard time when they figure out what happened?"

"I don't care if they do. It was worth it!"

"Even so, it might be wise to lay low for a couple of days," Daniel advised. "Give them time to convince themselves they weren't scared out of their wits."

"But they were, weren't they?" Hughie laughed again.

Daniel slung his haversack over his shoulder. "Well, I'd better be on my way. It was nice meeting you, Hughie. Remember today when you're older, and don't pick on boys smaller than you."

"'Cause it's more fun pickin' on boys older than you."

Daniel grinned.

"Sure you can't stay?" Hughie asked.

"Thanks, but I have to keep moving."

"'Cause of the men who are after you?"

"Aya."

"Will they ever stop chasin' you?"

Daniel sighed. "I don't know. I hope so."

Hughie extended his hand in a manly way. Daniel smiled and shook it, then walked away.

CHAPTER 27

Victory is sweeter when it's shared victory.

Daniel came to this conclusion as he walked in the woods. He didn't know who had enjoyed getting even with Dumps and Red more—him or Hughie. Every time Daniel got an image of Hughie's victory grin, it made him smile.

After they'd parted, Daniel wished he'd asked the boy about what was ahead. A town, to be sure. Red had mentioned a school and a schoolmaster, Mr. Tibbs. Or was it Tibbetts?

It didn't matter. But it did mean that with a schoolhouse there was a sizeable settlement nearby and a store where he could get food. Possibly even a tavern where he could get hot food. His stomach urged haste.

Then unpleasant images of the ruthlessness with which Epps had killed that man last night dampened Daniel's good feelings. They swayed his complaining stomach to caution. Epps might still be in the area.

Daniel straddled a fallen tree. Just as his foot touched down on the other side, he spied a man ahead. His back was to Daniel. He carried a rifle at the ready and moved with stealth. Daniel completed his vault over the tree and stood still.

Another man appeared, also armed and moving just like the first. Hunters.

Since they were moving away from him, Daniel figured his best course was to stay put until they were gone, which is exactly what he did.

"We've lost him," Asa said.

He sat in the carriage as Epps searched ahead. They hadn't heard the recorder for more than ten minutes.

"If there's one thing I've learned about tracking," Epps said, "it's that patience is a virtue that rarely goes unrewarded." He disappeared into a gully.

Asa got out of the carriage to stretch his legs.

"Lord, lead us to Daniel," he prayed.

Once the hunters were gone, Daniel moved on.

He didn't get far when he heard a low whistle. He stopped, and it stopped. He waited a minute, then continued, listening hard.

A few more steps and he heard it again. Surveying the woods, he saw nothing. The whistling stopped. Then there was a moan, long and drawn out.

Daniel moved toward the moan.

He came upon Dumps.

The boy was hiding behind a bush. Shaking it and moaning. Then shaking it and whistling, as if testing to see which sound he liked better.

"These boys don't give up, do they?" Daniel said under his breath.

To his right, Red and Hughie appeared.

The older boy was pulling his brother by the arm. "I'm tellin' you, Dumps has turned into a tree!" Red was saying.

Hughie tried to pull away. "He has not! Let me go!"

Red dragged him toward the bush where Dumps was hiding. Dumps was shaking it.

Again a hunter appeared.

The scene played in front of Daniel like a Greek tragedy. All the actors were in place. Three boys pulling pranks. One of them hiding in a bush. A hunter appeared with a loaded gun. A bush shook. The hunter shouldered his rifle.

Daniel yelled.

A puff of smoke rose from the rifle.

The bush stopped shaking.

The hunter turned. He must have realized what had happened, for Daniel could see it on his face.

Red and Hughie saw it too. After the shot, they halted and didn't move. Their faces were masks of disbelief.

This wasn't part of the prank.

Both Daniel and the hunter converged on the bush at a dead run. They reached it at the same time.

"I didn't know!" the hunter moaned. "All I saw was . . ."

Daniel dropped to his knees beside Dumps. The boy was curled up beneath the bush, as if he'd fallen asleep.

His belly rose and fell. A good sign.

Daniel reached under the bush and pulled the boy out by his shoulders. The boy moaned. His head moved side to side. His eyes remained closed. A large red spot stained his shirt on his left side, just above the belt.

"He's alive," Daniel said.

"It's the Taylor boy," the hunter said. "We need to get him to a doctor. I didn't know, mister! You have to believe me! I didn't know!"

When Daniel looked up, Red and Hughie were staring down in disbelief at Dumps's wound.

Daniel took Hughie by the arm. "I need you to do something for me. I need you to go and get his parents. You can do that?"

Hughie didn't move. His eyes were locked on the blood.

"Hughie!"

The smaller boy blinked. He turned his mournful gaze to Daniel.

"Can you do that for me? Go get his parents?"

Hughie nodded.

"I'll go with him," Red said.

The two boys ran off.

Lifting his head, Daniel saw another man standing there. The other hunter.

"I didn't see him in there, George," the first hunter was saying to him. "I didn't know it was a boy."

The second hunter put a hand on his friend's shoulder to steady him. "The boy needs a doctor. Can we move him, or should we get Doc and bring him here?"

"The wound isn't serious. He can be moved." The voice came from neither hunter.

Daniel looked up again . . . and into the eyes of Epps.

Dumps moaned. His eyes opened. He scrunched his face in pain and began to cry.

"Then let's get him to a doctor!" the first hunter cried.

Energy surged through Daniel. Every nerve told him to run. But he couldn't. He couldn't just leave Dumps here, not like this.

He told himself Epps wouldn't do anything with people around. As long as there were people around, he was safe. And if Epp's hands were busy—

"Mister, you take his shoulders," Daniel said.

Epps studied him with a satisfied expression.

"Yeah, you!" Daniel said. "I'll get his legs."

He didn't know what Epps would do. To Daniel's surprise, the killer bent down and grabbed Dumps under the arms. Daniel grabbed the boy's legs, and together they lifted him off the ground.

With the boy separating them, Daniel glanced up at Epps. This wasn't the first time they'd lifted a body. They'd lifted Emil Braxton the same way to place him in a coffin. From the smile on Epps's face, he seemed to be remembering the same thing.

"It's about a half-mile to the doctor," the hunter said.

"We can use my friend's carriage," Epps offered.

Daniel almost dropped the boy when he saw his uncle Asa, leaning on his cane and standing beside the carriage.

"Are you all right, son?" the hunter asked him.

"Aya." It was a reflex response. Daniel wasn't all right. The sight of his uncle with Epps had stunned him numb. Daniel's feet were moving, but he wasn't moving them.

Hughie and Red came running back. A man trailed behind them, and behind him a woman.

"Edward! Edward!" the woman was screaming.

The guilty hunter turned to the man. "Francis, I didn't see him! You have to believe me! I didn't see him!"

Dumps's father pushed past him to his boy. "Edward? Hold on, son. We'll get you to the doctor."

"There's a carriage just up the way," Daniel said.

The father nodded, then took charge. "Here, let me," he told Daniel, taking his son's legs.

"Maybe it would be best if you let the young man carry him," Epps said.

"I've got him," the father insisted.

His hands full, Epps could do nothing but continue toward the carriage.

Daniel stayed where he was and watched.

As the distance increased between Epps and Daniel, Epps shot him warning glances. Nobody else seemed to notice. Their attention was on Dumps.

Daniel caught Hughie's eye. The boy wore a knowing expression, as if he had taken in the way Epps regarded Daniel, and the way Daniel avoided Epps.

Everyone but Daniel had converged on the carriage. Uncle Asa had his head inside the carriage to arrange things to transport Dumps into town. He lifted his head . . . and exchanged glances with Daniel.

Then Daniel turned his back and headed into the woods.

"Daniel!" Epps barked.

But there was nothing the killer could do. He and the others were still a half-dozen feet from the carriage.

Daniel broke into a run.

"Stop him! Someone stop him!" Epps ordered.

A few heads turned, but Dumps had their attention.

As they loaded the boy into the carriage, Uncle Asa stepped clear. He faced Daniel. "Daniel? Daniel! Let's talk, son!"

Daniel slowed as he glanced back but kept running.

With Dumps in the carriage, and his hands free, Epps broke from the concerned townspeople and took after Daniel, his long legs churning.

Hughie bent down and picked up a stick. "Hey, Dumps! Don't forget your—" And at that second he stood up and ran smack into the long legs of the tall man, sending him flying through the air. He hit hard on the cold ground and rolled.

Daniel was just about to enter a thick patch of woods when he saw Epps and Hughie tumble. He stopped to see the outcome.

He was relieved to see Hughie get up, unhurt.

Epps rolled onto his knees, then got to his feet, favoring his right foot. He tested it. Hobbled. And fell.

The two hunters, having seen what happened, ran to Hughie to see if he was hurt. Then they ran to Epps. It took both of them, one under each arm, to help him back to the carriage.

The last thing Daniel saw before entering the thick woods was Hughie. The boy was smiling.

CHAPTER 28

Camilla Rush smoothed the front of her dress and checked her hair in the mirror on her way to the front door. Wrinkles at the corners of her eyes showed her age, as did her figure. She was rounder now than she'd ever been. But she chose not to dwell on that now.

Excitement had put a dash of color into her cheeks. With no one else to talk to day after day, she found herself looking forward to these late afternoon visits.

"Cyrus, come in. The water is hot, and I have fresh-made cookies."

"Oatmeal and raisin?" Cyrus removed his hat and handed it to her, along with his coat. They'd fallen into a routine.

"Are there any other kind?" Camilla laughed.

"Not as far as I'm concerned."

She hung up his coat and hat. He went to the tea tray and poured hot water into two cups.

"And how are you doing today, my dear?" he asked.

Over the weeks Cyrus's endearments had become more frequent and bolder. They had bothered Camilla at first. But she told herself that Cyrus didn't mean anything by them. He was just being a friend.

"I manage to keep myself busy," she replied. "Here, let me get that."

Cyrus sat while she served him. Sugar. Cream. He took only one cookie.

"Cyrus Gregg! You're not going to hurt my feelings, are you?"

With a smile, he helped himself to another cookie.

Camilla prepared herself tea and sat in a chair opposite him, even though he'd left room for her next to him on the sofa.

They sipped their tea in comfortable silence.

"Have you heard from Asa?" Cyrus asked.

He asked the same question every day, and every day it hurt to answer, because the answer was always the same.

"Nothing yet," she said.

"Camilla . . ."

Cyrus set his cup and saucer aside. What he was about to say was serious. Camilla knew this because Cyrus had set aside the second cookie with the tea.

"I'm beginning to grow concerned," he said.

Camilla stared at the tea in her cup. She made a concerted effort to hold back her emotions. Cyrus meant well, and she loved him for it. But all night and all day she tossed back and forth on a tempestuous sea of emotion. These afternoon teas were her sole respite—an island of peace. Must he throw her back into the sea so quickly?

"How long has it been now?" he asked. "Two weeks?"

"Three."

"And still no word."

Lifting her head, her chin set, Camilla fought back the pain inflicted by his statement of reality. "Asa and Daniel are in God's hands."

Cyrus leaned closer. "Let me do something to help. Let me send someone to locate them."

Camilla shook her head. "I'm confident Asa has his reasons for not sending word of his situation."

"Of course he does. My man will simply locate him and report back to me. I'll give him strict instructions not to interfere. He won't even make contact."

"I don't know," Camilla hedged. "If Asa knew we'd sent someone to check up on him . . ."

"He'll never know," Cyrus assured her.

Already on the edge of the sofa, Cyrus moved closer. He got on one knee before her, took her hand in his, and squeezed. "The only reason I'd do it is for your peace of mind, Camilla. It hurts me to see you torture yourself with uncertainty."

Camilla blushed, seeing Cyrus kneeling before her. "You've always been such a good friend."

"That means the world to me," Cyrus said. "You know how I feel about you. I've never stopped loving you."

He held her gaze. She turned her head and took her hand back.

Cyrus stood. "Then it's settled. The first thing I'll do when I return to my office is dispatch my man to locate Asa."

"Anything needing my attention?" Gregg barked as he strode into his office.

His secretary, a long-faced man in his twenties, jumped at the suddenness of Gregg's appearing.

"Um . . . aya. Congressman Matthews's assistant delivered a letter." He found the letter on his desk and held it out. "It requires your immediate—"

Gregg waved him off. "I'll deal with it later." He kept walking.

"I'll put it on your desk," the secretary said.

"Anything else?"

"Um—"

"Get me the production reports and payroll."

"Production reports for last week?"

"Of course for last week!"

In his private office, Cyrus Gregg removed his coat and hat. Standing at his desk, he leafed through a stack of papers.

His secretary came in with the production reports and payroll sheets. He placed them on Gregg's desk. "Will there be anything else, sir?"

"No. Nothing else."

The secretary started out, then turned back. "Oh! I almost forgot." He reached into his pocket and pulled out a well-traveled letter. "A man who said he was passing through Cumberland delivered this for you. It's addressed to Mrs. Camilla Rush. Should I have one of the shop boys run it out to her?"

"I'll take it," Gregg said. "And close the door."

He sat at his desk, placing the letter in front of him. Opening a drawer, he removed a bottle of whiskey and a glass and poured himself a drink. After taking a sip, he opened the letter addressed to Camilla.

My dearest Camilla,

I write from Syracuse, New York, finding it difficult to believe I've traveled this far and been gone this long. It seems every time I make a decision to abandon my pursuit, we come upon someone who has seen Daniel and once again he seems within reach.

The most recent sighting was yesterday. A local farmer discovered the boy sleeping in his barn and took pity on him. He and his wife fed Daniel breakfast. This godly family urged him to pursue a course of reconciliation. They prayed over him. As you might expect, their counsel fell on deaf ears.

After thanking the man and his wife for their kindness, we prayed together and I felt strengthened, though I don't know how much longer I can continue. My leg aches every day from the cold, and two days ago I awoke with a constricted chest and coughing.

I thank God every day for Robely. He's been a constant source of encouragement. I've taken to calling him Barnabas.

I covet your prayers, my dearest. I pray for you every night and, God willing, will be home soon.

Faithfully yours,

Asa

Cyrus took a sip of whiskey. At the bottom of the letter was a bold scrawl.

FURY

The fox is tiring. The hounds are closing. By the time this reaches you, the fox will be bagged. Not all hands will make it home.

Epps

After another sip, Cyrus Gregg crumpled the letter and got up. He tossed it into the fireplace and watched it burn.

He allowed himself a smile. He'd earned it. He'd turned disaster into blessing. With the boy dead, the threat was gone. And with Asa out of the way, he could openly court the woman who had possessed him since his youth.

The sky hung low and dark. Rain fell hard enough to bend the rim of Daniel's hat. His legs and lungs burned. Breaths came in painful gulps.

The Erie Canal and a packet boat separated him from his pursuers. Daniel had managed to cross over the canal and double back without their seeing him. At least he thought they hadn't seen him. The next few minutes would tell. Right now, they were closing on him.

Keeping pace with the packet boat, Daniel hid behind the cabin, moving with it, keeping it between him and the carriage on the other side of the canal. If he could pull this off, his uncle and Epps could travel miles before they realized what had happened.

Everyone on the boat was tucked away inside somewhere, staying out of the rain. All of them, that is, except a boy in a slicker who was riding one of three horses that pulled the boat.

As the carriage got closer, Daniel saw that his chances of pulling this off would be better if he was on the boat. Four feet of water separated them. With no one around to see him except the boy on the horse, Daniel leaped the span, landing on the deck. With his back pressed against the cabin, his chest still heaving, he hid from the carriage.

Having sacrificed better position for line of sight, however, Daniel was floating blindly. All he could do was wait and wait and wait, judging the time until the carriage passed. He heard nothing other than the beat of the rain and muffled laughter coming from inside the cabin. There were no shouts of discovery. No indication they had spotted him.

After what seemed forever, Daniel risked a peek. His heart heaved a sigh of relief as he saw the back of his uncle's carriage toddling down the road, heading the opposite direction.

He jumped ashore and continued his journey, sloshing beside the famous Erie Canal. For all its fame, there wasn't much to see. Not here, at least. He'd heard someone refer to this stretch between Syracuse and Utica as the "long level," because the water level neither rose nor fell enough to require a lock for seventy miles.

It was a dismal stretch of land. Inland from the canal lay stagnant swampland and hundreds of felled, rotting trees.

A burst of laughter from inside the cabin caught Daniel's attention. His head turned enough to catch sight of the carriage out of the corner of his eye, now smaller than a postal stamp . . . turning onto a bridge.

"No!"

Daniel stared in disbelief as his uncle's carriage crossed over the canal and, reaching the other side, reversed course. It was coming straight toward him!

"How? How?"

Gripped by panic and indecision, Daniel stood in the middle of the road, his arms limp with resignation.

Did they see him? At this distance, with the rain falling hard, could they recognize him?

Did it matter? Weariness covered him. His clothes clung to him, heavy and wet. Exhaustion had penetrated deep into his bones. He couldn't do this anymore.

Even if he chose to flee, where could he go? To one side was a canal forty feet wide; on the other side, a marsh littered with rotting timber. Ahead, the road stretched for as far as the eye could see. Even with fresh legs he couldn't outrun them.

Salvation—if it was to be found at all—lay on the packet boat. He leaped aboard.

His feet shuffled across the deck, resigned to his fate. He could hide, but they'd find him. He considered throwing open the cabin door and pleading his case. Would they believe him and protect him? Or would they hand him over to the adults—the killers?

Not willing to place himself at the mercy of strangers, Daniel lifted a cargo-hold door. He saw mountains of salt. The corners of the hold were dark. If he hid there . . . covered himself with . . .

"They'll find you in there."

Standing on deck was the boy Daniel had seen riding the horse in the rain. He appeared to be about Daniel's age.

"Give me your hat," the boy said, "and your coat."

The boy removed his own hat and slicker as he spoke, handing them to Daniel. "Put them on."

Daniel did. The hat was wider than his own. The slicker was warm from the boy's body.

"Do you know how to ride a horse?"

"Of course I know how to ride a horse."

"Good. Mount the lead horse. Keep your head down and the tow-line taut." The boy checked down the road at the carriage's progress. "Hurry!"

Daniel met his rescuer's eye. He saw intellect and a dash of adventure. "Thanks," he said.

Jumping to the bank, Daniel ran to the front horse and climbed on. As instructed, he kept his head down, tracking the carriage's progress by glancing over his shoulder.

Daniel discovered that a canal packet boat, while good for hauling tons of cargo, made for a sorry escape vehicle. A person on foot could overtake it. So it didn't take long for Uncle Asa's carriage to catch up.

Without being conspicuous, Daniel watched as the carriage matched the boat's speed.

"Hullo!" Epps hailed. He sat dry and cozy next to Uncle Asa.

The boy who had taken Daniel's hat and coat must have stashed them somewhere. He stood at the bow of the barge and returned Epps's hail.

Shouting through the rain, Epps said, "We're searching for a boy. A runaway. Sixteen years of age. We think he might have passed you on the other side of the canal about ten minutes ago. Did you happen to see him?"

"Wish I could help you," the boy at the bow shouted back. "But I took my post shortly before you arrived." He motioned toward Daniel with a thumb. "And he . . . excuse me a minute, gentlemen . . ." A sharp whistle split the air. "Theophilus! Show him who's boss! Keep that line taut!"

The towline, which had slacked, snapped taut.

Uncle Asa was intrigued. "His name's Theophilus?"

"Aya."

"Does that mean something?" Epps asked.

"From the Bible," Uncle Asa said. "It means, 'Friend of God.'" To the boy, "It's not a common name."

The boy shrugged. "It's the name he was given."

"Mind if we come aboard and look around?" Epps asked.

"Glad to have you. Visit for as long as you like. On a day like today, any distraction is welcomed."

Epps jumped out of the carriage and onto the boat. Uncle Asa stayed behind, keeping pace with the craft.

Daniel watched as Epps searched the deck, opened the cargo holds, then disappeared inside the cabin. The boy went with him, closing the door, leaving Daniel alone in the rain with his uncle.

A powerful urge came over Daniel to seize this opportunity and confront his uncle.

All right, Uncle Asa. Here I am. You want me dead? Then do it yourself. But you know what? I don't think you can do it. Like your friend, Cyrus Gregg, you have to hire someone to do your killing for you.

The cabin door opened and Epps stepped out. He stood on deck and surveyed the canal in both directions. His gaze settled on Daniel and lingered before moving to the swamp. Then he leaped to land and got into the carriage.

Having followed him out, the boy on the barge waved good-bye.

Daniel's hopes rose.

The carriage picked up speed. Daniel ducked his head as they passed him. And then they were gone. When it was safe, he climbed off the horse.

"I can't thank you enough," Daniel said, handing the boy his hat and slicker.

"Yours are in the storage chest to the right of the cabin," the boy said. "By the way, I'm Ben." He offered his hand.

Daniel shook the boy's hand. "Daniel. I suppose I owe you an explanation. You see, that's my uncle—"

Ben cut him off. "No explanation needed. God told me to help you, so I did."

Daniel didn't know what to say to that. The boy didn't look like he was trying to be humorous.

"All I can say is, you handled it well," Daniel said. "Whistling like that, telling me to keep the line taut."

The boy laughed. "I wasn't yelling at you. I was yelling at Theophilus—the horse."

Daniel laughed with him.

After retrieving his hat and coat, he thanked Ben again and wished him well.

"Which direction are you headed?" Ben asked.

"The opposite of them," Daniel replied.

"Godspeed, Daniel."

CHAPTER 29

Cyrus Gregg stood to one side of the drawing room so the women could do their work. He congratulated himself on his restraint. A wise man knew when to act and when to refrain from acting. This was a time for patience.

There was a soft knock on the door behind him. He turned and opened it.

"Martha . . . Abel . . . how good of you to come."

An elderly couple entered. Martha hurried past him, her mouth pressed into a thin line, and went straight to the other women. Abel stepped inside the door and hung back next to Cyrus Gregg in the dimly lit room. He was holding a pie. Blueberry from the smell of it.

White haired with a face of wrinkles, Abel Reynolds was an easygoing man, a deacon of the church. "Quite a shock," he murmured.

"Yes. Yes, it is," Cyrus Gregg replied.

The men spoke in hushed tones and without looking at each other. Gregg's eyes were fixed on the small circle of women in the middle of the room.

"From what I heard, you're the one that found out," Abel said.

"Aya."

"Bring Nola and Bea with you?"

"Aya. Figured I'd need help."

Abel nodded solemnly. "You're a good Christian man, Mr. Gregg."

"I try to be."

They watched the women for a time in silence.

Abel shuffled his feet. "Well, this is going to take a while . . ." He stepped toward the door. "I'm goin' to pick up some lumber at Henderson's, then I'll come back and pick up Martha. Can you see that . . . ?"

Abel hefted the pie, as if uncertain what to do with it. He seemed glad to hand it over when Gregg offered to take it.

"Much obliged," Abel said.

"Oh, Abel—Henderson just got a new shipment of mahogany for me," Cyrus Gregg said. "If you can use any of it, help yourself. And tell Henderson to charge you the price he gives me."

"Mighty kind of you, Mr. Gregg!" The old man's eyes sparkled over his good fortune. He thrust out a hand.

Juggling the pie, Gregg shook the old man's hand and then watched him exit.

Once again the only male in the room, Gregg set the pie on the dining-room table. He contented himself to stand in the background and observe.

Seated on the sofa, surrounded by four attending matrons, the widow Camilla Rush wept.

Yesterday he'd brought two women from the church with him when he broke the news to her about Asa and Daniel's tragic deaths.

With tact and solemnity he informed her of the report he'd received: that the remains of Asa and Daniel had been found in a Pennsylvania forest; that the cause of their deaths could not be determined because so little was left of the remains after the animals had gotten to them; but that pieces of Asa's cane and the boy's musical instrument were found with the bodies.

Today, as word spread of the deaths and the church responded with food and comfort, Cyrus Gregg assumed the role of family friend. He saw that guests were greeted and made himself available for any little thing that needed to be done, like putting a blueberry pie on the table.

He kept at arm's length from the mourners but always within sight.

Tomorrow he would offer to pay for the funeral, including the donation of two of his finest caskets, and attend to all the details. He would convince Camilla it was the least he could do for his close friend, Asa.

She would be grateful, though overcome with grief. Then, on Saturday, he would comfort her. A pat on the hand. A shoulder to cry on. A hug. Camilla would be lonely, and he would keep her company.

Cyrus Gregg gazed with compassion at his future bride. Her eyes were red and swollen, her cheeks stained with tears, yet still she looked adorable. The black dress against her pale skin was seductive.

Straw had worked its way down Daniel's back. He reached, a contorted effort, and pulled it out. He was getting good at it. Scratchy straw in inconvenient places was common among those who slept in haylofts.

Wanting to avoid the canal towns, he'd made his way to a place called Wright's Settlement, a community two miles northeast of Rome, New York.

The rain stopped shortly after he arrived. The sky cleared, and when night fell, so did the temperatures. Daniel found shelter in a large barn of a dairy farm. Spending the night with thirty cows wasn't his idea of an ideal arrangement, but it provided him shelter and hay for covers.

He burrowed down deep into the hay, became cozy and warm, and was drifting off when a ruckus awakened him—female squealing, male laughter, playful protestations, doors opening and closing, and all manner of happy outbursts.

The light from a swinging lantern cast crazy shadows among the rafters. A loud *thump* was followed by guffaws. From what Daniel could make out, there were at least two girls. He couldn't tell yet how many guys there were.

Once the light found a resting place, the shadows settled down. So did the merriment . . . somewhat.

Daniel's curiosity got the better of him. Elbowing back a layer of hay, he rolled over onto his knees and crawled to the edge of the loft, careful not to make a sound.

Lining the sides of the barn were two rows of cow backsides. The lantern had come to rest on a stool between them. Three young people sat in a circle around the lantern, two girls and a boy. The boy had his back to Daniel. He was rocking back and forth in convulsive laughter. The girls—one blonde, one brunette—seemed to be laughing at his laughter.

The blonde was stunning. Even from a distance, her eyes and the radiance of her face was unmistakable. Gloves could not conceal the elegance of her hands, nor her coat, the regal grace of her neck. Her laughter was the antidote to loneliness.

Next to her, the brunette was pretty in a wholesome way, with smiling dark eyes and dimples. She covered her mouth with a hand as she laughed.

From the back, all Daniel was able to determine of the guy was that he was average in size and—if the girls' reaction was any indication—he seemed to have a knack for making things funny.

Daniel found himself smiling, just watching them. The three were comfortable with each other, exhibiting an ease that comes from years of intimacy.

Out of the darkness, a moth swooped down and circled the lantern. The girls reacted to it with squeals and a frantic waving of hands. The moth, finding a greater light, took to circling the blonde. She jumped up, ducking and swatting and shrieking.

Daniel found her plight amusing, her laughter infectious, and the length of her legs captivating. He repositioned himself to get a better view by moving around a pillar. But as he did so, his recorder squirted out of his waistband and tumbled over the edge of the loft.

It was one of those moments when time slows and the inevitable crouches, ready to pounce.

The recorder somersaulted, its black, shiny finish catching the light of the lantern. It hit bottom with an awful clatter among stacks of milk pails before landing on the straw-strewn floor. The three jumped back from it, as if it was an adder, not a musical instrument.

The brunette was the first to look up into the loft. She grabbed a pitchfork. The young man, his eyes squinting into the darkness, held out his hand to the brunette. She handed him the pitchfork while the blonde bent down and picked up the recorder.

"Whoever is up there, come down!" the boy called, his voice steady.

Daniel's instinctive reaction to the announcement of his presence had been to shrink back into the shadows. From the way the three scanned the loft—their eyes not finding anything to fix upon—it was evident they couldn't see him.

Daniel's gut told him to sink deeper into the shadows and find some other way out of the loft than the ladder that had brought him here. His gut knew nothing of loyalty. It didn't seem to realize Daniel could never leave his recorder.

"I'm coming down," he said. "I'm unarmed. I don't wish to harm anyone."

He stood up in the loft. Three pairs of eyes fixed on him, tracking him to the ladder. As he climbed down, he felt vulnerable leading with his backside, knowing a three-pronged weapon was aimed at it.

"Turn around slowly," his captor said.

Daniel did as he was told. The first thing he saw were three angry prongs inches from his face.

"Daniel?"

The prongs fell away.

The face of his rescuer from the canal packet boat came into focus. Now he was all smiles.

"Ben?"

Ben turned to the ladies. "This is the fellow I was telling you about. You know, the friend of the Friend of God!"

Blank expressions.

"Theophilus!"

The brunette was the first to get the play on words, the blonde a second later.

She said, "You're a friend of Ben's horse?" Her blue eyes sparkled like gems in the dim light.

Daniel found himself staring at her longer than what is considered polite. When he realized it, he pulled his eyes away. "Sorry."

She smiled at him without offense, which he appreciated. But now he didn't know where to look. His eyes kept wanting to return to the blue gems.

"Her name is Lucy," the brunette said. She'd noticed Daniel's dilemma and found it humorous.

"Lucy," Daniel repeated. He gave a slight bow and the briefest of glances, because he knew that if his eyes lingered on hers for even an instant he might not be able to pull them away again.

"And this is Hannah," Ben said, introducing the brunette.

Daniel bowed and repeated her name.

"Hannah is my intended," Ben added.

"Really? Congratulations!" Daniel said with genuine enthusiasm. He was happy for himself. The pairing of Ben and Hannah left Lucy unescorted.

Ben lifted the pitchfork. "Can we expect company anytime soon?"

It took Daniel a few seconds to make the transition to his uncle and Epps. "Oh . . . no . . . I think I lost them. I haven't seen them since the canal."

"I believe you dropped this," Lucy said, holding out his recorder.

Taking it, he smiled. "I guess I should be angry at it for making such a rude introduction."

"Will you play it for us?" Lucy asked.

Daniel didn't play for other people. Until now he'd kept his music private. But when Lucy asked him to play, he knew he'd play for her.

The journey to Rome, New York, had taken a toll on Asa Rush. Epps could see it in the way the man slouched and the heaviness of his eyelids even after a night's sleep. He sensed his time with the educator was coming to an end.

Already he'd allowed Asa to live longer than he intended. His last correspondence to Cyrus Gregg indicated the man was as good as dead. It was a statement written with confidence. Epps could end Asa's life anytime. But he would do it when it was most convenient to him.

A day. Two at the most, he told himself.

He was going to miss Asa Rush. Talking to the man made him feel smart. Everyone else looked down their noses at him because of his lack of education. Everyone except Asa Rush.

"Center of town. That's what the boater said, isn't it?" Asa asked.

"There. On the corner." Epps pointed to the hotel.

"Sure I can't talk you into sharing a room with me?"

"Beds are too soft. They hurt my back."

"You can sleep on the floor."

"Thanks, but I prefer sleeping outdoors," Epps said.

"Suit yourself."

Asa steered the carriage to the front of the hotel. With a loud groan, he climbed down and fished behind the seat for his bag. Epps took the reins.

"Had I known it would be this far, we would have stayed in Utica," Asa said.

"All roads lead to Rome," Epps quipped. "You of all men should know that."

A good-natured smile lit Asa's face. "You constantly amaze me, Mr. Epps."

"Surprising people is part of my charm. See you in the morning."

CHAPTER 30

Daniel's music echoed among the barn rafters. Even the cows were taken by the solemn sounds, turning their heads to get a glimpse of the musician.

He played with his eyes closed, which wasn't unusual. This time, however, he closed them out of necessity. Open, he would stare at Lucy. And if he stared at Lucy, he'd lose all ability to concentrate.

They'd added a fourth stool around the lantern for him. He sat between the girls, which was a distraction even with his eyes shut. It was all he could do to focus on his composition—a low, meandering piece of soul-searching anguish.

"Mmmm. That was lovely," Lucy said when he finished.

"It made me sad, though," Hannah added.

"You can really play that thing," Ben exclaimed.

Daniel admired the recorder. "We've spent a lot of time together."

"Play another one!" Lucy urged him, brushing back strands of golden hair. "I could listen to you play all night."

Daniel smiled humbly, hoping to conceal the backflips his heart was doing. He flexed his hand. It was stiff from the cold without gloves. It hurt his joints to play, but it was a pain he was willing to endure as long as it fed the sparkle in Lucy's eyes.

Mentally selecting another song, he lifted the recorder to his lips.

The banging of the barn door interrupted.

"Your mother was right," a man boomed. "There's music coming from the barn. I told her she was imagining it."

His comment earned good-natured grins from Hannah, Lucy, and Ben, so Daniel risked one, too.

"Mr. Robbins!" Ben greeted him.

"Pa, this is Daniel," Hannah said.

Daniel stood. He shook Robbins's outstretched hand, the strong grip of a farmer.

The man was average height, stocky. He had friendly brown eyes and deep lines in his cheeks that suggested a happy nature. "You're a musician?" he asked with a loud voice.

"I play for my own enjoyment," Daniel said.

"He plays heavenly!" Lucy chimed.

Daniel didn't object to the compliment.

Speaking to no one in particular, Robbins said, "You're back from Western early. How was it tonight?"

Hannah was up off her stool. "Papa, it was amazing! I wish you would have come with us. Brother Finney's preaching was so powerful. And the Spirit . . . oh, Papa . . . the Spirit moved. Hundreds came to the Lord!"

"Hundreds!" Lucy agreed.

"We got so excited," Ben added, "we had to come back here to settle down."

Chuckling, Hannah took Ben's arm. "Papa, Ben was so funny. He said we were going to have to backslide in order to get sleep tonight."

Ben's eyes grew wide. "Mr. Robbins . . . I didn't mean anything by that. I was just . . ."

Robbins grinned. "Relax, son. I understand what you meant by it."

Daniel liked this man. Unlike other parents he knew, Robbins showed genuine affection for his daughter and her friends. And they to him.

Hannah turned to Daniel. "Have you heard Brother Finney preach?"

"Can't say that I have."

"But you've heard of the revival that's going on in Western, haven't you?" Ben asked him.

"Afraid not."

The three nearly came unglued. They all spoke at once, insisting that Daniel had to go to Western to hear Finney preach.

Daniel nodded and smiled, but inside all this talk of preaching and revival made him squirm.

"First time we went—," Ben said.

"About two weeks ago—," Hannah inserted.

"Sixteen days," Lucy corrected.

"We went to poke fun at what was happening. Thought we'd get a huge laugh watching a bunch of old people raising their hands and shouting and dancing."

"Four of us went," Lucy said.

"Arthur Hoyt went with us," Hannah explained, as though the name meant something to Daniel. It didn't.

Ben talked through the interruptions. "Once we got there, and Brother Finney started to preach—"

"The Spirit fell," Hannah said.

"It was wonderful and terrifying all at the same time!" Lucy exclaimed. "All of us felt it."

"All except Arthur," Hannah added.

"He felt it," Lucy objected. "He chose to fight it off."

"God opened our eyes, Daniel!" Ben exclaimed. "Since then, everything is different! We haven't been the same since."

"We've been going to Western every night." Lucy took Daniel's arm. "You should go with us, Daniel. Will you come with us tomorrow night?"

The barrage of narration came to an abrupt halt, awaiting Daniel's reply.

"I don't know how long I'll be here in the area," Daniel said weakly.

Robbins folded his arms, "Daniel, if you didn't meet these three scamps at Western, how did you manage to hook up with them?"

The three and Daniel exchanged glances.

"Actually," Ben said, "I met him on the canal route. Theophilus really took a shine to him."

Robbins guffawed. "Is that nag still alive?"

Ben laughed with him. "He's lead horse! Shows the others how it's done."

Robbins turned back to Daniel. "Where do you hail from, son?"

"Cumberland . . . most recently."

"Long way from home."

"Originally from New Haven."

"New Haven?" Robbins's face lit up. "I used to work at the docks in New Haven when I was your age. Maybe I know your family. What's your surname?"

"Cooper."

Robbins stared at him in earnest. "Cooper . . ."

"Yes, sir."

"You wouldn't happen to be related to Eli Cooper, would you? He's a minister in New Haven."

Daniel sobered. "My father."

"You don't say!" Robbins slapped his hands together with delight. "You're Eli Cooper's son?"

The news and Robbins's reaction to it prompted a fresh round of smiles among Daniel's new friends.

"Well, what do you know! How is he? The last I heard of your father, he was going to England on a preaching tour. And let me tell you, if anybody could turn those Brits back to God, it's your father!"

Daniel hesitated. "Um . . . my father's dead. He and my mother went down in the Atlantic on the return voyage."

It was as if he'd opened a door and let the cold air in. The worst hit by the news was Robbins.

"Oh my . . ." The man took a stumbling step.

Hannah grabbed his arm and steadied him. "Papa?"

"I'm . . . all right. It's just that Eli's been on my mind of late, what with everything that's happening in Western. Just yesterday morning . . ." He cleared his throat. "I prayed for him."

"Sit down, Papa." Hannah guided her father to a stool.

"No, that's . . . I'm fine."

Fine or not, he sat down. He rubbed his chin. His eyes had a far-off cast to them.

"And Asa Rush?" Robbins asked. "Is he—?"

"My uncle. He's still alive."

The irony of the inquiry was not lost on Daniel.

"Your uncle? That's right. Eli married Asa's sister."

The four young people stood in silence as Robbins retreated to a distant time and place.

"Did your father ever tell you the story of the guillotine revival?" Robbins asked.

"*Guillotine* revival?" Ben exclaimed.

"Aya," Daniel said without enthusiasm. "Whenever he was on tour, he preached on it."

"How about the time he shot your uncle Asa during a duel?"

"A *duel?*" Ben cried.

This was dusty history to Daniel.

"Can I tell them, or would you like to?" Robbins asked.

Daniel shrugged his indifference. He could see that Robbins wanted to tell the story, and that was fine by him.

"Tell you what," Robbins said, "I'll tell them about the guillotine revival. You can tell them later about the duel." He became as excited as a little boy. "Sit . . . sit . . . sit!"

With one stool less than the number of people present, Ben sat on the floor next to Hannah. She rested her arm on his shoulder.

Robbins began. "I was your age when I ran away from home, for reasons"—he looked down—"that are unimportant right now. It's enough to know that I was angry, hurt, and wanted to get off the farm and do something with my life. I wanted to go to sea. So I ran to Boston."

He laughed. "My first voyage was a short one. Boston to New Haven. I spent the entire time hanging over the side of the boat, swearing that if I ever made it back to solid land, I would never step foot on a boat again."

Daniel glanced at Lucy. As she listened to Robbins's story, her face radiated the light from the lantern with a soft, romantic glow.

Robbins continued. "So I got myself a job at the docks, loading and unloading cargo holds. It was hard work, and I lived with hard men, but it paid well for a man with no family to support. Now that was back in the days when the whole country was going crazy over all things French, including revolution. Everyone was calling each other, 'Citizen.' That sort of thing.

"So one day this guy—Benton . . . no, Benson—comes to the docks and says he'll pay us to drink ale, watch a real guillotine in action, and then do a little mischief around town. And we're thinking to ourselves, *Are you kidding?* We'd do that for free.

"Sure enough, that weekend, right there on the docks, is this guillotine. The genuine article, imported from France. We couldn't believe it! There were kegs of ale everywhere you looked, and we were all in a rather rambunctious mood by the time this guy stands up beside the guillotine and starts addressing the crowd. It became apparent that it was his job to get everyone riled up, and he was doing a pretty good job of it too. They even marched in a line of men who were scheduled to be guillotined!"

"No!" Ben exclaimed.

"That's when Eli Cooper—Daniel's father—took the platform to deliver the key speech. Benson had prepared us with a signal. When we heard the signal, we were to do a little mayhem in town. He told us to make it look spontaneous and natural." Robbins paused to remember. "The signal was to be, 'Citizens of America, unite!' When we heard Eli Cooper say those words, we were to go into the town, break a few windows, and do some other damage.

"Well, Eli gets up there and—we didn't know it at the time—but his good friend, Asa Rush, Daniel's uncle . . ."

For some reason, Ben glanced at Daniel with a puzzled expression.

". . . was in the front of the prisoner line to have his head chopped off. And he nearly did!" Tears welled in Robbins's eyes. "Oh, I wish all of you could have seen it. Eli was masterful. Full of the Spirit of God. Not only did he save his friend's life, but as the blade fell, he pulled Asa from the guillotine and gave the signal . . . only he changed it. He shouted, 'Citizens of America, repent!'"

Robbins gazed at the floor. "And the Spirit fell," he said with a choked voice. "I-I can't begin to describe to you what it was like. A huge invisible wave crashed down upon the whole lot of us, and I remember this incredible realization . . . this ponderous weight upon my chest and shoulders, knocking me to my knees. And I knew that, of all men there that day, *I* was the one who deserved to be placed under the blade of that guillotine.

"Eli Cooper preached, and we lined up—hundreds and hundreds of us—mounting the steps to that platform. Kneeling beside that guillotine. Confessing our sins. And Eli had each of us put our hand on the guillotine pillar . . ."

Robbins pursed his lips. Tears fell. He wiped them away with the back of his hand. The barn was dead silent. It was as though the whole world were holding its breath, waiting for him to continue.

"To this day, I remember what it felt like. The cool, rough wood. The way the whole structure shuddered as the blade released. The *whoosh* as it cut through air. The sudden, horrible *thud* as it hit bottom . . . and knowing, at that instant, at the base of that guillotine, that the old, despicable Lionel Robbins died."

He sniffed and smiled. "And then Eli Cooper said to me, 'Rise to new life.'" Another sniff. "And I did!"

Robbins drew a deep, ragged breath. "After that, everything changed. Not just with me, but across the whole country! It was as though one minute we were on the verge of revolution, and the next the whole world was different. Instead of hate, there was love. Instead of revolution, there was revival. Everything was fresh . . . new . . . exciting . . . good again."

He leaned toward his daughter. "That's why, when I heard about what was happening in Western, I urged you and your friends to go. I knew you went intending to mock the preacher. But I'd seen what revival could do to a dock full of rioters. I figured the Holy Spirit needn't feel threatened by the four of you."

For a time nobody spoke. The barn had taken on cathedral reverence.

Then Ben said to Daniel, "That man in the carriage. At the canal. You called him your uncle. The same uncle who almost had his head chopped off at the guillotine?"

Everyone was looking at him. Daniel grew uncomfortable.

"Aya."

"Your uncle Asa is here?" Robbins exclaimed. "I'd very much like to see him again!"

"He's n-not exactly with me," Daniel stammered. "I think he's—he's already gone back home."

Lionel Robbins's eyes quickened, the way a father's eyes do when he isn't sure he's being told the truth.

"Papa," Hannah said, "Daniel needs a place to sleep for a couple of nights. He can stay in our loft, can't he?"

Robbins turned to Daniel. "Is this true?"

"Aya."

The father-squint deepened.

"I'd be willing to work," Daniel offered.

Robbins relented. "Very well. I wish we could offer you better accommodations, but I'm afraid the loft is the best we can do for now."

"The loft will be fine. Thank you, sir." Daniel held out his hand.

Robbins took it and warmed to him. "It's a privilege for me to meet the son of Eli Cooper."

After Hannah's father departed, the evening broke up quickly.

"I must be getting home," Lucy said.

"I'll walk you back to town," Ben offered.

They said their good-byes to Daniel. He trailed behind them to the barn door, as though he were the host and this was his house.

He wanted to ask Lucy if she could stay longer, but he couldn't think of a way to phrase it that wasn't obvious. He could offer to walk her home himself, but then it would end up being him and Ben and Lucy.

Just then Lucy turned to him. "You don't have Jesus in your heart, do you?"

"Lucy!" Hannah frowned. "That's rather abrupt! Rude, in fact!"

But Lucy wasn't listening to Hannah. Her incredible blue eyes stared at Daniel, waiting for an answer.

"I'm afraid God and I aren't on speaking terms right now," he said.

"Pity." Turning, she walked out of the barn.

With an apologetic shrug, Ben said, "Lucy can be direct at times. See you tomorrow." He kissed Hannah on the cheek, then ran to catch up with Lucy.

"I'll leave the lantern," Hannah said by way of good night. "We milk the cows at five."

"In the morning?!" Daniel exclaimed.

Her eyebrows rose. "We tried doing it at five in the afternoon, but it kept interfering with the cow's tea time."

That got a smirk from Daniel.

"Good night, Mr. Cooper."

"Thank you," Daniel replied. "And thank you for asking your father if I could stay."

Hannah stood in the doorway. "I like your music. Maybe next time you could play something more cheerful."

In the dark, Daniel snuggled into the hay until he got comfortable. Having permission to be here made all the difference in the world. He didn't have to jump at every sound.

His mind ranged over the unexpected turn of events, and he found himself smiling.

Daniel liked Ben. He was quick of mind. Self-confident. Humorous. He wasn't like other fellows who turned everything into a competition, especially when girls were around.

Which, of course, made him think of Lucy . . . her sparkling blue eyes and milky skin and pearly teeth. Daniel inhaled deeply, intent on holding on to that image of Lucy until he fell asleep.

However, for some reason his mind kept drifting back to Hannah Robbins, framed in the barn doorway, her head cocked to one side, a playful smirk on her face.

CHAPTER 31

Morning clanged as Hannah Robbins tossed milk pails into the loft at five o'clock, waking Daniel with a barrage of empty metal buckets.

"Ow!" he complained, fending off one that would have hit him in the face.

"Wake up, music boy!" she called from below. "Cows don't milk themselves, you know. And bring those pails down with you. We're gonna need them."

After stacking the pails inside one another and pulling hay from his clothing, Daniel climbed down the ladder one-handed. "When I was a child, my mother used to sing me awake."

"Believe me, my singing would have hurt you a lot more than those pails. Besides, I'm not your mother. Start at that end; I'll start at this end, and we'll work toward each other." Hannah paused with her hands on her hips. "You do know how to milk a cow, don't you?"

"Of course I know how to milk a cow. It's just like a water pump. You grab the cow's tail and . . ." He took a tail in hand and began pumping it. The cow objected and tried to kick him.

"Funny boy."

"Just a little city-boy humor. You farm girls do know how to laugh in the morning, don't you?"

"Sure we do," Hannah said without a hint of a smile. "But only when we hear something funny." She positioned herself under the first cow and started milking.

Daniel picked up a pail and a stool. He looked at the pail and the cow, then sighed. Walking to the far end, he got to work.

"Do you normally milk all these cows yourself?" he said with a voice that would carry the length of the barn.

"Most days my eight-year-old sister helps me," came the reply. "If you're having trouble, I can ask her to help you."

Daniel scrunched his eyes shut a couple of times, trying to coax them into working. They weren't usually open this early in the morning.

"How long have you known Lucy?" he called out.

When Hannah didn't answer, Daniel wondered if she had even heard him.

But then she spoke. "I was wondering how long it'd take for you to ask about Lucy."

Had he been that obvious? He thought he'd shown restraint.

"Well . . . how'd I do? Now that you mentioned it."

"About what I'd expected," Hannah said. "A typical response time."

"So then, you're asked about Lucy a lot?"

Hannah laughed. "All my life. I've known Lucy since we were four years old."

Finished with the first cow, Daniel moved to the next. He risked a glance down the row. He couldn't see her, but he could hear rapid squirts of milk hitting the side of a pail.

Settling in beside the second cow, Daniel leaned into it, thinking it might be wise to wait and ask Ben about Lucy.

"Lucy Elizabeth Carrington." Hannah spoke as though she were reciting a memorized report in front of a classroom. "Attracts boys like moths to a flame. She'll tell you she doesn't like all the attention, but she does."

Daniel grinned, then felt silly about having romantic feelings with his hands full of udder and his cheek cozied up to cowhide.

"The mistake most boys make with her is thinking because she's pretty, she's not a real person. They treat her like she's a picture or a statue—just something nice to look at. They never find out that Lucy is loyal to a fault, tougher than any boy I know, and has a brain for mathematics." Hannah paused. "Surprised?"

"I-I'm not sure . . . m-mathematics?" Daniel stammered.

"Why do you think she loves your music?"

"Because I play well?"

Hannah laughed. "Typical self-centered boy. Lucy has always been attracted to music for two reasons: One, it's something she can't do. She tried to learn the violin once. It was awful. And that's another thing about her—she's competitive. She wants to be the best at whatever she does. The second reason she's attracted to music is that she loves the mathematics of it. She told me once she could not only hear the mathematics of the notes and tonal scales, but she could see it in her mind. She said it was like watching fireflies dance in precision."

"That's amazing! I've never heard of anyone who saw music visually."

"That's our Lucy. She is amazing. There's one thing more you need to know about her."

"What's that?" Daniel smiled at the thought Hannah was giving him tips to court Lucy.

"Since her faith has been revived, she can't tolerate fakes or hypocrites. Spiritual things are important to her now. She'll never go with a boy who doesn't believe in God as strongly as she does. That's why she dumped Arthur Hoyt. First he mocked her for believing in God. Then he promised to start attending church with her even though he doesn't believe, just so he could be with her. He thought she would be impressed with his grand gesture."

"I take it she wasn't."

"Do you want to know what she said to him?"

"Aya."

"She said, 'I'd sooner saddle up a mule and ride around pretending he's a thoroughbred than dress up a pagan man and go to church with him, pretending he's a Christian.'"

Daniel laughed.

"Go ahead, chuckle all you want, Romeo. But as long as you and God aren't speaking to each other—to use your words—you don't stand a chance with Lucy."

Camilla Rush stood in front of the bedroom mirror and assessed herself. She adjusted the black dress and straightened the veil, checked to make sure she had an extra handkerchief, and evaluated her eyes. They were red and swollen, and there was nothing she could do about them. But then, that's what veils were designed to cover.

Two coffins awaited her in the front room. She heard them being moved in downstairs while she dressed. Unwanted images of what was inside them tortured her mind. She bit her lower lip and tried not to think about it.

Cyrus Gregg's voice came to her rescue. He was using his business demeanor to direct the workers.

Camilla closed her eyes and thanked God for him. She didn't think she'd have been able to survive a double funeral without him.

Talking with Hannah made the time go quickly while milking the cows. It slowed to a crawl when Daniel helped Mr. Robbins scrub out some large milk vats. All Robbins wanted to talk about was how great Daniel's father and uncle were during their college days.

Breakfast was even more uncomfortable. Hannah had seven younger sisters, no brothers, and five minutes into the meal Mr. Robbins was called away, leaving Daniel alone at the table, the sole male among nine females. Despite their mother's repeated warnings, Hannah's sisters stared and giggled at him the entire meal.

Daniel was shoveling feed alongside Robbins when Ben came running up.

"Where's Hannah?" Ben gasped, out of breath.

"What's up, son?" Robbins asked.

"Finney! He's in town."

Robbins's entire demeanor changed in an instant—from workday dreary to childlike enthusiasm. "Rome? Finney's in Rome?"

"At Mr. Frank's hotel," Ben explained. "Everyone's headed there right now. I've never seen the road so busy with traffic."

"Will Lucy be there?" Daniel asked.

"Been thinking about her, have you?" Ben said in jest. "Don't know . . . I came here first."

"Hannah's in the house," Robbins said. "You can go fetch her."

Ben took off for the house.

Robbins called after him, "If her mother gives you grief, tell her I said she could go and we'll discuss it later." Turning to Daniel, he said, "You'll want to wash up before you go."

Daniel went back to work, sinking the shovel blade into the feed. "I'll stay here. You can use the help."

"You're right about that," Robbins replied, taking the shovel from Daniel. "But I have a feeling something good is going to happen in town today. One of us should be there to see it for ourselves."

Daniel took the shovel back. "I agree. I'll finish feeding the cows, and you can tell me what else needs to be done while you're in town."

Again the shovel exchanged hands as Robbins took it. "You've never seen a real revival, have you, son?"

"I grew up attending church services and religious meetings. There's nothing going to happen in town that I haven't already seen. And given the choice of attending another service or shoveling feed . . . well, I'd rather shovel feed."

"I see."

The two men locked gazes.

Daniel had another reason for not going, which he kept to himself. If he went, he would go to see Lucy, and from what Hannah told him, showing up at a religious meeting looking like some dressed-up pagan was the worst thing he could do to impress her. Better to see her after the meeting.

Hannah and Ben came running from the house, hand in hand. They looked happy together.

Daniel was glad for Ben. Hannah was an attractive girl in her own way. Daniel liked her smile and enjoyed sparring with her. She would be a good wife for Ben.

"Daniel here says he doesn't want to go with you," Robbins said as they approached.

"Not go?" Hannah exclaimed.

"You have to go!" Ben insisted.

The way they went after him, one would have thought they were hounds and Robbins had yelled, "Sic 'im!"

Daniel had no choice. They would not relent until he agreed to go with them. Even then they took no chances. Ben grabbed one arm, Hannah the other, and they escorted him away from the cows.

Glancing over his shoulder, Daniel saw Robbins standing there, holding two shovels, watching them leave with a satisfied smirk. He'd gotten his way, and he was proud of himself.

CHAPTER 32

When they reached the edge of town, the threesome split up. Hannah left the boys and went looking for Lucy, while the boys went to secure a spot for the four of them inside the hotel.

"You looked like a regular farmhand back there at the dairy," Ben said in jest.

"It's not the first time I've handled a shovel."

"How long do you think you'll stay?"

Daniel surveyed the town with an evaluating squint. "If things work out, I may settle here."

"Really? But last night you said . . ."

"Last night everyone was teaming up against me to drag me to a religious meeting. Is kidnapping the usual procedure to get people to attend church in these parts?"

Ben laughed but didn't apologize. "Do you think your uncle's still looking for you?"

"It's the other man I'm worried about," Daniel replied. "His name is Epps. My employer and my uncle have hired him to kill me."

"Kill you? Your uncle? Are you sure? From the way Mr. Robbins speaks of him—"

"He's changed."

"Is that possible? Can a man change that dramatically? From a courageous man of God to a killer? It seems so unlikely."

Daniel tried to be patient. Ben didn't know all he'd been through.

He said, "Epps—the man you saw riding with my uncle? His partner? I've seen him kill two people. Slit their throats. Do you still want to defend the man?"

Ben pursed his lips.

They walked in silence. Talk of Epps had made Daniel skittish. Each time a carriage approached from behind, he jumped.

"What about you?" Daniel asked, covering his jitters with conversation. "Are you going to settle down with Hannah? Take over her father's farm someday?"

A twinge at the corner of Ben's mouth suggested that Daniel had hit a nerve.

When Ben didn't answer right away, Daniel said, "Sorry. I'm getting too personal."

"No need to apologize. I like you."

Daniel basked in the comment. The feeling was mutual. He hadn't had someone he thought of as a friend since moving to Cumberland. In the short time he'd known Ben, he'd come to like him too. It was as though he'd known him for years.

Ben grimaced. "It's just that . . . please, don't tell Hannah, all right? But I'm not sure she's the right girl for me."

"But you look so happy together!"

"We are! I love Hannah. She's been my best friend since we were eight years old. It's just that, well, I don't feel attracted to her in a manly sort of way. Do you know what I mean?"

"Aya."

"The last thing I ever want to do is hurt her—or her father, for that matter. I like Mr. Robbins almost as much as I like Hannah. Strange, huh?"

"It's obvious he likes you."

"So you see my problem."

"Aya."

They strode side by side, their hands shoved into their pockets, mulling over Ben's dilemma.

"It gets worse," Ben said.

"Oh?"

Ben didn't elaborate. They walked a dozen or so steps before Daniel glanced over at him. Ben was looking back at him.

And Daniel knew. He couldn't explain how he knew, he just knew. "Lucy," he said.

Ben nodded. "Aya."

The hotel stood in the center of town on a corner. Daniel and Ben wove their way through the congested lobby into a large dining room that had been converted into a meeting hall with rows of chairs. It was already noisy and warm with people.

"You take that side; I'll take this side," Ben said.

Row by row they searched for four adjoining seats. There were single seats scattered here and there, an occasional set of two, but Daniel had yet to find three seats together. Four would be a miracle.

Waving arms from the far side of the room caught Daniel's attention. Ben was signaling him.

Abandoning his search, Daniel made his way to the other side. Ben had found two pair of chairs within a few rows of each other. He was bent over talking to some men who exchanged glances, shrugged, and got up. They relocated to empty chairs two rows behind them, leaving four adjacent chairs.

"Well done!" Daniel said.

The boys settled in, three rows from the front.

A door opened not a dozen feet from the boys. A tall, slim man in a gray suit stepped out, closed the door behind him, and surveyed the room before making his way to the lectern. He gripped a piece of paper in one hand.

"Is that Finney?" Daniel asked.

"No. Name's Gillett. I think he's from Western. At least that's where I've seen him before."

The speaker called for attention. With all the commotion in the room, he didn't get it easily.

"The carnal mind is enmity against God," Gillett shouted over the noise.

The din died, and the room came to order.

Satisfied his one-sentence sermon had earned him a hearing, Gillett began. "Reverend Finney has requested that I make the purpose of this meeting abundantly clear."

He spoke with a powerful voice. It was obvious the man was no stranger to public speaking.

"This is a meeting of inquiry," he said. "It is for those who are anxious about their spiritual state before God."

Daniel punched Ben's arm. "Did you know that's what this meeting was about?"

"Hey! Why did you hit me?"

"A meeting of inquiry? You brought me to a meeting of inquiry?" A pause. "What's a meeting of inquiry?"

"How should I know? I just heard that Finney was going to be here."

Ben turned his attention back to Gillett, but not before checking the back door for the girls.

Daniel glowered in his seat. He hadn't wanted to come to this meeting in the first place. And he certainly wasn't anxious about his spiritual state. He couldn't help feeling that Ben and Hannah had duped him.

As Gillett spoke, the room became a simmering pot of noise and commotion. The more he tried to put a lid on it, the more it seemed to reach the point of boiling over.

"You have no doubt heard about the revival at Western," Gillett said. "Many of you have questions. Some of you, I am sad to say, have been outspoken critics of Reverend Finney and his methods."

The room rumbled with a mixture of supportive and critical comments.

"Let me assure you that Reverend Finney is a man of God of the highest caliber. While some might question the methods by which he promotes revival, few can argue with the results."

Another rumble rippled through the congregation, enough to prompt Gillett to raise both hands. He had to shout to be heard.

"I assure you, his methods are spiritual ones. Allow me to enumerate: Reverend Finney believes in much prayer, both secret and social. He believes in public preaching. Personal conversation and visitation from house to house. And where inquirers have multiplied, he holds meetings whereby they are invited to assemble for instruction, suited to their necessities. These, and only these, are the methods Reverend Finney has used in attempting to secure the conversion of souls."

"There they are!" Daniel said, directing Ben's attention to the back of the room.

Hannah and Lucy stood in the doorway, arm in arm to keep from being separated. They stood on their tiptoes, surveying the congregation for a glimpse of Ben and Daniel. Even from a distance, Lucy commanded attention, a vision of grace and femininity.

Daniel stood so they might see him. When they didn't, he waved both arms over his head. Hannah saw him first. She whispered to Lucy, who looked his direction, saw him, smiled, and waved. Daniel's heart skipped a beat as the girls began making their way toward him.

Then it stopped beating altogether as the girls cleared the doorway.

Immediately behind them, leaning on his cane, stood his uncle Asa.

Daniel was still standing, still holding his hands over his head, though frozen now.

His uncle scanned the crowd in his direction.

Daniel dropped into his chair, hunkering down.

"What are you doing?" Ben cried.

The chair wasn't low enough. Daniel slid to the floor.

"My uncle!" Daniel whispered.

Ben stretched as tall as he could in his chair.

"Standing at the back door," Daniel directed him.

Ben turned that direction. "With the cane?"

"That's him. Did he see me?"

"He's looking this direction."

Daniel crawled on his hands and knees to the aisle.

Walking up the aisle from the back, both Hannah and Lucy saw him and scowled.

Up the aisle, in the other direction, was the door through which Gillett had entered. Daniel crawled toward it as fast as he could, crossing an open space in the front of the room. It couldn't be helped. There were two ways out of the room. Front and back. And his uncle was guarding the back.

At the door, Daniel reached for the latch, risking a glance over his shoulder. He could see his uncle, which meant his uncle could see him. Mercifully his uncle wasn't looking his direction.

In the aisle Ben crouched low. The girls turned their scowls to him. He said something to them Daniel couldn't hear and pointed at the empty seats. Both girls hissed at him. He shushed them and crawled after Daniel.

To frowns and "tut-tuts" from the front rows, the two boys crawled out of the dining room and shut the door behind them.

They found themselves in a storage room with chairs and tables stacked floor to ceiling against the walls. The only other door to the room was on the far side. To get there, they had to cross the room, which wouldn't have been a problem if it weren't for the fact that there was a man in the center of the room. He was on his knees, praying.

When the man gave no indication he'd heard the boys enter, Daniel decided to risk disturbing him. He figured if they were quiet, they could slip by the man unnoticed.

Daniel started to stand but was pulled from behind, back down to the floor. Ben shook his head and motioned for Daniel to follow him. He crawled into a corner of the room behind some tables. There was enough space in the corner for both boys to sit, but it was tight.

Ben pointed through the tables to the praying man and mouthed the word, "Finney!"

Robely Epps felt comfortable with the weight of the pistol. He examined the firing mechanism.

"I can give you a real good price on that one," the salesman said.

Epps said nothing. He didn't like the man. The salesman's eyes were set too close together and his nasal twang grated on Epps's nerves. Epps toyed with the idea of telling the man he wanted to fire the pistol before buying it and that salesmen were his favorite target.

He looked down the sight at the salesman.

The man tittered nervously and, despite Epps's glare, moved the barrel to one side. "Do you mind if I ask how you intend to use the pistol?"

"I shoot things."

"Yes, of course. What I meant was . . ."

"Not safe to travel," Epps said.

"You're one hundred percent right about that," the salesman said. "I know a man who, just last week, was traveling to Syracuse, which you would think was a safe road—what with the canal and all—but as he was getting to—"

"I'll take it," Epps said.

After paying for the pistol, Epps walked outside, removed it from its solid-cherry carrying case, tossed the case into the back of Asa's carriage, shoved the pistol into his waistband, and covered it with his coat.

He drove around behind the gun shop and loaded it. Then, with a snap of the reigns, he went to pick up Asa at the hotel.

CHAPTER 33

Asa felt someone at his elbow. He turned.

"What's going on here?" Epps scanned the packed hotel dining room with distaste.

"It's a religious meeting," Asa said.

"You think the boy's in there?"

"A religious meeting?" Asa scoffed. "That's the last place he'd be. I was waiting for you and got curious."

The two men walked through the lobby.

"What kept you?" Asa asked.

"Had some business to take care of."

Once they were outside, Asa climbed into the carriage. He took the reins. "What do you think? East?"

Epps had yet to get in. Looking up and down the street, he said, "It's been days since we've seen him. Suppose he could be anywhere by now."

"I think we're running out of time."

Epps stepped into the carriage. He tugged to get his coat situated. "My thoughts exactly. Time's just about up."

As they pulled away from the crowded hotel, Asa glanced back. Everywhere he looked he saw people with their heads bowed in prayer.

A sensation swept over him such as he had not felt in years.

With his knees tucked up to his chin, Daniel's back began to cramp. Next to him, Ben squirmed. They suffered in silence behind the stacked tables while Reverend Finney, who was most fervent in prayer, muttered, "O God . . . O God . . . help him, Jesus, help him!"

Ben whispered in Daniel's ear, "Should we be praying?"

Daniel replied with a reproving frown.

"It feels like we should be praying, that's all," Ben insisted.

The door to the dining room opened. Raucous and restless voices spilled into the storage room. The closing of the door cut them off.

For a time, all was quiet again, except for Finney's prayerful mumbling. Daniel and Ben exchanged glances. Had someone come in or not?

"Excuse me . . . Reverend Finney?"

Daniel recognized the voice. It was Gillett, the man who had addressed the gathering, defending Finney's revival methods. From his tone and the silence that preceded it, he was hesitant to interrupt the evangelist's prayers.

"Reverend Finney? Pardon me, but it's time . . ."

Finney didn't respond.

"I apologize for interrupting your prayers," Gillett said, "but the people are waiting."

"The room is full to capacity," Finney said. It sounded to Daniel like a statement, not a question.

"Yes, sir!" came the enthusiastic reply. "It's amazing that word has traveled so quickly. I saw people running to get here!"

Silence.

Daniel wished he could see Finney's reaction, which he assumed was exhilaration masked with piety. There wasn't a preacher in the world who wouldn't love to preach to a room that size, filled to capacity.

Ben also seemed curious to hear Finney's response. His ear was cocked, and he was listening hard.

"Ask them to leave," Finney said softly.

"What?" Gillett cried.

"The emotion is too high, Mr. Gillett. I fear an undesirable outburst. Please ask them to leave."

There was a shocked silence, then, "With all respect, Reverend Finney, I fear an undesirable outburst if I ask them to leave."

"Ask them to leave, Mr. Gillett," Finney insisted.

Silence. Then footsteps.

The door opened, the volume from the dining room increased, and the door closed, pinching it off.

While it was difficult to make out Gillett's words through the walls, the reaction of the people was clear enough. It sounded like a riot.

The door opened and closed quickly this time.

"Reverend Finney, you must make an appearance!" Gillett pleaded. "I fear the outcome if you do not speak to them."

"Trust in God, Mr. Gillett."

"While I am confident you believe you are doing what is right and good—"

"Ask them to leave, Mr. Gillett."

"Reverend Finney . . ."

Daniel didn't know what Finney did to stop Gillett's protest, but whatever he did, it worked.

The door opened and closed, signaling Gillett's departure.

On the other side of the wall the noise from the gathering grew so loud the walls shook.

This time when Gillett returned, it took a longer time for the door to close. Did Gillett have to force it closed to keep the people out? Daniel wondered.

"Reverend Finney . . ."

"Mr. Gillett, if they won't leave, ask them to pray."

"To pray?"

"No public prayers, but secretly or together as families. Ask them to pray unceasingly between now and seven o'clock this evening, at which time I will preach at your church."

Ben grinned excitedly. He gave Daniel a thumbs-up signal.

"Reverend Finney!" Gillett exclaimed. "Thank you! Thank you!"

Again Gillett left the room. This time, as he addressed the crowd, the noise on the other side of the wall subsided until it was as quiet as the proverbial calm after the storm.

When the door opened and closed this time, the only sound was the clicking of the latch.

"They're doing it," Gillett reported. "They're praying, just as you asked."

"Yes, Mr. Gillett. As they should."

Daniel closed his eyes with a prayer of his own—that the two men would leave the room so he could stand up and stretch out the knots in his back.

A commotion from the far side of the room interrupted him. From the sound of it, an entire regiment was storming the room.

"Reverend Gillett," a voice boomed. "Will you kindly tell me what's going on here?"

"Sheriff Beecher!" Gillett said. "Allow me to introduce to you Reverend Charles Finney."

"Finney? I've heard of you. You're the preacher that caused all the ruckus in Western."

"A revival, Sheriff," Gillett corrected him. "Reverend Finney has just agreed to preach at my church tonight."

"So what's going on out there?" the sheriff demanded.

"An inquiry meeting," Gillett answered. "As it turned out, the room was not large enough to accommodate the crowd, and when it threatened to get out of control, Reverend Finney asked everyone to leave."

"Just like that? He asked them to leave?"

"When they wouldn't leave, he asked them to pray."

"To pray?"

"That's what they're doing now, Sheriff. They're praying."

Footsteps could be heard crossing the room. Once again the door to the dining area opened, stayed that way for a minute, then closed.

The sheriff grunted. A favorable grunt, Daniel thought.

"Sheriff Beecher resides in Utica," Gillett explained. "Since we have two courthouses in the county, one at Utica and one here in Rome, he divides his time between the two towns."

"Sheriff," Finney greeted him.

"Mr. Gillett," the sheriff said. "I'd like a word with Reverend Finney in private, if you'll excuse us. Haskins, you and Rollins wait for me outside."

Two additional men accounted for the loud entrance earlier.

Gillett said, "Sheriff, if you've received any complaints about the noise from the meeting, you should talk to me."

"It's a personal matter, Mr. Gillett."

There was a scuffle of feet, followed by the closing of a door. The sheriff and Finney were alone in the room.

At least they thought they were alone.

Ben pulled on Daniel's sleeve, his eyes wide. He mouthed, "What do we do?"

Daniel didn't know. They'd been there so long, to reveal themselves now, and with the sheriff there. . . In his mind he could see only one ending. And it wasn't a happy one.

He pressed his forefinger to his lips.

Ben objected silently.

Daniel persisted, forefinger to lips.

Chairs scraped the wooden floor on the other side of the stacked-tables barrier as the two men sat down.

"How may I be of assistance, Sheriff?" Finney asked.

The sheriff cleared his throat. "I have something to tell you, Reverend Finney, and I don't want it to leave this room."

Finney must have made some kind of nonverbal assent, because the sheriff continued. "As Mr. Gillett indicated, I divide my time between

Utica and Rome, but I board at a hotel in Utica. With travelers coming and going, as you might expect, we have heard news from Western. Reports of the revival, so called."

The sheriff cleared his throat and scraped his chair. "I should tell you that the reports have been a nightly source of amusement and a good deal of laughter around the dinner table."

"You have participated in this amusement, Sheriff?" Finney asked.

"I have often been the instigator," the sheriff replied.

"Why do you tell me this?"

There was a pause, then, "I came to Rome today on official business, on a road I have traveled for more years than I care to count. Today, however, when I crossed the old canal—about a mile from here—a strange and powerful impression came over me. Awe so deep I could not shake it. How to describe it? It was as though God pervaded the whole atmosphere.

"The closer I came to town, the greater the feeling impressed itself upon me. I followed that feeling to this hotel. When Mr. Frank met me outside a short time ago and took my horse, I could see in his eyes that he was feeling exactly the same thing. And he could see it in me. Neither of us spoke. It was as though we were afraid to speak.

"To my surprise, the man with whom I have business was standing nearby. It's a minor matter, so Mr. Frank offered the use of his office. When we went inside, the gentleman could not attend to the business at hand. He rose from the table repeatedly and went to the window to divert his attention, to keep from weeping. I was grateful he did, for if he hadn't, I would have.

"There is such a tangible awe in this town, such solemnity, such a state of things as I have never witnessed in my life. As God is my witness: I will never speak lightly of the things of God again."

CHAPTER 34

"Daniel Cooper! I can't believe you sat there and listened to their conversation!"

Hannah gave the appearance of being offended but seemed more tantalized. She insisted on hearing everything he and Ben overheard. Her eyes lit up with every detail.

They walked side by side, just the two of them.

"What would you have done in our place?" Daniel countered.

"For one thing, I never would have been in your place! You will never see *me* crawling on my hands and knees down an aisle of a public meeting room."

"I told you . . . my uncle was there."

His voice was sharper than he'd intended. It wasn't that he felt threatened by her comments. If anything, he enjoyed sparring with her. But he was angry because while he was walking with Hannah, Ben was with Lucy.

The arrangement made sense. Ben and Lucy lived in town, while Daniel was staying at the Robbins's farm. But the logic of the pairing didn't make Daniel any less angry. He knew how Ben felt about Lucy.

"Well, I'm not convinced you should be running from your uncle . . . the way my father speaks of him."

That did it. It was the drop that burst the dam.

"Why is everyone always on his side?" Daniel thundered.

Hannah looked startled. She stopped walking.

Daniel knew he'd overreacted, but he couldn't contain his frustration any longer. "I'm tired of nobody believing me. That's how all this started. I saw Emil Braxton murdered! I saw Cyrus Gregg in the alley that night. Why won't anyone believe me? Then Cyrus Gregg had me nailed into a coffin so Epps could take me into the woods and kill me! Then I saw Epps kill a harmless man in the forest! And now my uncle and Epps have chased me all the way from Cumberland. For what? What possible reason could they have for pursuing me this far? Yet everyone keeps telling me what a great man my uncle is!"

His chest heaved with rage.

Hannah studied him. Her eyes became tender and moist. She cupped his cheek in her hand. "I believe you."

She spoke so softly that Daniel almost missed it.

"You believe me?"

Hannah nodded.

"But you said—"

"You poor boy," she murmured. "You have seen so much evil . . . been through so much. You've been running so long, you don't feel you can trust anybody. But you can trust us. Ben . . . Lucy . . . me . . . my father. You're among friends now. Can't you see that?"

Maybe it was because he was so tired, or that it had been so long since he'd had friends that weren't musical instruments, but Daniel found it difficult to hold back his emotions.

"Thank you," he mumbled. "You're right. I'm out of practice at being a friend. You may have to remind me of the rules from time to time."

The clatter of an approaching carriage interrupted them. Daniel's head snapped around. The carriage was large, with front and back seats. It slowed. Hannah greeted the driver, a weathered old man, and his equally weathered wife. She introduced Daniel to the Gowers, who owned the farm next to theirs.

Mr. Gower offered them a ride. Hannah refused with a sweet smile. As Mrs. Gower eyed her and then Daniel with amused interest, Hannah blushed.

As the carriage continued down the road, Daniel wondered if there would come a time when he no longer jumped at the sound of carriages. He told himself he'd be safe once they reached the farm. Why had Hannah refused the offer of a ride?

It was twilight. The heavenly canopy was translucent blue. They walked in silence. Hannah's hands had retreated into the warmth of a muff. The cold wind kissed her cheeks red.

"Is there a girl in Cumberland?" she asked without looking at him.

"Aya," he replied. "Plenty of girls in Cumberland."

A hand came out of the muff long enough to slap his shoulder. "You know what I mean."

He enjoyed the attack. "There is no girl in Cumberland waiting for me."

"Why not?"

"Such intimate questions," he teased her. "Very unbecoming in a lady."

"They're not intimate!" she protested. "I'm curious, that's all. Is there a law that prohibits curiosity?"

"No law. But I've heard it's fatal to felines."

"Are you going to answer the question?"

Daniel grimaced. "Whatever I say . . . you'll hit me."

"I will not."

"Will too."

"Just tell me!"

"All right. It's simple. They're too smart. They know better than to waste their time on someone like me."

She hit him.

"Ow! See? I knew you'd hit me."

"Well, you deserved it."

Daniel rubbed his shoulder, more for show than from pain. They walked a little farther.

Hannah broached a question. "Do . . . do you and Ben talk about me?"

Daniel sensed dangerous terrain ahead. He decided a guarded approach would be wise.

"Aya. We talk. Not a lot."

"What does he say about me?"

"I'm not sure I should—"

"He knows, doesn't he?"

Hannah wasn't even listening to him. Her head was down. "He knows that I don't . . . love him . . . romantically, I mean."

"You don't?"

He hadn't known Hannah, Ben, and Lucy for a very long time, yet everything he thought he knew about them was unraveling.

Shocked at his reply, Hannah's hands flew out of her muff to her mouth. "He *doesn't* know?" She turned away, unable to face him. "But the way he's been acting . . . oh, why did I say anything? I never should have told you!"

"You really don't love him?"

Her hands flopped helplessly at her sides. "What am I going to do?"

Daniel did a little hand-flopping of his own. Should he tell her? Ben had sworn him to confidence. If Hannah and Ben felt this way about each other, why were they telling him and not each other? He'd be doing them a favor to say something, wouldn't he?

On the other hand, if Ben knew Hannah didn't want to marry him, Ben would be free to pursue Lucy. So it was better to keep silent, wasn't it?

Hannah closed her eyes and tilted her head heavenward in silent agony. Daniel's chest hurt to see her like this.

"Well, say something!" she yelled in exasperation, her head still back, her eyes still closed.

"Um . . . are you talking to me or to God?"

Hannah's head rolled toward him. Her eyes opened. She laughed. "You really haven't been around girls much, have you?"

"It's that obvious?"

"Yes, dear, it is."

Shaking her head, she slipped her arm inside his and tugged him down the road. "So tell me. Are we going to have to hit you over the head to get you to go to the revival services tonight?"

Daniel wasn't sure what had happened or how she could change topics and moods so quickly. But it got him off the hook, so he liked it. All except for the new topic.

"I'd better not risk it. I'm still not sure where my—"

"Where your uncle is," she finished. "I've been thinking about that. You saw him at the hotel, right?"

"Aya."

"Was he there for the meeting of inquiry, or was he there because he lodged there last night?"

"I'm not sure. I haven't thought about that."

"Well, think about it. He's looking for you, right?"

"Right."

"So, given your deep-seated dread of religious meetings, does it make sense that he would look for you at that meeting?"

"Hmmm . . . I hadn't thought . . ."

"Aya. We've already established the fact that you're not thinking," she said with an impish grin.

"Hey! That was uncalled for!"

Hannah paid no mind to his protest. "Which means your uncle was there because he'd stayed the night. Now what if we got my father to check at the front desk and see if your uncle's still registered at the hotel? If he's checked out, it makes sense that he's moved on, doesn't it?"

"Not your father," Daniel objected. "Because if my uncle is there, he'll want to talk to him, and my uncle will convince him that I'm lying, and then your father will want to play peacemaker, and—"

"Whoa! Slow down. All right. If not my father, then . . ."

"Ben. We can get Ben to do it. No, wait . . . they've seen Ben. What if they recognize him?"

"He'll just have to be careful. Don't underestimate Ben."

"He saved me once already."

"Then it's settled. Once Ben learns that your uncle is no longer at the hotel, we can assume they've left town, and you'll be free to attend tonight's meeting."

"Aya, wait! You tricked me!"

But it was too late. And from the smile on Hannah's face, she knew exactly what she'd done.

Robely Epps stifled a yawn as Asa queried a local farmer they'd overtaken on the road. Asa was leaning against the side of the farmer's wagon. They'd been at it for nearly ten minutes. Slouched in the carriage, Epps waited as darkness crept over them.

During the last few weeks they'd learned that they fared better with the locals if Asa questioned them alone. Something about Epps's appearance made them nervous.

He grinned.

To himself, he said, *A time for honey, and a time for terror. Isn't that what the Good Book says?*

He repositioned himself on the seat. The pistol in his waistband dug into him. Muttering a curse, Epps repositioned it. He'd been fighting it all day.

Buying the pistol had been a mistake, something done in a moment of weakness. Cowards killed from a distance. Anyone could pull a trigger. It took a man to kill with a knife.

With a knife you had to get close to your victim. So close that—if he was quick enough and strong enough—he could kill you. What satisfaction was there in killing with a pistol? A mechanical thunder, the odor of gun powder . . . these were artificial sensations that could not compare to the animal pleasure a man sensed hearing another man's scream, smelling the fear in his sweat, overpowering his resistance, and then feeling the life drain from him until it was gone.

Laughter cut into Epps's reverie. Asa and the farmer had found something amusing.

Epps rebuked himself for getting too close to Asa. He enjoyed the man's company, though Epps thought him unrealistic about the realities of life. But he admired Asa's persistence to travel this far to track down a whiny, ungrateful, good-for-nothing nephew. Few men would do that for a son. His father never would have.

Leaning heavily on his cane, Asa limped back. The carriage tipped as he climbed in.

"He hasn't seen him," Asa reported.

Epps chuckled. "It took him that long to tell you he hasn't seen him?"

Asa laughed. The farmer had put Asa in a good mood.

"Turns out, he has a cousin that lives in Greenfield."

The town's name meant nothing to Epps. He waited for more.

"Greenfield, Massachusetts. I grew up there."

"Do you know his cousin?"

"I know the family. Don't recall ever meeting the cousin."

Asa slumped back, watching the back of the farmer's wagon as it ambled down the road. His good humor departed with the farmer.

"So where do we go from here?" Epps asked.

"Home. I'm done." The words themselves were weary.

"You've done more than most men in your situation," Epps said.

"And so have you, my friend."

Asa reached over and slapped Epps good-naturedly on the leg. As he did, Asa's forearm hit the butt of the concealed pistol.

Alarmed, Epps tensed.

"You've gone the extra mile, my friend." Asa showed no concern or curiosity over what was beneath Epps's coat.

"I've gone more than a mile," Epps said, keeping the conversation going.

Asa smiled. "You misunderstand. It's a biblical expression. To go the extra mile means—"

"Roman rule. Military occupation. The law required that locals assist a Roman soldier for a mile. Jesus taught that a good man would go two miles."

Asa shook his head in wonder. "This from a boy who never finished school? Robely Epps, all my professional life I have prayed that God would send me young men like you."

"Don't say that," Epps said.

"You not only have intelligence but determination. You can do anything you set your mind to, do you know that? What can I say to convince you to come back to Cumberland with me?"

Epps could feel his anger rising. Talk like that only made it more difficult for him to kill Asa. "Don't say things like that."

"Why not? I have faith in you. Somebody should have told you these things years ago. And it's still not too late. I could introduce you to some men in Cumberland. I have a good friend who—"

"Syracuse." Epps used the word as a stopper, to plug up the flow of words coming from Asa's mouth.

It worked.

Asa waited for more.

"Syracuse. My destiny lies in Syracuse."

Disappointment showed on Asa's face. But he recovered from it with the agility of a man experienced at handling disappointment. "Syracuse? When we first met, you told me you thought your fortune lay somewhere up here with the canal. So you've narrowed it down to Syracuse?"

"When we passed through it," Epps lied. "Utica . . . Rome . . . too small for my taste. I had a good feeling about Syracuse."

"Good!" Asa said with forced enthusiasm. "Good! Syracuse is a good choice." He grabbed the reigns and turned the carriage around.

"Tonight, we'll stay in Rome," Asa announced, "then tomorrow we head back. At least I have between Rome and Syracuse to try and twist your arm into coming back with me to Cumberland." He clucked his tongue and the horse responded.

Epps rode in silence. Sullen.

"Why the long face?" Asa asked him. "The last couple of days it's been obvious that something's been weighing on your mind. Now that the decision's made for Syracuse, you should feel relieved."

Epps took a deep breath. "I am."

"Well, someone ought to inform your face!" Asa said, laughing.

"It's a parting sadness. I'm going to miss your company."

That much was true.

"Well, there's one remedy to that," Asa added.

Epps ignored him.

They crossed an old canal bridge. As they did, a heavy sensation pressed down upon Epps, as though the atmosphere had become thick, making it difficult to breathe.

"You feel it too?" Asa asked. "It's hard to put your finger on, isn't it? But there's definitely something here. I felt something similar to it a long time ago, in New Haven."

CHAPTER 35

For not wanting to be in church, Daniel was having a good time. He'd settled into the pew with Hannah on his right and Lucy on his left. A disgruntled Ben sat on the other side of Hannah, between her and her father.

This was the seat Daniel had wanted. So had Ben. When they entered the church, Ben had jockeyed to position himself between the girls. Daniel had decided not to fight him for it.

Lucy had evidently noticed too. For reasons of her own, she had grabbed Daniel's arm, pulled him beside her, and orchestrated the seating.

"Daniel, you sit by me. Hannah, you next, then Ben."

They fell into line, and Ben took to sulking. Daniel wondered if Lucy knew how Hannah and Ben felt about each other.

The pews were packed. People stood in the aisles. Even though it was January, windows were open so those standing outside could hear.

Daniel's presence had been ordained when Ben reported that, according to the hotel front desk, Asa Rush had checked out earlier that day. The owner, Mr. Frank, told Ben that he had last seen Asa Rush with a tall, bearded man riding east.

Hannah grinned at the news.

On the way to the church it was decided—by Lucy and Hannah—that after the service they would all go to the Robbins's barn. There they could talk, and Daniel could play his recorder like he did the night they found him in the hayloft.

Daniel hadn't felt this relaxed since the night of Braxton's murder. His plan was to endure the sermon and enjoy the rest of the evening with his friends.

Hannah and Ben sat stiff and silent as they waited for the service to begin. Mr. Robbins stood in the aisle chatting with a sad-eyed man of about forty. He spoke with the animated gestures of a man who didn't get off the farm often enough.

Very much aware of Lucy's physical presence next to him, Daniel searched for something to say. Something witty. He glanced over at her, trying not to be obvious about it.

Lucy sat with perfect posture, head erect, her eyes closed, her lips moving ever so slightly.

Daniel whispered to her, "I think that's a record. Most people don't fall asleep until after the sermon begins."

Lucy frowned. Without opening her eyes, she shushed him. "I'm praying for you," she whispered back.

Daniel sat back, stung by the shush.

Well, at least she was thinking of him.

The buzz in the room dissipated as Reverend Gillett and Reverend Finney appeared on the front platform. While Daniel had seen Gillett before, for some reason he looked taller than he had this afternoon. He towered over Finney.

Gillett went to the pulpit. Finney took a seat.

Maybe it was the fact that they were in a church and not a converted dining room, but Gillett didn't have the same trouble getting the group's attention as he had at the hotel.

"At Reverend Finney's request," he said, "many of you have been much in prayer for this meeting. I have assured him of Rome's fervent desire that God grace our town with revival. Accordingly, he has agreed to address us on the subject of spiritual revival, and how we might promote revival here in Rome."

A general stir in the congregation suggested that not everyone liked the topic. Daniel had heard that some objected to the idea that revival was something that could be promoted. He looked to see Finney's reaction. His stoic expression remained unchanged.

"Furthermore," Gillett said, pressing on, "we have decided to dispense with the singing of hymns, to give Reverend Finney as much time as possible."

Daniel frowned. He would have preferred more hymns and less preaching.

"Reverend Finney," Gillett said, handing the pulpit over to the evangelist.

Charles Finney stood. In his midthirties, he had angular features and a high forehead. His eyes, clear and so piercing they could bore a hole through a tree, were his most striking feature. Finney carried a Bible, which he opened and placed in front of him on the pulpit.

"Our text for this evening is Hosea 10:12." His voice cut through the room like a knife.

Daniel glanced at his friends. All three were leaning forward, as if they were dying of thirst and this man was about to tell them where they could find an oasis.

"Break up your fallow ground;" Finney read, "for it is time to seek the Lord, till he come and rain righteousness upon you."

The carriage pulled up in front of the hotel. Asa handed the reigns to Epps. Out of courtesy to his friend, Asa didn't offer to share his room. Epps appeared to appreciate the nonoffer.

"Same time in the morning?" Epps asked.

"Aya," Asa grunted as he pulled a bag from the back of the carriage.

He noticed a wooden box that he hadn't seen before in the back of the carriage, but he didn't ask about it. It wasn't his, which meant it wasn't his business.

Bag in hand, Asa stepped away from the carriage.

Epps didn't look good.

"Are you all right?" Asa asked.

Epps shuddered. "I'll just be glad when we leave this place."

"Anxious to start your new life in Syracuse?"

Epps forced a grin. "Something like that." With a snap of the reigns, he drove away.

Asa toted his bag into the hotel, where the counter attendant greeted him by name.

"Thought you'd moved on," said the attendant.

"Change of plans," Asa said, scanning the lobby of the deserted hotel. "Quiet tonight."

"Aya," the attendant explained. "Everyone's at the church. Revival services. Finney's preaching."

Asa signed the register. "The preacher from Western."

"I heard he came out of the church at Evans Mills. But yeah, he's been making a stir in Western."

"Have you heard him? Is he a good preacher?"

The attendant handed Asa a key. "You're asking the wrong fellow. I'm of the opinion that the words *good* and *preacher* don't belong in the same sentence."

The attendant motioned to a boy to help Asa with his bags. Asa thanked him. He took a step toward his room, then turned back to the counter.

"Where is this church? I might wander over there later."

On the way to church, Mr. Robbins had told them that Finney had trained to become a lawyer. Daniel could see it. The man addressed the congregation as though they were a jury. "The Jews were a nation of farmers, and it is therefore a common thing in the Scriptures to refer for illustrations to their occupation, and to the scenes with which farmers and shepherds are familiar.

"What is it to break up fallow ground? To break up the fallow ground is to break up your hearts—to prepare your minds to bring forth fruit unto God. To break up the fallow ground is to bring the mind into such a state that it is fitted to receive the Word of God. You must begin by looking at your hearts. Many never seem to think about this. They pay no attention to their own hearts, and never know whether they are doing well in religion or not—whether they are gaining ground or going back—whether they are fruitful, or lying waste like the fallow ground.

"Examine thoroughly the state of your hearts, and see where you are—whether you are walking with God every day, or walking with the devil—whether you are serving God or serving the devil most—whether you are under the dominion of the prince of darkness, or of the Lord Jesus Christ."

Finney went on to describe fallow ground as cultivated land that is allowed to lie idle for a season. It's packed down, hard, and unproductive unless broken up. Breaking up such ground is a violent process whereby the farmer's blade cuts into the hardened surface and forcibly turns everything upside down, so that which has been hidden below is now brought to the surface.

Daniel didn't like this sermon. He believed that some things were buried for a reason and that they were best left buried.

"Break up all the ground and turn it over," Finney preached. "Do not balk it, as the farmers say; do not turn aside for little difficulties; drive the plow right through them, beam deep, and turn the ground all up, so that it may all be mellow and soft, and fit to receive the seed and bear fruit a hundredfold.

"It will do no good to preach to you while your hearts are in this hardened, and waste, and fallow state. The farmer might just as well sow his grain on the rock. This is the reason why there are so many fruitless professors in the church, and why there is so much outside machinery, and so little deep-toned feeling in the church. If you go on this way, the

Word of God will continue to harden you, and you will grow worse and worse, just as the rain and snow on an old fallow field makes the turf thicker, and the clods stronger."

Hannah whispered to Daniel, "Sit still!"

"I am sitting still!"

"You're fidgeting like a little boy."

She was right. Daniel hadn't noticed it until she said something. It gave him an idea. He started to get up.

Hannah yanked him back down. "Where do you think you're going?"

"Excuse me, but I have to step out."

"Do you see your uncle?"

"No."

"Then sit down."

She looped her arm in his and held him down. On the other side, Lucy did the same. Daniel found it to be a most delicious sensation to have a girl on each arm. Why did it have to be in church? He sat back.

Finney stepped to the side of the pulpit to press his point. "Take up your individual sins one by one, and look at them. I do not mean that you should just cast a glance at your past life, and see that it has been full of sins, and then go to God and make a sort of general confession, and ask for pardon. Go over them as carefully as a merchant goes over his books. Your sins were committed one by one; and as far as you can come at them, they ought to be reviewed and repented one by one. Now begin."

At this point, Finney began listing sins, beginning with sins of omission:

1. Ingratitude. You have received favors from God for which you have never exercised gratitude.

2. Want of love to God. Have you not given your heart to other loves; played the harlot, and offended Him?

3. Neglect of the Bible. Put down the cases when for days, and perhaps weeks—yea, months together—you had no pleasure in

God's Word.

4. Unbelief. Instances in which you have virtually charged the God of truth with lying, by your unbelief of His express promises and declarations.
5. Neglect of prayer.
6. Your want of love for the souls of your fellowmen. Look round upon your friends and relations, and remember how little compassion you have felt for them.
7. Your neglect of family duties.

From these sins, he turned to the sins of commission:

1. Worldly mindedness. What has been the state of your heart in regard to your worldly possessions? Have you looked at them as really yours?
2. Pride.
3. Envy.
4. Censoriousness. Instances in which you have had a bitter spirit, and spoke of Christians in a manner entirely devoid of charity and love.

The blade cut deep on that one. Daniel felt it down to his soul.

While Finney continued with his list—slander, levity, lying, cheating, hypocrisy, robbing God, bad temper, hindering others from being useful—Daniel no longer heard him.

His mind was thousands of miles away . . . far from land . . . bobbing on the turbulent Atlantic waves . . . with pieces of wreckage and human cargo . . . shirts, shoes, books, a pipe, a platter. Common items that are out of place floating in water, then dipping beneath the surface, then sinking, along with the people who once used them.

Though he'd never seen them before in life, he saw the faces of the people who had drowned that dreadful day over a year ago. Their flesh was tinted blue and green, their arms stretched wide in resignation to death. Fully clothed, they looked ridiculous in their shoes. What good were shoes to a man or woman in the ocean?

Two of the faces he recognized, despite the distortion of the water. Their images were so real to him, it was as though he were sinking with them.

Across time, his father gazed at him. Recognition filled his eyes—of Daniel's presence, of what was happening to him. His mother's gaze, too, was a tender good-bye. She spoke his name, her words becoming bubbles that never reached him.

Then, arms outstretched, his parents reached for each other, clasped hands, and sank into the inky depths.

And God's blade cut deep into Daniel's heart, a heart that had been packed down and hardened with anger and rage and tears and pain. The blade turned all these things up to the surface.

With the scream of a wounded animal, Daniel slid from the pew and onto his knees.

CHAPTER 36

Standing beside the pulpit, Finney pressed for a verdict: "How can you stand before God in the judgment, if your excuses are so mean that you cannot seriously think of bringing one of them before God in this world? O, sinner, that coming day will be far more searching and awful than anything you have seen yet.

"See that dense mass of sinners drawn up before the great white throne—as far as the eye can sweep they are surging up—a countless throng; and now they stand, and the awful trump of God summons them forward to bring forth their excuses for sin."

Daniel crouched on the floor between pews, his face buried in his hands. Hannah knelt beside him on one side, Lucy on the other. He heard their voices. Felt their warm hands on his back. He wished they would go away.

The weight of his sin pressed him against the floor. The blackness of the sin plunged him into despair.

All this time he'd blamed God for killing his parents. Thought Him cruel and barbarous, a capricious tyrant playing with life and death and having no greater feelings for them than a boy would have for his toy soldiers.

What kind of monster would kill the very people who'd dedicated themselves to serving Him? To teaching others about Him? To calling others to worship Him? What kind of a ruler would repay this kind of adoration by suffocating them in the sea and sending them to a watery grave?

But here, tonight, before God, his accusations were as substantial as ashes.

"Ho, sinners—any one of you, all—what have you to say why sentence should not be passed on you? Where are all those excuses you were once so free and bold to make? Where are they all? Why don't you make them now? Hark! God waits; He listens; there is silence in heaven—all through the congregated throng—for half an hour—an awful silence—that may be felt; but not a word—not a moving lip among the gathered myriads of sinners there; and now the great and dreadful Judge arises and lets loose His thunders. O, see the waves of dire damnation roll over those ocean-masses of self-condemned sinners."

It wasn't Daniel's parents who had sunk into the depths, he realized. It was him. He may be the one who was still breathing, but they were more alive now than he'd ever been.

His anger was a great weight, a ponderous chain that dragged him deeper and deeper into the depths.

"Did you ever see the judge rise from his bench in court to pass sentence of death on a criminal? There, see, the poor man reels—he falls prostrate—there is no longer any strength in him, for death is on him and his last hope has perished!

"O sinner, when that sentence from the dread throne shall fall on thee! Your excuses are as millstones around your neck as you plunge along down the sides of the pit to the nethermost hell!"

Voices surrounded Daniel, praying for him. Hannah. Lucy. Ben. Mr. Robbins. For him! They didn't even know him! They didn't know the magnitude of his sin, the blackness of his despair—or how it had pounded him, worn him down, day after day, like a relentless wave beating against rocky shoals.

They didn't know that he didn't deserve God's forgiveness. He didn't deserve to be called a Cooper. His petty, self-centered life had sullied his father's good name. What good was he to anyone?

Every time the preacher cried, "O sinner!" Daniel heard him say, "O Daniel!"

His guilt was evident. He knew it. The Judge knew it. He was without excuse. He deserved to die.

In Daniel's mind he could see the Judge rise from his bench, just as the preacher described. The Judge rose to pass sentence. There was no suspense. The verdict was not in question.

The omnipotent Judge raised his gavel and cried, *"Forgiven!"*

Daniel's head jolted up.

Forgiven!

He refused to believe it. Yet how many times had he heard his father preach it? Grace, grace, God's grace . . .

Forgiven!

Three times he heard the gavel sound. Three times he heard the verdict.

The chains fell from him.

Resigned to hopelessness, his heart flooded with relief and joy.

For the first time in as long as he could remember, Daniel wanted to live.

His face buried in his hands, he muttered, "The cross . . . the cross . . . the cross . . . the cross!"

Night never smelled as fresh.

Daniel stepped from the church giddy with life. He hadn't realized how great was the weight he'd been carrying around. He felt like he could fly.

What was it Ben had said the other night in the barn? *"We're going to have to backslide to get to sleep?"* The joke seemed funnier now that Daniel could identify with it.

Lucy, Hannah, and Ben were clustered around him, talking excitedly.

"Look at you!" Lucy exclaimed. "You can see the change! You see it, don't you, Hannah? He used to have a brooding aura about him."

"I was worried about you for a while," Ben said. "The way you dropped to the floor. The Spirit must have hit you hard."

Uncharacteristically quiet, Hannah smiled.

Daniel's mind raced ahead to the barn. He remembered the way the three of them had stormed into it the other night while he was sleeping in the hayloft. They were laughing and falling all over each other. At the time he had envied them. Now he was one of them.

He couldn't wait to get there tonight. To reenact that scene. To laugh. To have fun. To play his music. To steal glimpses of Lucy.

Lucy!

He glanced over at her and smiled.

She responded by taking his arm. Daniel's head swam. Could this night get any better?

People everywhere were in a good mood as they streamed out of the church and onto the road, walking together as families and side by side with friends. They were genial. Courteous. Strangers conversed with strangers as though they'd been lifelong friends.

For the first time Daniel understood why his father had labored so diligently to preach the Bible. Growing up, he'd always thought that the purpose of the Bible was to guilt people into being good. Not until tonight did he understand its miraculous power.

The Daniel who walked out of the church was a different Daniel from the one who had gone in.

A little ways in front of them, a group of people were saying their good-byes to go their separate ways. There was a lot of neck hugging and handshakes. Then, when they departed, it was as though a stage curtain opened.

And there, standing in what would be center stage, leaning on his cane, was Uncle Asa. Next to him stood a tall man with an imposing presence.

"Daniel?" his uncle said.

Daniel slowed. The others kept walking, then noticed something wrong. They turned to see why.

They saw what Daniel saw. Nobody spoke. Nobody moved.

Then Ben touched Daniel's arm. "Maybe it's time you stopped running. We're here with you."

Daniel took a step forward. "I'm not afraid."

He walked toward his uncle. His uncle walked toward him. They met in the middle of the street.

His uncle was the first to speak. "I've imagined this moment a thousand times—what I'd say to you when I finally found you. And now that you're here . . ." He took a deep breath. "Daniel, I don't pretend to understand . . ."

Daniel stepped forward. He put his arms around his uncle's neck and hugged him. "You never meant to hurt me. I know that now."

"Hurt you? Son, I'd give my life before I'd ever let anything hurt you."

Behind the hotel Epps stood in the shadows and watched Asa and the boy hugging each other. Epps's hand rested on the butt of the pistol in his waistband. His pulse quickened.

One tonight. One tomorrow.

One with a pistol. One with a knife.

He liked that the killing would have a sense of poetry to it, which the scene did not. The scene disturbed him. It lacked the conflict he'd expected to see.

Why wasn't Asa shouting?

Why wasn't the boy running?

It didn't make sense, and to a man who made his living anticipating the actions of his prey, surprises could be fatal.

At the same time, the scene accomplished something good. Seeing the uncle and boy reunited and amicable made it easier for him to kill the uncle.

While others might be heartened by this reunion, to Epps it was a scene of betrayal. Asa had gone over to the enemy. Epps should have known, should have seen it coming. He knew better than to trust the man. He'd allowed himself to be taken in by the man's flattery.

Epps drew the pistol from his waistband.

He'd save the knife for the boy.

In the center of the road, Asa and Daniel stepped back from each other.

Epps had an angle on them. The boy's back. Asa's front. The man wiped tears from his eyes.

Epps cocked the pistol.

The boy's friends held back, giving the two time alone and Epps a clear shot. He raised the pistol, leveling the sight on Asa's chest.

The movement of a man behind Asa caught Epps's attention. The man had tall, broad shoulders and was staring directly at Epps with a steely glare.

Epps evaluated his position. He was concealed. The man couldn't see him. It had to be coincidence that he was looking in Epps's direction.

Then the man took a step toward Epps. And another. Something about him commanded attention. Despite the fact that Epps was certain he was hidden from view, the man's eyes remained locked on him with a gaze that could be felt even at a distance.

Robely Epps lowered the pistol and eased deeper into the shadows. His retreating footfalls echoed in the alley.

CHAPTER 37

"I can't believe Asa Rush is sitting at my kitchen table."

Mr. Robbins circled the table pouring coffee and did a little dance that prompted a laugh from everyone except Hannah, who blushed and scolded him in a good-natured way.

"You think it's hard to believe Uncle Asa is sitting here. Imagine how it feels for me!" Daniel said.

Another round of laughs.

From the sounds coming from upstairs, the mood was equally joyous as Mrs. Robbins put the girls to bed. The pounding of girlish feet running up and down the hallway and high-pitched squeals was interrupted by the occasional motherly warnings and reproofs.

At the table, Robbins moved from person to person, filling coffee cups. Salvos of jest and banter flew back and forth. Daniel found himself smiling a lot and simply enjoying being where he was.

He amused himself watching his new friends dress up their coffee. Lucy added cream and two sugars; Hannah two sugars; Ben added double cream and three sugars, sneaking the last helping when he thought nobody was watching.

"Question," Uncle Asa said.

The declamation was his schoolmaster method of commanding

attention. It had always irritated Daniel. Tonight it didn't.

Attention around the table turned to Uncle Asa. Robbins poured the last cup of coffee—his—and set the pot aside. He took a seat next to his guest.

"Daniel," his uncle asked, "why didn't you run? You've been running from me for weeks. Why not tonight?"

Eyes turned to Daniel. Memory flashes of school played in his head, uncomfortable images of being singled out among his classmates. He ignored them. For some reason, he didn't mind being singled out tonight. The friendly gaze of everyone around the table didn't bother him.

"My first instinct was to run," he admitted.

"But you didn't. Why?"

Even now the recollection of his experience in the road brought a warm feeling. "It was your friend," Daniel said. "There was something about him. An assurance . . . a calmness. It's hard to describe, but the moment I saw him I knew I had nothing to fear."

"My friend?" Uncle Asa said.

"The man standing next to you."

Asa shook his head. "There was no one standing next to me."

Ben took exception. "No . . . there most definitely was someone standing beside you."

Asa chuckled. "I'm telling you, there was nobody standing beside me! I left the hotel alone. I stood alone."

"I saw him too," Lucy said. "He had the kindest eyes."

"And he was strong," Hannah added. "You could tell just by his bearing. He radiated . . . oh, I don't know . . . *confidence.* That's the best I can describe it."

Lucy gasped. "You don't suppose . . ." She shivered with excitement.

A ripple of awe like an electrical charge circled the table.

"Did anyone see where he went?" Ben asked. "I remember seeing him, but I don't remember seeing where he went after that."

"Now that you mention it . . . ," Daniel said.

"I was so caught up watching Daniel and his uncle . . . ," Hannah said.

"His work was finished," Lucy said.

Uncle Asa looked dubious. "If I were standing that close to an angel, don't you think I would have seen or felt something?"

"Not if you were in a backslidden condition," Daniel joked.

The table quieted. Everyone exchanged glances, as if uncertain how the great Asa Rush would react to such a statement.

He laughed. Not one of those polite laughs, but from the heart.

Everyone joined him.

Daniel couldn't remember ever laughing with his uncle. He liked it.

"Strange and mysterious things happen when the Spirit moves," Robbins said.

Although Daniel knew Mr. Robbins was referring to the possibility they'd seen an angel, he couldn't think of anything stranger at the moment than sitting at a table with his uncle and having a good time.

"After all that's happened, it's not surprising that it took a miracle to get Daniel and me together." Uncle Asa sobered. "I still find it hard to believe you thought I would be part of an attempt to kill you."

Daniel said, "If you'd seen Epps do the things I've seen him do, it wouldn't seem so far-fetched."

"Yes, well, about that . . . I've spent a good deal of time with Robely. He's intelligent, resourceful. To think he's capable of the things you claim he's done . . ."

Daniel tensed. Maybe things hadn't changed as much as he'd thought. He happened to glance at Hannah. She pleaded silently with him to keep calm.

"I'm not saying I don't believe you," his uncle said. "Your description of the man in the forest . . . it had to be Watkins—Timothy was his name, if I remember correctly—from the bank at Green Ridge. The poor man agreed to carry a message to Camilla for me, which makes me wonder now if she's received any of the messages I've sent her." Uncle Asa stared at the table in thought.

"This Epps fellow, where is he now?" Robbins asked.

Asa lifted his head and spoke in a detached voice. "Can't say for certain. He didn't like hotels, so he'd take my carriage and go off by himself. He'll pick me up in the morning. We'd planned to leave for Syracuse."

"If it's all the same to you," Robbins said, "I'm going to invite the sheriff to be there to meet this Epps when he arrives in the morning."

Daniel folded his arms and sat back in his chair. His uncle still didn't believe him. Not until the sheriff proved him right about Epps would his uncle believe him, which meant his uncle still didn't believe him about Cyrus Gregg, either.

Robbins threw his hands wide emphatically. "I'll tell you what I can't believe! I still can't believe I have Asa Rush and the son of Eli Cooper sitting at my kitchen table! And for both of them to appear right as another revival breaks out! God's hand is in it, that's all I have to say."

No one disagreed with him.

"Asa—what do you think of the revival?" Robbins asked. "In your opinion, how does it compare to the Yale revival?"

"I'm afraid I don't have enough evidence to form an opinion," Uncle Asa said. "But I sense something. God is here. But I have yet to witness anything directly."

"You've seen more than you're aware of," Robbins said.

"The angel," Lucy offered.

"I was thinking of those present at this table." Robbins smiled at his daughter.

"We're all a product of the revival, Mr. Rush," Hannah replied. "Lucy, Ben, myself—"

"—and Daniel," Ben inserted. "The revival's most notorious convert."

Daniel took the comment as it was intended, as a good-natured rib between friends. It made him feel accepted.

"Maybe if you heard more about the revival and Reverend Finney . . . ," Robbins suggested. "Let me tell you one of my favorite Finney stories."

He sat forward, arms on the table, in storyteller fashion. "I like this story because, having cut my teeth on the docks, I know how rough a neighborhood it can be. Then again, maybe I like the story because it shows the innate compassion of—"

"Papa," Hannah interrupted, "just tell the story!"

"Right." Robbins winked. To Asa he said, "Hannah's always looking out for me when her mother's not around. Even when she was little. One time—"

"Papa? The story?"

The way she spoke to her father and the playful way he responded to her stirred Daniel in a way that he couldn't begin to explain. Somehow the love of her father made Hannah more attractive. She had a glow about her. Daniel could hardly take his eyes off her.

"This incident took place in a harbor town before Finney became a Christian," Robbins began. "At the time, he had thoughts of enlisting in the navy. While he was walking along the boardwalk, this pretty young prostitute walks up to him and propositions him. Finney looks her in the eyes . . . she looks at him . . . and Finney breaks into tears, so overcome is he with the circumstances that would turn a lovely young girl into a prostitute! Seeing his compassion, the girl breaks into tears. Both of them stand there, weeping, on the docks. Finally they turn and go their separate ways."

"Ahhh!" Lucy said. "That's sweet!"

"Tell Mr. Rush the prayer meeting story in Western," Ben urged.

Robbins sat back in his chair. "You like that one, do you? Go ahead, Ben. You tell it."

From his startled expression, it was obvious that Ben hadn't expected to find himself the center of attention. But he warmed to it.

"Well, the way I heard it," he said, "a church in Western asked Reverend Finney to come and lead their prayer meeting. He agreed to attend but declined to lead it, preferring to hear them pray and talk. So one of the elders stood and opened the meeting by reading a chapter in the Bible and then leading them in a hymn. After that he launched into a prayer that became a very, very long prayer—more like a narration.

"The man told the Lord how they'd been holding prayer meetings weekly at the church for many years, and that they'd seen no answers to their prayers. After he was done, another elder stood and began to pray, going over the same ground. Then a third elder prayed in similar fashion. All the while Finney fidgeted, as if he could hardly contain himself.

"When they finished praying, before they dismissed the meeting, one of the elders turned to Mr. Finney and asked him if he would care to make any remarks to the group."

From the expression on their faces, Daniel could tell that Lucy and Hannah had heard this story before. They grinned in anticipation of what was to come.

"Well, Reverend Finney stood," Ben continued. "At first, he had no idea what he was going to say. Then, looking at them, he said, 'Would you mock God?' And he proceeded to tell them that God never shirks on a prayer, and that He had not answered their prayers because they didn't expect Him to answer their prayers."

"He said that?" Uncle Asa asked.

Robbins said, "The story comes from a reliable source—one of the elders himself. Go on, Ben."

There was a twinkle in Ben's eyes as he continued. "At first, they were angry. Some were so angry that they were ready to get up and walk out. Then the elder who opened the meeting burst into tears. 'Mr. Finney, it's all true! Every word of it is true!' Weeping, he fell to his knees.

"Before long, all the people in the room were on their knees, weeping and confessing and pouring out their hearts to God. Finney told them he believed that if they would unite and pray in faith that afternoon for an outpouring of God's Spirit, they would receive an answer from heaven sooner than they could get a message from Albany by the quickest post that could be sent.

"The people of the church prevailed on Finney to stay with them and preach to them, and when he saw the condition of their hearts, he consented to stay with them and preach that following Sunday. Well, the Spirit fell with great power that Sunday, and pretty soon Finney was preaching in businesses and hotels and schoolhouses. That's how the revival started in Western," Ben concluded in storyteller fashion. "And it did come sooner than a post from Albany."

"I didn't come after you to insist you return with me to Cumberland," Asa said.

Daniel and his uncle stood under the stars between the house and the barn. Ben was helping Mr. Robbins hitch up the horse. Hannah and Lucy were still in the house.

"Then why did you come after me?" Daniel asked.

"To make sure you were safe and to let you know that you will always have a home with me and your aunt."

"What about the money Cyrus Gregg claims I stole?"

"Did you steal it?"

"No."

His uncle nodded. "That's good enough for me."

"But you still don't believe me about Mr. Gregg."

The way his uncle sighed, it was obvious he didn't. "Cyrus Gregg has been a friend for years . . ."

Daniel turned to walk away.

His uncle caught him by the arm. "A man gives his friends the benefit of the doubt. Put yourself in my place. I don't know what's going on. I admit that. I thought I knew Robely Epps. Apparently I don't. He fooled me. But if he fooled me, isn't it possible that he's also fooled Cyrus Gregg?"

"What about family?" Daniel asked. "Aren't you supposed to give family the benefit of the doubt too?"

The carriage with Robbins and Ben emerged from the barn. Lucy and Hannah stepped from the house, bundled against the crisp January night.

Lucy, eyes sparkling, ran to Daniel and took him by the arm. "You're riding with us, aren't you?"

Daniel glanced at Ben sitting alone in the back of the carriage. There was plenty of room for three.

"No," Daniel said. "I think I'll stay here."

Lucy's lower lip protruded in a pout. Daniel didn't give her a chance to change his mind. He helped her into the back of the carriage beside a grinning Ben.

Uncle Asa climbed into the front seat next to Robbins. To Daniel he said, "I'd like you to come to town with Robbins in the morning. I'm sure the sheriff will have some questions for you regarding Robely."

"I'll be there," Daniel promised.

"From what Robbins has told me, there's a prayer meeting with this Finney fellow tomorrow afternoon. I'd like to hear him for myself. So I'll be staying an extra day."

Everyone said their good-byes.

As the carriage rattled down the road, Daniel and Hannah were left standing alone.

"I'll walk you into the barn," Hannah said, her arms folded, her shoulders hunched to ward off the cold.

Daniel shoved his hands into his pockets.

They fell into step.

He closed the huge barn door behind them while she lit a lantern.

"I suppose you'll be leaving with your uncle," Hannah said.

"Why would you suppose that?"

From her expression, his answer had surprised her.

"He came all this way . . . ," she began.

Daniel shook his head. "He doesn't expect me to return with him."

"He told you that?"

"Aya."

Hannah folded her arms again. Her posture made her appear motherly. "You should go back with him."

Now Daniel was surprised. "Why would you say something like that?"

"Family. He and your aunt need you."

"They don't need me."

"What about this Mr. Gregg? How is your uncle going to get to the truth if you're not there?"

Daniel shrugged off any implied responsibility. "Cyrus Gregg is my uncle's problem. Besides, I came all this way to find a new life. I can't leave now. I don't want to leave now."

Hannah looked away. "Lucy."

"No, not Lucy." Daniel stepped closer, stopping shy of touching her. "I want to stay because of you," he murmured.

For a long time Hannah said nothing.

Had she heard him?

Then she looked up. Her eyes were wet. And angry. "I can't believe you could be so cruel!"

Before Daniel could stop her, Hannah fled from the barn.

Am I wicked?

Camilla cut a piece of cake and put it on a plate. Cyrus Gregg could be heard moving about in the front room. It was late. Much later than was socially acceptable.

Camilla didn't care.

It was at night she suffered the most. Walking through the house in the dark. Lying in bed, listening to the creaks of the house, welcoming any sound she didn't make. She'd come to think of the creaks as the house talking to her. It was at night she craved a human voice.

"Would you like more tea?" she called.

"Can't have cake without tea," Gregg called back.

Camilla smiled. She lit the stove and put the kettle on, savoring the company. Within the hour she'd be alone in bed, her hand wandering over to Asa's side to feel the cold, empty space.

Would she ever adjust to being alone? Right now she couldn't imagine getting used to it. She had a hollow place in her chest that no amount of activity could fill.

But Gregg filled it. When he was around.

She wished he wouldn't leave her alone tonight.

Am I wicked? she thought.

CHAPTER 38

Early morning light streamed into the hotel lobby. Uncle Asa and Robbins stood off to the side, talking to the sheriff, when Hannah arrived with Lucy and Ben.

Daniel felt a twinge of pain when he looked at Hannah. She hadn't spoken to him the entire ride into town. Her father had done all the talking. Then, at his prompting, Hannah had gone immediately to Lucy's house. Robbins had insisted she not be at the hotel when Epps showed up.

Hannah's eagerness to leave so soon bothered Daniel. It was as if she was eager to get away from him.

"What did I miss?" Ben asked, hurrying in. "Where is he?"

"Epps never showed," Daniel replied. "They found my uncle's carriage abandoned near the canal road. It had an empty pistol case in the back."

"Empty?" Lucy said.

"Which means he still has the gun," Ben concluded, clearly enjoying the mystery. "Do you think he got wind the sheriff was looking for him?"

"How?" Daniel asked. "Nobody but us knew that the sheriff was going to be here. Not even the sheriff, until this morning."

He risked a glance at Hannah. The instant he caught her eye, she looked away.

He wracked his brain trying to figure out how he'd offended her. Girls liked being told when a guy was attracted to them, didn't they? Or had she interpreted his comment as a violation of her trust—since she'd told him she no longer liked Ben, but she hadn't yet told Ben, so technically she wasn't available? Had she taken offense because Daniel had acted prematurely?

In a way, it sort of made sense. Daniel wished there was some kind of rule book that documented these things. It would certainly save everyone a lot of grief.

Hannah grabbed Lucy by the arm and tugged her toward the dining room.

"We'll go save some seats," she said to no one in particular.

She wasn't fooling Daniel. It was still early. There were plenty of available seats. Hannah just didn't want to stand here with him.

When the girls were out of earshot, Daniel said, "You've got to tell her!"

"Tell who what?"

"Hannah! You have to tell her you don't want to be with her!"

Ben grimaced and shook his head. "Don't you think I've tried?"

"Try harder!" Daniel insisted.

As time for the prayer meeting drew near, Uncle Asa and Robbins concluded their business with the sheriff and joined the younger men.

"Where are the girls?" Robbins asked.

"Saving seats," Ben answered.

"What's the sheriff going to do?" Daniel asked.

"Not much he can do," his uncle replied. "He said he'll keep an eye open, alert the local businesses—that sort of thing. But I doubt it'll do much good. Epps is an expert woodsman. If he knows someone's looking for him, he'll disappear into the back country. He won't stay here in town."

With the hotel lobby getting crowded, the men decided it was time to join the girls in the dining room.

As they walked into the room, Daniel noticed it was set up the same as it had been for the meeting of inquiry. Excitement rushed through him at the thought of what was going to happen there in the next few hours. Then, in the next instant, he was amused. How much had Daniel Cooper changed that a prayer meeting could so excite him?

In the loft last night, after all the others had gone home and Hannah had stormed into the house, he had tried praying the way he used to pray. On his knees. Hands folded. He started with the memorized prayers he was taught as a child, hoping to warm up with them. But on his own, all he did was mumble one incoherent phrase after another. It felt so awkward and unnatural.

Then he had an idea. He prayed not with words, but with his recorder. He poured out his heart to God in music. After all, surely the God who understood Hebrew and Greek and Latin and all the languages of the world understood the language of music, didn't He?

Daniel had played and prayed late into the night—a deeply moving experience of suspended time and emotion and longing and praise, of spirits intertwining perfectly in harmony and companionship, as God had intended from the beginning when He said, "Let us make man in our image."

The annoying clang of the porter's bell yanked Daniel out of his reverie. Along with his uncle, Robbins, and Ben, he slipped into the stream of humanity that was flowing into the dining room.

Lucy assigned the boys seats when they arrived as she had done the night before at the revival. Hannah sat at the far end of the row next to the aisle, her hands in her lap, her head bowed. But her posture didn't fool Daniel. Lucy may have been the one directing the seating, but Hannah had a clear hand in it.

Lucy's seat was next to Hannah, then Ben, then Mr. Robbins, then Uncle Asa, and finally Daniel—as far from Hannah as possible.

Daniel accepted his exile without objection. He reminded himself that they'd come to pray, not to socialize.

The room was a beehive of excitement and activity. It wasn't like the tense, anxious mood of yesterday, during the meeting of inquiry. Today he could feel the Spirit. Something special was going to happen.

Mr. Gillett appeared at the podium and called the room to order. He explained that the purpose of the meeting was prayer, so they would forgo any reading of Scripture or singing and get right to the matter. He then introduced Reverend Finney and asked him to make similar comments as he had made at Western regarding prayer.

Finney stood. While Gillett spoke, there was an underlying hum of voices. As Finney approached the podium, the room hushed.

"As I told the good people of Western," Finney said, "I believe that if you will unite this afternoon in the prayer of faith to God for the immediate outpouring of His Spirit, you will receive an answer from heaven."

"Quicker than by post for Albany," Ben added. He whispered it loud enough for his row to hear.

The preliminaries over, they started praying. In some parts of the room clusters formed. Others prayed in family groups. Scattered throughout the room, couples and trios prayed together. A general buzz engulfed the room, occasionally interrupted by someone standing and voicing a prayer that all could hear.

Daniel followed the example of Ben and Robbins and his uncle by turning around, facing his chair, and kneeling with folded hands on the seat.

He prayed, "Dear God . . ." but got no further than that. He tried again. "Our Father, who art in heaven . . ." and came up dry.

On the far side of the room a man stood and prayed for a wayward son. Another man prayed for his wife, who was ill.

Daniel rested his forehead against the seat. He wondered what people would think if he stood up and began playing a prayer to God on his recorder.

The chair next to him jostled as his uncle stood. Daniel looked up.

His uncle's head tilted heavenward. His eyes were closed. He began to pray.

Uncle Asa's words flowed like a stream. He thanked God for helping him locate Daniel. He began to pray for Aunt Camilla.

And then another man in the back of the room stood.

Daniel's heart lurched the instant he recognized Epps.

Like the apocalyptic beast rising out of the sea, the killer rose above the surface of those bowed in prayer. From his waistband he drew a pistol and, with one fluid motion, aimed it at Uncle Asa's chest.

Asa's eyes were closed. He couldn't see the threat, Daniel knew.

But somehow Uncle Asa sensed it, or an angel alerted him, or something, because before Daniel could react, his uncle's eyes opened.

"Robely?"

Epps cocked the pistol.

His uncle, still using his speaking voice, which he'd been using to pray, began quoting the psalmist: "Yea, though I walk through the valley of the shadow of death . . ."

Shoving the chair away, Daniel scrambled to his feet, rising up in front of his uncle. He took up the psalm, his voice blending with his uncle's voice: ". . . I will fear no evil . . ."

Chairs that hindered flew aside as Robbins and Ben stood, shielding Daniel, who shielded his uncle. Their voices joined, ". . . for thou art with me . . ."

The commotion alerted others, who also stood. They added their voices. "Thou preparest a table before me in the presence of mine enemies: thou anointest my head with oil; my cup runneth over."

Robely Epps, undeterred, continued to stand with pistol aimed.

"Surely goodness and mercy shall follow me . . ."

His arm began to shake.

". . . all the days of my life . . ."

The pistol wavered, as if it was too heavy and weighed his arm down.

". . . and I shall dwell in the house of the Lord . . ."

The weapon clattered to the floor.

". . . forever."

Robely Epps was shaking all over. His hands flew to his face as he let out a long, mournful wail that sent a shiver through Daniel. Then the killer sank to his knees, weeping profusely.

Someone retrieved the pistol from the floor.

Those who were close to Epps surrounded him, kneeling beside him, placing their hands on his head and shoulders and back, praying for him.

From the center of the prayers came Epps's wail, "I'm lost! I'm lost! I'm lost!"

Daniel found that he, too, was shaking.

"I've never seen a braver act," a smiling Robbins told Daniel, clapping him hard on the shoulder.

"Me? What about you and Ben?" Daniel insisted.

"Just following your example, son."

Hands grabbed Daniel's shoulders. The next thing he knew he was encircled by his uncle's arms in a hug that squeezed the breath from him.

Lucy was crying and laughing. Hannah stood at a distance, her arms folded, but she was looking at Daniel and smiling.

The entire room felt electric with the Spirit. The incident had served as a catalyst for people to pray harder and louder and longer.

Daniel's uncle tried to get to Robely Epps, but by the time he had worked his way through the layers that surrounded him, the sheriff had arrived to remove Epps from the room.

Epps offered no resistance. As he stood to his feet, he kept his head bowed. His hair covered his face as he was led from the room.

"Where will they take him?" Uncle Asa asked.

"Jailhouse," Robbins replied. "You want to talk to him, don't you?"

"Aya."

"I'll take you later."

"Much obliged." Uncle Asa took a deep breath. "I don't do this kind of thing every day. I could use some air."

Robbins led him out of the room, meandering toward the back door around kneeling, praying people.

"That was really something!" Ben told Daniel.

"Thanks."

"You're a hero." Lucy kissed him on the cheek.

Daniel blushed.

Hannah was right behind her. She put her arms around Daniel's neck, her cheek against his cheek.

"There's hope for you yet," she whispered.

CHAPTER 39

"You're hopeless!" Hannah yelled.

"What brought that on?"

Daniel looked up, pitchfork poised. It was morning. He'd been mucking out the stalls in the barn when Hannah barged in.

Following the prayer meeting yesterday, he and his uncle had spent a delightful day with the Robbins family, Ben, and Lucy. That evening Finney had preached again to a crowded church with similar results. The whole town had turned religious, and Uncle Asa was convinced the revival was genuine.

The only disappointing part of the day had come when Uncle Asa and Robbins went to see Epps in jail. The sheriff told them the man had gone insane. He was curled up in the corner of the jail cell and ignored any attempts to converse with him.

Uncle Asa had insisted Epps would talk to him, so the sheriff agreed to let him try. But once inside, Uncle Asa fared no better than the others. Epps rocked back and forth, ranting meaningless phrases, and talking only to phantoms.

Late into the night Daniel had talked with his uncle in the hotel lobby. They had said their good-byes.

By the time Daniel got back to the Robbins's farm, everyone else had retired for the night.

"What are you still doing here?" Hannah demanded.

"I'm glad to see my presence fills you with such happiness," Daniel replied, returning to work.

Hannah marched to the edge of the stall. Arms folded across her chest, she glared at him. "Your uncle's leaving this morning, right?"

"Aya. Probably on his way by now."

"So?"

She wasn't going to let him off easy. Daniel leaned on the pitchfork. "So?" he repeated.

"Aren't you going with him?"

"No."

Her eyes flashed anger. "Why not?"

"My uncle's capable of making the journey himself."

"Are you so certain of that? On his way here he had a traveling companion. Someone to look out for him."

Daniel grinned. "Are you sure you want to use that argument? My uncle had a killer with him. Besides, we've already had this conversation. There's nothing for me in Cumberland." He resumed mucking.

"Yes, we have had this conversation," she countered, "only I thought you'd grown up a little since then. Apparently I was wrong."

Again Daniel straightened up. "What do you mean by that?"

Before she could answer, Robbins pulled into the barn driving his wagon. He leaped down from the seat. "Well . . . your uncle's on his way!" he said jovially.

When no response was forthcoming, he eyed Hannah. Evidently he read his daughter's expression and realized he'd driven into the middle of something, for his own expression changed. He started unhitching the horse and talked nonstop as he worked.

"Happened to find two families traveling as far as Harrisburg . . . cousins of the Blakelys over on River Street, just east of the fort. You went to school with the Blakely boy, didn't you, Hannah?"

Her father didn't give any indication he expected an answer. He appeared to be familiar with her mood.

"As it turned out," he continued, "they were delighted to have Asa travel with them. Turns out her father is a preacher in Providence. So Asa won't have to make the long journey alone. I feel better about that."

Hannah shot a glance at Daniel, who tried not to smile.

He said to Robbins, "So then, it worked out good for everyone, didn't it?"

"Aya," Robbins said, leading the horse to his stall. "God has a way of working things out for all concerned."

Hannah harrumphed and stomped out of the barn.

Her father looked after her. "Anything I should know about?" he asked Daniel.

"She's angry because I didn't go with my uncle back to Cumberland."

Robbins nodded. He didn't appear too concerned. "She's a lot like her mother. Word of advice? Batten down the hatches, my boy."

After helping Robbins push the wagon to where it was stored when not in use, Daniel returned to mucking and Robbins went into the house.

Daniel wasn't alone for long.

Hannah marched in, quoting Scripture: "'I will put my laws into their mind, and write them in their hearts: and I will be to them a God, and they shall be to me a people.'" She set her jaw and awaited his response.

"From the Bible, right?" Daniel said.

"The book of Hebrews. It goes on to say, 'And they shall not teach every man his neighbour, and every man his brother, saying, Know the Lord: for all shall know me, from the least to the greatest.'" Again, she awaited his response.

"What's your point?" Daniel asked.

"My point is—I shouldn't have to tell you to go with your uncle to Cumberland!"

Daniel shook his head. "You drew that conclusion from that verse?"

She let loose a frustrated sigh, as though he was purposely playing ignorant to try her patience. He wasn't. Maybe he was dumb, but he didn't see what the one had to do with the other.

"It's like when you were a child," she explained. "Your parents taught you rules that were meant to keep you from hurting yourself. Rules like, don't play with sharp knives. But when you grew up, there came a time when they no longer had to tell you not to play with sharp knives. You knew not to play with sharp knives."

The subject of knives brought Epps to mind. Daniel was tempted to say he wished someone had taught Epps not to play with knives when he was a little boy, but he thought it would only make her angrier.

"Don't you see?" she cried. "There came a time when God no longer had to remind His people of right and wrong, nor did they have to teach it to their neighbors, because He placed the law in their hearts. Which means that I shouldn't have to tell you that going with your uncle is the right thing to do. You should *know* it's the right thing to do . . . and you should do it *because* it's the right thing to do! You're not a little boy anymore."

Her words hit him hard.

She must have noticed. "What?" she asked.

"Hughie."

Hannah shook her head. "I don't understand."

"A boy I met in the forest. His brother and another older boy were being mean to him."

"What happened?"

"I helped him."

Hannah smiled.

He understood now.

"Nobody had to tell you to help him."

"It was the right thing to do." Daniel grew thoughtful. "I'm not the only one Cyrus Gregg is being mean to. He's not my uncle's friend."

"Only your uncle doesn't know it."

Daniel straightened himself with resolve. "He will soon enough."

"You're going back to Cumberland."

"It's the right thing to do," Daniel said. "Only—"

Hannah frowned. "Only what?"

"I'd rather stay."

She nodded. "Sometimes you have to do the adult thing. Lucy will still be here when you get back."

"When I come back, it won't be for Lucy."

Hannah's eyes flashed fury. She raised a warning finger in his direction. "Don't do that, Daniel! It's mean!"

"What is it with you?" He threw the pitchfork aside.

But before he could say anything else, Ben came running into the barn out of breath. "He's escaped!" Ben bent over, gulping air.

Hannah rushed to him. She put her hand on his back and bent over so she was on his level. "Take deep breaths. And then tell us—"

"Epps." Daniel didn't need to be told.

Ben nodded. "Epps."

"How do you know?" Daniel asked.

"Was coming this way," Ben said, still laboring for air, "ran into some men who are . . . looking for him . . . deputies. Said he came to himself this morning and was . . . real calm like . . . and asked for some men to pray with him . . . and somehow got a weapon and almost—"

"Slit a man's throat," Daniel inserted.

"Aya. And then he ran away. They're out looking for him."

"They won't find him," Daniel said.

"What makes you say that?" Ben asked.

"Because he's an expert woodsman, for one thing. But also because he's probably no longer in the area."

"Do you think he'll go after your uncle?" Hannah asked.

Daniel started for the loft to get his things. "Aya."

CHAPTER 40

"You're in a good mood today, Mr. Gregg," his secretary said by way of greeting.

"It's a good day to be alive," Gregg said.

"It may get even better. A letter from Representative Holt arrived while you were out. I put it on your desk."

Cyrus Gregg closed his office door behind him. He'd refrained from smiling in front of his secretary. Now, rubbing his hands together in celebration, he hurried to his desk.

Holding the letter in his hand, he savored the moment, relishing the missive's point of origin—Washington, D.C. Finally unable to contain his excitement any longer, he opened the envelope and read Holt's report.

His good mood increased with each sentence. In two weeks the United States House of Representatives would vote on funding for his canal. It was going to pass. Holt had the votes. Cyrus Gregg's dream of a water highway linking Cumberland to the Ohio Canal was going to become a reality.

Gregg folded the letter. He started whistling a joyful little ditty from his childhood.

He couldn't wait to tell Camilla. Maybe he wouldn't wait. Maybe he'd ride out to her place later this afternoon and surprise her.

For the last few weeks everything had gone his way. Ever since the funeral.

His eyes fell on a calendar. He smiled. Today was an anniversary of sorts. It was a month to the day that they had buried Asa Rush.

As he'd expected, Asa's death had been hard on Camilla. But also, as he'd expected, she was beginning to show signs of emerging from her grief. Custom allowed her eleven more months of bereavement, which meant they could be married after the first of next year. He wondered if she'd want to have a spring wedding.

There was a soft knock on the door.

"I'm busy!" Gregg barked.

The door opened anyway. His secretary stuck his long face in the doorway. "Mr. Epps is here to see you," he said in a trembling voice. "I tried to explain to him that you were busy. He's most insistent."

"Show him in," Gregg said reluctantly. "And Heinrich? If you let another person through that door, I'll have you stuffed and mounted over my mantle."

"Yes sir."

Cyrus Gregg slipped the congressional letter under his desk blotter. Epps, filthy and surly, strolled into the office.

"The least you could have done is clean up before coming to my office," Gregg said with distaste. "This is a business establishment."

"You've got greater problems than offending the sensibilities of your clientele." Epps pulled a chair to the front of the desk and propped up a foot.

Gregg bit back a complaint. An animal-like glint in Epps's eyes warned him it was unwise to expect the woodsman to act like a gentleman.

"What are you talking about?" Gregg asked.

"Asa Rush is still alive."

"What?"

"So's the boy."

A flash of anger nearly pushed Gregg over the line that separated rational thought from irrational acts of violence. He was standing, holding a lead paperweight, before he was even aware he'd picked it up.

Epps's hand moved instinctively under his coat.

Gregg made a show of putting down the paperweight peacefully and taking his seat. "Let's stay calm," he said with forced civility.

"That temper's going to get you killed one of these days." Epps removed his hand from his coat.

Gregg ignored the prediction. There was only one thing he wanted to hear from Epps right now.

"What happened?" he demanded. "The last message I received from you indicated they were as good as dead."

"Things changed. The wind shifted. What does it matter? All that matters is that I have everything under control."

"What does it matter?" Gregg yelled. "We buried two empty caskets a month ago! Everyone around here thinks that Asa and the boy are dead! How am I going to explain Asa Rush riding into the center of town?"

Epps sat up. "What in blazes did you do a fool thing like that for?"

Cyrus Gregg felt his face redden. He wasn't accustomed to having his judgment being called into question.

"I had my reasons," he said with authority. "What did you mean when you said you have everything under control?"

"Just that. I have everything under control," Epps insisted, despite Gregg's revelation. "Asa Rush is three hours outside Cumberland."

Cyrus Gregg's anger returned. It brought panic with it. Only by supreme effort was he able to contain them. "You know this for certain?"

"I told you. I have everything under control."

"Explain it to me."

Epps nodded. "Fair enough. The boy managed to elude us for weeks. Mostly luck, though he got help from locals at times . . ."

Gregg clenched his jaw so tight it hurt. "Skip to the part of what you plan to do about Asa Rush."

"Afraid I can't do that," Epps insisted. "To understand how it's all going to play out, you have to understand what's happened to this point."

Gregg granted him the point with reluctance.

Epps said, "You pay me to know what people are going to do even before they do it. That's how I—"

"I pay you to remove people who are a threat to me."

Epps glared at him for a minute, then must have thought better of debating the point. "When we finally caught up with the boy, he'd inserted himself into a family, making it harder to reach him. Harder still because of the town. I tell you, something strange and unnatural was going on in that town." Epps shuddered. "It was thick . . . oppressive . . . know what I mean?"

"No. Continue."

"Eliminating them in Rome proved to be impossible. There were too many people in the streets at the oddest hours. I had to think of a way to flush Asa and the boy out. So I had myself a religious conversion at one of their prayer meetings."

"You what?"

"It was necessary. I had to assume that when Asa found the boy, the boy told him about me. So I knew Asa wouldn't trust me anymore. Well, if there's one thing that crowd likes more than anything else, it's a broken sinner. So I gave them one. Did it in front of the whole town. Didn't give him a chance to talk to me there, to counsel me . . . or whatever it is they do. So now, when Asa sees me, he won't be afraid of me. You see, I'm a converted sinner—a brother. His guard will be down."

"But why Cumberland? It's too risky. Why not on the road?"

Epps narrowed his eyes. "It wasn't risky until I found out you'd already buried him!" Then, in a calmer tone, he added, "Anyway, that was the plan at first. But then Asa joined up with this family all the way to Harrisburg and from there met up with a couple of men. I was going to kill all three of them, but then I got to thinking it would be better here, even more so after what you just told me."

"Better? I don't see it."

Epps expelled a sigh of forced patience, the kind a teacher might use on a dumb student.

Cyrus Gregg didn't like it.

"Suppose someone were to find their remains. How would you explain the two fresh graves in the churchyard?"

Gregg had to concede that Epps had a point.

"Here," Epps said, indicating the casket shop, "we have the resources to dispatch of their remains where no one will find them."

The woodsman had thought it through. Gregg had to give him that much. But that didn't mean Epps was off the hook. He should have killed Asa and the boy weeks ago.

"Tell me your plan."

Epps nodded. A slight smirk crossed his face, as if he were pleased Gregg was with him to this point. "The first place Asa will go is to his house. As soon as I leave here, I'll go to his house, dispatch his wife, and wait for him."

"No!" Gregg jumped out of his chair.

Epps frowned.

Cyrus Gregg didn't care. "I'll take care of Cam—of his wife. You're not to touch her, do you understand?"

From his expression Epps understood. In fact, he understood more than Gregg wanted him to understand.

"This is what we'll do," Gregg said, taking charge. He'd had enough of Epps's bumbling. "Go around to the shop and tell the head shop boy that I want him to stack the six caskets that are against the south wall in the alley. Don't let him give you any excuses. Tell him I want those six caskets in the alley before he goes home or he'll be inspecting one of them tomorrow from the inside. Then ride out to Asa's house. His wife won't be there—"

"How—"

"Never mind how!" Gregg snapped. "If she's there, wait for her to leave before entering the house. Do you understand? Under no circumstances are you to have any contact with her."

Epps nodded, but he clearly didn't like what he was hearing.

"When Asa arrives, do whatever you need to do to get him to come to the back alley. Take one of the caskets. You can transport him in it, if you need to. But no blood. Do you understand? I don't want any blood at his house. It will raise suspicion. We will take care of that in the alley. Then we'll load the other five caskets onto the wagon. That way we can transport his body and it will look like one of my deliveries. Do you understand?" It was Cyrus Gregg's turn to adopt the role of the impatient teacher.

From Epps's expression, he didn't like it any more than Gregg did.

"You are not to deviate from this plan," Gregg ordered. "Now, what about the boy—Daniel?"

Epps was grinding his teeth. He stopped long enough to say, "The boy didn't leave with his uncle, but he *will* come back to Cumberland."

"How do you know?"

"I told you. I make my living by knowing what my prey will do even before they know it."

"When will he come?"

"Days. A week. I can't say for sure. All I know is that he'll come, and I'll be waiting for him. I assume you have a casket he can use?"

Cyrus Gregg ignored Epps's insolent tone. "You'd better be right about this."

"I always am."

"All right." Given the time factor, Gregg didn't have any other choice. "Go. There's a wagon out back."

Epps stood. The tension between them was electric. Gregg insolated himself against it with a stern expression and clenched fists. He walked Epps to the office door and shut it behind him.

As soon as the door was closed, he rushed to his desk, pulled out a sheet of paper, and began writing.

"Heinrich!" he bellowed.

His skinny secretary made an instant appearance. "Yes sir?"

Cyrus Gregg ignored his secretary and continued writing until he had finished the note. Then, after folding it, he shouted again, "Heinrich!"

Next to him, the secretary jumped.

"Take this to Mrs. Rush," Gregg ordered. "Make sure she understands that I need the pie within the hour, as soon as she can get it to my house."

"But sir, it takes longer than an hour to bake a pie."

"Do I look stupid to you?" Gregg shouted. "The pie is already made! All you have to do is see that she takes it to my house. Better yet, go with her. Stay with her and make sure she gets to the house safely."

"Sir, why don't I pick up the pie and deliver it myself? That way we wouldn't have to trouble Mrs.—"

"Just do what I say!" Gregg bellowed. "See that the pie and Mrs. Rush are at my house within the hour, or you will be looking for another job. And I assure you, with my recommendation, the only job you'll get is shoveling horse manure. Am I making myself clear?"

"Yes sir!" Heinrich took the note and stumbled all over himself to get out of the office.

Alone in his office, Cyrus Gregg noticed his hands were shaking. What had started out as a day of promise had turned into a nightmare, thanks to the inept Epps.

Walking around to the business side of his desk, Gregg opened a drawer. He removed a small pistol and loaded it.

CHAPTER 41

Epps slouched in the wagon, reins in hand. He kept a sharp watch on the Rush house. Two figures passed alternately in front of the windows. One female. One male.

He recognized the male as Cyrus Gregg's secretary. The woman he'd never seen before. Had to be Asa's wife.

At the sight of the woman Asa loved, warm feelings rose within Epps—feelings based on memories of conversations with Asa on the road to Syracuse.

Epps killed them off. He had no feelings now.

As much as he hated to admit it, Gregg was right, though Epps would never admit it to the dandified casket maker. He'd botched this assignment badly. He'd let his feelings override his instincts.

That would be remedied shortly.

The front door opened. Gregg's man and the woman stepped from the house. Epps watched as the skinny secretary assisted her into a carriage and they drove off.

It would be a mistake to let her live. Gregg's feelings for her were jeopardizing business.

Epps flicked the reins. The horse responded, pulling the wagon from behind the bushes that had provided cover. Epps steered toward the back of the barn. Best to keep the wagon out of sight.

A folded tarp was in the back of the wagon. He thought Gregg's suggestion of a casket an unwarranted risk. It drew too much attention to itself and from here on out, Epps was going to do things his way.

He cursed himself for letting things get out of hand with Asa and the boy. That wouldn't happen again. After dispatching Asa, he'd come back tonight and take care of the wife. It was time Epps cleaned up his mess.

The woman's death wasn't a matter of revenge, nor was it a matter of sending a signal to Gregg, though it would serve that purpose. Her death was a necessity. Epps couldn't risk Gregg's emotional involvement with her. Neither could Gregg, but apparently he was blinded to that fact. Epps wasn't. In fact, for the first time in weeks he saw things clearly.

Once the wagon was secured, Epps bounded up the front steps and through the front door. The aroma of warm blueberry pie greeted him.

He scanned the interior. A parlor with a fireplace to the left. Dining table to the right with an open doorway to the kitchen. In front of him stairs to the second floor.

Gregg said the house would be empty. Epps would check for himself. He wanted no surprises. He moved methodically from room to room, his long coat swishing as he walked. He took note of everything.

The neatness of the rooms. The access to knives and other potential weapons in the kitchen. The pantry. Closets. Windows and the terrain outside. Once he was upstairs, baking smells gave way to powders and perfume in the master bedroom. Outside the window of the second bedroom, presumably the boy's, a tree had been cut down.

Not only did the house look empty, it sounded empty. Satisfied, Epps made his way downstairs. He sat in the parlor on a small sofa that faced the front windows. From here, he could monitor Asa's arrival.

Next to the sofa was a Pembroke table with an open Bible. Epps picked it up. In the front it bore the owner's name: Camilla Buel Rush.

There was an inscription.

My dearest Camilla,

In the face of life's uncertainties, two things are certain:
God's abundant grace and my everlasting love for you.

Asa Rush

Christmas, 1811

Turning the page, Epps came across the family record. There was a single entry on the *Births* page—

Timothy Eli Rush, November 3, 1811

And a single entry on the *Deaths* page—

Timothy Eli Rush, November 3, 1811

Epps flipped through the Bible. In several places Camilla had recorded comments in the margins of the text. Epps ignored the printed text and read the handwritten comments, keeping one eye on the window for Asa's arrival.

Home had never looked so good.

As the carriage rounded the final bend and the house came into view, an involuntary sigh escaped Asa's lips. The sun was low in the sky, stretching the house's shadow toward him like welcoming arms.

Asa felt gritty, bone-weary, hungry, and his leg ached something awful. All he wanted was a bath, a meal, and a hug from his wife—and not necessarily in that order.

She, of course, would want to talk. To hear everything that happened to him while he was away. To tell him of her experiences while he was gone. She would want to know all about Daniel. It was a conversation he wanted to have . . . only not tonight. He didn't have the strength.

He wanted to climb into his own bed and sleep like the dead for a couple of days.

The carriage came to a stop in front of the house. Asa groaned as he climbed out. He told himself he should go straight into the barn and take care of the horse and carriage before he sat down, but he wasn't listening.

He looked to the door as he retrieved his cane, expecting Camilla to come charging out of the door, but the front door remained closed. She must be in the kitchen or upstairs and didn't hear him.

A serenity settled over him as he climbed the front steps. That comfortable peace a man feels nowhere else but home. He smelled blueberry pie and smiled as he opened the door.

But instead of Camilla . . .

"Robely!"

Epps sat on the sofa with an open Bible in his hands. "Hope you don't mind me waiting for you here. Your wife said I could. She had to leave. Something about taking a pie to a sick friend."

"Oh . . ." Asa tried not to show his disappointment. Not only was Camilla not here, but neither was the pie. "How did you know I would be home today?"

Epps set the Bible aside and stood. "Saw you on the road."

"Why didn't you join me? You know I would have welcomed your company."

A knowing smile formed on Epps's face.

"Truth be told, I was ashamed. Saw that you were in the company of good folks and didn't want to put you in a spot where you felt you had to pretend you were my friend."

"Robely! I'd never be ashamed of you."

Epps looked away. "You don't know what I've done."

"Whatever it is, all that changed in Rome, the moment you—"

"And you don't know Cyrus Gregg. He's not your friend, Asa."

Asa stepped farther into the room. He was too tired to be having this discussion.

"I need to set things right," Epps said. "And I need to do it tonight. You can't imagine the sleepless nights I've had since Rome. Asa, will you help me?"

Asa took a hard look at Epps. Camilla wasn't at home. Maybe now would be the best time to do this. "What do you want me to do?"

"Come with me to Gregg's place of business. That way he can speak for himself. But I'm telling you, I have to get this off my chest. I respect you, and I want to make things right by you."

"Very well," Asa said. "Let me leave a note for Camilla."

He hobbled to a small cabinet and took out pencil and paper. Going to the dining room table, he set his cane aside and started to compose his note.

The blow to the back of Asa's head didn't knock him unconscious. He remembered hitting his forehead on the dining room table before passing out.

CHAPTER 42

A canvas shroud covered Asa. He tasted blood and dirt. His head felt like it would explode if he moved it. His cheek pressed against the ground.

Beyond the shroud he heard voices.

"You left the carriage at his house?"

"Don't speak to me like I'm one of your shop boys! I know what I'm doing. First I'll take care of the body. Then I'll get rid of the carriage."

Asa recognized both voices.

"What if someone sees it?" Cyrus Gregg asked. "Tell me you at least hid it in the barn!"

"You're the one that got the woman out of the way," Robely Epps said. "She won't go back there, will she?"

"When I take care of something, it gets done," Gregg insisted.

"Then what are you crying about?" Robely countered.

Asa heard what sounded like hollow wooden boxes being moved. He eased back the shroud—even the thought of sudden movement was painful—to see Cyrus Gregg and Robely Epps lifting opposite ends of a casket. They moved it from a vertical stack of a half-dozen caskets and lay it horizontally on the ground.

Asa recognized where he was—the alley behind Cyrus Gregg's casket shop.

The movement of the shroud startled Cyrus. He dropped his end of

293

the casket. Robely cursed at him for being clumsy.

Asa propped himself up on one arm. That was as far as he got before his head fell off . . . or at least felt like it did. He grabbed it and moaned.

Cyrus pointed at Asa as though he were some kind of critter. "Epps . . . Epps . . . Epps . . ."

"I see him." Epps lowered his end of the casket. "He's not going anywhere."

"What's going on here, Cyrus?" Asa asked. "Or is it better I not know? And Robely, am I mistaken, or did you clobber me on the back of the head in my own house?"

Cyrus backed away toward the mouth of the alley. "There's no use in doing anything foolish, Asa. Just go quietly."

Asa blinked back pain. "Am I going somewhere, Cyrus?"

Epps unsheathed his hunting knife.

"Oh," Asa said.

"Now don't make a mess like you did last time," Cyrus told his killer.

"Are you doing this, or am I?" Epps said testily.

"You're worried about getting my blood all over the alley, is that it?" Asa asked. "Here—maybe this will help."

Instinctively he reached around for his cane. When he couldn't find it, he used a nearby barrel to pull himself up.

Epps took a step toward him.

Asa backed him off with an upraised hand. "Patience, Robely."

Epps kept a wary eye on him.

Reaching down, Asa snatched up the canvas tarp. He dragged it over to the casket and lifted the lid. With nothing fastening the lid to the body of the casket, it slid off to the opposite side with a clatter.

Bending over, Asa lined the casket with the tarp, smoothing it on the bottom with his hands, draping the edges over the sides. When it was situated just right, he stepped into the casket and—grabbing the sides with his hands—lowered himself, first into a sitting position, then completely reclined.

"There," he said. "Now when Robely cuts my throat, the canvas will catch the blood. No mess."

Cyrus walked to the casket. "Your theatrics won't make a difference this time, Asa," he said with a sneer. "They may have worked in the past—dueling, guillotines, and the like—but you're not dealing with weak, impressionable minds today." Turning to Epps, he ordered, "Kill him."

Peering up from inside the casket, Asa asked, "How many of these are you going to fill in order to get what you want, Cyrus?"

Cyrus Gregg stared down at him. "As many as it takes."

Seeing the Rush house brought mixed feelings to Daniel. It reminded him of past battles and foretold of battles to come. Convincing Uncle Asa and Aunt Camilla of Cyrus Gregg's well-disguised evil nature would not be easy. But it was something he had to do. He knew that now.

From Syracuse to Cumberland he'd thought of little else . . . Hannah being the exception. He had to admit he'd thought a lot about her. He'd prayed. He'd steeled himself for the battles ahead. And now he was ready. His uncle and aunt may not like what he had to tell them, but one way or another he was going to convince them for their own protection.

Uncle Asa's horse was tied up in front of the house. Daniel investigated inside the carriage. Everything appeared to be as it was when his uncle was traveling, even the wooden pistol case. Had his uncle just recently arrived home?

Daniel smiled to himself. He'd made better time than he'd thought.

Taking the front steps two at a time, Daniel landed on the porch. *Lord, it begins,* he prayed. *Guide my thoughts and tongue. Ummm . . . and my temper.*

He swung open the door. "Aunt Camilla? Uncle Asa? It's me, Daniel."

Familiarity of surroundings greeted him. The parlor was as he remembered it. She wasn't there now, but in his mind's eye Daniel could see his aunt sitting on the sofa, her Bible open on her lap, a cup of tea on the table.

"Aunt Camilla?"

Daniel found no one in the kitchen. He noticed a pencil on the dining-room table. There was no paper.

"Uncle Asa?" he called upstairs, then followed the words to the second story.

The bedrooms were empty. Bounding down the stairs, he went outside. There was no one in the barn. He walked around the house, ending up back in front next to the carriage.

It was the carriage that bothered him. Uncle Asa couldn't have gone far walking, especially after a trip. He would have taken the carriage.

Of course, there was the possibility a friend from church had been here when he'd arrived. And that Uncle Asa and Aunt Camilla could have ridden away with them.

Daniel examined the dirt for tracks and found some. They were wide—more like wagon tracks—and they went in the direction of town.

His hands on his hips, Daniel stared that direction. The colors were deep. Everything had an orange tint to it. The sun touched the tips of trees on the horizon.

Hefting his haversack on his shoulder, Daniel went back inside the house and tossed the haversack onto the floor by the door. The instant he did, he heard his uncle's voice in his head, telling him to take it up to his room.

Daniel exhaled. His uncle wasn't even here, and already they were battling. Daniel was tempted to leave the haversack on the floor. That's what he used to do. He'd leave it there just to get on his uncle's nerves.

But things were different now. Daniel was different. He reached down and grabbed the haversack.

That's when he saw it—under the dining-room table. Uncle Asa's cane.

Intuition seized Daniel's heart with an icy grip.

The front door banged hard enough to loosen its hinges as he burst out of the house and jumped into the carriage.

At first Uncle Asa's tired horse objected to going anywhere. Maybe it sensed Daniel's fear. But something Daniel said or did convinced the horse to make one more trip.

The pounding in Asa's head made it difficult for him to think. But even with the pain he knew enough.

He knew that it was two against one, and he was in the minority.

He knew that while Cyrus and Robely were acting in concert to kill him, they didn't like each other.

He knew that if he didn't do something soon, he would die.

The whole climbing-into-the-casket thing had been to buy time. But that purchase was about to expire. Somehow he needed to win one of them to his side and make the odds two to one in his favor. But which one?

"What's this all about, Cyrus?" Asa said. "If you're going to kill me, you owe me that much."

"Now is not the time to get into that," Cyrus replied.

Asa forced a chuckle. "Then how about if we make it another time. Say Tuesday, lunch?"

Cyrus was not amused. "He's stalling. Kill him."

Epps was on the wrong side of the casket. He moved around behind Asa to get into position.

Asa propped himself up, arms on the wooden sides. He bared his throat. "Does that make it easier for you, Robely?"

The killer did not reply. He got down on one knee and grabbed Asa by the hair.

"Just one thing," Asa said. "In Rome . . . the prayer meeting . . . was that an act?"

"Yes. It was an act."

"Hmmm, that's disappointing."

"You sound like my father," Epps growled.

"No, Robely, you misunderstand. I'm not disappointed *in* you. I'm disappointed *for* you. I thought you'd found something of great value that day, and now that I learn you didn't, I'm sad for you."

Robely jerked Asa's head back.

"Was that an act in the forest too?" Asa asked. "Were you pretending to be my friend?"

The grip on his hair eased.

"Because I wasn't pretending. All my professional life I prayed God would send me young men like you. I've never met a man with as much innate intelligence. You're too smart to be someone's hired hand. I hope someday you realize your potential."

"You idiot!" Cyrus shouted. "Can't you see what he's doing? Kill him and let's be done with this!"

In the distance Asa heard the clatter of a fast-approaching carriage.

"Wait," Cyrus said.

Epps kept hold of Asa's hair but hid the knife behind him.

Cyrus crept toward the front corner of the alley. "Would you look at that!" He flattened himself against the wall as the carriage came to a halt.

It was Daniel! Asa's heart leapt in hope . . . then in fear.

Daniel jumped out and started toward the shop door before he altered his course quickly toward the alley.

Had he seen what was happening? Asa wondered.

"Uncle Asa!"

Daniel ran into the alley, past Cyrus, without even seeing him.

"No, Daniel!" Asa yelled. "Behind—"

His head was jerked back, cutting off the last of the warning.

Daniel whirled around.

A smiling Cyrus greeted him with a drawn pistol.

"I told you I'm never wrong," Epps said.

It took Asa a moment to piece it together. "You played us. Anticipated our movements. Brilliant."

"Now we finish this before anyone else comes," a triumphant Cyrus said. Waving the pistol, he pointed to Asa, then Daniel. "First him, then the boy."

Daniel's eyes were darting from Epps to Asa to Cyrus to the knife that had reappeared. Asa knew he had one chance, doubtless a dying effort, to create a diversion so Daniel could have a chance to escape.

Up until now he'd supported his own weight with his arms on the sides of the casket. Folding his arms to his side, he dropped down.

Taken by surprise, Epps yelped and countered by pulling up on Asa's hair. Asa felt some of it rip out.

Grabbing Epps's knife arm with both hands, Asa held it at a distance, all the while kicking and twisting and shouting, "Run, Daniel! Run!"

Cyrus Gregg swung the pistol to cover Uncle Asa.

Daniel's first reaction when his uncle took up the fight was to jump Epps and join the struggle for the knife.

Then his uncle ordered him to run. But by the time Daniel understood what his uncle was doing, it was too late.

One step and Gregg swung the pistol back at him, blocking his departure. Daniel took a long look down the barrel of the gun, then dove behind a stack of barrels, the same stack he'd hidden behind the night of Emil Braxton's murder.

His efforts evoked laughter from Cyrus Gregg. "There's no door back there. No hole to crawl into. No place to go!"

Daniel's chest was heaving. His eyes searched frantically for something . . . *anything* he could use as a weapon. But, like the night of the murder, there was nothing but a brick wall on one side and a stack of barrels on the other.

He scrambled into a sitting position. Could he lure Gregg closer? Tumble the barrels over and possibly make good his escape that way?

Daniel found a peeking place between two of the barrels. Gregg was too far away at the mouth of the alley.

"Slit the man's throat," Gregg said. "Then drag the boy out from behind the barrels and do him. I'll get another casket."

Gregg shoved the weapon into his waistband and moved toward the stacked row of caskets.

"My name's Asa Rush, Cyrus," Uncle Asa said, no longer struggling. "We've been friends for nearly two decades. Do you have to reduce me to a nameless body to kill me?"

From his place of hiding, Daniel knew he had to do something. But what? What could he do? They had all the weapons. He and his uncle didn't have a prayer.

No, that wasn't right. Prayer was *all* they had. But was it enough?

Daniel folded his hands and touched them with his sweaty brow. "Our Father . . . dear Father . . . Holy Father . . . Holy God . . ."

He squeezed his hands in frustration. He wasn't good at this!

But he was good at . . .

Daniel reached for his recorder. With trembling hands and trembling lips, he began to play a prayer to God.

"You worry too much, Heinrich!" Camilla laughed.

It was the end of a workday. The streets were nearly deserted. Most everyone was home by now, their thoughts having turned to the evening meal.

Cyrus Gregg's nervous secretary shook his head. "You don't know Mr. Gregg like I do. He shouts a lot."

"Well, he doesn't shout at me. Trust me. Mr. Gregg will be surprised and delighted."

But Heinrich was not convinced. "Surprised, yes. I'm not sure I've ever heard anyone use the words *delighted* and *Mr. Gregg* in the same sentence before."

"I take full responsibility," Camilla said. "I'll tell him I insisted you drive me to his office. If for no other reason than we can walk home together. He needs to walk, to counter the effect of all those pieces of pies he's been eating."

Heinrich was not appeased. "He told me to see to it that you stayed at his house."

"Will you stop worrying!" Camilla laughed.

Just as the Gregg's Caskets of Cumberland sign came into view, Camilla thought she heard something.

"You are the only person in the world," Heinrich said, "who can say things to Mr. Gregg without—"

"Hush!" Camilla sat up and listened hard.

"What is it you—?"

"Hush!"

Horror swept over her. Tears flooded her eyes.

"Daniel!"

Before Heinrich could stop the carriage, she was out of the carriage and running down the street, around the side of Cyrus Gregg's shop, in the direction of the music.

CHAPTER 43

"Shut him up!" Cyrus Gregg yelled, dancing in place, desperate to stop the music. "Epps . . . the boy . . . shut him up. Make him stop!"

Epps released Asa to go after Daniel.

Asa wasted no time. He scrambled to get out of the casket.

Two things stopped him. Epps shoved him down from behind. And Cyrus's pistol made a reappearance.

The way Asa saw it, he could die by a slit throat or a bullet to the brain. He chose the bullet. If his good friend Cyrus Gregg wanted him dead, he was going to have to kill him himself.

Asa relaxed, feigning resignation to his fate. He'd wait until Epps was out of arm's reach, then he'd shout a warning to Daniel and lunge at the no-good Gregg.

It was a desperate plan at a desperate time. Asa trusted God for whatever future he had left.

Head down, Asa checked Epps's progress out of the corner of his eye. Epps's back was turned so he could focus on Daniel.

This was the moment Asa had anticipated. If he was going to make a move, now was the time.

"Asa!" Camilla's voice was more of a scream than anything else.

Asa's breath caught in his throat at the sight of his beloved. This couldn't be happening!

"Camilla . . . no!"

Asa was halfway out of the casket when he saw her. He stopped and dropped to one knee as Cyrus seized Camilla by the wrist and pulled her to him. Cyrus swung her around so that he held her from behind. He pressed the pistol against her neck.

"No! Don't!" Asa yelled, afraid to move. "Don't hurt her!"

Behind the barrels, Daniel squeezed his eyes shut and played his heart to God. Something told him to shut out everything he heard or thought he heard, and to concentrate on playing.

Nothing but playing.

Playing was the best thing he could do.

The *only* thing he could do that would make a difference.

So he played. He played with all his heart. He played like he'd never played before.

"Are you going to kill me, Cyrus?" Camilla asked, her tone icy.

She'd regained a measure of control, but only a measure. The sight of her dead husband sitting up in a casket—alive—was almost too much for her. And hearing her unseen nephew playing a recorder as though from the grave nearly made her swoon. But Cyrus pressing a gun against her neck? That was something else altogether. It made her furious.

"Well, Cyrus? Either explain to me what's going on here, or pull the trigger. I don't see that you have any other choices. Was that your plan all along? To kill me?"

Just then Heinrich came around the corner. "Mr. Gregg, did you want me to lock up the front—landsakes' alive! What . . . oh!"

He stopped short when he saw Camilla.

"Mr. Gregg, please don't be angry with her," the secretary begged. "She only wanted to surprise you, that's all! She didn't mean any harm!"

Cyrus Gregg was sweating profusely. His eyes bulged at the activity in the alley. He didn't know which crisis to address first.

"Father! Over here!" another voice called. "I told you it was Daniel! Here's Mr. Rush—oh, and Mr. Epps! Hello, Mr. Epps!"

Hannah Robbins appeared from nowhere.

Asa tried to warn her away. "Hannah! Go! Turn around and go! Go now!" he pleaded.

But it was too late. Hannah took it all in—the row of caskets, the music, a disheveled Asa on one knee in a coffin, a woman held hostage with a pistol to her neck.

Ben was right on her heels, holding a laughing Lucy's hand. The laughter died quickly.

A jovial Robbins was right behind them. "Asa! Hannah said she heard Daniel's . . . oh!"

"Robbins, get them out of here. Now!" Asa shouted.

The music stopped. Daniel stood. He stepped from behind the barrels.

"Hannah? What are you—?"

"Daniel?"

"Shut up! Everyone shut up!" Cyrus Gregg ordered, waving the pistol wildly.

A few more residents of Cumberland gathered at the mouth of the alley, drawn to the music and the shouting.

"It's over, Cyrus," Asa said. With the help of the side of the casket, he stood up.

"No, no, I will *not* admit defeat!" Cyrus yelled.

Asa spread his hands wide. "You can't kill all of us."

Cyrus was shaking so hard, it frightened Camilla. She let out a whimper.

Robely Epps hadn't moved since Camilla had blundered into the alley. The knife still in his hand, he'd made no further effort to get Daniel or to restrain Asa.

Now he took a step toward Cyrus Gregg, challenging him. "I know what you plan to do." He sheathed his knife. "You forget. I make a living predicting what people will do before they do it. But it won't work. This time nobody will believe you." He spread his hands wide, palms forward. "It won't work."

At that instant, Asa realized what Cyrus was about to do. But there was nothing he could do to stop it.

"Epps! I'm warning you!" Cyrus yelled. "Drop the knife!"

The thunder of the pistol echoed in the alley. A puff of white-blue smoke rose from the gun.

Hit in the chest, Robely Epps dropped to his knees.

Asa rushed to Epps's side and caught him as he fell. It took all of his strength to lower the big man gently to the ground.

Epps looked up at him. "You're the only man to show me respect. I wish I'd been a better friend."

Robely Epps closed his eyes and was gone.

"You saw it! All of you saw it!" Cyrus proclaimed.

He released Camilla, who bolted to her husband. Asa put a protective arm around her as she buried her face in his chest and wept.

"That man," Gregg ranted, "that man was about to knife my good friend Asa Rush. You all saw it! I had to shoot him! I had to! To save Asa's life!"

The sheriff appeared, pushing his way through the growing crowd at the mouth of the alley. "What's going on here, Mr. Gregg?"

"Sheriff," Gregg said, moving toward him, quick to plead his case, "the man on the ground is Robely Epps, a known criminal. He was about to do harm to Asa Rush, and would have, had I not happened upon them. I had no choice but to shoot him."

Cyrus Gregg's demeanor, his movements, his speech were once again that of a respected and powerful businessman.

The sheriff responded accordingly. "Then it's a good thing you happened to be here," he said to Gregg.

"He's lying to you, Sheriff." Daniel stepped forward. "That's not what happened at all. Epps worked for Mr. Gregg."

"That's ridiculous, Sheriff. Look at the man. Does he look like the kind of man I would hire?"

"Son," the sheriff said, "maybe it's best if I take it from here."

"Listen to the boy, Sheriff," Asa said.

"Epps is the kind of man you hire when you want to kill someone," Daniel explained. "I saw them kill Emil Braxton. And then he and Cyrus

Gregg tried to kill me and my uncle."

"This is absurd!" Cyrus bellowed. "It's a pack of lies from a known liar!"

"You take that back!" Hannah fired, lunging at Cyrus Gregg. She might have done some damage had her father not restrained her.

Cyrus stood toe to toe with Daniel. "I don't know what you're up to, boy. But in the long run, it comes down to my word against yours. Who do you think people are going to believe?"

"I believe my nephew," Asa said. Struggling to get to his feet, he stood beside Daniel.

"I believe Daniel." Camilla took her husband's hand.

"So do I," Hannah said.

One by one, Hannah, Lucy, Ben, and Robbins moved to stand beside Daniel.

"Sheriff?" Heinrich stepped forward. "This is going to cost me my job, but I don't want to work for a man who puts a gun to a woman's throat. There are some ledgers in Mr. Gregg's office that might interest you. They document a series of bribes to a number of U.S. senators and congressmen."

"Cyrus Gregg," the sheriff said, taking the businessman by the arm, "I think we need to have a little talk."

CHAPTER 44

"It was a classic battle between the powers of light and the powers of darkness, between eternal good and ultimate evil . . ."

Robbins circled the Rush's dining-room table filling teacup after teacup as he narrated his version of the day's events.

Earlier, when they walked through the door, Camilla had fallen instinctively into the role of hostess. But Robbins had taken her by the shoulders and led her to the seat next to Asa. Robbins insisted he knew how to heat water for tea. He informed her that, on a day like today, her place was next to her husband.

Camilla didn't object. She scooted her chair up against her husband's, linked her arm in his, and lay her cheek on his shoulder. Tears came frequently with each fresh realization that Asa and Daniel were alive. She hadn't moved from her position through two servings of tea.

Ben and Lucy sat next to each other. They held hands under the table. Lucy kept nudging Ben, whispering to him that she thought Asa and Camilla looked cute together.

Hannah sat next to Lucy. She couldn't miss the hand-holding and the whispers, but those gestures didn't appear to upset her. Obviously there had been some developments along the journey from Rome to Cumberland. Daniel figured Hannah would fill him in on the news later.

307

For now Robbins held the floor as well as the tea pot, and he was relishing both roles.

"Cyrus Gregg and Robely Epps never stood a chance. They were outmatched and overpowered from the start. What good are mere guns and knives when Daniel, son of Eli Cooper, came charging into the fray armed with his recorder and the Spirit of God?"

"Robbins, what exactly are you doing here?" Asa asked.

Robbins, taken aback, stood with pot in hand. "I thought it was obvious. I'm pouring tea."

"Here in Cumberland, I mean," Asa clarified. "Don't get me wrong, I'm glad to see you. It's a little unexpected, that's all."

"You can blame Hannah for that," Robbins said with a wink.

"Me?" Hannah protested.

"A couple of days after you left," Robbins explained, "my daughter approaches me and starts telling me how God writes the law on men's hearts, so they no longer had to be told what to do, or to teach their neighbors what to do."

"That's exactly what happens in revival," Asa said, using his professor's voice. "No longer do men have to be reminded what is right and wrong. It's stamped on their hearts."

"Exactly!" Robbins emphasized. "And then she launches into this looonnngggg sermon—"

"Papa!"

"—about how a man shouldn't have to be told to do the right thing. No, he does it for no other reason than it's the right thing to do!"

"I think I've heard that sermon," Daniel quipped.

His comment earned him a playful punch on the arm from Hannah.

"Next thing I know," Robbins concluded, "the four of us are packed into my carriage and driving south."

"But how is coming to Cumberland the right thing to do?" Asa asked.

Robbins gazed at him in all seriousness. "A friend in need . . ."

Uncle Asa blinked back emotion. "Thank you. Thank you. It's been a long time since I've had a friend who would go to such lengths for me."

"Anyway, as I told my three young bodyguards during our journey," Robbins continued, "this is Asa Rush we're going to help. So don't be surprised if we come across a French guillotine or a revolution or a presidential assassination attempt or a duel along the way. And no sooner had we rolled into town, and what do we find? Asa Rush kneeling in a casket in an alley, a man with a knife behind him, and a man with a gun in front of him!"

Daniel laughed with the rest of them, happy to have the good times he'd had in Rome imported into his uncle's house.

"Mrs. Rush," Lucy said, "I think it's incredible the way you've held up through all of this. You have been so courageous!"

Aunt Camilla ventured a smile. She gazed lovingly at Asa. "A few weeks ago I buried him. And now here he—"

She couldn't finish for the tears.

Asa put his arm around her. Lucy apologized profusely, explaining that she'd meant it as a compliment.

Daniel scooted his chair back. "Excuse me. I need some air." He was halfway to the door before he asked, "Hannah, would you like to join me?"

Amused glances circled the table. Hannah blushed, then stood. Daniel pulled on his coat and helped her with hers.

Opening the door, he offered her his hand. With a coy smile Daniel had not seen before—but he liked it . . . a lot—Hannah slipped her hand into his as they walked outside.

The sky was clear. The stars sparkled with promise.

Daniel led her to the side of the house. A rectangle of light from his upstairs window stretched across the ground. They walked to the re-maining stump of a tree that had once served as a ladder for him. Daniel sat on half and offered Hannah the other half.

"This tree seemed a lot taller when I was younger," Daniel quipped.

Hannah laughed.

They sat in silence. It was the first time Daniel had ever sat next to a girl and felt comfortable. He liked it. He wanted to do it more often.

"You were amazing," Hannah said.

Daniel glanced at her to see if she was making fun of him. Her expression said she wasn't.

"In Rome, when you described all that you'd been through . . . well, I have to admit, being so distant from it all, I thought you were exaggerating. It didn't seem real. But in that alley . . ." Hannah shook her head. "Lucy's right. We can't begin to imagine all that you and your aunt and uncle have been through."

They'd unclasped hands when they sat down. Now Hannah slid her hand under Daniel's arm and sought his hand again. Their fingers intertwined.

"I know I'm dumb for saying this," Daniel said. "Just when we're getting along so well and everything . . ." He paused. "Twice now, when I said it, you got angry with me."

Hannah lowered her head.

"But back in Rome . . ."

He stopped. He decided he didn't want to ruin this moment.

"Go ahead," Hannah whispered. "Say it."

"When I said I wanted to stay for you and not for Lucy, I didn't mean to be cruel. I meant what I said."

"I know," Hannah said.

"Then why did you . . . ?"

"I didn't believe you. I've known Lucy all my life. No boy has ever chosen me over Lucy. *Ever.* I didn't know how to handle it."

Daniel squeezed her hand.

Hannah sniffed and wiped away tears, but it was all right. Her eyes were smiling.

"Play something for me?" she asked.

"I'd rather not . . ."

"Please?"

"If I play, it means I have to let go of your hand. And I like holding it."

Hannah smiled. "If I promise you can hold my hand again after you play, will you play for me?"

"You have to promise."

"I give you my word."

"Because I don't want to give up your hand now and then find out later that it was some kind of trick." He grinned.

She pulled her hand away and slapped his shoulder with it. "And play something happy—or romantic. Not one of those dirges you seem to like so much."

Daniel took the recorder from his waistband, put the mouthpiece to his lips, and played a tune that he'd created to remind himself of Hannah.

Within moments they had company. First Ben and Lucy, then Robbins, then Uncle Asa and Aunt Camilla.

Once again, Daniel's black recorder, Judas, had betrayed him by attracting an unwanted audience. But this time, he didn't mind.

AUTHORS' NOTES

In any novel of this genre, the blending of the historical and the fictional is a balancing act. Our goal is to transport you back in time so you might experience what it was like to live in 1825–1826 and to witness the wondrous events of God that unfolded in what has been called the Burned-Over District of New York for the fires of revival that swept through the towns.

The historical threads that are woven throughout this story include some major events as well as minor details that we found interesting—

The washing machines described in chapter 6 are descriptions of actual patent drawings from this time period. They can be found in the National Archives.

For the cave scenes, we created a composite of two actual Maryland caves: the Round Top Summit Cave and the Schetromph Cave.

The practical joke Red and Dumps played on the younger Hughie in chapter 25 was crafted from an ancient myth recorded by Ovid in his collection of myths titled *Metamorphoses*. Ovid has been required reading in schools for centuries, and the practical joke seemed to be just the kind of thing a couple of boys with time on their hands would do with their required reading material.

Cumberland, Maryland, and Rome, New York, have played major roles in American history—the one historically, and the other as the scene of revival. Also mentioned in the text are the cities of Syracuse, Utica, and Wright's Settlement.

Of major historical significance are the canals—the Erie Canal being the most famous, along with the no-less-significant but lesser-known Patowmack Canal. The town of Matildaville existed as portrayed in the story. Its life and death was linked to the Patowmack Canal.

While there was talk of extending the Potowmack Canal from Cumberland to the Ohio River, it never became reality. Cyrus Gregg's plan to link the Ohio River to the Atlantic Ocean was a fictional representation of these unrealized dreams. Of special interest was the fascination of these canal waterways in their heyday, along with the possibility of constructing a transcontinental canal system. At the time, these canals were an unbelievable technological breakthrough for transportation and shipping. The tragedy of the canal systems is that they were so quickly overshadowed by the emergence of the steam engine and a railroad system. Men who had sunk their hopes and dreams into the canals lost fortunes almost overnight.

As for historical characters in the novel, the legendary revival preacher Charles Finney is most prominent. His methods of revival—controversial and revolutionary at the time—became the basis for many succeeding evangelists, including Billy Sunday and Billy Graham. Scenes for the novel were drawn from his autobiography, including the hotel, the sheriff's testimony, and the revival in Western. Finney's sermon quotes are from actual transcripts.

Even before this novel was conceived, Finney's sermon "How to Promote Revival" had influenced Jack's life as a minister. So he is particularly pleased to quote from it just so he might share it with you.

Someone has said, "If you are in earnest about starting revival, draw a circle on the ground, step inside and pray, 'Lord, begin a revival within this circle.'" Finney's sermon on how to promote a revival was, and still is, a valuable tool for the serious seeker of revival.

The fictional thread in the story was crafted in an attempt to convey the emotions and thoughts that an average Christian might have had in such extraordinary circumstances.

Fictional characters include: Daniel Cooper and his trials and conversion, Asa and Camilla Rush (Asa making a reappearance from the previous novel, *Storm*), Cyrus Gregg and Gregg's Caskets of Cumberland, Robely Epps, Robbins, Hannah, Ben, and Lucy.

For more information about The Great Awakening and this series, go online to www.thegreatawakenings.org.

FOR THE REST OF THE STORY,

READ

PROOF

1857–1858

CHAPTER 1

BY

BILL BRIGHT & JACK CAVANAUGH

THE GREAT AWAKENINGS SERIES

CHAPTER 1

Harrison Shaw tugged at the sleeves of his dress coat. Actually, it wasn't his coat. It belonged to the Newsboys' Lodge in Brooklyn. All the guys used it for important occasions. Isaac Hirsch wore it to his bar mitzvah. Murry Simon got married in it. Luckily for Murry—or perhaps for Murry's bride—the coat was his size. Isaac wasn't so lucky. When he wore it, the sleeves hung well past his knuckles. He looked like he was playing dress-up with his father's coat. Harrison had the opposite problem. The sleeves didn't begin to cover his bony wrists. He tugged on them again just before reaching for the door knocker.

Hollow brass lion's eyes stared back at him. His coat sleeve rode up his arm as he lifted the lion's jaw to strike the knocker pad. The metal was cold. He shivered—not from the chill of brass in early winter, but from nervous excitement. This was the first time he'd been this far uptown. It had been an intimidating journey as he'd walked past one stately mansion after another. "Millionaire Row," they called it. If the boys at the lodge could only see him now.

Nervously, he shoved a hand into his trousers pocket and fingered a lone coin. An 1831 silver dollar with a nick on the edge. It had been his good-luck piece for as long as he could remember.

The latch sounded. The door opened.

A house servant appeared. She was so short her gaze hit him in the

319

belly and worked its way up, the way it would if she were gazing at a church steeple.

"Deliveries in back," she said, closing the door.

Harrison found himself once again face to face with the brass lion. The lion was smirking at him.

He knocked a second time, this time bending over to speak to the female servant on her level.

The door opened.

"I'm not a delivery boy," he blurted. He spoke the words so quickly—to get them out before she had time to close the door again—that they came out as a single word: "I'mnotadeliveryboy."

His words hit a middle-aged man in the waistcoat.

"Congratulations, sir," said the house servant, looking down at him.

Cringing, Harrison pulled himself up to full height. The servant, distinguished, with gray temples, extended his hand, palm up.

Harrison grabbed the servant's hand and shook it. "Nice to meet you. Name's Harrison Shaw. I'm expected."

The servant stared at Harrison's hand as though it were a three-day old fish. "Your calling card, sir."

"Oh! Calling card!" Harrison retracted his hand sheepishly. He felt his pockets, even though he knew there were no calling cards to be found.

The servant stood motionless. Pigeons could have landed on his arm.

"Um . . . where I live we don't use a lot of calling cards," Harrison said.

"Shocking, sir."

"If you could just check with Mr. Jarves, I'm sure my name's on a list somewhere, or I could run home and get a note from my guardian . . . a letter of introduction . . . that is, if you really need something in writing."

The servant lowered his hand and stepped back. With a heavy sigh, he said, "This way, sir."

Earlier that morning, when Harrison, now in his midtwenties, had climbed out of bed, he knew that the events of this day could very well chart the course of his professional career in New York's dog-eat-dog legal system. He'd worked hard to get this far, and today could very well be the payoff he'd so often dreamed of. Had he known that stepping across the threshold of this Fifth Avenue mansion would launch him down a series of rapids in a boat without an oar, he might not have crossed it so eagerly.

Never in his life had Harrison stood in such an entryway. Four white marble Corinthian columns thrust upward to the heavens. Literally. Overhead cherubs looked down mischievously at him from cotton clouds set against a domed blue sky. Gawking upward, he turned full circle, his feet gliding effortlessly on a floor smooth as glass.

All of a sudden Harrison realized he and the cherubs were alone. The house servant had moved on. He ran to catch up.

Harrison followed his escort at a steady clip through two rooms, both of them larger than the common room at the Newsboys' Lodge, then down a carpeted hallway lined with portraits of well-dressed people who glared at him disapprovingly as he passed.

The servant opened two floor-to-ceiling doors and motioned Harrison into a sitting room. "Wait here. Don't touch anything." The massive doors closed.

Harrison found himself alone in a room that resembled a museum. He wasn't surprised. Jimmy Wessler had warned him that rich people liked to collect a lot of strange and unusual artifacts, not just paintings and statues of ancient Greeks like most people thought. Jimmy knew about this kind of stuff because his uncle was a lawyer for rich people in Albany.

For twenty minutes Harrison remained firmly planted where the house servant had left him, suffering the scratchy constraints of his stiff upturned collar with no complaint as his head swiveled this way and that. Then his curiosity got the better of him, and he inched closer to a polished round table to get a better look at a white porcelain elephant. Just beyond the elephant was an oriental jade chess set; and beyond it, a vase with a painting of a crouching black jaguar. And before Harrison knew it, he had penetrated the room's interior. But he wasn't touching anything.

Floor-to-ceiling windows flanked him on the left, framed by red velvet curtains. Beyond the windows was a small orchard of trees with naked branches. A soft light fell on him and the room's strange assortment of collectibles.

Painfully aware that he didn't have the money to replace anything he broke, Harrison navigated the room's clutter, zigzagging around embroidered footstools, plump sofas and chairs, little tables loaded with trinkets, and cabinets jammed full of porcelain and glass animals.

Oil paintings hung on the walls from long wires that stretched to the ceiling. Pastorals mostly. Metal plates mounted on the frames identified both painting and artist. *The Voyage of Life*, by Thomas Cole, captivated him with its depiction of a young man, tiller firmly in hand, sailing the river of life. The thrust of the young man's chin and his billowing clothes suggested adventure and determination. In the distance a shining castle beckoned him. An angelic being watched over him from the shore. So intent was the youth on his goal, he didn't see the choppy seas and rough water ahead.

Other paintings in the room were interesting but not as dramatic. There were several by Frederick Church depicting scenes of South America and a pastoral landscape by Asher B. Durand that hung in a prominent location. Harrison had never heard of any of these painters before.

Next to the Durand painting hung a scuffed wooden frame that was not displaying a painting. Inside the frame was a piece of paper that showed a crease from being folded over and was now yellowed with age. A letter, penned in French. The signature fascinated him: Marquis de Lafayette. A chill of excitement passed through Harrison at the realization he was inches from a page of correspondence that had been penned by the hand of a true Revolutionary War hero. A relative of Jarves's perhaps?

Something else caught his eye. Something down low on a table. Harrison turned his head to see a stuffed bird beneath a glass bell looking up at him. Its eyes had a murderous glint in them, as though death had come upon it suddenly and it was intent on revenge.

The creature was small and gray with black markings around its eyes so that it appeared to be wearing a mask. Its eyes locked on to him with hypnotic force, and for an instant, Harrison knew the helpless sensation prey feel when they know they're going to die. The moment was beyond unnerving.

Harrison gave the table a wide berth. The bird's eyes seemed to follow him.

Now that he thought about it, the whole house was a bit unnerving—the peeping angels in the entryway, the unsmiling portraits in the hallway, the bird restrained under glass. The unsettled feeling in his gut was more than simply being unaccustomed to the trappings of wealth. There was an underlying dark anxiety about the place. He suddenly found himself craving fresh air—fresh *outside* air.

But he couldn't just leave. Mr. Bowen and the boys back at the lodge were counting on him. What would he tell them—he got scared and ran away before the interview?

He took a deep breath and put some distance between him and the bird, looking for something to distract him. Something that didn't have eyes.

He found what he was looking for beneath another glass bell jar. A pocket watch dangled on a gold chain. It was obviously of sentimental value to Mr. Jarves, because while the watch looked expensive, it was damaged. Its backside was charred; a portion of the crystal was clouded from smoke. The hands of the watch were stilled, frozen at sixteen minutes past one o'clock.

As Harrison bent over to examine it, he noticed something new to the room. Something that hadn't been there when he'd entered. He was certain of it. An odor. What intrigued him was that the odor obviously didn't belong in this museum of musty drapes and old wood and scary stuffed birds beneath bell jars.

The door latch rattled. The massive doors swung open. The house servant who had deposited him in the room eyed Harrison suspiciously. Harrison raised his hands to indicate he hadn't touched anything.

Everything about the house servant said, *Follow me.* Verbalizing it would have been redundant. The servant turned, and Harrison dutifully fell in step behind him.

Their journey was short. They stepped across the hallway, where the house servant opened a second pair of double wooden doors.

ABOUT THE AUTHORS

Bill Bright passed away in 2003, but his enduring legacy continues. He was heavily involved in the development of this series with his team from Bright Media and Jack Cavanaugh.

Known worldwide for his love of Jesus Christ and dedication to sharing the message of God's grace in everything he did, Bill Bright founded Campus Crusade for Christ International. From a small beginning in 1951, the organization he began had, in 2002, more than 25,000 full-time staff and over 553,000 trained volunteer staff in 196 countries in areas representing 99.6 percent of the world's population. What began as a campus ministry now covers almost every segment of society, with more than seventy special ministries and projects that reach out to students, inner cities, governments, prisons, families, the military, executives, musicians, athletes, and many others.

Each ministry is designed to help fulfill the Great Commission, Christ's command to carry the gospel to the entire world. The film *Jesus*, which Bright conceived and funded through Campus Crusade for Christ, is the most widely viewed film ever produced. It has been translated into more than 730 languages and viewed by more than 4.5 billion people in 234 countries, with 300 additional languages currently being translated. More than 148 million people have indicated making salvation decisions for Christ after viewing it live. Additional tens of millions are believed to have made similar decisions through television and radio versions of the *Jesus* film.

Dr. Bright held six honorary doctorate degrees: a Doctor of Laws from the Jeonbug National University of Korea, a Doctor of Divinity from John Brown University, a Doctor of Letters from Houghton University, a Doctor of Divinity from the Los Angeles Bible College and Seminary, a Doctor of Divinity from Montreat-Anderson College, and a Doctor of Laws from Pepperdine University. In 1971 he was named outstanding alumnus of his alma mater, Northeastern State University. He was listed in Who's Who in Religion and Who's Who in Community Service (England) and received numerous other recognitions. In 1973 Dr. Bright received a special award from Religious Heritage of America for his work with youth, and in 1982 received the Golden Angel Award as International Churchman of the Year.

Together with his wife, Vonette, he received the Jubilate Christian Achievement Award, 1982–1983, for outstanding leadership and dedication in furthering the gospel through the work of Campus Crusade and the Great Commission Prayer Crusade. In addition to having many other responsibilities, Bright served as chairman of the Year of the Bible Foundation, and he also chaired the National Committee for the National Year of the Bible in 1983, with President Ronald Reagan serving as honorary chairman. When Bright was named the 1996 recipient of the one-million-dollar Templeton Prize for Progress in Religion, he dedicated all of the proceeds of the award toward training Christians internationally in the spiritual benefits of fasting and prayer, and for the fulfillment of the Great Commission. Bright was also inducted into the Oklahoma Hall of Fame in November 1996.

In the last two years of his life, Bright received the first Lifetime Achievement Award from his alma mater, Northeastern State University.

He was also a corecipient, with his wife, of the Lifetime Inspiration Award from Religious Heritage of America Foundation. In addition, he received the Lifetime Achievement Award from both the National Association of Evangelicals and the Evangelical Christian Publishers Association, which also bestowed on him the Chairman's Award. He was inducted into the National Religious Broadcasters Hall of Fame in 2002. Dr. Bright authored more than one hundred books and booklets, as well as thousands of articles and pamphlets that have been distributed by the millions in most major languages.

Bill Bright celebrated being married to Vonette Zachary Bright for fifty-four years. They have two married sons, Zac and Brad, who are both actively involved in ministry today, and four grandchildren.

 **Jack Cavanaugh** is an award-winning, full-time author who has published twenty-two books to date, mostly historical fiction. His eight-volume American Family Portrait series spans the history of our nation from the arrival of the Puritans to the Vietnam War. He has also written novels about South Africa, the English versions of the Bible, and German Christians who resisted Hitler. He has published with Victor/Chariot-Victor, Moody, Zondervan, Bethany House, and Fleming H. Revell. His books have been translated into six languages.

The Puritans was a Gold Medallion finalist in 1995. It received the San Diego Book Award for Best Historical in 1994, and the Best Book of the Year Award in 1995 by the San Diego Christian Writers' Guild.

The Patriots won the San Diego Christian Writers' Guild Best Fiction award in 1996.

Glimpses of Truth was a Christy Award finalist in International Fiction in 2000.

While Mortals Sleep won the Christy Award for International

Fiction in 2002; the Gold Medal in *ForeWord* magazine's Book of the Year contest in 2001; and the Excellence in Media's Silver Angel Award in 2002.

His Watchful Eye was a Christy Award winner in International Fiction in 2003.

Beyond the Sacred Page was a Christy Award finalist in Historical Fiction in 2004.

Fire has been nominated for *ForeWord* magazine's Book of the Year for 2006.

Jack has been writing full-time since 1993. A student of the novel for nearly a quarter of a century, he takes his craft seriously, continuing to study and teach at Christian writers' conferences. He is the former pastor of three Southern Baptist churches in San Diego county. He draws upon his theological background for the spiritual elements of his books. Jack has three grown children. He and his wife live in Southern California.

Enjoyment Guarantee

If you are not totally satisfied with this book, simply return it to us along with your receipt, a statement of what you didn't like about the book, and your name and address within 60 days of purchase to Howard Books, 3117 North 7th Street, West Monroe, LA 71291-2227, and we will gladly reimburse you for the cost of the book.